Praise for *The Novelist*

"Although Hunt is known for her competency, this novel also shows poignancy and imagination."

—*Publishers Weekly*

"A great novel to pick up at the end of a hectic day, crisp writing and spiritual candor mark *The Novelist* as another winner for Ms. Hunt."

—www.infuzemag.com

"Angela Hunt does a remarkable job of portraying a "normal" family caught in the grips of mental illness and its associated behaviors. *The Novelist* is a heartfelt, thought-provoking look at a family's faith and actions in a challenging situation."

—BrownBookLoft.com

"I inhaled this book in one day and was sad to see it end."

—bookloons.com

"*The Novelist* is a well-written, imaginative read."

—*Homelife* magazine

"Angela Hunt's books always make me think, and *The Novelist* gave me much to ponder. This book is two stories for the price of one, and both made me feel as if I was looking into a mirror. Her creativity and skill always amaze me."
—Terri Blackstock, author of the Cape Refuge and Newpointe 911 Series

"Angie Hunt has done it again. *The Novelist* is unique. Innovative. Touching. Thought-provoking. Behold characters breathed into life by the Novelist . . . and gain a rich perspective on your own story."
—Randy Alcorn, author of *Safely Home* and *Heaven*

"For those who love to read fiction and for those who love to write it, *The Novelist* is sure to delight. Ms. Hunt has penned an innovative and fascinating look into the relationship between creator and creation that both surprised and captivated me. But even more, the wondrous story of the Author's love for His creation shines throughout."
—Robin Lee Hatcher, author of *The Victory Club* and *Loving Libby*

"With *The Novelist*, readers have a triple blessing in store: a moving story of one woman's angst-ridden journey toward authenticity, a powerful allegory of original sin and eternal redemption, and a clear outline of the storytelling process itself. An exceptional work of fiction with a life-changing message for every reader."

—Liz Curtis Higgs, best-selling author of *Thorn in My Heart*

"Angela Hunt is a master storyteller who continually raises the bar. With its story-within-a-story format and allegorical elements, *The Novelist* will make you take a deeper look at yourself, and will break your heart for those who don't know the Truth."

—Deborah Raney, author of *Over the Waters* and *A Nest of Sparrows*

"*The Novelist* not only provides great insights for anyone interested in writers and the creative process, but Angela Hunt has written a rich and powerful allegory exploring the Great Author's own love, power, and process."

—Bill Myers, author of *The Presence*

"*The Novelist* invokes a simple but essential truth: that the greatest story ever told would be impossible without the greatest storyteller. Angela Hunt has given us a heart-sourced work of fiction that offers truth at every turn, and a frank and rare trip to the other side of the keyboard. Highly recommended for those who view the popular novelist's life with stars in their eyes . . . as well as those who understand the business well enough to know better."

—Tom Morrisey, author of *Deep Blue* and *Dark Fathom*

"I loved Angela's *The Novelist*! Readers need to be warned that their work will pile up because it is impossible to put the book down until the last page is devoured."

—Marilyn Meberg, best-selling author of
God At Your Wits' End and speaker for Women of Faith

"Reading *The Novelist* is like watching one of the better episodes of "The Twilight Zone"—without all the creepiness. The story behind the story and the story within the story are skillfully interwoven in yet another thought-provoking parable from Angela Hunt."

—Jane Orcutt, author of *Dear Baby Girl*

"*The Novelist* is Angela Hunt at the very top of her form. I was deeply moved by this story, and absolutely captivated by the skill with which this story is told. Rich in heart and profound in spiritual insight, *The Novelist* is a book you will remember long after you finish the last page."

—James Scott Bell, bestselling author of
Sins of the Fathers and *Glimpses of Paradise*

the Novelist

OTHER NOVELS BY ANGELA HUNT

Unspoken

The Truth Teller

The Awakening

The Debt

The Canopy

The Pearl

The Justice

The Note

The Immortal

The Shadow Women

The Silver Sword

The Golden Cross

The Velvet Shadow

The Emerald Isle

Dreamers

Brothers

Journey

For a complete listing, visit
www.angelahuntbooks.com.

the Novelist

Her story is only half the story.

ANGELA
HUNT

WestBow
PRESS

A Division of Thomas Nelson Publishers
Since 1798

visit us at www.westbowpress.com

Published by WestBow Press, Nashville, Tennessee, in association with the literary agency of Alive Communications, Inc., 7680 Goddard Street, Suite 200,
Colorado Springs, Colorado 80920.

WestBow Press books may be purchased in bulk for educational, business,
fund-raising, or sales promotional use. For information, please e-mail
SpecialMarkets@thomasnelson.com.

Scripture quotations are taken from the Holy Bible, New Living Translation,
copyright © 1996. Used by permission of Tyndale House Publishers, Inc.,
Wheaton, Illinois 60189. All rights reserved.

Publisher's Note: This novel is a work of fiction. Names, characters, places, and
incidents are either products of the author's imagination or used fictitiously. All
characters are fictional, and any similarity to people living or dead is purely
coincidental.

Library of Congress Cataloging-in-Publication Data

Hunt, Angela Elwell, 1957-
    The novelist : her story is only half the story / Angela Hunt.
    p. cm.
    ISBN 0-8499-4483-X (hc)
    ISBN 1-5955-4158-6 (tp)
    1. Women novelists—Fiction. 2. Mothers and sons—Fiction. I. Title.
    PS3558.U46747N685 2006
    813'.54—dc22

2005010207

Printed in the United States of America
06 07 08 09 10 RRD 9 8 7 6 5 4 3 2 1

[The novel] happens because
the storyteller's own experience of men and
things, whether for good or ill . . . ,
has moved him to an emotion so passionate
that he can no longer keep it shut up in his heart.

—MURASAKI SHIKIBU

One

I must be crazy, I tell myself, to stick my neck in a noose on my birthday. My husband, Carl, thinks my gesture is gracious and long overdue, so he kisses my cheek and bows gallantly before opening the door of my '85 Mercedes roadster. "Knock 'em dead, dear. I can't wait to hear all about it."

My twenty-one-year-old son, Zachary, is in one of his joking moods—in fact, he's been extra-friendly and charming all day, a much-appreciated birthday gift. "I'm glad my name isn't on that class roster," he says, slipping his hands into his jeans pockets. Barefoot, he does a side-stepping little dance that tells me he's anxious to finish this family farewell so he can go out with his friends. "I'd hate to have you as a professor."

"Your mother is a wonderful teacher." Carl smiles into my eyes. "Those people at the community college are lucky to have her."

I slide into the low seat of the car and punch the garage door opener. "You guys can go ahead and eat some cake if you get hungry. Don't wait on me."

Carl shakes his head. "Nonsense. We're going to sing and blow out candles when you get back."

"It's not really a big deal."

"It's a huge deal. How often does my best girl turn fifty-four?"

I roll my eyes and slip my key into the ignition.

"Hey, Mom?"

I look at Zack, enormously grateful for another opportunity to linger at home. "Yes?"

"You're teaching under your pen name, right?"

The question puzzles me until I consider its source. I've agreed to teach a course at the local college . . . which means some of my son's

I

friends might be in my class. Though I know Zack's proud of me, he's not exactly thrilled with the kind of books I write.

I give him a reassuring smile. "Don't worry, Son. I'll be Jordan Casey 'til the clock strikes nine."

He blows out his cheeks in exaggerated relief. "Dodged a bullet."

"You should be proud of your mother," Carl says.

"I am, but—"

I turn the key, allowing the rumble of the roadster's engine to drown out the father-son discussion. It's a debate I've heard before.

"Hey." I hang my elbow over the door. "If Patty or Shannon calls—"

"I'll tell them to call again after nine."

"Better make that nine thirty. I'm not sure how soon I'll be able to get away."

Carl nods as another flock of doubts swoops down to shadow my good intentions. Why on earth did I agree to teach this class? Patty and Shannon, my daughters, both live on the East Coast, which means they aren't likely to stay up if I miss their calls. Neither will forget my birthday, but Patricia is a busy lawyer, and Shannon's two little ones wear her out . . .

"Tell the girls I'll call them tomorrow."

I blow Carl a kiss, then slip the car into reverse and edge into the night.

 two

Curled into himself, the character rests in a beam of light while soft darkness supports his fragile form. A voice strikes his ear like a wave, vibrating inside his head as the light gilds his bare skin. He is conscious only of warmth, words, and an assurance that he is safe . . . and valued.

He gasps and inhales a first breath of brightness. Why he is, what he is, and where he is . . . none of these things matter yet. He is . . .

William, a whispering voice tells him. He is William Case, and he is alive. He has been fashioned for a purpose, so he is not to fear. The one who willed him into being will guide him to his destiny . . .

"I have outlined a plan for you . . ."

The words patter like water droplets on his inexperienced ears, registering without resonating. He blinks his dazzled eyes and brings his hand toward his face, smiling as the fingers bend and bow to his will.

Alive. Before he was alive he knew nothing, but now he blinks and bends and hears while a rush of information streams through his head. A flood of words spills before his eyes, each representing something he will need to know. Images accompany the words, bright pictures of objects his eyes have never seen.

When the procession ceases, he turns in the light, but he sees nothing beyond the edge of its beam. He feels only warmth; he hears nothing but the faint creak of his untested joints as they obey his commands.

So he waits.

Three

I open the door into a room of students jabbering like a flock of crows, but the noise fades as I thread my way through an aisle cluttered with backpacks, purses, and sneakered feet. I stop at the front of the room where a whiteboard, table, and lectern wait.

I can feel the pressure of eyes on my back like an itch. They probably think I'm a secretary, come to tell them the famous Jordan Casey has been unavoidably detained.

I wish.

I turn and drop my purse onto the table, then grip the lectern with both hands. "Good evening." I lift my gaze for the first time. "This class is 'An Introduction to Novel Writing.' If you're looking for womens' studies, chemistry, or badminton, you may now excuse yourself."

My students stare at me with questioning eyes until I smile, then they chuckle.

"Seriously," a kid about Zachary's age calls above the laughter, "when's he coming?"

Just as I expected. "The class doesn't begin until seven," I tell him. "I'll explain everything then."

As a pair of latecomers shuffle in, I step back and study the assembled group. Most of my students appear to be in their early twenties, but middle age has settled over at least a half dozen of them. A thin woman at the back of the room looks to be at least sixty.

I suppose Zachary was right to worry that one of his friends might be in my class. The place is crowded with young men waiting to meet Jordan Casey, dashing author of the testosterone-laced Rex Tower novels. They are not expecting to meet Jordan Casey Kerrigan, middle-aged wife and mother of three.

I lower my gaze, purposefully keeping my face smooth and blank as the remaining minutes tick by. Though Zachary and my career were conceived in the same year, my son is not my biggest fan. I thought my unanticipated baby and unexpected career would complement each other, but my son resents my fictional alter ego, and my writing suffers from the demands of my troublesome son.

When the clock on the wall advances to seven, a man in the front pointedly clears his throat. I immediately recognize him and his companion. "Dr. Whitson, Dr. Bell, I'm honored you would attend."

Dr. Avery Whitson, president of Truckee Meadows Community College, rises from his seat. "I wanted to come tonight," he says, turning to address the students, "and personally thank Jordan Casey for this great privilege. It's not often we get writers of her caliber to visit our campus. Her willingness to join our faculty this semester has honored us beyond words."

I hear gasps of astonishment as I step forward and clasp Whitson's hand. "Thank you, sir. The honor is mine."

I'm puzzled when Whitson holds my grip a moment longer than necessary, but the reason becomes clear when a camera flashes. I bare my teeth in a belated smile, knowing one of these shots will appear in the next school newspaper, probably along with reviews of both my latest novel and my teaching style.

"Have a good class," Whitson says, still playing to the audience. "If you need anything, don't hesitate to call my office."

As the college president leaves, photographer in tow, I acknowledge the other dignitary. "Dr. Bell, thank you for coming."

The chairman of the English Department nods, but a flush colors his cheeks. When he doesn't move to give a speech or shake my hand, I return to the lectern. If the English professor is sticking around, he probably wants to write a novel. Who doesn't?

Linking my hands behind my back, I turn my attention to my students. Between thirty and forty faces stare back at me, eyes brimming with varying levels of curiosity, desire, and drive.

I draw a deep breath. "Before we begin our official study, I thought it might be nice to have a time of questions and answers. I'd like to know what you'd like to learn in this course, and you may have questions you'd like to ask up front. If so, this is the time to ask them."

A wave of silence greets my suggestion, followed by a timid hand. I recognize the young man who spoke earlier. "Yes?"

"You're a woman."

The class laughs when I respond with wide eyes and a dropped jaw. "Really?"

He blushes. "I mean, everyone thinks Jordan Casey is a man."

"Not everyone, surely. My publisher knows I'm a woman. So does my agent."

The student grins. "Come on, that's not fair. I think you all are connin' us. Like, why don't they put your picture on the back cover?"

I lift my hand, conceding his point. "I'll admit having a gender-neutral name may be an advantage when you write about a superspy. But my gender isn't the main reason my picture isn't on my books."

The young man lifts a brow. "And the main reason is?"

"I'm one of those women who prefers to guard her privacy. Why should my gender be an issue? There are plenty of men who write about women."

"Yeah, but most women write that mushy romance stuff. Rex Tower is never mushy."

"I beg to differ. Rex has his tender moments." I rest one elbow on the lectern and smile at my interrogator. "What's your name?"

"Zappariello," he answers. "Michael, but everyone calls me Mike."

"Well, Mike, I'm a firm believer in writing whatever you want to write. When I began my first Rex Tower novel, I was raising two daughters and had just learned that I was expecting a son. At that point in my life, I was more interested in snips and snails than sugar and spice."

Mike Zappariello and I have broken the ice. Hands fill the air now, so I move across the rows, trying to keep my answers short and simple.

"Where do you get your ideas?"

"From life—and from the newspaper, books, and that thing called inspiration."

"Do you write every day?"

"Every day but Saturday and my birthday. I try never to work on my birthday, but occasionally things come up."

"Will you ever write about anything besides Rex Tower?"

I tilt my head. "I'm not sure. I can't leave Rex behind until I've exhausted my Tower ideas, and that hasn't happened yet. I like Rex too much to dump him."

"How many books have you written so far?"

"Twenty, one for every year since 1984. Only nineteen of them have been released; the other is scheduled for publication this coming May."

"How many have been made into movies?"

I stop to count on my fingers. "Ten, I think, though almost all of them have been optioned—meaning someone bought the rights in the hope of making a movie."

"Are you rich?"

The blunt question makes me laugh. "We're . . . comfortable. I've been a schoolteacher and a novelist, and I can definitely say that writing novels has been more lucrative than teaching. But I've read that the average freelance writer in America earns less than five thousand dollars a year, so I've been blessed."

A young lady in the far corner of the room blushes when I catch her eye. "You wanted to ask something?"

She nods uncertainly. "I was wondering—how do you make it come together? I get ideas all the time, but I don't know how to turn them into stories."

I'm grateful for the question—at last, someone who might actually want to be a writer—but how can I explain a process I don't fully understand? Part of my livelihood springs from craft, but beneath the skill lie the stories, delicate and detailed snowflakes that drop into my brain at inexplicable times and for no apparent reason. I can no more control the process that births my art than I can control the weather.

I can only hope that some of the people in this room will have the same gift . . . and the courage to implement it.

"The ideas will come together," I begin, "when you gain an understanding of the structure that lies beneath stories. When you understand the bone structure of a plot skeleton, you'll know how to build a story."

"What about characters?" the older woman asks. "Do you base them on people you know?"

"You mean take advantage of my crazy Uncle Joe?" I shake my head. "Not really. Most of the time characters pop into my head, complete with names and occupations . . . and they wait until I'm ready to use them." I look around. "That reminds me of another topic I wanted to discuss tonight—why did you sign up for this class? Are you here because you wanted to talk about Rex Tower, or are you here because you'd like to write a novel of your own?"

When my students look at each other with chagrinned smiles, I realize I have a mixed group. Some of them came because they wanted to meet Rex Tower's creator; that group probably won't come back. But the others might tough it out.

I smile as a surge of hope brightens my mood. "Let me say that while some people will disagree, I think it is entirely possible for one person to teach another to write a novel. The desire to create is easy to kindle. It springs from our souls, where it echoes the drive of the one who made us. Many of us are desperate to see what worlds our minds can invent; we long for the company of characters we fashion from bits of background, emotion, and intellect. This part of the creative process is magic. It's the reason some of you are here."

I lower my voice and lean on the lectern's slanting surface. "If what I've just said sounds like nonsense, and you're here because you think a novelist's life consists of pixie dust, million-dollar paychecks, and cocktail parties, you're mistaken. The life of a writer is tedious and trying. My days—except on rare occasions like this—are spent in the company

7

of dusty books, a finicky computer, and a journal of scribbled notes. If you think being a novelist involves exchanging confidences with a mystical muse, I'm sorry to disappoint you. I don't live in a garret, nor do I think my career is particularly romantic. I work several hours a day to write a rough draft, and rewriting is even more labor-intensive."

I can't help noticing Michael Zappariello's reaction to my statement. A flicker of shock widens his eyes, and something—panic, perhaps?—tightens the corners of his mouth.

I soften my voice. "I can't teach you how to kindle the passion that propels a writer from a vague idea to a compelling book. But if you can accept the responsibility for maintaining your desire and commit yourself to the hard work of rewriting, I can teach you how to turn ideas into stories and stories into novels."

I smile as hope flickers back into Mike's face. "Over the years, I've learned that creating a story is analogous to building a structure. Once you learn how to use the proper tools and follow a blueprint, you can construct anything from a doghouse to a Victorian mansion. Writing is no different. Once you learn to construct a proper sentence, a paragraph, and a plot, you can write anything from a picture book to an epic novel. More than any other form, however, a novel demands persistence, patience, and a certain amount of perversity."

I laugh, but few of my students seem to appreciate my humor. Dr. Bell shifts in his chair while a pair of young women whisper to each other. Are they hoping to slip out as soon as I turn my back?

"The work can be trying," I add, hoping I haven't murdered their motivation, "but it's not impossible. I usually spend between three and five months on a full-length novel. I've been writing so long that I've worked out a system to make things easier."

One of the girls, a redhead with a pale complexion, lifts her hand.

I acknowledge her with a nod. "May I have your name, please?"

"Kristal Palma." She bites her lip. "You can write an entire book in three months? How is that possible? I mean, didn't Harper Lee spend years on *To Kill a Mockingbird*? And they say the work of writing *Gone with the Wind* wore Margaret Mitchell out."

I sigh. "I can't speak for anyone else, but I've found that writing only becomes difficult when writers fail to plan. Some create a full cast of characters and thrust them into a story without having the slightest idea where they're going. Before I begin, I create a detailed outline. I hold my characters and their environment firmly in my grip. I know what will happen to them at each stage of the journey so I don't waste time wondering about what comes next."

"So you're an outline person," Mike offers, tugging at the scruff on his chin. "An OP."

"Um—yes. I'm going to show you how to create realistic personalities, a unique story world, and a serviceable plot. I can teach you how to write a good story. It's not difficult."

When the disgruntled expression on Dr. Bell's face shifts into definite lines of disapproval, I have a feeling I've destroyed a mystique he's coveted for years.

"Writing can be simple," I say, smiling at the professor, "and before the semester is finished, I will explain each step of the creative process. You will find that novelists, like the great and powerful Oz, are a bit like puppet masters behind a curtain."

I press my palms together and step back. "If there are no other questions—"

"Ms. Casey?" A young man in the second row waves for my attention.

I lift my chin. The student is a big kid, tall, wide-shouldered, and athletic-looking—the kind of sassy jock who always irritated me in my high school teaching days.

I meet his gaze. "May I ask your name?"

"Morley," the kid says. "Ian Morley." He stretches a long leg into the aisle and regards me with a half smile. "First, I should tell you I've read almost all your books."

If that comment had come from anyone else, I'd have thanked him and moved on. Something in this kid's smirk, though, tells me he's not about to deliver an accolade.

I prop an elbow on the lectern. "Did you enjoy them?"

A corner of the kid's broad mouth twitches. "They held my interest, sure, but not because of Rex Tower. I read your books because I enjoy the technical stuff."

"You don't like Rex Tower?" The African-American girl to Morley's left glares at him. "How can you not like a superhero?"

The kid shrugs. "We're supposed to be honest with her, right?"

"Please." Despite my growing annoyance, I wave Morley on. "I appreciate candor."

The kid sinks deeper into his chair. "Your plots are okay. But Rex Tower is, like, plastic man. He never changes, he never learns anything, and he never fails. I can't identify with him. He's not the sort of guy I'd want to invite over for a beer."

"But that's what's so cool about him," a tattooed student calls. "Tower is Superman. He always saves the day—and wipes out a few hundred bad guys while he's doing it."

Morley scrapes his hand over his short red hair. "That's another problem—the bad guys are predictable. I mean, in your early books they were all Russian, and in your last books they've all been Islamic terrorists."

"What about *Maximum Tower*?" the red-haired girl says. "In that book, Rex was battling mad scientists who wanted to release nanobots into the world's blood supply so they could eat people up from the inside."

Comments begin to fly like spit wads.

"That was cool."

"Stop, don't tell me! I haven't read that one!"

"Did you read the one where the bad guys planted C-four in the White House? Awesome!"

I lift my hand to regain control. "That's enough, I think. We don't want to spoil anything for people who haven't read the entire Tower library." I shift my gaze to Ian Morley. "I'm sorry you don't find my novels compelling. But something about them must work, because each new novel sells more than the last."

"That's why I read them. I've thought about being a writer myself, so I'm always trying to figure out what makes a novel work." Morley folds one arm across his chest, then glances at the girl across the aisle. "I'm not trying to be rude. But I think readers should be honest."

I step back behind the lectern. "Well, Mr. Morley, I shall look forward to reading some of your honest ideas."

Dr. Bell twists in his seat, his dark brows bristling. "May I add something?"

I gesture to the lectern. "Would you like to take the floor?"

The English professor remains in his seat, but he turns and addresses Morley in the thunderous tones of a preacher at the pulpit. "I think, Ian, that your dissatisfaction arises not from Ms. Casey's writing, but from her chosen genre. Rex Tower is an action hero. People who go to Tower movies don't expect to see sweeping changes in the hero's character—they expect to see amazing gadgets, beautiful women, and a protagonist who thinks, shoots, and maneuvers faster than anyone else."

"Oh, I'll admit that Tower is perfect for the screen," Morley answers, straightening. "But a novel is supposed to be different. Wasn't it Red Smith who said that writing was sitting down at a typewriter and opening a vein? No offense, Ms. Casey, but I don't think you open any veins as you write your books."

For a moment I can't speak, then I have to stifle a guffaw. And Carl thought my students would be starstruck! He won't believe me when I tell him that a jock in a tank top has accused me of not *bleeding* enough in my work.

Taking pains to maintain a pleasant tone, I try to answer: "You don't know me, Mr. Morley, so I don't think you can judge how much of myself I put into my books."

"No, no, please don't be mad." A blush rises from the back of his neck. "But think about it—I never imagined you were a woman. I never knew you had a family. Because Tower is so unattached, I thought Jordan Casey had to be an ex-Navy SEAL who lives out in the woods with nothing but a hunting dog to keep him company."

I smile when the rest of the class laughs, but Morley's words have raised a welt on my heart. Is my work really that . . . detached? Tower champions truth, justice, and democracy, ideals I strongly support. Surely my books don't need to reveal anything more personal.

I return my attention to the class. "Writers must make certain choices up front, and years ago I chose to write action novels. I could write something more personal if I wanted to."

Morley's eyes glint at me. "Could you?"

"Of course."

"Then why don't you?"

The challenge hangs in midair, bold and blatant, while overhead a faulty fluorescent bulb flickers and buzzes like a wasp.

I close my eyes. I didn't expect anything like this. Over the years, I've received my share of critical fan letters, but I've never been personally challenged.

Then again, I've rarely allowed readers to get this close.

I open my eyes and clear my throat. "In our next class"—I scan the room, deliberately avoiding Morley's vicinity—"we'll discuss how a writer decides what sort of book to write. When we meet again, I'd like you to have a concept sketched out on paper—an idea you'd like to write about."

I slide a hand into my jacket pocket. "If you'll excuse me now, there's a birthday cake waiting for me at home."

I lower my head and charge the back door, ignoring the curious glances cast in my direction.

Four

Zachary is out with his friends when I arrive home—no surprise there—but Carl is waiting with my birthday cake, candles, and a goblet filled with my favorite fizzy beverage, Diet Coke.

At the kitchen bar, I prop my head on my hand as my husband turns off the lights, then fumbles his way toward me. "Here." I laugh and reach for his arm. "I don't want you to fall and break something on my birthday. We older folks have to be careful."

"Fifty-four is not old."

"Spoken like someone who's fifty-six."

He sits on the bar stool next to me, then flicks the propane lighter. I don't know how Carl does it, but as he smiles and delicately touches the tip of the lighter to each wick, my husband manages to make the act of lighting fifty-four candles a bona fide romantic experience.

When all the candles are burning, he looks at me, his face alight with the cake's glow. "Make a wish, sweetheart."

I close my eyes and whisper the same prayer I offer every year: that God would bless my children and grandchildren; that my husband would remain healthy and by my side.

When I open my eyes, Carl leans toward me. "What'd you wish?"

"I'm not supposed to tell."

The corner of his mouth quirks as he strokes my arm. "You don't have to. I know you like a book."

I inhale a deep breath and blow on the candles, drawing on deep reserves as I puff at the last sputtering wicks. As Carl rises to turn on the lights, I lean back and realize he's right—he *does* know me like a book. He's probably the only living person who does.

"Now," he says, coming to help me pluck candles out of the cake, "tell me about your class."

I shrug and drop a pink candle onto an empty plate. "It was fine. About forty students, I think, though I'm sure the group will be smaller next time."

"Lots of Rex Tower groupies?"

"A few. They were surprised, of course, to see a grandmother behind the lectern."

Carl laughs. "I wish Zachary could have been there. He'd have been impressed to realize his mother can draw a crowd."

"I don't know about that, though I could have used some emotional support. One young man wasn't at all complimentary of my books."

Carl makes a face, then pointedly flexes his bicep. "Want me to teach him some manners?"

I snort. "He wasn't exactly rude; he was . . . writerly. He's spent too much time wallowing in angst, I think. He quoted that bit about how writers are supposed to sit down and open a vein, so apparently I haven't bled enough to suit him."

"With your high body counts, I don't see how anyone could say—"

"He wasn't referring to bloodshed in the story; he was talking about self-revelation. I suspect he's heard other writers mention how they suffer for their art and all that. What he'd never heard before tonight is that it's possible to tell a story without exsanguinating yourself in the process."

Carl drops the last candle onto the edge of the cake stand, then lifts a knife to cut the first slice. "Have you ever thought that maybe the kid is right?"

Carl doesn't often offer comments about my writing, so this feels a little intrusive. "What are you saying?"

"I'm not saying anything." He draws the blade through a generous swirl of icing. "I'm playing devil's advocate. Have you ever thought about putting more of your heart in your books?"

He drops a generous slice of cake onto a plate and offers it to me.

"That's far too much."

Carl sets the cake aside. "For instance—"

"Yes?"

"You're a believer, but Rex Tower never even thinks about God. Maybe you could address that in your books—you know, without being preachy."

I say nothing as he cuts a smaller slice. It's easy for him to think in terms of religious belief; after all, he's been a seminary professor for the last seven years. Theology is his bread and butter, but my career revolves around a fedora-wearing spy who makes mincemeat of evil masterminds while defending truth, liberty, and the American way.

Carl slides the second plate toward me, then looks around as if he expects the rest of the family to pop in and want a piece.

I pick up a fork. "Did Shannon or Patricia call?"

"Both of them, not half an hour after you left. They said to wish you a happy birthday, and I told them you'd give them a ring tomorrow."

I look down as tears fill my eyes. I'm not usually this high-strung, but my anxiety about tonight's class and Carl's comment have left me feeling a little unsettled.

Carl takes a bite, then nods. "This cake is good. Not dry like last year's."

I drag my fork through the frosting, then squint at my husband. "My readers would have a collective hissy fit if Rex started going to church."

My husband blinks, then swallows. "I'm no expert on books, hon. I don't know how those things work. All I know is your relationship with God either permeates your life or it doesn't."

My spine stiffens. "Are you saying—"

"I'm saying that you have an honest relationship with God. Don't you think your novels would be deeper if you included some of that reality in your stories?"

I want to be irritated, but it's my birthday. And my husband is right—he knows *nothing* about popular fiction.

I shake my head and smile. "Novels are not soapboxes, Carl. Besides, my life is boring. Why do you think I invented Rex Tower?"

Carl opens his mouth to reply but halts at the sound of a slamming car door. As one, we look at the clock, then at each other.

"He's early," I say.

"Maybe he came home because it's your birthday."

"I doubt it—maybe he just *really* wants a piece of cake."

We laugh, but as the front door opens, I feel my shoulders tighten. What is it about parenting young adults? When they're not home we worry about where they are; when they come home, we worry about where they've been. At twenty-one, Zack no longer has a curfew, but neither Carl nor I can sleep until we hear the door alarm and know our son is safe under our roof.

So why is Zack home now?

"Hey, Momsers!" Wearing a wide smile, our son buzzes into the kitchen and wraps his arms around me. I relax and lean back against him, but I can't help turning to search his eyes. They are bright, the pupils small and black. Is that normal for a young man coming in from the dark?

I pat his arm. "You want some cake?"

"Naw, not hungry. Just came in to wish you happy birthday."

I cringe as Zack plants a loud, smacky kiss on my cheek. He grins at his father as he releases me. "What's up, Popster? You want a kiss too?"

Carl lifts a hand to protest, but Zack wraps an arm around his father's shoulders, then rakes his broad hand through the wisps on Carl's head. "Hey, hey, hey! For Dad's birthday, Mom, why don't you get him a hair transplant? Dad, what'd you get Mom?"

I point to the jeweler's box on the counter, but Zack has already left Carl and is accosting the refrigerator. He stands before the open door, one leg twitching to a rhythm only he can hear, then he slams the door and whirls away, heading for the hallway and the stairs.

"Happy B-day, Mom!" he calls, taking the steps two at a time.

I watch until he turns the corner, then my eyes meet Carl's. "He wasn't drinking," he says, his shoulders relaxing. "I didn't smell anything on his breath."

I nod, silently agreeing. We've had our problems with Zack in the past, but this was a good night. Maybe he *did* come home early for my sake.

Happy birthday to me.

Five

"Why don't you?"

Ian Morley's question shimmers on the air like gasoline fumes, blurring the books on my office shelves. Carl's question rises to join it, pushing all other thoughts from my head.

"You have an honest relationship with God. Don't you think your novels would be deeper if you included some of that reality in your stories?"

I tighten my hand into a fist and pound the desktop. It's Tuesday morning, and I have a to-do list ten feet long, but I can't seem to think about anything but those two annoying queries.

Why don't I put more of my reality into my novels? Because the reading public clamors for Rex Tower, and no novelist in her right mind would abandon the character who keeps food on her table and a roof over her family's head.

I swivel toward the window and watch the groundskeeper skimming leaves from the pool. A few years ago I toyed with the idea of writing something different. I reminded my agent that John Grisham managed to break out of the legal genre with *A Painted House* and *Skipping Christmas;* my agent rebutted by saying that Grisham could sell a rhyming grocery list.

Because I'm not Grisham, I continued to write about Rex Tower.

Our dog, a 250-pound hunk of mastiff named Dubya, lifts his head as I turn away from the window. I drop my hand to his broad head and give him a scratch.

Maybe Ian Morley and Carl have a point. Maybe I am too protective, not only of my family, but of myself. I'm an introvert by nature; I've always been content to let life approach me. Perhaps that's why Rex Tower is such a go-getter—he's everything I'm not.

I stop scratching the dog as another thought strikes: *What sort of example am I being to my son?* He has been skeptical of Christianity ever since Carl and I began to follow the Lord. Though I've always tried to be honest about my failings under Zack's watchful eye, now I have to wonder—*Does he view my reluctance to merge my faith and my work as selling out? Does he think I'm ashamed of God?*

As always, thoughts of Zachary bring pain. Like an old wound that aches in damp weather, I can't think of my son without remembering what we've endured on his account. He's been doing well these past five weeks; he seems glad to be home again. He was certainly upbeat last night, and his restless energy must have persisted. The quiet beep that signals the opening of our front door woke us from a dead sleep; apparently Zachary went out at one and returned home at five. He says he and his friends go to an all-night diner to "shoot the breeze," but I'm never sure what he does.

I wish I could trust him completely.

Someday when he's a father, he'll experience the sleepless nights, the worry, the fear. Then he'll finally understand what he's put us through.

I look at the dog, who is regarding me with the open smile of a relaxed beast. "I wish you could go out with Zack. You'd keep an eye on him, wouldn't you?"

Dubya closes his eyes, willing to agree with anything as long as I keep scratching.

"Sorry, sweetie. I need to get to work." I give the dog one last rub, then pull a yellow legal pad from beneath a stack of books. On it I have sketched a rough outline of a class syllabus, but—

"Why don't you?"

The challenge continues to echo in my ear. Why not answer it? I don't have to begin another Tower novel until summer, so why couldn't I write something different now? Students learn more from watching a demonstration than by jotting down instructions, so why not let them witness the act of creation? I could write a novel and spread the work over the semester. By example I could demonstrate that anyone with patience, perseverance, and even a tiny bit of imagination can write a book.

I pick up my pen and plot my course:

Session 1: What makes a good idea?
Session 2: What genre best fits your story?

An anticipatory shiver ripples through my limbs. I will write a new kind of book—shoot, if Carl wants truth, I'll write an *allegory*. I'll take a spiritual concept and spin it into a novel. I'll create a story world unlike anything I've ever invented, populate it with characters, then turn the fictitious world upside down with a predicament. Every week I'll share my progress with the class. In time they'll see that creating a story is no more difficult for a novelist than measuring is for a carpenter.

And if, by heaven, even one student has a smidgen of talent, that young man or woman could catch the vision and write something publishable. In a couple of years, I might open a novel and read an inscription on the dedication page: *For Jordan Casey, who ripped writing from the garret and moved it into the classroom . . . Thanks.*

I rest my cheek on my hand and feel a smile curve against my palm. I might actually enjoy teaching this class. I might—

I catch my breath as my germinating idea sprouts yet another tendril. I can give this manuscript to Zack. Though my son has never been thrilled to have a mother who writes at the top of a male-oriented genre, he *does* read my manuscripts, sometimes even offering to proof them for mistakes.

I will write a story for my son. If I fill it with spiritual wisdom, maybe through vicarious experience he'll learn what he has not been able to accept firsthand.

I close my eyes. Zack was eleven when his Aunt Alicia, Carl's sister, succumbed to breast cancer. Alicia's faith, vibrant even in the face of death, convinced me and Carl that faith was something we needed, but Zack had not been able to see past the loss of his favorite aunt. In the months and years since Alicia's home-going, Carl and I have baby-stepped toward spiritual maturity while Zack seems determined to leap-frog away from God.

How many Sunday mornings have I gone upstairs and begged him to come to church with us? Threats and bribery pulled him out of bed on a few occasions, but by the time we slipped into a pew with our sullen son, neither Carl nor I felt like worshipping. After a while, we stopped nagging.

But I have never stopped praying.

My son no longer listens when I try to tell him what God says about living a successful life, but he does love to read.

As excited as a diver who has just stumbled across an encrusted treasure chest, I press my hand to my forehead and try to think of topics that might work in a contemporary allegory. My thoughts skitter from one Bible story to another, then I remember a half-formed character I haven't yet used—*William*.

I can write a story to demonstrate how bad choices destroy and evil corrupts . . . a modern retelling of the temptation in the Garden. The title comes to me in a flash: *The Ambassador*.

Zack's chief temptation is alcohol, so I won't use that; I'll use something similarly addictive . . . like gambling. Since we live only a few hours from Las Vegas, my students will appreciate the casino connection.

The concept comes, not in a blazing burst of illumination, but like a miniscule pinhole of light. Slowly it grows, meeting a theme here, connecting with a unique setting there, merging with a symbol to support the story premise . . .

Two pages of notes later, the conception is complete. I lean back and smile as I imagine Morley's reaction to my presentation. Nothing is more personal than religion, so if Morley wants to peek at the underpinnings of my life, I'll give him an eyeful. Since Carl wants me to write about spiritual things, I'll underline this story with themes of sin and redemption.

And if my son reads this manuscript and understands that God can grant a second chance for everyone who makes a mistake, all the work will have been worth it.

Eager to begin, I stand and reach toward the shelf where Carl keeps his old theology books.

Six

Like a sea mammal seeking fresh air, he swims up through the fog between sleeping and waking, then opens his eyes. A pebbled surface looms above him, an area gleaming with the faint light from an open . . . He glances toward a glass rectangle in the wall as memory supplies the missing word: *window*.

The surface is a *ceiling*, he is lying in a *bed*, and this must be his *home*.

He sits up. The world shifts dizzily until he swings his feet from beneath a thin covering, and the cool kiss of the wooden floor establishes reality. His eyes glimpse movement as he turns; after an instinctive stab of fear, he realizes he is looking at a *mirror*, so the naked man in the glass must be . . . him.

He is William Case. The name comes to him on a wave of memory.

Staring at the reflective glass, he sees his mouth fall open. So . . . this is the face he's been given. He glances at his hands and thin legs. They are familiar; he's seen them before. But he's never seen this face.

He pushes himself off the bed and steps to the mirror on legs that tremble beneath the unaccustomed weight of his body. He leans on a wooden chest under the mirror, bracing his torso on spindly arms while he gazes at the pale mask crowned by hair the color of darkness.

He opens his mouth, touches his teeth, peers into the tunnels of his nose. He has never seen any face, so he does not know if his is ordinary or exceptional or horrid. He likes it well enough. The fair skin magnifies the darkness of his hair and eyes; the teeth, white and even, are a pleasant contrast to the faintly pink lips. The nose is clear-cut and more than adequate for respiration; the forehead wide enough to shield the brain holding the knowledge he's been given.

He searches that brain for some hint of what comes next, but he is overwhelmed by an urgent need to move into the small space beyond another door—the *bathroom,* memory informs him, where he will find a *toilet.*

After a few minutes, during which he instinctively tends to the urges of his new body, he steps toward another door. He opens it and discovers a closet outfitted with a thick wooden pole from which several pieces of clothing dangle on wire frames. He runs his fingertips over the frames, counting two sets of pants, two shirts, a jacket. Two shoes sit on the floor, each stuffed with a lump that proves, upon investigation, to be a sock. On a shelf above the pole, his questing fingers discover a leather belt and two pairs of short white pants—*underwear* or *briefs.*

The author has thought of everything.

Slowly adjusting to wakefulness, he smiles as he runs the sensitive pads of his palms over the clothing. Amazing how one fabric soothes while another scratches. And the colors! A red shirt and a white one, black pants and navy. How confusing to have choice! But if he can choose between words, why should he be surprised to discover he's allowed to choose between colors? He laughs, then flinches at the unexpectedly solid sound of his voice.

He sinks to the edge of the bed, overcome with awe at the wonder of this world. Some deep sector of his brain, a fragment not occupied with the pressing problem of picking the proper pants, wonders why he has been placed in this confusing situation. But that voice falls silent as he returns to the closet and pulls out the navy pants, white shirt, underwear, belt, and blue socks. He tosses these things onto the bed, then rakes his hands through his hair and stares at the assortment.

He should put on the pants—no, the underwear first, *then* the pants. The socks, *then* the shoes. The shirt, then, if necessary, the jacket. He dresses carefully, taking care not to break the buttons or the zipper, following the order that seems best.

When he is wearing one of each category in the closet, he opens a third door and steps into the space beyond.

The walls of this room have been painted a warm yellow. The hue cheers him, reminding him of something from a time before this, and the smooth surface of a wooden table feels good beneath his hand. He looks around, spying a sink, metal cabinets, and several chairs. White curtains flutter over a wide window that has been opened to allow a stream of fresh air into the room.

The author's doing, surely. The creator of this world has arranged even the smallest details.

William presses his hands to the windowsill and looks out. The space outside is bright and warm, gilded in the same sunny tones as this room. Sound fills the air—a wind ruffles the grass along the road and rustles the tall, leafy trees along the cobblestone street. Yellow flowers nod along the brick pathway while ornate lamps sway above people on the path. For an instant he is so surprised to see other people—and relieved to note that they have dressed in the same order—that he can barely keep the words in his head from jumbling into a pile of nonsense.

Two men stroll by, huddled together in mumbled conversation, then they cross the street and approach a large brick building with wide windows beneath a red-and-white-striped awning. Someone has painted words on the glass, and William is thrilled to discover he can read them: *Casey's Machine Company.*

At the sight of the building, a buried thought tickles his brain. He is about to concentrate and bring it up, but another person passes in front of his window—a stranger who looks nothing like him or the two men.

Woman, his brain assures him, while his senses reel as he beholds the embodiment of the word. This amazing creature is somewhat like him, but she's smaller and far more appealing. Her skin glows in the sun's light, and dark hair crowns her head in thick masses of curls. His body is angular, his legs spindly; her form is curved and graceful and soft.

From somewhere down the street, a deep voice calls, "Raquel!" She turns, her eyes searching as she looks for the one who spoke. When her gaze crosses William's, she smiles . . . and he feels his legs buckle at the seam.

He sinks into one of the chairs by the table. *Knee*, the voice in his brain whispers. *The seam of your leg is your knee.* But he no longer cares about language lessons. He keeps his gaze glued to the woman until a tall, heavy man with puffy white hair extends his arm to her. She smiles at him—fortunate fellow!—and he walks with her across the street, then opens the door and steps back to let the woman enter first.

William feels a sudden urge to visit that building.

He shoots from the chair. As he strides toward the exit, he spies a slip of paper tacked to the door frame.

Welcome to Paradise! Rent is due the first of next month. You will need a job; check with the company across the street.
Welcome, William!

A message from his creator, surely. He pulls the note from the wood and rubs his finger across the paper, then sniffs it, hoping to catch some trace of the author.

He smells nothing but paper, but that's okay. Though he's not quite sure what a job requires, he folds the note and slips it into his pocket. He is inexperienced and uncertain, yet he knows one thing: if the woman called Raquel also has a job across the street, this place really is Paradise.

 Seven

Wrapped in a cocoon of anticipation, I survey the faces of my students. "I know I asked you to come to class with a concept for a novel"—I smile—"but I want you to hold on to those ideas for a while. I've had another thought about how to teach this course, and I hope you'll be as excited about this approach as I am."

I look around, noticing that the crowd has thinned, as I expected. "I've decided," I continue, "that since the best learning occurs by doing, we will not only talk about novels, but we will write one—you and I, all of us. You will work on your novel in small steps; I will write mine between class sessions. I don't expect our projects to give Grisham or King much competition, but I will write a novella, and at the very least, each of you will produce an outline, a synopsis, a cast of characters, and a first chapter."

I pause as exclamations of alarm ripple through the room. Amid the sounds of shock, Kristal Palma squeaks, Ian Morley groans, and several students hang their heads as if already conceding defeat.

I lift a chiding finger. "Writing a novel is not the impossible activity you may imagine it to be. The professional novelist does invest a lot of time, soul-searching, and personal artistry, but I'm not asking you to write the great American epic. I'm asking you to begin a novella. I believe you can do it."

From the second row, my least-favorite pupil waves for my attention. "Yes, Mr. Morley?"

"I thought this class was supposed to be about your stuff."

"My *stuff*?" I arch a brow. "Why would we study my work when yours is bound to be more fascinating?"

The class twitters at my sarcasm. Though I'm a little ashamed of myself for stooping to toss such a barb, ten years of public high school teaching have quickened my verbal reflexes.

"Ms. Casey?" The African-American girl raises her hand. When I ask her name, she introduces herself as Linda Frankel. "I was wondering— how are we supposed to find time to write a book?"

I chuckle. "Good question, Linda. After all, we live busy lives; we have friendships to maintain and television to watch. Let me ask you"— I look directly at an older woman in the third row—"How do *you* find time for the things you want to do?"

The woman tugs at her turtleneck as color flames in her lined cheeks. "I make time for it."

"Thank you." I smile. "Your name?"

"Edna Sardilli," she says, her voice clear and crisp.

"And why, Edna," I persist, "did you sign up for this class?"

She shifts in her seat, obviously uncomfortable as the center of attention, but age has granted her a dignity the younger students lack.

"I signed up," she says, lifting her chin, "because I want to write my life's story for my grandchildren. My story will be true, of course, but I want it to be interesting, like a novel."

I thank her with my eyes. "That is a perfect answer. We make time for things that are important to us. We make time for writing in the same way we make time for eating, sleeping, and television. You wouldn't be here if you weren't interested in writing, so let's apply our minds to the task. Now . . ." I step to the table where I have spread my notes. "First we'll talk about what makes a good idea, then we'll discuss plotting."

And so I teach. My students seem receptive; pens drive furiously over paper as I explain the qualities of an interesting concept and then move into basic plot forms.

After I explain that the dramatic question—will the protagonist reach his goal?—should span the story, Ian Morley lifts his hand.

I brace myself against the young man's skeptical gaze. "Would you like to make a comment, Mr. Morley?"

The student shrugs. "I don't see how that applies to your books. I mean, Rex Tower always reaches his goal, and his goal is always the same. He saves the world in every novel."

Beneath a rising tide of indignation, I inhale a deliberate breath. "Tower *does* consistently achieve his primary goal, but the reader keeps reading to see *how* he does it. And he *doesn't* always achieve his secondary goals. In *Tower of Power*, for instance, he didn't save the president's daughter, the woman he had begun to love. He couldn't disarm the nuclear bomb and save the girl at the same time."

"Too bad he wasn't Superman," Mike Zappariello quips. "He could fly counterclockwise around the world and turn back time."

I cross my arms. "One of the silliest ideas I've ever seen on screen. If you *could* turn back time, you'd restore everything to its former situation. So even though Tower might save the president's daughter in such a scenario, he wouldn't be able to disarm the nuclear bomb. So would he selfishly accomplish his secondary goal and doom New York City? I think not. Tower might be predictable, but he is not selfish. Now . . ." I glance at my legal pad. "Once you have a goal for your character, what should be your next consideration?"

I prop one elbow on the lectern, half-smiling while my students consult their notes as if the answer might magically appear there.

"Think." I lean forward. "Would we have an interesting story if our protagonist declared his goal and accomplished it in the next scene?"

"No," Kristal Palma says. "That'd be boring."

"Thank you. Yes, it would be boring, for the writer *and* the reader. So our plot needs complications. Your hero needs complications, too, because he should grow and learn something over the course of the story. In the best novels, the lead character becomes older, wiser, more mature. Though this sounds frightfully educational, he learns a lesson."

"Rex Tower doesn't change."

Without looking, I know where the comment originated. Ian Morley seems determined to needle me at every opportunity.

"The Tower books are not character novels"—I turn to look at my most outspoken student—"but even though they are plot-driven, Tower does change in certain areas—he learns new ways of defeating the enemy, and he also loses friends and associates in each adventure. In *Tilting Tower*, for instance, he lost Mr. Smith, his special weapons designer. Smith had the misfortune to be in Tower's car when terrorists blew up a suitcase bomb hidden in the trunk."

"He lost his shrink in *Tower of Terror*," Linda Frankel adds. The young woman grins when I meet her gaze. "He'd been visiting the doctor for weeks, right, after the rough time he had in *Electric Tower*? The psychologist had been helping Rex, and then, blam! Dr. Molotov took her out just for spite."

I make an imaginary check in the air. "Excellent insight. And notice how the lovely psychologist's murder functions as an inciting incident. Her death sent Tower over the edge, resulting in full-scale war between Tower and Molotov's forces."

Voices interrupt and hands flutter, but I shake my head. "I'd love to discuss specific stories with you, but we must keep moving. All right—we have a main character with two needs. An inciting incident thrusts him into the story world. This setting should be unique, a place unfamiliar to your average reader. You may go backward or forward in time, send your reader to another country or another planet. You may take your reader to the world of a gorilla linguist or set your story in the canopy of the rain forest. You may color your hero's perceptions by giving him an unusual disease; you may place him in a typical city but surround him with quirky friends. The choice is up to you, but the thing you cannot afford to be is ordinary."

I hesitate, half-expecting a derisive comment from Ian Morley, but apparently the young man finds Rex Tower's world sufficiently unusual.

I'm watching the knocking knees of a hyperactive youth in the front row when a woman in the back lifts her hand. The movement is so small I barely catch it. "Will you give me your name, please?"

The woman, who could have been anywhere from forty to sixty, touches her collar-length hair. "I'm Johanna Sicorsky."

I make a mental note. "And your question?"

"Well . . ." Her dark brows draw together. "What if you want to write about a regular person?"

I step into the aisle to better see the petite woman. Far from ordinary herself, Johanna's unlined face is dominated by wide brown eyes and framed by hair as white as my mother's.

"You can write about ordinary people," I say, softening my voice, "but you should give them extraordinary characteristics—a special talent, for instance, or unusual courage. Most people read for escape and entertainment. The more distinctive your characters and setting are, the more entertained your reader will be."

As I look around, waiting for another question, I can't help thinking about Morley's suggestion that I reveal more of myself in my books. I'm nothing *but* ordinary, a fact that has undoubtedly registered in his argumentative brain. I have only two talents: a knack for writing and an ability to make mouthwatering hamburgers. I'd be a boring protagonist in anybody's book.

When no one else speaks, I continue to outline a basic plot that moves from a goal through complications to the bleakest moment.

Edna Sardilli raises her hand. "Is the bleakest moment like the time when Tower lost the special mask he needed to breathe in the room contaminated with that deadly virus? He had only ten seconds to get in and shut off the dispersal unit, but he lost the mask when it blew out the broken window in that skyscraper—"

"*The Tower Grid*," I interrupt. "Yes, that's definitely a bleakest moment scenario. Since you've remembered that much, can you tell me what happened next?"

The older woman grimaces. "Um . . . didn't someone hand him a coffee filter?"

"Exactly." I repress the urge to blow the woman a kiss. Always nice to hear from someone who's read my books and doesn't feel the need to criticize. "A clerk from the office handed Tower a used coffee filter, and I'd already established that the specially engineered virus couldn't handle the acid content of day-old coffee."

I scan the rest of the class. "When your hero faces his bleakest moment, he will need help. It will come from two places—first from an outside source, then from inside himself. The outside source—and this can be anyone from a friend to a computer—usually teaches the hero something or provides assistance. This aid may trigger a memory or propel the protagonist toward an epiphany. But with this assistance, your hero is able to overcome the despair of his bleakest moment. He will then decide to quit or press on, leading to a lesson learned, the resolution, and the end of your story. Any questions?"

Ian Morley taps the tip of his pen against his chin, looking thoughtful, while Dr. Bell nods. Linda Frankel smiles as she makes notes. The blue-jeaned kid in the first row finally stops knocking his knees. I hope the cessation of unconscious movement doesn't signal a loss of conscious brain activity.

"This structure will become clear as we work on our plots." I move to the dry-erase board. "What I want you to do for our next class is create the protagonist of your novella. You're going to give him two needs—one obvious, one hidden. Later you will sketch out a rough plot, beginning with the character's inciting incident and concluding with his bleakest moment when he needs help—and gets it."

I uncap a marker and face the wall. "As you will see, I have created the following plot points for my story. This is still rough, but I'll fill in the details after I spend a little time with my characters."

I scrawl my outline on the board, then drop the marker into the tray. When I turn, I find my students wearing looks of dazed horror.

"What?" My gaze sweeps from one row to the next. "Can't you read my printing?"

The blue-jeaned knee-knocker shakes his head. "It's gonna be too hard. Writing's your job, not ours."

I fold my hands. "I don't believe I've caught your name."

The kid looks at me through half-closed lids. "Joseph Thronebury."

"Well, Joseph, writing a story is no harder than eating a cow. You must do it, though, one bite at a time." I force a smile. "I'm only asking you to eat a steak, and I'm going to demonstrate every step. Perhaps I should begin by telling you a little something about the protagonist I've created for my class project."

Ian Morley's eyes gleam with a taunting light. "We're not using Rex Tower?"

I manufacture a laugh. "My protagonist's name is William Case. He's an average-looking fellow—dark hair, medium height, brown eyes. He's about five foot eleven, clean shaven, a little on the thin side. If he were to walk into this room, you'd assume he was in his midtwenties, but people in his story world don't grow and mature as we do. I wanted William to be physically unremarkable because the focus of this story will not be physical strength or daring. The center of this story is a *concept.*"

"Might be a stretch," Morley calls, thrusting a long leg into the aisle.

I look at the lectern and force myself to ignore the insult. If this were my high school classroom, I'd march over to Morley's desk, point toward the hallway, and demand that he hike himself down to the assistant principal's office. But this isn't high school. It's college, and I am a guest professor in a temporary gig.

I've raised three children, so I can handle Morley.

I lift my chin and smile at the other students. "I've decided to take some good advice and write about an idea that is personally important to me. It's going to be an inspirational allegory—the characters will represent something else, either a real person or a concept. I'm also going to add a bit of Las Vegas flavor."

"Vegas?" Mike Zappariello looks up at me. "Let me guess—Wayne Newton will be a character."

I laugh. "Thanks, but I don't think so. Now"—I glance around—"would anyone like to suggest an obvious need with which I could begin the first chapter?"

Kristal Palma studies her fingernails; Edna Sardilli plucks the collar of her turtleneck and avoids my eyes. When my gaze crosses the classroom, Linda Frankel looks like a rabbit caught in a trap, and Joseph Thronebury's knees begin to knock again.

Finally, an Asian girl lifts her hand. "I know what I need," she says, shrugging a slender shoulder. "A job."

"Excellent—a job is nice and simple. So William Case's obvious need at the beginning of the story will be to make a living in his world. His hidden need should be something more profound—any suggestions?"

A library stillness settles over the room, with nothing but the tick of the clock to disturb it.

I prop an elbow on the lectern. "How about this—William needs to discover *why* he was created. I can't think of a more existential need. That question bedevils all of us at one time or another."

And I think it's been troubling my son.

I search the room, hoping for signs of affirmation, but most of my students are putting away pens, closing their notebooks, and turning toward the aisles.

I glance up at the clock—dismissal time. My class has mentally checked out.

I cross my arms and step back. "All right, then. I hope to have character profiles to share with you on Friday. From you, though, I'd like at least a paragraph describing a unique story world—a place, occupation, or situation in which you might like to set a novel. I'd also like you to tell me about your protagonist and his two needs—one hidden, one obvious."

They stand and begin to slip away, but on the off chance someone is still listening, I continue. "Don't forget that your protagonist must carry the action in your story. If he balks, remember, *you are the creator*."

I stand at the lectern, waiting for any further questions, but my students have heard enough. Now they want to talk to each other.

All except Ian Morley. That young man is still at his desk, his eyes fastened to the whiteboard and my hastily sketched plot outline.

Should I ask if he has a question about what he's reading?

No, not tonight. I've already borne my share of caustic comments.

Zack has grown up with an author mother. Because he and my career were conceived practically in the same month, for years he never realized my work was anything out of the ordinary.

When he was in second grade, his class invited parents to come talk about their careers. Carl couldn't attend because he was in school at the time, so I reserved the morning and drove over to Hunsberger Elementary.

Squeezed into one of the kid-sized desks, I watched Zack shuffle to the front of the classroom to introduce me. "My dad is in school all day, like me," he announced, his face a study in resigned disappointment. "So he couldn't come. My mom works, so she came."

His teacher, a pleasant woman with the patience of a saint, urged him on. "And what does your mother do, Zack?"

Zack sighed heavily. "She sits at a computer all day and all night. She types books."

The teacher sent me a knowing grin. "I think your mother is an author. Would you like to be an author when you grow up?"

Zack shook his head. "No. She has the most boringest job in the world."

The moon hides her face behind a gauzy scarf of cloud as the roadster rumbles down the curving road that leads me home. No lights burn at our closest neighbors' house, but the Jeffersons are spending the winter in Hawaii. If not for our son and a certain college class, we might be wintering there too.

But that's not fair. I have to admit I've enjoyed teaching, and I'm excited about my new project. And as for Zack . . . well, we had to bring him home. If we'd left him in Salt Lake City, he'd have failed another semester and wasted another six months. Here in Reno, we can help him get back on his feet. Carl's friend Jim McNeil has already given him a job at Bennigan's, and Zack has agreed to go back to school for the summer term.

I turn into the driveway and press the button that activates our electronic gate, then tap my thumbs against the steering wheel as the stately gates swing open. While I'm waiting, something at the base of the privacy wall moves and catches my eye.

We're used to seeing wildlife out here, but this doesn't look like a coyote. I fumble with a switch, and then, in the unforgiving brightness of my high beams, I see a man slumped against the stuccoed wall. His head is down, his shoulders slumped, his jacket littered with grass and mud.

A frisson of alarm tightens every nerve. Who is this, a transient or a stalker? I am reaching for my cell phone, ready to summon an ambulance or the police, when the man turns his head and lifts one hand to block the light.

The stranger is my son.

"Zack!" I shove the car into park and spill out, rushing to his side. The reek of alcohol assaults my nostrils as I catch his chin and search his face. No blood, no cuts, no visible wounds . . . He's not hurt; he's drunk.

My mood veers from fear to fury. What kind of friend dumps a young man beside the road? It's early yet, barely nine thirty, but if I hadn't had class, Zack might have lain out here until morning.

"Zack." I speak in as stern a voice as I can muster. "Son, wake up. Do you hear me?"

Squinting against the light, he mumbles something, then his head rolls into my shadow and his eyes open. "Mom." His voice is thick and heavy. "What are you doing here?"

"I'm taking you inside. Get up."

It's not easy, but between wheedling and sharp commands, I pull Zack to his feet and walk him to the car, where he falls into the passenger seat and slumps over the center console. I slam his door, then hurry to the driver's side, where I have to shove my barely conscious son off the gearshift.

The writer in me makes a mental note: *this is what hauling a dead body would feel like.*

When I finally manage to prop Zack against the passenger door, I place my hand on the gearshift and gulp in deep breaths. Sweat is trickling down my back, soaking the blouse beneath my jacket. Now I reek of alcohol, too, and my limbs are trembling with exhaustion.

A sense of foreboding descends as I drive toward the house. It can't be happening again, yet here's our son, drunk and senseless. What happened tonight? He's had a good month; lately he's been as cheerful as a baby bird. He's been to at least two AA meetings since coming home, and I had begun to think he had finally turned a corner.

I slam my hand against the steering wheel as a wave of resentment crests and crashes. What is *wrong* with this kid? We've done everything we know to do for him; we've answered every reasonable request. He seems appreciative, happy, and stable, then something like *this* happens . . .

I fumble for the garage door opener as tears burn my eyes. After twenty-one years of parenting this child, I have decided I know nothing about raising boys. The girls were never any problem; Patty and Shannon have both been goal-setters and high achievers. Zachary, on the other hand, has driven me to my knees more times than I can remember.

The garage door creaks and rises; as I pull in, the door to the kitchen opens. Carl stands in the rectangle of light, his posture relaxed and welcoming, but his pleasant expression shifts to shock when he sees who's riding shotgun.

I shut off the engine and open my door as Carl comes down the steps. "What the—"

"I found him by the gate. Apparently one of his friends dumped him there."

"Is he—"

"He's okay, but he's drunk. Completely soused."

A glint of resolve enters my husband's eyes as he strides forward to pull our son from the car. Zack looks up when Carl's hand falls on his shoulder. His confused expression melts into a goofy smile when he sees his father's face.

At least some part of his brain is still functioning.

"Dad," he says, his words slurred and slow, "sorry you missed the party. I woulda called you, but you weren't home."

Carl bends to catch my eye. "I've been here all night."

"I know."

As Carl pries Zack from the seat, a crumpled slip of paper falls from my son's pocket to the carpeted floor. I pick it up and smooth it, then hold it under the dome light. It's a receipt from Bennigan's, a long list of dinners and drinks. The total amount charged is over six hundred dollars.

I blink, certain my tired eyes are playing tricks on me. But no, there are three numerals to the left of the decimal point, and this is my son's signature.

"Zack," I call, hoping my voice will penetrate his stupor, "did you meet friends at Bennigan's?"

Zack leans against his father as a crooked smile crosses his face. "Jes put it on my tab."

"Oh, I will," I assure him, meaning every word. When Carl looks at me with a question in his eyes, I flash the receipt. "Over six hundred dollars—I wouldn't be surprised if he sprang for five or six tables tonight."

Carl shakes his head, then half-leads, half-drags Zack into the house.

I follow, pausing only to lower the garage door before going into the kitchen. Some rational part of my brain reminds me that coming home drunk isn't the worst thing a young man could do, but I feel like we're sinking back into a nightmare.

After dropping my purse on the counter, I look through the divider that separates the kitchen from the living room. Zack and Carl are on the stairs, my son leaning heavily on his father as they negotiate the steps.

He won't remember any of this in the morning. But forgetfulness won't erase that credit card charge or relieve the nauseated feeling in my gut.

I sink into a chair and bury my head in my hands. What are we supposed to do now, ground him? Kick him out? If I thought either of those things would solve the problem and teach him to take responsibility, I wouldn't hesitate, but we've tried those things before and nothing changed.

I love my son, honestly I do, but I despise this behavior. The last time we dealt with it, I found myself hating Zack . . . and hating myself for feeling that emotion.

34

Mothers aren't supposed to despise their sons. But I don't know how to love Zachary when he behaves this way.

A tangle of bells jangles as the machine company door closes behind William. Almost instantly, the white-haired man thrusts his head out from behind a tall black box. He grins. "Hello, stranger. Can I help you?"

William gestures toward the home he's just left. "Um, I found a note. And I need a job."

"I'm sure you do." The man steps forward, revealing a paunchy stomach beneath a smudged apron, which he uses to wipe his hands. "We need someone to tend the machines. The job won't make you rich, but it'll put food on the table and keep a roof over your head."

William slips his hand into his pocket. "That's what I need. I think."

The fellow drops his apron, then shoots William a sideward look he can't read. "Wait a minute." He glances out the window. "Did you come from the newcomers' apartments?"

William nods.

A tremor passes over the big man's face. "Are you visiting Paradise from another town? Or are you . . . new?"

A spasm of alarm shoots through his middle, but William manages to answer. "I'm new, and I don't know—"

"You're a newcomer!" The big man whoops and dances a little jig. William steps back, his sense of panic growing until the other man stops dancing and presses his hand to his chest. "I didn't think you'd ever get here. Welcome."

The other man extends his thick hand and regards William with watery eyes. "I'm Ross Ramirez, manager of Casey's Machine Company."

William takes the man's hand and introduces himself.

"William Case." Ramirez repeats the name with satisfaction. "I knew you would come. I told the others you'd be here on the first day of the fourth month, just as Casey said. And here you are, our representative. Ambassador William."

For an instant William feels a surge of adrenaline. An idea blossoms at the front of his brain but is trampled in a rush of confusion.

Yet the title feels right. "Ambassador," he whispers, fitting the word to his tongue. Didn't the author plan this?

Ramirez claps his hand on William's shoulder. "You have the gift," he says, leading William down an aisle between the machines. "The gift of design, the gift of creativity. I don't have it. But here you are, just as Casey promised."

A piece of the puzzle snaps into place. "Casey . . . is the author?"

Ramirez laughs. "Right you are. The creator of everything and everyone in Paradise."

Not knowing what else to do, William nods. "I think I should tell you I don't know anything about machines. As you've probably guessed, I don't know much about anything."

Ramirez chuckles. "We all arrive in Paradise as ignorant as dirt. But don't worry; we'll make sure you learn everything you need to know. Your gift will take care of the rest. Now—how are you coming with the language?"

William sighs. "I'm doing okay, I guess. Sometimes the words get tangled in my head, but they always seem to sort themselves out."

"That'll happen until you get the hang of the lingo. Casey has given us knowledge about all kinds of things. Sometimes you have to concentrate to find the understanding you need, but it'll come."

He turns on the ball of his foot, a surprisingly graceful gesture for a man of his size, then motions toward the boxy cabinets along the walls. "This is Casey's Machine Company." His voice booms in the enclosed space. "We make and sell mechanical games people play for enjoyment. The operating principle is simple—you put in a silver coin, you receive a valuable gift. You put in a gold coin, you receive a *more* valuable gift. Casey believes people should reap what they sow. Let me show you what I mean."

He walks over to a rectangular machine against the wall. The lower part of the cabinet has been painted bright red; the upper section is a clear plastic cube. Inside the cube, a slim ballerina spins on a circular platform, her arms extended.

Ramirez jingles something in his pocket and fondly pats the machine. "This is a good one." He slides a silver coin into a slot at the top of the box. William leans forward as the coin rolls around a narrow track, then drops into the dancer's outstretched hand. At the touch of silver, the doll's eyes open, her arm lifts, and the coin shoots into a canister at the back of the machine.

Ramirez's eyes glow with admiration. "She never misses. This one's a thing of beauty."

William watches, fascinated, as the coin clunks into a container and triggers a door at the back of the cabinet. The dancer keeps spinning as the door opens and a train emerges, smoke billowing from its miniature smokestack as it follows a winding track to the front of the box. A car behind the engine carries a small stuffed bear; when the train reaches its destination, the track tilts, the ballerina stops spinning, and the stuffed bear drops through an opening and vanishes from sight.

"It's yours." Ramirez points to a shiny panel at the bottom of the machine. "Consider it a welcoming gift."

William pushes the swinging panel aside and pulls out the bear. He doesn't think it's what he needs to pay the rent, but it is a cute little thing.

"If I had put in a gold coin," Ramirez explains, moving to another machine, "I'd have received a fancier toy or even a book. Casey's games are designed to surprise the player, but they never cheat. They always reward us with something bigger or better."

He points to another machine, this one painted in hues of blue. A miniature waterfall flows from the back wall, splashing over rocks and tiny green trees.

"Casey's games are also designed to celebrate this world," Ramirez says. "This one is called *Nature Falls*. It rewards players with precious stones, polished rocks, and the occasional fertile egg. Marilyn won an egg a few weeks ago; now she's living with a canary."

"Marilyn?" William wonders if she is anything like the beauty who preceded him into the building.

"One of our sweetest and most faithful customers—you'll meet her soon, I'm sure." Ramirez lifts a hand, taking in all the games with one grand gesture. "These are Casey's inventions. The author designed them, Stan manufactures them, I oversee the game room. What we need now is someone to help us create new games, and you're the one Casey sent. Other towns have been waiting for new models."

William stares at the incredibly detailed *Nature Falls* game, where a tiny fish is trying his best to swim upstream. "Other towns play these machines too?"

"Casey's work is known all over the world." Ramirez beams with pride. "We get orders all the time."

"Then why did Casey stop designing?"

"Not my place to ask questions," Ramirez whispers, "but I think the creator is working on something else."

William is about to nod, but he is nearly knocked off his feet when Ramirez slaps him on the back. "Come on and let me introduce you to the rest of the staff. We'll get you a pair of coveralls too—don't want you to dirty your own clothes as you learn how the games are put together."

William's pulse increases as he follows Ramirez through a swinging door marked *Employees Only*. They step into an open space occupied by a table and four chairs. A bench runs along one wall while a set of cubicles occupies the other. On the wall above the bench, someone has painted a huge triangle with an eye in the center.

Ramirez gestures to the space. "This is our employees' area. The restrooms are over there"—he points to a pair of doors at his right—"and the office is over here. If you can't find me in the factory or the game room, I'm sure to be in the office."

William's heart skips a beat when he turns toward the left. A large picture window looks into the office, and through the glass he sees . . . her.

"That's—"

"Raquel Santiago." Ramirez grins. "She's our financial clerk, and she does a bit of typing for me now and then." He wriggles his thick fingers. "Never got the hang of a typewriter. My paws barely fit on the keys."

William forces himself to study Ramirez, hoping he won't see the gleam of possession in the manager's eyes. No, the man is striding forward with an air of nonchalance, a feat that would be impossible if he realized the most desirable woman in this world sat only a few feet away.

The manager opens the door and leans into the office. "Raquel? I want you to meet someone. The ambassador has finally arrived."

Rattled by Ramirez's announcement and Raquel's proximity, William steps forward. He gives her a wobbly smile and offers his free hand.

She comes from behind the desk and accepts it. "William." Her skin feels cool and smooth in his grip. "Nice to have you with us."

"Nice to be here." In an instant of inspired spontaneity, he offers her the stuffed bear. "You look like someone who might enjoy this."

The words have no sooner left his lips than he is overwhelmed with regret—she probably hates bears, she'll be insulted by his gift, she might have a dozen of these things jammed into her desk drawer—but she takes the toy with a smile that lingers on him. "Thanks. You're sweet."

William glances over his shoulder, certain that Ramirez is about to mention that Raquel is his wife, his daughter, or his personal property, but the manager has already moved back into the employees' area.

"Um"—William jerks his head toward the doorway—"I guess I'd better follow the boss."

"The boss?" She smiles, sending a dimple winking in her left cheek. "*You're* the ambassador. But okay, I'll see you later."

William follows Ramirez, his head ringing with Raquel's words. What did she mean by that parting comment?

"Here," Ramirez says, pointing to one of the cubicles, "you'll find a pair of coveralls for when you begin to work. You don't have to worry about leaving your things in there; no one will bother them."

William looks at the compartment, empty except for a folded orange jumpsuit.

"Back here"—Ramirez pushes his way through a swinging door— "is the factory."

William follows Ramirez into a room so filled with noise he is tempted to clap his hands over his ears. The air vibrates with the hiss and clank of automatic machinery, while from somewhere beyond the assembly line, saws shriek and a siren warbles. Long tables stand off to the right, cluttered with various mechanical parts and miniature objects. Empty cabinets line the front wall, the shells of games-to-be, and above the vacant frames, another eyeball-in-pyramid looks down on the confusion.

Ramirez pulls a set of earphones from a shelf, then leans in to yell at William. "I'll show you around, but save your questions until we go back to the break room. No sense in us screaming at each other."

William adjusts his headset, then sighs in relief. The contraption does muffle the noise, but it also blocks Ramirez's voice. Still, the big man talks nearly nonstop as they walk down the line.

The assembly line is totally automatic and completely mechanized. Robotic arms fasten pieces together; mechanical tools fasten and weld and wire. An automatic sprayer applies paint to the cabinet bases, while a polisher shines the acrylic cubes that house the moving parts.

The factory is almost too much for William to take in. By the time they complete the tour of just one line, he's grateful that being the ambassador apparently has nothing to do with automation.

At one point Ramirez lifts his brows, obviously asking a question. William shakes his head, then Ramirez grins and motions toward a small corner office. In this cubbyhole they find another man in an orange jumpsuit. When the stranger stands, William notices that they are about the same height. The new man's face is smooth and unlined, his waistline trim, but his deep-set eyes seem more experienced than Ramirez's. He gives William a confident smile, then picks up a clipboard and a pen. A moment later he flashes a crude sign: *Stan Silva, Master Mechanic and Resident Know-It-All.*

William laughs. Ramirez jerks his thumb toward the fellow, shakes his head in good-natured resignation, and motions toward the exit.

They remove their earphones in the employees' area, which now rings with silence. Ramirez tosses his headset onto the table. "Stan is quite a character, but he's the genius who set up our automated assembly line. He's responsible for putting together every machine that rolls out of this place." Ramirez suddenly places his hands on his hips. "Well, look at that—Raquel's been busy."

The back of William's neck heats as he studies the row of cubicles. While Ramirez and William have toured the factory, someone—apparently Raquel—has painted William's name on the wood framing his space. The thought that she would do something for him leaves William breathless.

"Well, now." Ramirez folds his hands. "That's the grand tour. I don't expect you to do anything today, but we'll look for you first thing tomorrow morning. We have a couple of regular customers who like to stop by on their way to work, and I'd like to introduce you."

Feeling more assured than before, William nods. "I'll be here."

"I think," the manager says, "you'll like working here. Now"—he glances at his watch—"I'll let you go. You need to get some rest, and I need to make sure Casey intended the fish in *Nature Falls* to swim upstream."

William forces a smile as Ramirez holds the door leading into the game room. He would like to linger and talk to Raquel, but the manager obviously expects him to leave.

It probably wouldn't be wise to disappoint on his first day.

After sending Raquel a small smile, William waves farewell to Ramirez and heads home.

Nine

William sits in the kitchen of his apartment, his elbows propped on the table, his head in his hands. He is staring out the window at an image of the triangle-and-eye someone has painted on a sign across the street.

He yawns and lets his forehead fall to the tabletop. He closes his eyes, preferring to dwell on visions of the lovely girl across the street than to ponder the meaning of a mysterious symbol.

As he is about to drift into a doze, the muffled sound of a female voice rouses him. He sits up, startled, and looks out his window. Raquel

Santiago is leaving the machine company with Stan Silva by her side. No longer wearing his orange jumpsuit, Stan swaggers in a nice suit, a smile on his face . . . and Raquel's hand on his arm.

William steps back, his hope crumpling as if squeezed by a fist. What does it mean, this touching of hands and arms? Raquel couldn't be with Stan, could she? If she likes Stan, will she have room in her heart for William?

He moves closer to the window, pressing his fingertips to the warm glass as he peers out. The sun is setting behind the machine company building, and the street has filled with people of all shapes and sizes— women of varying ages and hair colors, men hustling along with books and bags and briefcases. As interesting as these people are, none of the women can compare to Raquel, and none of the men are as intimidating as Stan.

William pulls his jacket from the hook by the door and shrugs his way into it. Squinting against the bright sun, he steps onto the sidewalk and peers in the direction where Raquel and Stan have vanished. Dozens of small houses line the street to the south, pleasant-looking pastel buildings with wide porches festooned with ferns and flowers. Raquel is no longer in sight, and William fears he'll look silly if he tries to figure out which house is hers . . . but perhaps he won't have to snoop. Paradise is a small town. Surely someone will tell him what he needs to know.

William turns right, then tips his head to read the sign hanging over the building next door: *Eden's Repast, Home of the Best Organic Cooking in Paradise.*

His stomach growls at the thought of food, and he realizes he hasn't eaten. Ever. But eating is beneficial; food is important. So he pastes on an unsteady smile and heads toward the restaurant.

The place is small, not much larger than his apartment, with a row of booths by the windows and a line of stools before a gleaming counter. Stainless steel equipment lines the back wall, and the mingled aromas of food and drink make William's knees go wobbly. Somehow he staggers to the bar and sits down. Before reaching for the menu, he searches his pocket—there! Two gold coins have been fastened to the fabric. Surely that's enough to buy a meal in this place.

William tugs the plastic-covered menu from between a domed sugar dispenser and a napkin holder, then frowns at the cover. The restaurant's name has been printed above the pyramid and its unblinking eye.

A pink-haired waitress comes over, pen and pad in hand. She smiles. "Can I help you?"

"Yes." Certain that a pleasant expression will help him win acceptance, William returns her smile, then flips open the menu and scans the contents.

"Um . . . what's good?"

She leans against the counter. "What do you like?"

"I don't know."

For an instant she stares, dull eyed, then her brows lift. "You must be a newcomer."

William's cheeks heat under the intensity of her gaze. "Yes."

"Then you don't want anything from the menu, hon; you want a nice bowl of broth. Best to break in the stomach gently."

She scratches something on her pad, then halts in midstroke.

"Today," she says, her voice going hoarse, "is the first day of the fourth month."

William closes the menu. "So I've heard."

"Then . . ." Her hand flies to her mouth. "Ohmygoodness, are you *him*?"

"Him who?"

"The ambassador who's supposed to come. The one Ross Ramirez is always talking about."

"I don't know," he says. "I probably know less than anybody in this town."

She props her elbow on the counter and regards him with wide eyes. "You may not feel like the ambassador now, but you will. Ross says so."

William clears his throat and searches for another topic of conversation. His gaze lights on the menu, so he taps the picture of the pyramid eye. "Maybe you can tell me what this means. I see it all over the place."

She glances at the image. "That's Casey's eye. It's to remind us the creator is always watching."

"Really?" William glances around, half-expecting to see some wise old man propped up in a booth.

The waitress giggles. "You're funny."

"Well?" He glances left to right, then leans toward her. "Have you ever seen him?"

"Who?"

"Casey."

She shakes her head. "Not me. But others have, I think."

"Who?"

"Well . . . Ramirez, for one. He's always telling me Casey said this or that."

"*How* does he see him? Do they meet behind the machine company or what?"

Annoyance struggles with humor on her fine-boned face. "I don't know. I've never asked." She straightens, then pulls a dishcloth from beneath the counter and swipes the countertop. "Why don't you ask him yourself?"

"I will." William gives her another smile as his stomach grumbles. "If I don't first pass out from hunger."

"Oh. Sorry." She tears the top sheet from her order pad and turns to slide it through the kitchen window. "Bowl of broth, Hank, and hurry, will you, hon? Got a newcomer out here, and he's hungry."

She leaves to pour coffee for another man and woman at the end of the bar. While she tends to them, William swivels on his stool and looks around the restaurant. Another couple sits in a booth near the window; a woman is sipping coffee at the far end of the counter. This might be the perfect place to ask about Raquel—if he can trust the waitress not to laugh out loud when she figures out why he's asking.

Then again, maybe he should wait. If all goes well at the machine company, maybe he won't have to ask. After all, this morning he thought he sensed a quiet attraction between him and Raquel, so maybe she thinks of Stan Silva only as a good friend.

The pink-haired lady comes back. "You're going to think I have no manners." She extends her hand. "I'm Eden. That's my husband, Hank, in the kitchen. We run this place."

William shakes her hand. "I'm William."

"Good to know you, Ambassador William."

"I still don't understand what that means."

"Doesn't matter. Casey does." She crosses her arms on the counter. "So. Got a job yet?"

"Yes," he answers, glad that he's managed to accomplish something. "I'll be working at the machine company."

"I shoulda figured that. But you better be careful."

"What do you mean?"

She shrugs. "Don't you remember what you read in the paper? You're our representative. We choose what you choose."

"Does that mean everyone has to have broth for dinner?"

She laughs. "I don't know what it means. Maybe Ramirez does."

He's about to ask something else, but Hank bellows her name. Eden hurries to the kitchen window; a moment later she sets a bowl of steaming broth on the counter.

"It's on the house," she says, smiling. "Seein' that it's your first meal and all. The least we can do for the ambassador."

William wants to insist he doesn't deserve anything special, but his starving body won't be distracted. Ignoring the utensils on the counter, he picks up the bowl and drinks the luscious liquid in long, slow swallows.

Delicious.

en

When I open my eyes the next morning, for a long moment I can't remember what day it is. Monday? Sunday? No . . . Thursday. Another writing day and the day after a horrible night.

I lift my head and peer through the morning gloom. The bathroom door is edged in light, so Carl is up and in the shower. He'll grab a cup of coffee and glance at the paper and be out of here before eight—long before our son rises with what's sure to be a nasty hangover.

I fall back to my pillow and stare at the ceiling. *Lord, I don't know why you've brought us back to this place, but you're gonna have to give me strength.*

The people at my church say that prayer changes everything. While I don't doubt that prayer has the power to change people, in between answers you still have to deal with the here and now. I can ask God to change my son and show Zack the error of his ways, but I still have to find a way to cope with the man-boy upstairs.

I toss off the heavy comforter and tiptoe through the bathroom, squinting against the light as I twiddle my fingers at the man in the shower. A small door off the bathroom leads into my office, so I go to my desk and power on my computer. While the hard drive whirrs and clicks, I look out across our manicured lawn. Anyone driving by would think this is a peaceful house. Amazing how deceptive a dawn-shrouded landscape can be.

I pass the morning in my usual routine: I feed Dubya, read the *Reno Gazette-Journal* while eating my crumpets and jam, let the dog out. I sweep the area around the dog's bed, let Dubya back in, wander into the library, and pull my Bible from the desk by the window. I read the daily selection, jot a few benumbed reactions in my journal, then bow my head.

Prayer doesn't come easily this morning. May heaven help me, but the experience of last night has awakened feelings and fears I've successfully repressed. Adrenaline boils beneath my drowsy brain; anger lurks beneath my morning silence.

I ask the Lord to bless Patricia in her work; Travis, Shannon, and their girls in their routine; Carl at the school; and me at my desk. I would ask the Lord to bless Zachary, too, but at this moment I'd honestly prefer that God knock him over the head.

Carl comes out of the kitchen and presses a kiss to my cheek. "Love you," he calls.

I manage to whisper the same before he strides through the foyer and out the door.

I drop my pencil, then scrub my hands through my hair in the hope a scalp massage will stimulate my brain. I don't like to admit it, but I'm finding it difficult to be creative. Perhaps it's the pressure of competition—I've told my class to invent a unique story setting, so I can't have them coming up with ideas better than the world I've created for William Case.

My vision of Paradise will have to knock their socks off. Not only that, but William has to live in an environment totally different from Rex Tower's. If I stray too far from the conventional, however, I'll spend half the book explaining why *two* moons light the night sky and a year consists of six months instead of the usual twelve.

Sighing, I pick up my pencil and scratch through a note that reads "Consider talking animals?" Better by far to plant William in a community resembling small-town America. I can add a few oddities that might eventually play into the plot, but I don't want to waste words on unimportant explanations. This novel, after all, is about something far more important than talking animals and double moons.

Dubya and I both look up as the door alarm beeps softly. A moment later Carl comes into my study, one hand tugging at his tie.

"Is he up?"

Maybe my creativity has been blocked by thoughts of my wayward offspring.

I push away from the desk, knowing I'm done for the day. "I haven't heard a peep out of him. I guess he's still sleeping it off."

A worry line appears between Carl's brows. "Have you checked on him?"

"Oh, he's breathing. I went up about nine and again at two. He was still in his clothes, sound asleep."

Carl yanks his tie out of his collar, then drops it on my desk. He tips his head toward the stairs. "You want to come with me?"

I shake my head. "He's all yours."

My husband sighs and heads for the staircase while I cross my arms and try to control my wavering emotions. My gaze gravitates to a photo on the corner of my desk—Patty and Shannon, ages eleven and nine, laughing on a park bench while two-year-old Zachary stretches across their laps and mugs for the camera.

We never intended to have a third child—I was perfectly happy with two girls, but God had other plans. I was less than thrilled about teaching through a third pregnancy, but God took care of that too.

When complications arose and my doctor prescribed bed rest, I decided to pass the time learning how to write a novel. By the time Zachary was born, I'd tapped out the initial adventure of Rex Tower, American super-spy and former Navy SEAL.

I'd harbored few hopes for *American Tower*, my apprentice novel, but the first agent I contacted adored the book. With contagious enthusiasm, he presented the manuscript to Dalton & Sons, whose head honchos gave me a contract and hired a minor movie actor to swagger through the aisles of the American Booksellers Convention as Rex Tower. The publisher's marketing savvy, combined with the actor's rugged good looks, satisfied an American hunger for a contemporary Superman. The resulting success has kept my name near the top of every *New York Times* annual best-seller list since 1985.

If only I could be successful with my son.

Zachary hasn't always been in trouble. Through elementary and middle school, he was the light of our lives, the jokester at every family occasion. No one was brighter or more energetic than he was, no one more up for adventure.

I used to watch my son and imagine that as a boy Rex Tower had been like Zack . . . and dream that my son would grow up to be like my literary hero. But something happened in Zack's high school years—bad friends, bad choices, bad consequences. He had his first DUI arrest at seventeen, resulting in the impounding of his car, ninety-six hours of required community service, a $1,000 fine, compulsory attendance at DUI school, and a ninety-day revocation of his license.

We thought Zack had learned his lesson, but he was arrested for DUI again his senior year. The second judge slapped Zack with the usual fines and penalties, then added a thirty-day stay at a rehab facility, a year of weekly participation in Alcoholics Anonymous, and a court-ordered program requiring random urine tests three times a week. We had to get special permission for the drug tests to be administered in Salt Lake City, where Zack was a freshman at the University of Utah. I've often wondered if that added pressure contributed to his poor grades.

Though he passed every court-ordered drug test, college life didn't agree with Zachary. He failed nearly every class that first year, blaming his lack of success on a noisy dorm and poor study habits. We found him an apartment in Salt Lake and handpicked a roommate from a list of applicants, hoping he'd fare better during his second year.

Back in Reno, we thought Zack was doing well—we didn't hear from him for long stretches, but when we did catch him on the phone, he seemed upbeat and cheerful. One weekend, though, we paid our son a surprise visit and found him completely disoriented. His roommate, Clay, told us Zack hadn't slept in days; we could see that our son was so tired he could barely walk.

The result of stress, we told ourselves. He was under too much pressure, not eating properly, and not pacing himself. In time, he'd adjust. We went to the grocery and brought back bags of real food, then gave Clay a check for five hundred dollars to replenish the pantry. We spoke to Zack's adviser and suggested that he recommend a lighter class load. We asked Clay to call us if we were needed.

Several months passed in relative peace and quiet. Carl taught; I worked on my twentieth Tower novel. "We finally have an empty nest," I e-mailed a friend, "and we like it a lot."

Just before Thanksgiving, however, we received a frantic call from Zack's roommate. Our son was outside in the parking lot, Clay said, being beaten by a gang of men he'd never seen before.

"Have you called the police?"

"Um, I dunno if I should. I dunno what Zack's doin' down there."

His unspoken implication waved like a red flag. *If this is a drug buy gone bad, Zack wouldn't want the cops around . . .*

We told Clay to call 911, then we jumped in the car and drove the 450 miles to Salt Lake City. We found Zack in his apartment with an egg-shaped lump on the back of his head. Clay couldn't identify any of the thugs in the parking lot, and Zack wouldn't.

Our bruised and bloodied son wept in our arms and agreed to come home, but we hadn't been on the interstate more than an hour before he became belligerent and tried to climb out of our moving car. Not knowing what else to do, Carl and I took him back to Salt Lake. Zack *had* to be using drugs, but his roommate either hadn't seen evidence of drug use or wouldn't tell us what he'd seen.

What could we do? Over the Thanksgiving weekend, we begged and prayed and pleaded, but Zack refused to admit he had a problem.

God, though, works in mysterious ways. On Sunday night, the day before we had to go back to Reno, Zack was arrested for driving under the influence. He protested, insisting he'd been exhausted, not drunk, when he ran his car into a ditch, but we bailed him out and convinced him to come home. Slow down, we said. Work a little, earn some cash, take only as many courses as you want.

Privately, Carl and I thanked God that Zack's citation had been issued in Utah, not Nevada, where he already had two DUI convictions. No one had to remind us how fortunate we were that our son had not caused any serious accidents.

Zack came home. He took the job at Bennigan's and reconnected with old friends. Over Christmas he charmed and entertained us.

But now the bubble has burst.

I knock my fist against my forehead as my mind burns with painful memories. The last two years have been bearable because we didn't have to encounter Zack's problems on a daily basis. Though we worried about him, I had my writing to distract me; Carl had his teaching. Our careers were God-given life rafts, keeping us afloat in a stormy sea.

How can I write *and* deal with Zachary?

"It's too much," I whisper into my hands. "Lord, you know this is more than I can handle."

No answer disturbs the stillness of my office; no sound comes from upstairs.

Eleven

William slips into the roomy orange coveralls and fastens the snaps. The garment hangs on his slender frame, but after a few more meals at Eden's, he's bound to fill out the waistline. The hem drags on the floor, though, and he's not sure he'll ever be taller.

Pausing before the mirror in the men's room, he gives his reflection a critical squint. Now that he's had a chance to look around Paradise, he knows his looks aren't anything special. But as long as his face doesn't send Raquel running in horror, he can accept it.

Curious, he investigates his surroundings. A bottle of degreaser sits on the counter. When he crouches and opens the cabinet doors, he finds extra toilet paper, a bundle of brown paper towels, a can of air freshener, a canister of drain cleaner, and a plunger. Apparently, Casey's Machine Company employees handle the janitorial and maintenance work too.

He looks up as the door opens. Stan Silva comes in, a smile creasing his face when he sees William. "Finding everything you need?" he asks, moving to the sink.

"Um, yeah. I was just looking around."

"If you need anything you can't find, give a shout."

"Thanks."

Stan lathers his hands with a squirt of degreaser. "Ready to start work?"

William stands and slips his hands into the pockets of his coveralls. "I guess so. I still don't understand exactly what I'm supposed to do."

Stan grins as he scrubs grime from his hands. "Ramirez will explain everything. So relax and stay cool."

Together they walk into the employees' break area. William tries to be as cool as Stan says, but his heart leaps into his throat when Raquel shoots a smile through the office window. He feels a warm glow flow through him, then he can't help but wonder—was that smile meant for him or Stan?

He doesn't have time to consider the question. The door to the game room swings open, and Ramirez enters, a grin on his broad face. "Morning, William, Stan. How are you two this fine day?"

Stan moves to his cubicle. "Doing great, boss."

"William?" Ramirez lifts a silvery brow. "Finding everything you need?"

"Yes."

The manager beams. "That's good."

"Ross?"

William looks over to see Raquel standing in the office doorway. "Don't we need to go over those reports?" she asks.

Ramirez rubs his hands together. "Indeed we do. William, will you be okay if I leave you with Stan?"

William looks at his coworker, who grins again. "Sure."

"Fine. Stan will demonstrate the inner workings of a machine while I meet with Raquel. You and I can talk later."

Ramirez flashes a parting smile, then strides toward the office. William sighs. How wonderful it would be to work in the office, knowing Raquel sat only a few feet away . . .

When Ramirez closes the door, Stan erupts in laughter.

"What?" Heat steals into William's face as he turns. "Something funny?"

"You are, man. I can read your face like a book."

"Really? And what are you reading?"

Stan claps his hand on William's shoulder. "She is gorgeous, isn't she? Probably the prettiest woman in Paradise."

William is about to protest, but Stan is probably right. Maybe he should work harder at controlling his facial expressions.

Still laughing, Stan shoulders his way through the door that leads to the machine factory. William tosses his folded clothes into his cubicle, then curls his belt into a circle and sets it on his shirt.

He's about to follow the mechanic, but a red blur in his peripheral vision snags his attention. To the left of the restroom entrance stands a third door, an opening nearly obscured by shadows and a tall garbage can. The door bears a sign painted in stiff red letters: NO ADMITTANCE. Leaving nothing to chance, someone has secured the door with a padlock and hasp.

Staring at the sign, William is overcome by a sense, unanchored but strong, that the door is important.

He glances toward the office, where Ramirez leans over Raquel's desk, a paper in his hand. The boss isn't watching.

William steps closer and peers over the garbage can. He didn't notice the door yesterday, but Ramirez gave him such a quick tour that he didn't examine anything carefully. This is only one door in a town filled with them, but this is the first lock he's seen. On an island where every door opens freely, why has Ramirez locked this one?

William walks to the bench, then sits and rolls up the hem of his coveralls. As he folds the fabric, he steals a glance at the office.

Ramirez has disappeared into the inner room, but Raquel sits at her station, her eyes intent on her typewriter. The little bear he gave her sits on the corner of her desk.

In an instant, he makes his decision.

"Excuse me, Raquel?"

Her brown eyes widen as she meets his gaze. "You need something, William?"

He leans on the door frame. "I have a question—this door behind me, the one near the corner. Why is it locked?"

Her brows wrinkle. "It's always been like that. Casey must have locked it."

"But why? What's in that room?"

She lifts one lovely shoulder in a shrug. "I've never asked."

He crosses his arms, a little amazed that someone so interesting could be so uninterested in a puzzle right outside her office. "Does Ramirez ever go in there?"

"I've never seen him go anywhere near it."

William studies her, wondering if he should press further, but maybe he shouldn't stick his nose where it doesn't belong. After all, this is his first day on the job, and he has a lot to learn. After he has proven himself, maybe Ramirez will take him aside and explain this little mystery.

"William?"

"Yeah?"

Her eyes are bright, expectant. "Anything else you need? I could get almost anything for you . . . if you want me to, that is."

He shakes his head. "I'm okay. I'm good. Thanks."

He slips his hands into his pockets and nods to Raquel, then stops by his cubicle to pick up his protective earphones. He will tour the factory and fill his brain with information about Casey's machines, but he will not forget the locked door.

After a detailed journey through the guts of an *Under the Seas* game, William's head buzzes with the names and images of more than fifty mechanical parts. He can barely tell an arm switch from a kick switch, a hopper knife from a hopper wiper, a pinwheel from a screw-operated brake.

Stan laughs at his confusion. "Don't worry, I'm the one who puts things together," he tells William in a rare silence. He has shut down the mechanical assembly line so they can talk. "You only need to know how things work."

He leads William into his cubbyhole office, then opens a drawer and pulls out several curled diagrams. "Take a look if you want." He nods toward the pages. "The original schematics, drawn by Casey's own hand . . . or so I've been told."

The implied doubt in his comment makes William pause. "You're not sure?"

The mechanic picks up a wheel from a coin intake mechanism and polishes it. "You know, don't you, that Ramirez expects you to design new games."

William's breath catches in his lungs. "Not anytime soon, I hope."

Stan gives him a lopsided smile. "What are you waiting for, Mr. Ambassador? You're supposed to be the one who leads the way."

William's not sure what he means by that, but perhaps he can find an answer in the detailed schematics Stan has given him. Wondering if his less-than-brilliant approach to the job has revealed his lack of preparation, he carries the stapled pages to the break room, where he can read in quiet . . . and occasionally peek at Raquel through the window.

Sitting cross-legged on the bench, he flips to a section titled "How to Repair What Is Broken."

To gain a basic understanding of the electronic functions and philosophy underlying the operation of Casey's machines, it is advisable for new employees to run the series of tests described on page 8 and ending on page 15. To aid in troubleshooting, pages 16–20 explain the malfunction codes that will be displayed in the LED screen.

William looks up, baffled. What is troubleshooting? And why do the machines need malfunction codes?

He looks up to see if Ramirez is nearby, then he walks to the office door. A welcoming smile lights Raquel's face.

He leans into the room. "Is the boss around?"

"He's at lunch."

"Okay, then . . . Can I ask *you* something?"

"Sure." A flush colors her face as she crosses her arms. "What do you need?"

"Some direction, maybe." Emboldened by her smile, he moves closer. "Has anything ever gone wrong with the machines?"

Lines of concentration deepen along her brows. "What do you mean?"

"Well—has Stan or Ramirez ever had to fix them?"

"Fix?"

"Repair, restore, replace. Rewire, reconfigure, refurbish."

"Wow." Her eyes twinkle like stars. "You must be the smartest man to ever come through that door."

She hasn't answered his question, but she has made him feel good. He stands there, blinking in pleased surprise, until she reaches into her drawer and pulls out a silver coin. "I know what will make you feel better." She presses the coin into his hand. "You need to play one of the yellow machines."

He gives Raquel a puzzled frown. "You want me to go play a game?"

She points toward the game room. "Any of the machines with a yellow cabinet. Go on." She shoos him out the door. "You can thank me later."

Moving in blind obedience, William heads into the game room. A few of the games are occupied; from the doorway he can hear the clink and clack of mechanical gears.

He walks to the far wall, where yellow machines are mixed among a row of red, blue, and green games. He slides the coin into the slot of a game called *Sun, Moons, and Stars*, then grips the Plexiglas sides of the transparent cube atop the yellow base.

A light shines from the interior of the darkened box, illuminating a three-dimensional tree. While he watches, a silver-throated bird appears from within a hollow of the tree trunk. The background darkens and the twin moons of Paradise climb from the velvety horizon.

As a bright sprinkling of stars gleams through the night, the bird begins to sing.

The crystalline beauty of the song catches William by surprise. The tremulous whistle rises from the little warbler's throat and pierces the plastic walls, shooting straight into William's heart. He knows the sound comes from a matching pair of stereo speakers, but whoever wrote the nightingale's song is . . . a genius.

Spellbound, he listens until the song ends, then lets his forehead fall to the Plexiglas. Does all music affect people this way, or is this a particularly gifted design? Either way, Raquel was right. The song has lightened his mood.

The sound of low, cackling laughter breaks into his thoughts. He lifts his head and sees a white-haired woman off to his right, a smile on her lips and a knowing expression in her blue eyes. She wears baggy pants, a matching shirt, and a sun visor. On her arm she carries a flowered bag from which two sets of eyes peer at William—the eyes, he sees upon closer examination, belong to a tiny dog and cat.

"The song knocked me out, too, the first time I heard it." Her sparkling eyes sink into nets of wrinkles as she smiles. "I couldn't understand why, but I had to sit down and collect myself. Left me weak in the knees."

William uses his sleeve to wipe his handprints from the glass. "Sorry. I'm not used to a lot of things."

"I know." Her smile deepens. "I'm Marilyn Barron, and these are my companions, Carlo and Marlo." She lifts the lid of her ventilated bag and pats the dog and cat. "And you are?"

"William." He takes her small hand.

"Nice to meet you, William. Welcome to Paradise."

"Thank you." He snaps his fingers as a memory surfaces. "You're the woman who won the canary."

Her eyes compress as she smiles. "Oh yes. It was such fun to take care of the fledgling."

"And how is the bird?"

She lifts her hand and flutters her fingers. "Gone. When he was strong enough, I set him free. I like to think of him nesting in a tree somewhere, singing for anyone who'll take the time to listen."

Remembering his manners, William gestures to the machine, then pauses to wipe a smudge from the place where his forehead rested on the glass. "If you want to play this one, it's all yours."

"There's no need. One of the nicest things about the yellow machines is that when one person gives, everyone around enjoys the reward. There's nothing like a lovely song to set the tone for the day."

William steps to the next machine and wipes its window as Marilyn moves to the next yellow game, then lowers her bag to the floor. This one, *Sahara Sunrise,* accepts her silver coin, then the background brightens, the stars fade, and the sky flushes with a hundred shades of rose. A thinner tree sprouts from the floor of the box and another bird appears, this one colored in rainbow hues. This warbler sings a different song, but its tune is no less breathtaking than the nightingale's.

While the dog yowls and the cat purrs in accompaniment, William shakes his head in amused wonder. He's not sure how he's supposed to design machines as incredible as these, but watching Marilyn has given him an idea.

When he skimmed through the schematics, he saw a section with pictures of animals and birds and sunsets and storms. Why not use the existing technology to spin off a game featuring a giant sea horse? Or the wonders of thunder and hail?

He turns and hurries to the break room, where the pages wait on the bench. His brain has suddenly become a lightning rod for ideas.

Twelve

I'm warming leftovers in the kitchen when I finally hear my husband's heavy creak on the steps. I turn and lean against the granite counter, bracing myself for bad news.

I expect Carl's eyes to be angry when he slides onto a stool at the counter. Instead, they're watery and red-rimmed.

"What happened?" I search his face. "What'd he say?"

Carl pushes a leather-bound volume toward me. "Have you seen this?"

What is it, some kind of pornography? I step closer to look at the book. "Where'd that come from?"

"His dresser, under a stack of shorts. It's a journal."

I give my husband a swift look. "Zack keeps a journal?"

"Apparently. Some of the entries go back two years. He must have started it in Salt Lake." Carl pulls a handkerchief from his pocket and dabs at his eyes. "It's . . . Well, you should look at it, Jordy."

Something in me recoils at the thought. "I'm not sure we should be reading his personal thoughts."

Carl presses his hands to his face for a long moment, then lowers them and looks at me. "If not us, who? Who else cares as much about this kid?"

When his eyes fill with fresh tears, my heart leaps into the back of my throat. "Good grief, Carl, what did you read in that thing?"

"He wants to kill himself. He's written pages and pages about how he has no life and no one cares. He says he might as well be dead."

For a moment the book and countertop meld in a spinning blur, then, slowly, I blink the room back into focus. "That's impossible. No one has more to live for—"

"He needs help, hon. We've got to do something."

"*Do* something?" I choke on the words. "What can we do that we haven't done? We've hired lawyers, put him in rehab, bribed roommates, and called in favors to find him a job. How much more can we do?"

Carl is weeping now, tears flowing freely over his cheeks. "There's one thing we haven't tried."

I stare at him, baffled, but I understand when his hand falls on the journal.

"Oh no." I force a laugh. "Our son does not need a shrink."

"There's no shame in seeking professional counseling, Jordan. The boy needs help."

"For *drinking*? We'll make sure he gets back to AA. He's been hit or miss over the last year, so if he gets involved again—"

"AA's not going to give him a reason to live." Carl strokes the journal. "He has problems."

"He's an alcoholic, pure and simple. We know this. *He* knows this. He does fine except for those times when he falls off the wagon."

"Maybe something is driving him to take that first drink. Something we've missed all these years."

"That's not possible." I pick up a dish towel and scrub at the counter. "We're good parents. Even though we didn't know what we were doing, Patty and Shannon turned out okay. We didn't mess up our kids."

"If we had, would you let your pride stand between Zack and the help he needs?"

The question snaps like a whip, stinging my conscience. Am I being prideful? After all we've been through, I find it hard to believe I have an ounce of pride left. I have begged police officers, groveled before judges, pleaded with probation officers and rehab counselors . . .

"It's not pride." I swipe at a tear trickling down my cheek. "A few years ago I might have been too proud, but not now."

"Then why don't you want Zack to see a counselor?"

Around us, the house falls silent, as if it is listening. The refrigerator ceases to hum, the dishwasher takes a break in its wash cycle, the convection oven stops blowing exhaust.

"I don't want him to see a shrink," I begin, my voice wavering, "because that would make Zack see himself as *broken*. And he's not broken, not by a long shot. He's made a few mistakes."

With the weariness of the world in his eyes, Carl pushes the book in my direction. "Read it, then tell me what you think."

He leaves me in the kitchen with my son's secret thoughts and a dinner that will not be eaten tonight.

Thirteen

By the time Ramirez steps into the employees' break room to tell the new employee it's time for lunch, William has sketched out three rough ideas: *White Snow Power,* in which the reward will tumble down as a snowy mountain sheers away in an avalanche; *Catch the Croc,* in which the reward will be plucked from the toothy mouth of a crocodile after the player has put a noose around the animal's neck; and *Under the Ostrich,* which requires a player to pluck an egg from the big bird's nest and find the prize within.

He can't resist showing the designs to Ramirez, who takes them, clucks thoughtfully, then hands them back. "I see Casey in this work," he says, his smile gathering up his heavy cheeks. "Well done."

As he walks away, William drops the sketches to the table, unable to explain why the manager's comment has left him feeling . . . dissatisfied. Of course he sees Casey in the design; William's ideas for the avalanche, the croc, and the bird came from existing schematics. But in those bold lines and clever captions, couldn't he see at least a little of *William*?

He bites down hard on his lip, then lowers his head and wanders into the game room. This space has emptied in the last few minutes, and through the front windows he notices that Eden's Repast is bustling with the lunch crowd. From the wide window he can see Ramirez's broad back on a stool and Stan Silva sitting next to him.

That means . . . A flush of pleasure warms his blood when William realizes he and Raquel are alone in the building. He has brought his lunch—an apple and a package of almond butter crackers in a paper bag—and earlier this morning he spied a similar bag on Raquel's desk.

His dissatisfaction with Ramirez vanishes as he hurries to the break room.

Raquel looks up from her magazine as the swinging door opens and William appears. He barely glances at her as he moves to his cubicle, then he asks, "Mind if I join you?"

She gives him what she hopes is a nonchalant shrug. "Do as you please." As an afterthought, she gives him a smile, which he returns in full measure.

She can't help peeking at him as he pulls out a chair. Could he really be the man intended for her? She doesn't know him well, but he does seem to like her. And while he's not as confident as Stan or as wise as Ramirez, he has a charming quality all his own.

Stan once told her to take what she wants. And of all the men in Paradise, she wants this one.

He's nice.

He's talented.

And he has a *title*.

She lowers her gaze when he glances her way. "Have you already eaten?" he asks.

She waves the soda can in her left hand. "I'm not hungry."

"Oh." He opens his lunch bag and takes out a package of crackers, then fumbles with the wrapper. She smothers a smile as he works to open the crinkly cellophane; apparently he is trying to be quiet and not disturb her.

Feeling generous, she lowers her magazine. "So"—she shifts to face him—"how do you like the place?"

He rips the package open, spilling crackers onto the table. "The machine company?"

She smiles. "No, silly. What do you think of Paradise?"

His throat bobs as he swallows. "It's okay. It's great, actually. The people are nice. Some of them are really interesting."

Raquel crosses her arms. "You must have met Marilyn Barron."

"I did. She likes the yellow machines."

"She likes *all* the machines. She comes every morning before work and every night before she goes home. She adores the musical games especially. I suppose you met her animals too. She never goes any- where without them."

William, whose mouth is now full of food, nods. Raquel crosses her legs and can't help noticing how a flood of red is creeping up from the back of his neck, touching his ears, now brushing his jawline . . .

Either this man likes her or he has a severe allergy to almond butter.

He swallows and holds out the wrapper, which still contains two crackers. "Would you like one?"

"No, thank you. Those things are too bland for my taste. I prefer foods with a little more zip."

When he looks away, she feels a moment's guilt for having rejected his offering. "You know," she adds, propping her elbow on the table, "it's easy to meet everyone in Paradise if you work here. Most of the people here don't go anywhere or do anything special. They get up, walk to work, do their jobs, walk home, and eat their dinners. Day after day, they do the same old things."

William swallows again. "Isn't that what we're supposed to do?"

She shrugs. "Maybe. But don't you ever wonder if we're missing something? I mean, look at this." She picks up the magazine and flips through the glossy pages. "See these women? Do they look like they spend their days counting coins in an office?"

William gives the pages a perfunctory glance, then takes in the magazine with wide eyes. "Where'd that come from?"

"Someone from Oceanside left it behind. No one in Paradise sells anything like this."

William crosses one arm across his chest and picks up another cracker. "Those ladies are nice, I guess."

"Nice? Is that all?"

"Okay, they're pretty. But none of them are as pretty as you."

She gives him a quick glance. His eyes are open and sincere; his forehead smooth and wide. If that's the look of love . . . it's not terribly exciting.

"I think these pictures are beautiful." She turns the magazine to view a scene from a different perspective. "I mean, look at these women! This one is walking along a beach; this one is wrapped in fur while she eats chocolates. What a life!"

She points to a photo of a woman standing on spiky heels, her thin dress fluttering in a breeze, her hand lifted as hundreds of faces peer at her from behind a curving velvet rope. Those people adore that woman; Raquel can see it in their eyes. She would like to be adored, but no one in Paradise will clamor to watch her type memos or count the day's coin intake.

"Aren't you happy here?" William asks.

Her gaze flies up at him. For a moment she's surprised he would dare to ask the question out loud. No one in Paradise questions Casey's methods; no one talks about secret ambitions. No one ever admits to being unhappy.

William's question is like a tunnel with a dozen secret compartments. She stands on the threshold, ready to venture with him into uncharted territory, but not sure she should.

"Are you?" she whispers.

For a moment he studies her with a curious intensity, then he looks down and flips a page of the magazine. "In these pictures, what are these women doing?"

So he's decided to retreat and change the subject. Raquel leans back in her chair. "Those women are living the good life."

"And you're not?"

"Well . . . what do you think?"

His gaze delves into hers again as awareness thickens between them. Yearnings and emotions curl in the room like smoke, but neither will clothe their thoughts in words. That would be disloyal. Wrong.

"Casey has created us," she says. "Casey placed us here, so here is where we belong." She arches a brow. "Right?"

William looks around as if he fears someone might be listening, then he lowers his voice. "Would you ever want to leave Paradise?"

She can almost feel the intense stare of the painted eye on the wall as she leans toward him. "I might leave . . . if the right opportunity came along."

"Where would you go? What would you do?"

For a moment she is irritated by his lack of imagination, then she remembers he has not seen much of the outside world. "All I know," she whispers, "is I think I'd be happier somewhere else. I'd like to cross the bridge and go into Oceanside, maybe even farther. I'd like to live in a big house on the beach. I could hold parties there and meet beautiful people . . . people who actually do things like the women in these pictures."

She closes her eyes. "Maybe," she breathes, "you'll be my ticket out of here, Mr. Ambassador. Do you think that's possible?"

When she looks at him, she knows he has taken the bait. His hand grips hers, his touch burning her skin.

"Do you," he asks, "think you could love me?"

Thoroughly enjoying the danger and excitement of the moment, she lowers her gaze to conceal the light that must be leaping in her eyes. "If you find a way to set me free, William, I'll be yours forever."

He leans forward and brushes her cheek with a kiss. The feeling unsettles her even as it brings a flush of heat to her skin.

"I need to go," she says, standing. "Gotta type letters, work on the books, count a few stacks of coins. Because life in Paradise is fun, fun, fun, and it is busy. Gotta stay busy for Casey, you know."

He leans back, watching her with mingled desire and sorrow in his eyes. She is troubled by a moment of guilt, but if he has to feel sad before he'll move forward . . .

"I may be new," he says suddenly, halting her in midstep. "But I'm not helpless. If I can find a way, I'll free you from that desk. I promise."

"Of course you will," she answers. "Because you're the ambassador."

I stand outside Zachary's room, my fingertips pressed to the closed door as if they could pick up mental vibrations and translate the thoughts moving through my son's head. After knocking softly and hearing no response, I turn the handle and look in.

Though it is five o'clock on Monday afternoon, my son still lies beneath a snarl of sheets and blankets. A foot protrudes from the edge of his plaid comforter. As I walk closer I see his hands gripping the pillow. His eyes are closed, his hair dark against the ivory bed linens.

He has slept for two days.

I bend close to listen for the sounds of deep breathing. Yesterday I thought he was sleeping off a dilly of a hangover; today I'm not so sure.

I lift a stack of clean shorts from the top of his dresser, then place the journal where Carl says he found it. After taking one last look at my son, I slip out of the room and close the door.

The tears come before I have taken two steps. Standing in the hallway outside his room, I cover my face with my hands and shudder in a silent sob. My heart cries out while my lips speak the only words that come to mind: "God, why are you doing this to us?"

Since reading my son's diary, the air in our house has thickened with the dullness of despair.

I curled up with the book last night after dinner, not wanting to pry, but determined to discover what had upset my husband. Between those pages I saw my son—bright, busy, active—but I also discovered a stranger, a young man filled with guilt and bereft of hope. If I hadn't recognized references to people and places, I would have sworn that Zack's roommate penned the plodding, depressing entries. On those pages even Zack's handwriting altered, slanting moodily toward the left, sometimes drooping toward the bottom of the unlined page. These pages held the ramblings of an angst-filled, pessimistic, emotional adolescent whose illogical comments made me want to fly up the stairs and confront the source of these crazy ideas.

Crazy. There's a word I won't be using in the near future. After reading the journal, I agreed with Carl—we have to enlist a professional counselor to help our son. I don't know how to proceed, but we can't wait much longer.

The references to suicide alarmed me, of course, but the repetitive comments about the worthlessness of life convinced me that Zack was only venting. He never mentioned making a suicide plan; he never admitted taking any action that would lead me to believe he was serious. Suicide and death are common enough themes these days, inhabiting everything from the rock music Zack favors to television shows. Writing about it seems only a step away from moaning about the joylessness of life.

Our son has made mistakes in the past, but those mistakes don't have to shadow the rest of his life. By learning to make good choices, he can correct his course. He doesn't have to dwell in depression.

My deepest prayer, of course, is that he would say yes to the God who has hounded him for years. But Zack is stubborn . . . like me.

The chime of the grandfather clock interrupts my thoughts. I have to pull something together for dinner, then I have to get to the college.

Though it's tempting to stay home and fret about my son, I have other responsibilities.

Tonight, when every thought of Zack brings fresh tears, I thank God for them.

When Zack was in fifth grade, he and the boy next door, Randy Jefferson, decided to organize a neighborhood circus. They set a date, decided what sorts of acts to include ("Do you have a trained dog? A talking parrot? Maybe you can wiggle your ears or touch your tongue to your nose!") and selected a location (our house). After printing flyers on our computer, the boys distributed their announcements to every house on our street. They rose early on the big day, hauled every chair around the pool to the front lawn, and waited for other children to show up.

I watched from the front window, not knowing how to explain that neighborhood circuses belonged more to the days of *Leave It to Beaver* than 1994. The circus was supposed to begin at ten, yet at 9:55, the only boys in our front yard were Zack and Randy.

At ten o'clock sharp, the Jeffersons' Mercedes nosed through our gate. Maris and Duke climbed out, bringing their standard poodle, Frisbee, on a leash. Zack ran into the house to get Justus, Dubya's predecessor, and I talked Shannon into climbing out of bed and into a robe to watch her little brother's circus.

The five of us—Carl, myself, Shannon, Maris, and Duke—sat on the lawn and watched Randy and Zack coax their dogs through a series of tricks, the most flamboyant of which was "Drool! Let's see some slobber! Yeah, let's hear it for the drool hounds!"

Shannon rolled her eyes, but we parents dutifully applauded each trick. My son, whom I'd always thought of as flighty and hyperactive, basked in the limelight as if he belonged there. Dancer, entertainer, announcer, animal trainer—he filled every role and loved it.

I leaned back in my lawn chair, kicking my foot to the rhythm pounding from the boom box and wondering at the expression of sheer joy on Zack's face.

For some reason I feel jittery as I follow the sidewalk that leads to my classroom. My nerves are tight; my thoughts and emotions centered on my son. I am an overfilled water balloon—the slightest prick and I will explode.

The writer in me makes a mental note: *this is how emotional catastrophe feels.*

I pause outside the door of my classroom and run down the list of reasons why I will not crack up in class: None of my students is likely to ask me about Zack. I know this material; I could teach it on autopilot. This class is a relief; an opportunity to get out of the house and think about something other than the problems at home.

Promptly at seven, I open the door and announce that for the next two hours we will discuss characterization. "Some writers," I continue, ignoring my students' shuffling as I walk to the lectern, "like to assemble long biographies of their major characters, including birthplace, birth date, astrological sign, family history, and the like. I prefer a technique my husband taught me. It's simple, quick, and relatively painless."

When a couple of students perk up at the mention of my husband, I feel a moment's guilt for not mentioning Carl sooner.

"My wonderful spouse," I say, eager to correct my oversight, "teaches theology at the Seminary of St. Augustine. He's the one who acquainted me with the Myers-Briggs system of personality profiling."

I lower my purse to the table, slip my sweater from my shoulders, and pull my notes from my folio. Joseph Thronebury, still in the front row, grins up at me. "Wow. You came in, like, in charge."

"It's called *in medias res*," I tell him. "Literally, in the midst of things. A little reminder that you should always begin a scene in the middle of the action."

Half of my students look at me with puzzled expressions, but Ian Morley is chuckling as he takes notes.

Who knows what he's thinking?

I glance at my legal pad and continue: "I used to sweat over my characters, straining to imagine their traits and quirks. Now, instead of trying to analyze people I don't yet know, I ask myself four questions that correspond to the four elements of the Myers-Briggs personality inventory. Once I have the four qualities I need for each character, I can pick up any of the dozens of books written on this assessment system and learn anything I care to know about my story people."

I move across the front of the classroom, distributing a handout that includes an overview of the sixteen different Myers-Briggs personality types. "This sheet will give you all the information you need to know. When you've read it, look up, and we'll go on."

As heads bow across the classroom, I cross my arms and pace silently at the front. Zack was still sleeping when I left the house; Carl and I had debated whether we should let him rest or wake him and ask him to come downstairs.

"It's not healthy for him to sleep for days on end," I pointed out. "He's not eating!"

"I don't think he's going to starve," Carl argued. "When he's hungry, he'll come down."

"I think we should wake him."

"Now?"

"No—maybe when I get back."

The thought of telling my son he needs to see a mental health professional leaves me with a knot in my stomach.

"Ms. Casey?"

The voice jerks me back to reality. I blink and look around. "Yes?"

Linda Frankel waves for my attention. "I think everyone has finished reading."

They have. Every head has lifted, every pair of eyes is staring at me. What emotions have flitted over my face in the last five minutes?

"All right." I walk to the lectern. "Keep those sheets handy while we talk about character cards."

I wait as pens click and notebooks open again.

"I keep all the pertinent information about a character on a single note card," I explain, "including his appearance, personality type, quirks, history, and family background. On the back, I usually tape his picture."

Kristal Palma laughs. "Where do you get pictures?"

"The JCPenney catalog is a good source," I tell her. "Magazines.

Sometimes you can find head shots online. It doesn't really matter where the picture comes from, as long as you have a mental image of what your character looks like."

To provide an example, I read William Case's physical description to my class, then lower the biography card. Sari Soutar, an Asian girl who always sits near the wall, sighs. "Wow. I can almost *see* him."

I lift a finger to acknowledge her point. "Exactly. Good character description provokes a visual image in the reader's mind. But don't tell us your character is tall or brunette; *show* him knocking his bony knees or peering at the sky through bangs the color of his muddy eyes. Your character must see, hear, taste, touch, and smell. Sometimes he will experience hunches with a kind of extrasensory perception. Your reader will relate to these impressions and your words will paint a picture that can be more involving than scenes presented in film and theater. Those media, after all, deal primarily with only *two* senses, sight and sound."

I glance at Ian Morley, but apparently that young man has heard nothing to merit a critical comment—either that, or he is reserving his sarcasm for a more opportune moment.

Dr. Bell lifts his hand. "I always assumed novelists used their acquaintances as a basis for their characters. I know you've said you never use real people, but it seems natural to take people you've met and mix their qualities with someone else's. Have you ever done that?"

"Well"—I pause to think—"if I have, it was for a minor character. The funny thing is that most people don't recognize themselves. Makes me wonder if we ever see ourselves the way other people see us."

Ian Morley lifts a finger. "Just wondering—"

"Yes?"

The student strokes his chin. "What personality type is Rex Tower?"

I slip a hand into my coat pocket. "What do you think he is?"

Morley laughs. "I don't know. But he seems more like a robot than a person."

Deep in the camouflaging pocket, my hand curls into a claw, but the smile I give Morley is confident and bright. "Tower is an ESTJ, a natural administrator. He's organized, exacting, socially deft, gregarious, dependable, and always appropriate. When he's asked to save the country, the president, or the NBA's leading scorer, he says yes without hesitation, then he goes out and does it. He enjoys parties, conversation with beautiful and intelligent women, fine food and clothing, but he is also devoutly monogamous, reserving himself for his wife, Rebecca, who's been in a coma since the eleventh book, *Tower Unleashed.*"

"That's so sweet," Linda Frankel says, her eyes glittering. "I cried when they got married. That was in *Tower of London*, right?"

I smile, delighted by the young woman's recall. "Tower had gone to England to help Scotland Yard with a problem. That's where he met Rebecca de George."

Edna Sardilli inclines her head. "We could use more of that kind of commitment in literature. Some of the books they're writing today are . . . Well, they're silly. Real people don't hop in and out of the sack like bedbugs."

When Kristal and Sari giggle at the older woman's comment, I decide it's time to move on.

"Enough about personalities." I move back to the lectern and glance at my notes. "Back to the story under construction."

I pick up William's biography card and suddenly see his physical description with new eyes: brown hair, medium height, slender frame, intense eyes, wide forehead.

Without realizing it, I have written my son into my story. Did I do it because I want Zachary to learn what William will learn . . . or because I want Zack to possess William's innocence?

My heart squeezes so tight I can barely draw breath, but I force out a string of words: "William's story takes place in a small town, so the cast is—"

My voice catches, then breaks. My face twists, my eyes screw tight to trap the sudden rush of tears, but there are too many. They roll recklessly down my face, hot spurts of grief and frustration.

I lower my head and bring up one hand to cover my embarrassment. My students are going to think I've lost my mind. Dr. Bell will think I need counseling. And if any of these people write for the student paper, next week's headline might be "Celebrity Professor Suffers Breakdown in Class" . . .

Gotta get ahold of myself.

I stand motionless in the astonished silence until I find my voice.

"Menopause," I manage to croak, forcing a smile as I lower my hand. "Unpredictable emotions, you know."

I catch Johanna Sicorsky's eye and am warmed by the sympathy in her gaze. Kristal Palma hands me a tissue, which I gratefully accept. I turn away to mop my face, then tuck the tissue into my jacket pocket and attempt to continue.

"As I was saying—or trying to say—William's story unfolds on a small canvas. There's a reason for this."

I discuss the advantages of a limited cast in a wavering voice, then several students offer examples of well-known novels that could have benefited from a careful culling of characters.

I am about to praise Judith Guest's wonderful novel, *Ordinary People*, but as I form a mental picture of that heroic young protagonist, I remember that Conrad was suicidal . . . and a psychiatric patient.

I stand in silence, my tears barely dammed, and swallow the urge to speak of Conrad Jarrett. Two rogue tears well up and overflow; I feel them slip down my cheeks as the closing of notebooks and gathering of book bags begin.

I look up at the clock, hoping to draw my students' attention away from my wet face. "That's all the time we have." *Thank heaven.*

I lower my watery gaze. "When we meet again on Friday"—my voice catches, but this time I manage to soldier on—"I'd like each of you to enlarge your protagonist's description by including his Myers-Briggs profile. Answer the four questions, determine his personality type, and go to the library to find out more about him. Bring your reports to class."

A chorus of groans greets this announcement, but I wave briefly, then gather my things and hurry for the door.

I make it as far as the parking lot before I hear the quick slap of leather on concrete. "Ms. Casey?"

I turn to see Johanna Sicorsky approaching, her notebook tucked under her arm.

I pull my keys from my purse as I wait. When she reaches me, I give her a patient smile. "Can I help you?"

She steps forward, moving into my personal space. Her eyes search my face, seeming to reach into my thoughts. I would back away, but my car blocks my exit.

"I know menopause," Johanna finally says, her hand coming to rest on my shoulder, "and I know broken hearts. I'll be praying for you, Jordan."

Her use of my first name, coupled with her light touch, unfurls streamers of emotion I thought I had packed away. I gulp hard as fresh tears slip down my cheeks, then cling to the slender woman who has risked showing mercy to a near-stranger in the parking lot.

Ramirez calls William into the factory, where Raquel and Stan are waiting just inside the door. The first thing William notices is the silence—for some reason, the mechanical assembly line has stopped. Stan is wearing his closed-mouth grin, and Raquel is almost dancing with excitement.

Something is up.

"They wanted to be here for this," Ramirez explains, dropping his hands on William's shoulders. "Step to the right, please—there. Now, Stan."

The mechanic jerks on a cord; a silk cloth falls away from what William had assumed was a machine prepared for shipping.

"Oh my." A new and unexpected warmth surges through him as he beholds his design, *White Snow Power*. "You actually made it?"

Stan's grin widens. "*You* made it. I've been working around the clock to have this ready."

William steps forward and runs his palm over the smooth Plexiglas surrounding the arctic scene. "Does it work?"

Ramirez's approving smile deepens into laughter. "Somebody give the boy a coin, please."

Raquel presses a silver circle into William's palm, holding his hand an instant longer than necessary. He drops the coin into the slot, then steps back as the motor churns a pile of glittery white flakes into a whirling cone of snow. A trio of penguins waddle from left to right in the foreground, while dark clouds move in to color the horizon.

He can't stop a shiver. Though he knows it's impossible, he feels as though the temperature in the factory has dropped at least ten degrees. The wind howls, the storm twists, and cold mist seeps from beneath the bottom of the machine cabinet.

Raquel gasps. "Wow. That's a nice touch."

Ramirez pats his shoulder. "Brilliant. Absolutely brilliant."

Then the sun appears. The spinning snow settles, the penguins waddle from right to left, this time with babies in tow, and all is peaceful until one of the little penguins sneezes. A rumbling begins, rattling the penguins and the frost and the packed snow on the mountain; then the mountain's snowy face sheers away. As the avalanche crashes against the Plexiglas, he glimpses his reward—a black camera.

William turns wide eyes upon Ramirez. "For me?"

The boss winks. "We figured you could use one—you never know when an idea is going to strike, right? You can take pictures to inspire other ideas."

William grins as the camera drops into a padded receptacle. Raquel bends to retrieve it, then gently places it in his hands.

"Go on," Ramirez says, urging him toward the door. "Go out, take some pictures, pick up some new ideas. Stan's working on your other sketches, and he says we'll have more new machines within the week."

William is too grateful and overwhelmed to respond with anything other than unquestioning obedience.

An hour later, William is in the game room snapping pictures of customers. Marilyn has come in to play *Sun, Moons, and Stars*, but as he looks at her through the camera's viewfinder, something seems wrong.

He lowers the camera and studies her more closely, then realizes what's missing. Her little dog, Carlo, sits in the flowered carrier, but the other half of the bag is empty.

He glances around to be sure the cat hasn't escaped, but when he crouches down all he sees are machine cabinets and the occasional pair of human legs.

When the nightingale has finished warbling his melody, he lets Marilyn enjoy a moment of silence, then he approaches. The thump of Carlo's wagging tail rouses his friend from her reverie. "Oh! William," she says, opening her eyes. "How good to see you."

"You look nice today, Marilyn."

She blushes, one hand rising to her rouged cheek. "You're sweet to say so."

"I was wondering, though"—he points to the pet carrier—"where's Marlo? It's not like her to stay home while you and Carlo go out."

Marilyn chuckles. "Didn't I tell you? Marlo is a mama now. Papa Carlo is about to bust his buttons. We have three babies, all of them healthy and adorable."

"Babies! Your dog and your cat—"

"Had dittens," Marilyn finishes. "They'll be sterile hybrids, of course, like mules. But they are the most *precious* things imaginable. Loyal as dogs and clean as cats. Dittens make the best pets."

"You have *dittens*?" Raquel asks.

William looks up as she approaches, her fingers splayed across her chest. "I've never seen one, but I heard Eden talking about them the other day."

"We have three." Marilyn lifts her chin. "The babies have Marlo's gray coloring and Carlo's spots. They're absolutely adorable."

Raquel releases a dramatic sigh. "How wonderful. When they're big enough, could you bring them in?"

Marilyn's brow furrows. "I don't know. They'll be small and helpless for a while yet."

"Please? I'd love to see one."

Marilyn glances at her watch. "My, how the time has flown. I'd better get home to check on the babies."

Aware that the conversation has grown awkward, William offers Marilyn his elbow. "Let me see you out."

When they reach the exit, he opens the door for her, then steps onto the sidewalk and glances up at the blue sky. "Beautiful day."

"It's lovely."

"That's great news about your animals."

"I'm over the moon about it."

"I'm curious, though—when a ditten grows up, does it become a *dat*?"

She chuckles. "What else?"

William drives to the point. "Marilyn, are you planning to keep all three dittens?"

She screws up her face as if she's about to cry. "I'm afraid I'm going to have to sell them. I hate to, but you know how it is. I can't see how I'd manage with more animals—my little carrier only holds two."

"I'd like to buy one."

Her mouth shapes into a perfect O. "Why, you'd make a wonderful caretaker for one of my beloved beauties. But . . ." Her smile fades slightly. "I should warn you, they won't be inexpensive. My ditten money is part of my livelihood, so they aren't the cheapest pets you could get."

William shifts tactics. "I don't have a lot of money, but I could pay you a little each week. Maybe I should explain—I'd be buying it to give to Raquel."

A tiny line appears between Marilyn's brows. "But I don't know her as well as I know you."

"I know she'd take good care of it and bring it to work—so you see, it'd almost be like I was a part-owner. I'd see the little guy every day, and so would you, if you come by the game room."

She presses her lips together, then nods. "When the babies are strong enough, I'll let you look at them. Then you can decide if they're worth the cost. If you decide to buy, you can give a ditten to that girl, but you have to promise you'll keep an eye on it. I can't have my animals feeling lost or lonely. They are my special gift from Casey, and they mean the world to me."

"You don't have to worry, Marilyn." William gives her a smile and basks in the radiating warmth of the sunny street. "It'd be my pleasure to check up on Raquel and her ditten for you."

Sixteen

Wrested from Paradise by the strong scent of Starbucks coffee, I tear my gaze from the computer screen and swivel in my chair. Carl stands by my desk, a steaming mug in his hand. "Want to take a break?"

I don't, but Carl wouldn't have come in if he didn't want my attention. And I've been sitting in this seat for—good grief, five hours?

"My goodness, where did the time go?" I accept the mug he offers and sip the fragrant brew.

Carl leans against the door frame. "He's up. He's in the kitchen, making a sandwich."

I lower the mug as understanding dawns. Zachary has finally come out of his room—six days after we put him to bed in a drunken stupor.

I stare at my husband across a sudden ringing silence. "Are you ready to talk to him now?"

I thought we were going to talk to Zack Friday night, but Carl had had second thoughts by the time I returned from school. If Zack needed sleep, he should get it, he argued. Since I was an emotional wreck, I didn't protest.

Saturday came and went with no sign of our son. I went up to his room at lunchtime and discovered a trail of Pop Tart wrappers on the floor, so I knew he'd been up to eat—probably in the dead of night.

By Sunday afternoon Zack's room was beginning to smell. Carl and I argued over Sunday dinner about whether we should get him up and force him to talk; once again, Carl prevailed.

But now the boy is up . . . and apparently planning to rejoin the family.

I swallow hard. "Should we let him eat first? If he gets upset and goes back to his room—"

"We'll let him eat," Carl says. "Then we have to be honest with him." He pulls a business card from his pocket and drops it on my desk. "That's a counselor one of my students recommended. He's a young guy, and I think he'd be good for Zachary."

Bracing myself for a confrontation, I leave the world of Paradise and follow Carl into the kitchen.

Zachary is sitting in the second of three chairs at our kitchen counter, his hands folded above a sandwich on a plate. He's wearing flannel pajama pants and a T-shirt, clothing he must have pulled on sometime between days two and three.

"Zack," Carl says.

Our son turns his head, and for a moment I'm shocked. Despite the Pop Tarts and whatever else he ate during his late-night visits to the pantry, he's lost weight. His face is sharply angled and bony, his uncombed brown hair a sharp contrast to his pallid skin. The T-shirt hangs from his shoulders, and his hands seem too big for his arms.

"Hey, Dad, Mom." Zack offers us a weak smile. "What year is it?"

My pity veers to sudden irritation. "Is that supposed to be funny? You've had us worried sick!"

He looks back at his sandwich. "Sorry. Guess I slept too long."

Carl slides into the empty chair at Zack's right. "What's wrong, Son? You know you can tell us anything."

Zack shakes his head. "I'm fine, Dad."

Though the other empty chair beckons, I can't approach. Instead, I lean against the counter and cross my arms. "We need to talk about last week—maybe it feels like yesterday to you. I came home and found you nearly passed out by the gate. What kind of friends have you been running around with? They get you to drink, which you know you can't handle; they sucker you into paying for six hundred dollars worth of food; then they dump you by the side of the road? You could have been hit by a car; you could have been killed—"

Carl catches my eye and lifts both hands in a *don't shoot* pose. I know he's warning me to give the kid a break, but who's going to give *us* a break? We're the parents, the ones who've suffered years of this unacceptable behavior.

"Zack"—Carl places his hand on Zack's arm—"we read your journal."

Despite Zack's weariness, anger flashes from his eyes. "You had no business reading that!"

"We care about you." Carl girds his voice with steel. "We care enough to see that you get help. There's a man we think can help you—"

"There's nothing wrong with me."

"This man's a professional counselor. Your mother and I think you need to talk to him."

Zack stands so quickly that the movement sends his chair crashing to the tile floor. "No!" He turns and runs for the stairs, then takes them two at a time.

"Zack!" I start to run after him—with the adrenaline coursing through my bloodstream, I think I might actually catch him—but Carl snags my arm.

"Give him time." His creditable attempt at calm is marred only by the thickness in his voice. "You resisted the idea at first too. He needs to think about it."

I close my eyes, bracing myself for the sound of a slamming door. When it comes, I can't help feeling grateful that the lion has returned to his cave.

I have a cave too. My only sanctuary.

"If you need me," I tell Carl, "I'll be in my office."

Back in my study, I sink into my chair and swivel away from the door. I don't want to see Zack or Carl; I'm tired of talking, arguing, and thinking about my son's impossible problems.

For a long while I close my eyes and focus on taking deep breaths, then I force myself to concentrate on the task at hand. Relegating thoughts of Zachary to a closet of my mind, I reread my last paragraph and ease back into Paradise, where people speak plainly and problems are simple.

Seventeen

Over the next few days, William fills his hours with thoughts of Raquel and the joyful expression that will fill her eyes when he presents her with the ditten.

William *thinks* she likes him. She might even admire him because the factory now hums with the manufacture of machines that he designed. Ramirez keeps saying he can see Casey in every line of William's games, but William can see himself too. His sense of humor is evident in the line of waddling penguins in *White Snow Power*; his commitment to perseverance is obvious in *Catch the Croc*.

Best of all, his machines are a hit. Business picks up at lunch; people stop to test their skill at snagging an ostrich egg before going over to Eden's to talk about the machine company's new games. The coin box Ramirez carries to the office every night looks a little fuller, so William knows he's pulling his weight.

He hopes Raquel is pleased.

When he's not mining the schematics for new game ideas, he looks at photos he's snapped and waits for inspiration to strike. He has taken pictures of the tidy houses south of the machine company, the neat garden furrows behind Eden's Repast, and the place where Main Street intersects a wide expanse of white beach at the southernmost tip of the island. A *Welcome to Paradise* sign stands by the bridge, a small wooden placard in keeping with the tone of the town.

The cliffs at the opposite end of the island would inspire anyone, but William hasn't decided how to work them into a game. Raquel accompanied him to the cliffs one afternoon after work. Like giggling children they walked down the cobblestone road and paused at the place where the steep walls of blue-black stone fall away to a shining sweep of sea. For a long moment they didn't speak, then Raquel led him down a path cut through the rugged rock. After much twisting and turning, he found himself on a stone promontory, a ledge barely wide enough for two. They sat a long time, the granite cliff at their backs and nothing but sea and sunset sky before them.

Raquel took his hand. "This will be our special place."

His heart bounded upward at her touch. "Lookout Ledge," he managed to answer. "The place where we can see almost everything Casey created."

William can't imagine a game detailed enough to contain the majesty of that splendid sight.

His yearning to create new and better games inevitably leads his thoughts to the machine company's mysterious locked door. He dreams of it, he stares at it, he ruminates about it. Once he sketched out a design for a game featuring a mysterious portal, but the sight of the design on paper sent an inexplicable shudder down his spine.

An opportunity arrives, however, when he enters the employees' area and breathes in the sharp tang of dill pickles. That can mean only one thing—today Ramirez is eating lunch with the employees.

A moment later the boss confirms William's hunch. As he crouches by his cubicle, Ramirez comes out of his office and takes a seat at the table next to Stan, lunch bag in hand. When Raquel slips into the ladies' room, William figures this is his chance to ask about the forbidden door without being embarrassed in front of her.

"Hey, Ross," he says, feigning nonchalance as he grabs his lunch and slides into a chair, "what's with the door behind the garbage can?" He points toward the padlocked entry as if he has just noticed it. "What's in that room?"

Ramirez doesn't even glance up. He pulls a giant pickle from its paper wrapping, holds the pickle between his thumb and forefinger for a moment of silent admiration, then gives William a rueful smile. "You'll discover the answer soon enough."

The manager bites into the pickle, then lifts his brows as the telephone rings. Munching double-time, he scoops up the remains of his lunch and hurries into the office.

William shifts his gaze to Stan, who has bent double with silent laughter. "What's so funny?"

The mechanic snorts. "If you want to know what's inside the room, open the door."

"But it's locked."

"And we work in a machine factory. Picking a padlock isn't hard. Finding the key wouldn't be hard, either."

William unfolds the waxed paper around his sandwich as Stan tosses his trash into the bin. "Hey," he calls, stopping Stan before he can leave. "If it's so easy, why haven't *you* picked the lock?"

The man sends him a lopsided grin. "I know what's in the room. A game."

William's jaw drops. "You've known all along?"

"This is a game factory. What else would be in there?"

William frets the wrinkles out of a waxed paper corner. "If it *is* a game, why isn't it out front with the others?"

Stan shrugs. "I don't know. Ask Ramirez."

"I tried that."

"Then good luck finding the answer."

William glances at the clock. He has three minutes remaining on his lunch hour, not long enough to venture inside the locked room, but long enough to think about it.

Maybe the *No Admittance* sign has been there so long it's no longer applicable. Maybe the game inside—if a game lies beyond the door—isn't quite finished, but someone with his creative gift could make it work. Stan is a mechanical whiz, and William has learned a lot since his first day at the company. Ramirez was right about his gift—it has kicked in, along with a curiosity that keeps drawing him toward a certain corner . . .

Sighing, he grabs his earphones and follows Stan into the factory.

Eighteen

I wait until the sound of my words fades from the classroom, then tighten my grip on the last page. An unexpected sense of anxiety seized me as I read; a fear born of insecurity. An odd voice in my head, snide and smooth, told me not to worry about the opinions of mere students, but a primal fear made my voice quiver and urged me to keep my gaze lowered.

Now I wait. No applause from my class, but no jeers, either. I wouldn't have been surprised to hear a taunt or two from Ian Morley, because my first drafts usually lack polish and precision. But I hear only the rataplan of rain on the roof, see only the jiggle of Joseph Thronebury's hyperactive knees beyond the edge of the page.

I drop the manuscript and peer over the top of my reading glasses, then blink at the sight of more than a dozen uplifted hands. They listened . . . and they have questions.

I stack the manuscript on the table. My class has grown smaller over the last few weeks, but what it lost in size, it seems to have gained in enthusiasm.

I meet Linda Frankel's gaze. "Miss Frankel?"

The young woman straightens in her chair. "What I want to know," she says, a brassy note in her voice, "is how you can get away with pink hair, double moons, and dittens. Is this supposed to be a fantasy?"

I grin. "It *is* a unique world, isn't it? I wanted something slightly off kilter, but not too unreal. A few odd touches are all I need to let the reader know this story isn't taking place on planet Earth."

"We're not in Kansas anymore, Toto," Michael Zappariello deadpans.

I nod. "I toyed with several ideas—thought about having Paradise operate on a six-month annual calendar or a twelve-hour day; considered mixing up the races so they sprang from different continents and claimed opposite histories. I played with inventing several new types of animals and briefly considered creating a new language. With each scenario, though, I had to ask, 'Will this advance the story?' If the idea didn't do something to deepen plot or character, I decided it wasn't worth pursuing."

Johanna Sicorsky flutters her fingers to catch my attention. "These other towns you've mentioned—"

"Like Oceanside?"

"Right. You said you wanted a limited canvas, but you've mentioned other towns beyond the island. How do they fit into the story?"

I slide a hand into my pocket. "Think of those other cities as existing in 'Casey's Realm'—the universe of my imagination. Over the years I've set novels in London, New York, and Washington, as well as fictional towns that only exist in my books. Those cities are reality-based, of course. Paradise operates under special rules."

A smile nudges its way into the corner of her mouth. "I see."

"What about that eye of God image?" Dr. Bell pulls the stem of his glasses away from his mouth long enough to draw a triangle in the air. "Are you referring to the picture on the back of a dollar bill?"

"Probably. The idea came to me, though, from something I once read in a book. Apparently, in the days prior to World War II, it was common to see that sort of symbol in public places. The image was supposed to remind people that the eye of God was upon the place, so cursing would not be allowed." I give him a rueful smile. "I can't imagine seeing such an emblem painted at our local superstore, can you?"

I answer several other questions, then glance at my watch. "We don't have much time, but if you have those descriptive paragraphs I asked you to write, please bring them to me before you go."

At our last meeting I told my students to write a single scene in which they evoked at least four of the five senses. We've been working together six weeks now, and I've seen marked improvement in most of them. Those who have stayed with the class have begun to exercise their imaginations, and fewer of them seem intimidated by the idea of putting words to paper.

I dismiss them five minutes early, then stand at the front of the room to collect papers and exchange small talk. Linda Frankel, Johanna Sicorsky, Dr. Bell, and Sari Soutar have written paragraphs over a page in length; Ian Morley managed to scratch out a paragraph under the heading "Water Tower." "Interesting title," I remark, scanning his work.

Ian grins at me and moves on. Our verbal battles have softened, and I find myself growing almost fond of the young man. In many ways, he reminds me of Zachary. They're both bright and active; they both evidence a low tolerance for procedures and routines. Both Ian and Zack love being the center of attention, but life is not a three-ring circus, and they are not ringmasters.

Kristal Palma, I notice, slips out of the classroom without handing in an assignment, as do Mike Zappariello and Joseph Thronebury. Edna Sardilli, for whom I've harbored high hopes, did not show up for class tonight.

My cell phone begins playing a calypso as the clock marks the hour. Stepping away from a knot of lingering students, I pull the phone from my purse and punch the receive button.

"Hello?"

"Jordan!" The deep voice of Winston McIntyre, my agent, rumbles through the phone. "Carl said you'd be free at nine. Got a minute?"

"As a matter of fact"—I turn to see Johanna Sicorsky pull away from the others—"I don't, not yet. Can I call you back?"

"Of course, but don't forget. I've got big news. A great offer."

I hang up, but Winston's announcement has piqued my interest. I'm not expecting any big news—my last release, *Tower Invasion*, has already been optioned by Columbia TriStar, and my next novel, an as-yet-untitled story pitting Tower against a saboteur aboard the space station, isn't due for another nine months. Winston could be calling about foreign rights, of course, or news of some kind of an award—

The Nobel Prize?

Wouldn't that frost Ian Morley's cupcakes? I cough out a laugh, then cover my mouth to stifle any further guffaws.

I turn and find Ms. Sicorsky waiting for me.

"Johanna." I smile. "Do you have a question?"

A slight flush marks her narrow face as she hands me a manila envelope. "I wondered if you'd mind taking a look at this story—*The Tale of Peter McPossum*. My grandchildren like it, so I thought it might make a nice picture book. Trouble is, I don't have any idea how to go about getting it published."

Though it pains me to repay her kindness with a refusal, I hand the envelope back to her. "I'm sorry, Johanna, but picture books aren't my field of expertise."

"But you know good writing—"

"And I have a policy against reading unpublished manuscripts. I'd hate it if one day I came up with a similar idea and you thought I stole it from you. But I know what you *can* do—go to the library and find a book on how to write children's picture books."

Surprise radiates from her dark eyes. "There are books about that?"

"There are books about *everything*. You might find as many as half a dozen on how to write picture books. You need to study the blueprint for that genre, then you need to approach a children's publisher or an agent. Those are the only opinions that matter when it comes to publication."

She takes the manuscript and thanks me, but when a muscle twitches in her jaw, I know she hasn't shared everything on her mind.

I lower my head to catch her gaze. "Something else you wanted to say?"

Her smile is friendly, almost apologetic. "I don't mean to pry, but I wondered—how are you feeling these days? You know . . . about your menopause."

I'm embarrassed, but I grimace in good humor. "Well, life is what it is. We've been in a holding pattern for the last month. Things aren't great, but they've been worse."

She smiles, her eyes soft with kind concern. "I've been praying for you. I'll keep at it."

I catch her hand and squeeze it. "Thanks."

I sigh as she walks away. I'd like nothing better than to unload all my Zack frustrations on a sympathetic ear, but this isn't the place, and Johanna, sweet as she is, isn't the person. Carl and I have tried to protect Zack by not broadcasting his problems. I've even wondered if I'm revealing too much by writing *The Ambassador*, because the parallels between my protagonist and my easily tempted son are obvious to anyone who knows us.

After making sure none of the remaining students need to speak to me, I gather my materials and leave the room, keeping my head down as I move through the hall and into the parking lot. My celebrity no longer matters to my class, but occasionally other people on campus run over to ask for an autograph. I usually don't mind obliging, but tonight I want to get to my car and call Winston.

I dump my papers into the passenger seat and slide into the Mercedes, then lock the driver's door. I punch in my agent's number and settle back to wait, but Winston answers on the first ring.

"Jordan! You sitting down?"

"No choice—I'm in the car."

"You're not driving, are you? I'd hate for you to crash when you hear this."

"Don't worry; I'm in a parking lot. What's the big news?"

Winston's laughter floats out of the phone. "Listen, I just talked to Francis. He wants another Tower novel—not a replacement for an already contracted book, but a special project. He needs it soon, though, because they want the book to tie in with the Winter Olympics."

I press my palm to my forehead as my thoughts scamper. My editor,

Francis Clifton, always wants more Tower novels, but he has never asked for one in a hurry. "When are the Winter Olympics?"

"Next February, in Turin, Italy. That's why this project has to be a rush job, and that's why they're willing to pay—are you ready for this?—$3.3 million. For *one* book."

I sit in pleased surprise as threes and zeroes dance before my eyes. Nearly three and a half million dollars for one book? I've signed multi-million dollar contracts before, but they've been for four or five books, and the work has been spread over several years. I handed in *The Queen's Tower* last December, so I had planned to take a few months off before beginning the space station story . . . until Carl talked me into teaching this class.

I close my eyes. "When would they need the manuscript?"

"They'd like it by July first. But since they've already come up with the premise and title, I'm thinking the art and marketing departments could get started without a manuscript in-house. I think we could get them to accept August first as a deadline."

Unbidden, words creep from my throat. "I can't do it."

Winston laughs. "Must be static on the line. I thought I heard you say—"

"I said I can't do it." I sink lower in my seat. "Believe me, I'd *like* to do it, but I can't. I'm teaching a community college class, so I'll be tied up until mid-May."

"Tell me you're joking." Winston's voice has gone hoarse with shock. "What are you doing at a community college?"

I look out the window as a pair of students walk by, stuck to each other like Velcro. "I'm not doing it for the money, I can promise you that."

"Then what?"

"I gave my word. I signed a contract."

"Listen, Jordan." My agent's voice holds a note halfway between disbelief and pleading. "What is it, two nights a week?"

"Three."

"Whatever. Teach if you want, but write this story—think of it as your day job. You're fast, you work well under pressure, and I'll bet Francis would be willing to hire somebody to help with the research. You won't have to go to Turin—shoot, *I'll* go to Turin for you; I'll take pictures and tons of notes. All I need is your signature on the contract."

I massage my temple, where the faint throb of a headache has begun to pound. "I wish it were that simple. But I figured my class would learn best by watching me write something, so I've started a novel for them. It's a complicated kind of allegory, and it's kept me busy these last few weeks."

Winston snorts. "Let them watch you write *Tower on Ice*. Let them watch you sign the contract and drive to the bank; let them read about this deal in the papers. Because it's going to be big, you know. Dalton & Sons has wised up to cross-marketing, and the IOC is willing to put money behind this venture. Nobody watches the Olympics on TV anymore, so some brilliant marketer figured, 'Hey! Why not send Rex Tower, America's favorite tough guy, to the games?'"

I laughed. "That's incredible."

"You bet it is—it's going to be a *huge* launch. They're talking about filming scenes from the book and using the footage for commercials during the Olympic broadcasts. I'm telling you, this is going to be huge—no, bigger than huge. This is going to be *titanic*."

I exhale slowly. Wouldn't my students understand? After all, it's not like any of *them* would refuse an opportunity to earn over three million dollars in a few months. I could still let them watch the process, though I'd have to dust off Rex Tower's superhero cape and revert to my tried-and-true plot formula. The females in my class would enjoy sighing over Tower, but Ian Morley would think I'd sold out—and he'd be right.

I'd be trading a story that could change my son's heart for $3.3 million. A sorry bargain.

If I set aside the William Case story, it would sit on a shelf as I pursued my next Tower novel, and the next, and the next. I'd probably never pick up *The Ambassador* again.

"Listen, Winston," I say, straightening in my seat, "it's late, and I don't want Carl to worry. Let's pretend this offer never came in, okay? Tell Francis I can't fit another book into my schedule."

"But—"

"I need to run, Winston. Take care."

I click off the power and toss the phone onto the passenger seat, then grip the steering wheel.

What have I just done? The same stubborn honor and commitment that make Rex Tower a laughingstock among more jaded people has congealed around me, Tower's creator. Even if I never finish *The Ambassador*, I can't take my publisher's offer because I can't deal with a rushed Tower novel, this college class, and my troubled son.

Aye, there's the rub. Even with God's grace, a woman can only handle so much. Lately I've felt like looking up to heaven, drawing my hand across my throat, and calling, "Enough, already!"

After cranking the engine, I turn to make sure the way is clear, then back out of the parking space. As the car noses toward home, I wonder if Winston called the house and told Carl about the deal on the table —and what my husband's reaction would be.

I have a strong hunch he'd agree with what I've decided.

Nineteen

On Tuesday morning, among the e-mails waiting in my private mailbox is one from JSicorsky@aol.com. I stare at the address, puzzled, and hope Johanna hasn't decided to send a picture book manuscript for my evaluation.

The message is not at all what I expected.

Dear Ms. Casey:

I don't think I've told you that I like to garden. I raise plants in pots mostly because I'm limited to what I can grow on my apartment balcony. I've had the most success with tomatoes, which seem to love Reno's sun.

I've learned one thing about tomatoes—if I try to pick them while they are green, they resist. If I insist on pulling, I may damage the fruit or the stem. But if I wait until the fruit has been ripened by the sun, even a gentle tug will make the tomato tumble into my hand.

I hope you'll accept this as my way of showing appreciation for all you've been teaching me.

Johanna Sicorsky

Puzzled and more than a little disturbed, I read the e-mail a second time. What *is* this? At first I thought Johanna was sending me a sample of creative writing, but by the third paragraph I realized it was a simple letter.

About tomatoes.

I hate tomatoes. And I don't garden. So why in the world . . .

I lean back in my chair and rest my chin on my hand, thinking about the woman who sent this to me. Johanna—dark eyes, white hair, serene expression. The one student who saw through my flimsy excuse and realized my pain.

The student who prays for me.

What is she trying to tell me? That she's not ready to write and I'm pushing too hard? That I shouldn't have refused to look at her manuscript?

I lean forward and slide the mouse over the X that will delete the message, then decide to save it for a few days. I'll want to remember the details if she mentions it after class.

I close my e-mail and open my work-in-progress. With the sound-track to *Forrest Gump* playing in the background, I close my eyes and visualize the scene I've sketched on a note card. The machine company's break room would be silent and still, cloaked in shadows. William would be on edge, his limbs taut with repressed energy.

I have just dropped my hands to the keyboard when Carl raps on the door. I look up, momentarily jarred by the change of scenery.

He leans against the door frame and tucks his hands under his arms. "Winston's called three times."

"I was afraid of that."

"He thinks you're crazy for turning down that Olympic project."

"Maybe I am." I turn in my seat. "But he doesn't know what we're dealing with at home."

Carl drops into the chair opposite my desk. "How's the story coming?"

"Okay. But I keep seeing Zack in every scene."

In the last month, Zack has pretty much stuck close to home, leaving only to go to work, then coming home to crash. Though he hasn't mentioned going to a counselor, we've been proud of him for avoiding the friends who influence him to drink.

But Sunday night he stayed out until 4:00 a.m. The door alarm woke us when he came in, but neither Carl nor I had the heart to get up and see if Zack had been drinking.

I'm sure he was, though, because he went to his room and hasn't come out since. He was supposed to work yesterday, but Carl wouldn't let me wake him in time for his shift. I paced outside Zack's room for an hour, furious with my husband *and* my son.

Carl cracks his knuckles, then looks at me. "He's up, you know."

My jaw drops. "Rumplestiltskin is awake?"

"He's watching TV upstairs. I think he even took a shower."

I shake my head. "So what was that, thirty hours in bed? If he's awake, he's lucid. We need to go up and have a family conference. If he doesn't get on a regular schedule, he's going to lose his job—"

"Let him lose it."

"But he needs to learn responsibility."

"He'll never learn from his mistakes if we don't let him make a few."

A bitter laugh rises from my throat. "He's already made more than a few. The kid would be in jail if we hadn't hired him a good lawyer and agreed to put him in rehab."

"All the same, Jordy, you can't organize his life forever. You have to—"

Carl falls silent as a shadow moves in from the hall. As one, we look up to see Zachary standing in the doorway.

"Mom. Dad." He steps into the room and leans against the wall, giving us a smile that seems about 90 percent bravado and 10 percent regret. "I'm sorry I missed work yesterday."

My smile is tight-lipped. "You're going to have to take that up with Mr. McNeil."

He nods. "I will. But I've been thinking."

Carl lifts a brow. "About . . . ?"

"About everything you've said. Yeah, maybe I do need to talk to someone. The way I've been acting . . . it's not right. I know it."

"Zachary." I stand and go to him, folding his angular body into my arms. For a moment he is stiff and distant—he is *William*—then something in him breaks and he is once again the son I have loved and kissed and comforted through a lifetime.

When he begins to weep, Carl stands, too, draping his arms around us. "I'm so sorry, Son," he says in a cracked whisper, "that we didn't see how you were hurting. We should have known."

When Zack cries even harder, I'm so crushed by the sound of my son's brokenness that I can't speak. When I finally find my voice, I promise to make an appointment with a counselor as soon as possible.

After a long while, Zack wipes his woebegone face with his sleeve, and Carl cracks a smile. "Hungry? Want me to go rustle up some grub?"

My men head for the kitchen while I drop back into my chair and reach for a tissue. I watch as they walk down the hallway and turn the corner; then I lower my head onto my hand.

We've had a breakthrough. I don't know what triggered it, but I'm grateful all the same.

Determined to seize the moment, I pull the counselor's business card from my desk drawer and phone the office. The first available appointment is 11:00 a.m., Thursday, February 17. In two days.

I tell the receptionist to book the appointment for Zachary Kerrigan; then I hang up and wipe the remaining dampness from my lower lashes.

I turn and look at the computer, where William's story waits. *My* William, my son, has just found the courage to turn away from the forbidden room . . . so do I need to continue with this book?

For a moment I toy with the thought of setting *The Ambassador* aside, but I promised my students I'd produce a complete story. Besides, I'm not the sort who can walk away from a half-finished anything. I gain about two pounds per year because I can't push away a half-finished dessert, and I once painted around my sleeping husband because I couldn't sleep in a half-painted bedroom.

Carl and Zack may be able to walk away from partially completed projects, but I can't. And as hopeful as I am that Zack's attitude signals a major change in his life, getting him to a counselor is only a first step.

He needs so much more.

In a flash of insight, I understand Johanna's note. For years I have tried to persuade Zack that he should find good friends, study the Bible, embrace our beliefs, and live as a Christian . . . but *if I try to pick them while they are green, they resist. If I insist on pulling, I may damage the fruit or the stem. But if I wait until the fruit has been ripened by the sun, even a gentle tug will make the tomato tumble into my hand.*

I'm not the sun. And the fruit is not yet ready to fall into my hands.

I glance at the scene card again and then rest my fingers on the keyboard. I will finish *The Ambassador* because the Spirit who ripens hearts may still use this story to influence my son. Zack needs more than the strength to turn from temptation. He needs a new heart.

Drawing a deep breath, I begin to type.

Twenty

In the empty men's room, William slips out of his coveralls and pulls on his jeans. Ramirez has asked to see all the company employees before closing, and William needs to hurry. From behind the bathroom door, he can hear voices in the break room.

Stan and Raquel are sitting around the table when he steps out. Ramirez stands beneath the painted eye on the wall. He nods as William approaches.

"Casey," he begins without preamble, "has called me away for a few days—I'm not sure how long I'll be gone. But I'm to go into the wilds to fast and prepare myself. Something important will happen soon, and I need to be ready."

"So"—Stan taps his fingers briefly on the table—"who are you leaving in charge of the company?"

Ramirez acknowledges the question with a perplexed look. "Casey's in charge, as always. Stan, you keep working production; William, you keep creating new games; Raquel, count the coins and update the records. Nothing should change, nothing at all."

The manager spreads his hands. "Anything else?"

The question is met with silence. Stan gets up and pats Ramirez on the shoulder; Raquel returns to her office.

William walks to Raquel's office and says good-bye, then makes a point of waving to Ramirez before striding to the entrance. He opens the door, sending the jingle of the bells onto the sidewalk, then he ducks back inside the building and crouches behind a *Moons on the Mountains* machine.

He doesn't have to wait long. Stan leaves almost immediately. A few minutes later Raquel comes out of the office and exits without looking around. Ramirez turns off the lights and steps into the factory to throw the game room circuit breaker, which cuts power to the machines. An eerie silence descends, broken only when Ramirez lumbers toward the front door. His watch thunks against the glass as he turns the *Open* sign to *Closed*, then he leaves the building.

By eight fifteen William is alone inside Casey's Machine Company —and as nervous as a mouse. He stands, cringing as his knees snap in the silence, then he creeps to the break room. An emergency light glows above the factory door, and a small lamp burns on Raquel's desk.

By the glow of these little lights, he runs his hand along the wooden base of his cubicle, wincing when his finger encounters the thin wire he hid there earlier in the day. No one noticed when he took it; he doubts anyone would have cared. In Paradise, where coin boxes, diaries, and all doors save one remain unlocked, no one suspects anyone of hidden motives.

He positions the wire between his thumb and index finger, then holds it up to the light. Fear blows down the back of his neck as the tip gleams red in the glow of the exit sign.

He is the ambassador, representative, and envoy. And he is about to do something no one in Paradise has yet garnered the courage to do.

He glances around to be sure he is still alone, then walks to the locked door and reaches for the flashlight Stan keeps in his cubicle. With the flashlight in one hand, William grasps the padlock and studies it. He sees only one opening, a narrow slash at the bottom, so he sets the flashlight on the stack of cubicles and shines the light toward the door.

Holding the lock with his left hand, he forces the wire into the opening with his right. He jabs it into the lock several times, but the wire finds no purchase in the mechanism. He yelps, startling himself, when he miscalculates and stabs his finger. He shakes his wounded hand and tries to throw off the pain, then brings his throbbing flesh to his mouth. He tastes blood.

"This is not going to work." His voice sounds like thunder in the thick silence. Refocusing, he tosses the wire into the trash can and moves to the middle of the break room.

The answer to his problem is simple. The padlock must have a key; as manager, Ramirez must possess it. And since the boss leaves everything affiliated with the business in his office, the key must be in his desk—probably in the top drawer.

An impulse urges William forward—enter Raquel's office, step into Ramirez's. Open the desk drawer, find the key. Easy as breathing.

Yet another voice holds him back: *Trying to open the lock with a wire is bad; trespassing in Ramirez's office is worse. If he comes in and finds the key gone, he'll know who took it.*

No, he won't. William can put the key back, so Ramirez will never know anything. But surely the ambassador is entitled to know what's in the locked room.

Though his heart beats heavily, each thump like a blow to his chest, he follows his inclination and moves into Ramirez's office. He turns on the lamp at the corner of the desk, then leans down and opens the top drawer.

In the corner, amid paper clips, pens, and a half-eaten roll of mints, gleams a gold key. William picks it up, blows dust from the edge, and spins to leave, but a sight stops him in his tracks.

Ramirez has painted the all-seeing eye above his door. The eye watches, impassive and silent, and for an instant William hesitates.

Should he continue? He could return the key and go home; no one would know. But he has already set a plan in motion, and his desire to continue is stronger than his desire to please.

He lifts his chin and carries the key to the locked door. The key fits smoothly into the lock. He flinches as the mechanism pops open with a metallic click.

Swallowing the lump that rises in his throat, William removes the lock from the hasp. His ears fill with the screech of metal as he lifts the plate that fastens the door to the hasp. The door groans as he pushes it open and steps into the forbidden room.

No lights burn overhead, yet shadows dance on the ceiling. A barrier of concrete blocks stands a few feet behind the door, obstructing his view of whatever waits inside, but an opening to his right entices like a riddle. Beyond the opening, gold and red beams flash over the walls in a strobic rhythm.

As William moves forward with a silent tread, his ears fill with a kind of growling, jugular music unlike anything he's ever heard from the yellow machines. Something is happening inside his head. The noises are distorted, fizzy, out of sync. Then, from nowhere, comes a voice that strikes deep in the pit of his stomach.

Hey, William . . . wanna bet your life?

He hesitates, the hair on his arms lifting in a shudder. For some reason he is suddenly certain this room is a test and a trap, and he has tumbled into it like an unreasoning animal. When he rounds the corner, he will look up and see Casey. His creator made him and gave him a title, but he has proven he is not fit to be the ambassador.

William hangs his head, drowning in a surge of guilt. He's done wrong; he has broken the rules; he has ignored the sign and the warning and the lock. He has stolen a key; he has plotted and schemed; he has resented Ramirez and Casey and their rules . . .

He hesitates when nothing happens. He's not struck down, the light doesn't advance, no wave of chilly disapproval sweeps toward him. He's still here, still balancing on the threshold of a mystery.

After gulping a quick breath, he peers around the corner. Stan is right—a machine rests against the far wall, a device larger and brighter and louder than anything in the game room. Showy red and gold lights flash around its curved upper rim; the picture of a smiling man in a black cape and tall hat shines from the smooth surface of the lower cabinet. Wheels spin beneath a clear cover, and all the while a dark rhythm pounds like William's heart, drawing him closer with every step.

"Come on in." Before his eyes, a rectangular black screen fills with color. The man in the cape twirls, his smile broadening. "Welcome, friend. I've been waiting for you."

William tilts his head, amazed at the technology. The voice is unfamiliar, so neither Stan nor Ramirez recorded the vocal loop. Someone has done an incredible job of coordinating the sound and animation; this game, though a bit bizarre, could compete with any currently in the front room.

So why has it been locked away?

He steps back and eyes the machine with a critical squint. This game rests on a different type of base than the others; it seems to have been molded of a glossy material he doesn't recognize. The surfaces have been polished to a mirrorlike shine, and when he looks *at* it instead of *through* it, he can see his narrow eyes and jutting chin reflected in its sheen.

"Greetings, friend," the mechanical man says, his image swaying on the video screen. "Would you like to play my little game?"

The animated figure bends and taps the end of his cane to the lower edge of the screen. Instantly, the rectangle explodes with color, a virtual rain of multicolored stars. When the stars finish falling, the name of the game remains on-screen—*You Bet Your Life*.

Curious, William steps closer, scanning the on-screen image. The technology in the game room is impressive, but this is something altogether different. The image appears three-dimensional, and when it speaks, the man in black sounds as if he is whispering in William's ear.

"Don't be shy," the video taunts. "Come on, Ambassador, take your best shot. It's time to pay and play."

The friendly address is like a slug to the center of William's chest. How did this game become . . . personalized?

"Come now, William," the man says, the warmth of his smile echoing in his voice. "Surely you're not surprised I know your name?"

William takes a wincing little breath. "You're so . . . advanced."

"Of course I am. I'm the best. That's why I'm reserved for very special players." The magician whispers these last words in a confidential tone.

The man's smile widens when William steps forward. "Ready to play with the magician?"

William glances over his shoulder; he is still quite alone. No harm, then, in playing along.

He turns back to the machine. "What is this game?"

The magician uses the end of his cane to tip his hat at a jaunty angle, then he winks. "It's *You Bet Your Life*, noggin head. You read the name on the screen."

"How much?" William bends to examine the coin slot. "Do you require silver or gold?"

Music fills the air as the video image begins to sing: "To play one day, your soul you pay. To play again, you must let me win."

As if on cue, bells jingle and whistles blow. William steps back and gapes as the screen explodes in more fireworks. The magician divides and multiplies; soon there are at least a hundred caped men dancing on the screen, each of them tipping his hat and waving as he passes by.

William is flummoxed. Who programmed this thing? Ramirez couldn't design a game like this in a hundred years. Stan can make almost anything if given a blueprint and schematic, but he'd be clueless about this. So unless some other genius has passed through Paradise—

Wait. Could *Casey* have invented this? This game is different from the others, but William can see signs of Casey's creative touch. Or maybe someone else has been here . . . someone trained by Casey, perhaps, but with a distinctively darker nature.

William moistens his dry lips as the music fades, and the dancing magicians fold back into one. "Um . . . I'm not sure I understand how this game works."

"Don't worry." The magician leans toward him, his eyes looming huge in the screen, his eyebrows wagging. "It's as easy as rolling off a wagon, tumbling from the stars, falling from grace. I'll teach you everything you need to know."

William takes a half step back, too startled to respond.

"Come on," the animated imp insists. "Step right up and watch the screen. No money down, nothing to buy, satisfaction guar-an-*teed*! Just surrender your soul and tell me what you want to win. The sky's the limit!"

William doesn't understand what the clown means by surrendering his soul, but what is a soul, anyway? He's never seen one. He's never felt one. His soul, if it exists, has done nothing for him.

So why not play along with this wild and crazy game?

"Ready, Freddy?" The magician removes his top hat, then thrusts his gloved hand inside and pulls out a fistful of alphabet letters. Laughing, he throws them at William, but they hit the screen and splatter into three words: *health, wealth,* and *happiness.*

"Oh, goodie!" The magician rubs his hands together. "What'll it be, William, my man? Which of these three things would you like to win?"

"So . . . winning is a sure thing?"

"Few things in life are a sure thing, William, but my game will not disappoint. Pick a word, any word. If you win, you win big. If you lose, you lose little. How can you go wrong?"

William stares at the three words, uncertain how to proceed. Wager his health? What would it mean if he loses? He could become unwell, he supposes, but he's never known a single moment of sickness, and neither has anyone else in Paradise.

Wager his wealth? Ha! As if he has great wealth to lose. He's still trying to figure out how to pay Marilyn what she wants for the ditten. His meager salary will only stretch so far.

As for happiness . . . is he happy now? He doesn't have Raquel, a fact that frequently makes him miserable. He lives in an apartment while others live in houses, so he *could* be more prosperous. So if this current unsatisfied state is happiness, then perhaps happiness is not such a great thing. But if happiness is relative, losing any hope of Raquel would be far worse than pining for her.

After deliberating, he lifts his hand and touches the word *wealth.* Surely he can afford to lose a coin or two.

"He wagers his wealth," the magician announces, grinning. "Interesting choice, William. Now spin!"

William blinks as a bank of blinking lightbulbs slides aside, revealing three reels and a lever. He grasps the lever and pulls, then holds his breath as the reels flash before his eyes, spinning round and round, their images a blur he can't follow.

The first reel stops on a picture: *cherry.*

The second reel: *cherry.*

The third reel slows to a crawl, showing him pictures of an apple, a banana, and an orange, then finally slides to a cherry.

"We have a winnah!" The magician breaks into a soft shoe routine while lights flash and confetti rains from a vent in the ceiling. William grins, caught up in the theatrical silliness, then gasps as gold coins begin to stream from a chute at the machine's base. He holds out his cupped hands, but in no time the load is spilling onto the floor. He stuffs handfuls of gold into his pockets, then laughs aloud. Why is he frantic? He is alone here; he's the only person with courage enough to risk this game.

As the gold coins tumble and collect at his feet, he realizes he can buy the ditten for Raquel with no trouble. Wait—why stop at a ditten? With this much gold, he can buy Raquel the life she wants. They could leave Paradise and buy a house on the beach near Oceanside. She could quit her job and spend her days basking in the sun, playing the lady of leisure to her heart's content.

"Congratulations." The magician's voice cuts through the rattle of the cascading coins. "That's a lot of moolah for a man barely past his beginning. I suppose you have big plans?"

"The biggest." William grins and resists the urge to pinch himself. Things like this only happen in dreams and, apparently, locked rooms. What else has Casey been hiding?

"Want to play again?" The magician cocks a brow. "Come on, William, don't take my money and run. There's more to be had."

As if by magic, three words again appear on the screen: *wealth, happiness, love.*

"What'll you wager next, Mr. Ambassador?" His voice narrows to a nasal drone. "Come on, my friend, make your decision. I don't have all night, you know."

"You don't?" The question is rhetorical; William is already considering his choices. He now has something to lose if he wagers wealth, but how could a video image sweep down and gather the coins on the floor? What would the machine do, empty his pockets? Impossible. Nearly as impossible as the likelihood of a game increasing his happiness or helping him win Raquel's love.

"Come on, where's the harm?" the man in black teases, winking again. "This is only a game."

The magician might be nothing but a bit of animated code, but William has to admit he's been effective so far. So effective, in fact, William is certain he's discovered the reason this game has been locked away. This machine is off limits because anyone who plays and wins could end up bankrupting the company.

Yet he is enthralled by its possibilities.

"Love." He touches the word, for how can he lose what he doesn't yet have? "I'd like to see you get that for me."

The magician smiles. "Go ahead, William. Try your luck."

William pulls the lever.

The reels spin again, moving too quickly for his eyes to discern anything more than a smear of color. Around him, the room seems to hold its breath.

The first reel stops: *apple*.

The second reel: *apple*.

The third: *apple*.

"You win!"

William laughs, fully expecting the magician to tell him that love is something one human can win only from another. But instead of offering a lecture, the machine begins to hum. William steps away, afraid the game is in the midst of some sort of meltdown, then the humming stops and he hears a faint *clunk* in the tray at the base. When he glances down he sees that the machine has printed a glossy portrait of Raquel.

He lets out a whistle of pure admiration and bends to pick up his prize. "Pretty swift. But not exactly what I'm supposed to win."

The magician's mercurial black eyes sharpen. "Isn't it?"

William holds the picture closer to the flashing lights and catches his breath as the image on the page begins to *move*. The Raquel of his dreams smiles and holds out her arms, her hips gently swaying to the rhythm of the mechanical music.

"She wants you," the magician says, his smile throwing off the shadows of his face. "And you can have her whenever you like."

"It's not Raquel." He meets the magician's glittering gaze. "This isn't love; it's only a picture of the woman I love."

"Oh ye of little faith." The man's mouth curls in a furtive smile.

"Trust me, William. Tomorrow you'll find your wager fulfilled, your fondest wishes granted. Love is yours if you want it . . . because I never fail to deliver on my promises."

"Who *are* you?"

The man doesn't answer but slips his hands into his pockets and turns as if to walk away. As William blinks in stunned silence, the magician glances back, his eyes bright with speculation, his smile partly sly as if he has a secret. "Want to play one more time before I go?"

"I think you've given me more than enough."

"Oh, come on." The man's bottom lip edges forward in an exaggerated pout. "You're not going to leave me empty-handed, are you? Besides, you're far from the man Raquel wants."

Alarm ripples along William's spine. "She wants a man of means, and you've taken care of that."

"Oh, you can win her attention," the magician answers, "with the hologram and all that gold. But love grows cold, my friend, unless you feed it, and only continued success can keep a woman like Raquel satisfied. How do you plan on maintaining your prosperity when your glittering stockpile is gone?"

The question hangs in the space between them, shimmering like the lights reflected in the machine's polished surface. The magician is right. When this money runs out, Raquel might run out too.

"What else do I need?" William smiles, waiting for the magician to respond, but the conjurer stares at him with implacable concentration, then reaches into his hat, withdraws another collection of letters, and tosses them onto the screen. As before, they rearrange themselves into three words: *health, success, wealth*.

William fixates on the word *success*. His short life hasn't exactly set Paradise afire, so what does he have to lose? Besides, isn't success the root of happiness? Raquel wants money and a life of ease, but she knows she needs a successful man to furnish those things. Her love would fade when his money ran out, but success would prevent both disasters.

He has nothing to lose. So far, the title *Ambassador* has done nothing for him but invite strange comments and odd looks. Yet this meaningless, paltry life could become truly significant with only a touch of success.

"Forget it," the magician says, apparently interpreting his hesitation as reluctance. "If you don't want to play again—"

"I'll play." William touches the word *success*, then grabs the lever and closes his eyes. *Please, please let me win*. He jerks the lever downward, then leans over the machine with both hands pressed to the cold glass, *willing* the reels to spin to the result he desperately desires.

He doesn't open his eyes until he hears the third *click* of a stopped reel. Quickly he glances left to right—*orange, orange, orange*.

"Yes!" He beats the air with his fists, then dances along with the beat pulsing from the stereo speakers. The cascade of lights flashes, confetti rains again, and his holographic Raquel sways with the grace of a palm tree as she beckons and celebrates his *success*.

When the merriment finally ends, a sheaf of paper slides into the tray at the base of the machine.

"What's that?"

With an exaggerated wince of remorse, the magician edges closer. "The key to your success," he says. "You ought to recognize it."

William stoops to retrieve his reward and finds himself holding a sketch. He glances at the magician, who is watching with an amused expression. "Go ahead—it won't bite."

William turns the cover page and brings the diagram closer. He is holding a schematic for a new game, a model unlike anything Casey's Machine Company has ever produced. Across the top of the page, in bold italics, is a caveat: *Remember the basic principle of machine gaming: the house always wins*.

"Incredible." He moves toward the lights in order to read the fine print. "It's . . . Well, the game is a bit like this one—"

"Not quite," the magician drawls. "I'm unique. But the game is revolutionary. Build it, William, and people will come. They will play, they will pay, and you will find success—enough to satisfy even your rapacious little Raquel."

William nods without looking at the video screen; his imagination has been captured by the mechanical drawing. The layout is simple and far less involved than some of their current games, but the underlying philosophy is radically different. Instead of exchanging something for something, this game offers only the *chance* to win.

ANGELA HUNT

"Take a risk?" he whispers.

"Amazing, how people respond to that offer." A look of malign satisfaction creeps over the magician's features, a look almost of gloating. "You'll find that most people would rather explore the possibility of winning on their own terms than settling for the predictability of Casey's games."

William is only half-listening. The schematic commands his attention, for not only does it reveal how the game is designed and wired, but it also contains information on how to adjust the machine so it is either tight or loose in its payouts. A tight machine will make money for the house, the instructions tell him, and a loose machine will make customers happy.

And happy customers play all kinds of machines.

A strange, cold excitement fills William's head as he rolls the schematic for safekeeping. He turns to thank the magician, but the video screen has gone blank. Enough light remains, though, for him to gather his winnings and remove every last coin from the forbidden room.

Twenty-one

I lift my gaze, meet Sari Soutar's wide eyes, and decide the chapter works. Ian Morley remains silent over in the jeering section, and for once Dr. Bell does not look as though he could have done as well himself.

I set the chapter aside and make a deliberate effort to switch from author to teacher mode. "Let's review. Who can describe William's ordinary world?"

After an interval of heavy silence, Sari raises her hand. "His ordinary world was the apartment and the machine company. And maybe Main Street."

I nod, grateful that at least one student has grasped a key concept.

"And the inciting incident? What force propelled William in a different direction?"

"The machine," Dr. Bell called. "The magician's game moved the story forward."

I tilt my head. "Is the inciting incident the machine itself, or something about the machine? After all, the machine had been in the locked room a long time. William could have ignored it indefinitely. Our story would remain entrenched in the ordinary world until—"

"William decided to *play* the machine." Ian Morley grins. "Once he played it, everything changed."

I give my favorite critic a wide smile. "Two points, Mr. Morley. You are correct. For all intents and purposes, the die is cast at the moment of William's decision. I want my readers to see how one bad choice can set a string of events in motion. Now, after an inciting incident, the protagonist usually establishes a goal—did William Case formulate a goal in the scene I read?"

Several foreheads furrow, then Johanna Sicorsky leans into the aisle to catch my eye. "He took his winnings and decided to use that mechanical diagram. I'm not sure what he's going to do with it, but I think he's going to go after Raquel and anything else he can get."

I cross my arms. "I suppose you'll have to stay tuned until I write the next few chapters. But yes, you have all put your fingers on the proper pulse points. The story opened with William Case in his ordinary world—a world nothing like this one, but ordinary for William. One day he heard about a locked room and an illicit machine. The information interested him, but not until he decided to enter the room and play the game did the story turn in a new direction. Now our protagonist is in a different place; the action has changed his situation."

I glance up at the clock. "Until next time, happy mulling. Think about your main characters—and what you want them to learn as they grow and mature."

I don't linger to talk but grab my notes and smile my way out of the room. For once, none of my students wave for my attention, so I quicken my pace as I head toward the parking lot.

Tomorrow is Zack's first meeting with the counselor, and something tells me he might be nervous. I want to get home, fix him a cup of cocoa, and make sure he's okay. I don't want to hover, but I want to be nearby in case he gets cold feet.

He cannot miss this appointment.

When Zack's eighth-grade English teacher requested a parent/teacher conference, I was certain my son had committed some terrible crime. I wasn't prepared for the paper Mr. Fielding handed me. "Excellent!" he had written across the top. "You have real talent, Zack!"

I met the teacher's gaze and frowned. "Is there a problem with this paper?"

"No, not at all." Mr. Fielding folded his hands on his desk. "I just thought you should know that your son is exhibiting unusual talent in creative writing. I don't know how much your family emphasizes the language arts at home, but I think Zack could benefit from some additional exposure to literature."

I pursed my lips into a silent O and lowered the paper. Obviously, Mr. Fielding was unaware of Zack Kerrigan's connection to Jordan Casey and Carl Kerrigan, seminary professor.

"Mr. Fielding, I can assure you that we *do* expose Zack to books."

"Do you?" He eyed me with a critical squint. "Zack seems to resist reading, writing, everything I encourage him to pursue. I think he's been pressured to pursue athletic-type activities more than literary, which is a real shame. The boy has a gift."

I tilt my head and nod. "Thank you for telling us. This comes as quite a surprise."

"Children are capable of surprising things." Mr. Fielding leaned back, a satisfied smile on his face. "And parents are often the last to know."

Because Carl has a class, I accompany Zack to the counselor's office. So far, it's been a good day. Zack got up, ate breakfast, and dressed in plenty of time for our appointment. Though he's not excited about baring his soul to a stranger (who would be?), he hasn't complained, either.

My confidence dips a bit when we sit in the waiting room for half an hour. The receptionist hides behind a window of frosted glass, occasionally peeking out to assure us that Mr. Glazier is running late.

Beside me, Zack picks up a dog-eared copy of *Sports Illustrated*. He takes in each glossy page with one glance, then flips to another as his right heel thumps against the carpet with a woodpecker's persistence.

Finally, a door opens. The thirtysomething man standing in the doorway smiles when he catches my eye, then he looks at Zachary. "Zack Kerrigan?"

Zack stands.

The man extends his hand. "I'm Otto Glazier. It's a pleasure to meet you."

They move into the hallway, and the door closes. I relax and settle into my chair, content to let them take as long as they like. I've brought a book to read, so I don't care if Mr. Glazier takes two hours to begin repairing my son.

Forty minutes later, I glance up from my book as the door opens again. Glazier looks at me and smiles. "Mrs. Kerrigan?"

"Yes."

"Would you mind joining us?"

"Of—of course not." I fumble for my purse, grab my book, and follow him to a space that's furnished more like a living room than an office. Zack sits in an upholstered chair, but he barely glances at me when I come in.

I take the seat Glazier indicates and lean on the arm as he sits in a chair facing me and Zack. "Your son and I have had a nice chat," he says, giving me a smile that seems deliberate and professional. "I can see that Zack has been well loved by you and your husband. Zack knows he has disappointed you in the past, and he's willing to try harder to make good choices in the future."

I look at Zachary, hoping for some sign of confirmation, but he is looking at his hands.

"Zack knows he's an alcoholic," Glazier continues, "and he understands that he *cannot* drink. He knows that certain drugs can be dangerously addictive for him too."

"Do you, Zack? Do you really understand?"

For the first time, Zack meets my gaze. "Sure I do, Mom."

I press my lips together, still uncertain, but Glazier seems to have everything under control. "We're going to work on some coping mechanisms and redirectional activities to help Zack," he says. "We don't want him to become a recluse, so we're going to help him learn how to socialize without drinking. We're going to develop his self-esteem so he doesn't have to use chemical substances to boost his confidence or numb his pain. We're going to meet twice a week in the beginning, then we'll taper off and see how Zack's progressing."

I nod. Glazier is going to do what Carl and I have tried to do for years, but perhaps Zack will pay more attention when the advice comes from a man we're paying by the hour.

Glazier leans toward my son. "Zack, would you mind if I spoke to your mother for a few minutes? Go out to the lobby and ask the receptionist for a soft drink. She has almost anything you could want in a mini-fridge by her desk."

Unbridled relief floods my son's face. Without a backward glance he stands and strides away, leaving me alone with the counselor.

Now, perhaps I can get a straight answer. I cross my legs and meet Glazier's gaze head-on. "What's wrong with my son? Every time my husband and I think we've made progress with him, Zack goes off with his friends and ends up on a drinking binge."

Glazier crosses his legs, too, and brings his hands together, fingertips lightly touching. "You have an amazing family, Mrs. Kerrigan: two high-achieving daughters, a husband who's a seminary professor, and you—who could doubt *your* success?"

Why is he telling me what I already know? I'm about to ask why we're wasting time, but he doesn't give me a chance to speak. "It's my feeling that Zachary has been intimidated by the people in his life, particularly the females. His older sister—is that Shannon?"

"Patricia." I correct him. "Patty is the oldest."

Glazier waves an apology and glances at a scrawled legal pad. "Yes. Patricia is a high-powered lawyer, a woman in a male-dominated field. Zack says he can't remember a time when Patricia wasn't strong enough to beat him up."

I sit back, momentarily confused. "Patty left home when Zack was nine. I don't see how—"

"For whatever reason, she intimidates him."

"What about Shannon?" I counter. "Shannon is a homemaker, not a career woman—"

"Zack also thinks of your other daughter as a high achiever. He says she made straight A's, was a cheerleader, and won awards right and left."

Unable to deny the facts, I fall silent.

Glazier spreads his hands. "You see? Zack may be an exceptional kid, but throughout his life he's felt overshadowed by these extraordinarily successful girls. Add to that a father who's more academic than athletic—"

"Hold on," I interrupt. "My husband has always made time for our son. Anytime Zack wants to, Carl will go outside to throw a football or whatever. He offered to coach Little League when Zack was younger—"

"But his heart wasn't in it." Glazier lifts a brow. "Am I right?"

He is. My life-of-the-party husband loves to socialize, but sports have always been at the bottom of his priority list.

"I'm not saying your husband isn't masculine," Glazier continues. "But from Zack's perspective, Carl's interests fell more in line with the girls' activities."

I stare at the ceiling, unable to believe what I'm hearing. Carl always has said he'd do anything Zack wanted to do, but Zack rarely asked to do athletic kinds of things. Have we misread him?

"And you," Glazier says, with a significant lifting of his brows, "you have excelled in a rare occupation and attained a status few writers enjoy. I was astounded when Zack told me you are Jordan Casey."

For the first time, the mention of my pen name makes me want to crawl under a rock.

"Not only are you an incredibly successful writer, but you write in a genre dominated by men. Your books feature an idealized man's man, a glorified superhero. While Zack is proud of your accomplishments, something in him despairs of ever living up to your standards. How can he compare with Rex Tower?"

"Wait." I hold up my hand. "You make it sound as though Zack has been emasculated or something, and that hasn't happened."

"Not emasculated, but hurt. Wounded. I have a feeling deep wells of hurt and anger exist in your son, things we won't discover for some time."

Sitting there, I feel as if there are hands on my heart, slowly twisting the hope from it. Glazier seems to think that Patricia, Shannon, Carl, and I have sabotaged Zachary. I know we have done nothing to hurt him purposefully, but perhaps we have unintentionally done damage . . .

Broken, I look up and meet his gaze. "What should we do?"

Glazier adjusts his smile. "For now, I think you should ease up on your son. Don't ask so much of him. Let him develop at his own pace. From what I've gathered, you have come from a strict, ordered background, but that sort of environment isn't the best situation for Zack. Let him breathe a bit. And make sure he keeps his appointment next week."

Nodding in weary submission, I stand and thank Mr. Glazier for his time.

Twenty-two

The maître d' at Le Coûteux, the most elegant restaurant in Oceanside, bows when he spies the beautiful woman on William's arm. The man had greeted William with mere polite attention when he phoned in the reservation; now the host bends and scrapes when William slips him a gold coin and asks to be seated at a table with a view of the beach.

"William," Raquel teases, dropping her hand on his arm when the host finally leaves them alone, "I never knew you were so brilliant."

He lifts his shoulder in what he hopes is a modest shrug and captures her hand with his. "So . . . you really liked it?"

"I think it's marvelous! Much better than anything in the game room now."

Earlier this afternoon, with only Stan in attendance, he had escorted Raquel into the factory and unveiled his new machine. He called it *Wondrous Raquel*, with a subtitle etched on the belly glass: *Good Things Come to Those Who Wait*. The machine featured a video screen onto which he'd projected a copy of the Raquel hologram. As he had hoped, Raquel had been entranced, delighted as much by the machine's dazzling effects as by the supply of gold coins he gave her.

What gorgeous woman wouldn't be pleased to see herself celebrated in living color?

Emboldened by her response, William had pressed his luck and invited her to dinner. Stan recommended Le Coûteux in Oceanside. Though he admitted he'd never been to the restaurant himself, he assured William the place had a reputation for wonderful food and a sublime atmosphere.

Now Raquel looks at him, her gaze as soft as a caress. "This is all so unexpected," she says, gesturing to their surroundings. "I was beginning to think I'd never venture out of Paradise. But when you came I caught a glimmer of hope, and here we are—"

"I've loved you since the first day I saw you." The words leapfrog over his tongue, pushing past common sense, reticence, and discretion. "I looked out my apartment window and saw you on the street. In that instant, Raquel, I knew you were meant for me."

She averts her gaze as a tear slips onto her lower lashes. "I've always thought you were special, William. And I've always wondered if you were meant—"

"For what?"

She shakes her head. "Never mind."

Two days ago, this decidedly neutral response would have crushed him. Now he smiles, remembering the stash of gold hidden in his apartment. "I think *life* holds potential, Raquel, and I want you to share it with me. I want you at my side, because I have big plans. I'm going to buy a furnished house on the beach."

Her mouth opens. "Outside Paradise?"

"Miles outside. I went out this afternoon to look at a place—it's a huge estate with six bedrooms, a library, a modern kitchen, everything you could want. It's a beautiful home, and I'm ready to buy it, but I don't want to live there alone. I want you to live with me."

"Are you *crazy*?" She squeezes his arm while light dances in her eyes. "William, I can't believe—how can you afford a place like that?"

"Let's just say I believe in myself." He leans closer. "And I believe in my new machine. I'm going to mass-produce it, fill the game room with others like it, and export the new models to other towns. *Wondrous Raquel* will be a great success, I know it."

"I know it too. I do!"

He is resisting a wild urge to draw her into his arms when a shadow enters her brown eyes. "What's wrong?"

She shakes her head. "Ross won't like it. He's so set in his ways, such a stickler about people getting something for every coin they spend in the game room. He'll say the new game violates Casey's principles—"

"Ramirez is out of touch." William waves her worries away. "I'm talking about the future. When Ramirez sees how people take to my new machine, he'll change his tune."

"And if he doesn't?"

"If he doesn't," he says, pressing his hand to hers so they are palm-to-palm, "then we'll convince him to adjust his point of view." Their fingers interweave and lock; then he brings their woven hands to his lips and kisses her fingertips.

Something inside him turns over when she blushes. With his free arm he draws her close.

"I love you, Raquel," he whispers into her hair. "I want to share my life and all I've been given with you. So I need to know—will you join me?"

She pulls away. "This is so sudden."

"Life can change in a heartbeat."

"But good things come to those who wait. Isn't that what your machine says?"

Caught by his own words, he chuckles. "You're right," he admits, releasing her hand. "And I can wait. But not forever, because you're driving me crazy. I don't know how much longer I can stand not knowing you're mine."

She gazes at him, affection and alarm warring in her eyes. "Something's happened to you."

"*You've* happened to me."

"No, it's something else. You've never talked like this before. No one has. You're . . . different."

If she only knew. He draws a deep breath, forcibly curbing his enthusiasm, and picks up the menu. "I'm the same man who fell in love with you on his first day in Paradise." He meets her eyes above the ragged parchment. "I'll always be that man. But I'm going to be a *successful* man, and I want you to be with me. It's as simple as that."

She lifts her menu, too, but as she studies the selections, he feels the occasional dart of her gaze. She is intrigued, but he's probably frightened her with his sudden request for commitment.

All right, then. Good things *do* come to those who wait, and he's prepared to give her time—but not too much.

The magician has shown him that good things also come to those who actively pursue their desires.

Raquel is staring dreamily at a snarl of words in Ross's handwriting when William raps on the window of her office. She looks up and is surprised to see Marilyn Barron in the employees' break area. Her reservations about this infraction of the rules vanishes when she spies the big-eared, bright-eyed fuzz ball in Marilyn's arms.

"Oh!" Raquel rises and flies into the break room, her hands extended. "May I hold him?"

"Certainly," Marilyn chirps.

Raquel holds the little creature aloft, then brings him down to caress her cheek. "He's the softest thing! So adorable! You're so lucky to have him."

For some reason Raquel doesn't understand, Marilyn winks at William.

Ignoring the old woman, Raquel croons to the ditten and kisses the tip of his nose. "Does he have a name?"

A half smile crosses Marilyn's face. "Not yet. I thought you should name him."

"Why me?"

"Because he's yours. A gift from this thoughtful fellow here."

For the second time in as many days, Raquel's mind goes blank with shock. "William? *You* got him for me?"

"He did," Marilyn answers. "And dittens don't come cheap, you know. But this guy had me reserve one as soon as they were born. He's been waiting for the little things to grow big enough to leave their mother."

This must be a sign. This love was meant to be.

Marilyn keeps talking, but Raquel pays no attention. She throws her free arm around William's neck, nearly knocking the man off his feet.

She lifts her lips to William's, and when they connect she's not sure she can stand the dizzying current racing through her.

When their lips separate, Raquel lowers her head to his shoulder. "Yes, William, I'll live with you. Wherever you want me to be, I'm there."

Careful of the little animal, William wraps his arms around her.

Raquel melts in his embrace. At last her worries about the future are over. William will take care of her. He's ambitious, and he's proven that he can break free of the boundaries that have kept her in one place since her beginning.

She now has a partner—and a ditten. Life is sweet.

Reality intrudes when the telephone rings. William sighs when Raquel reluctantly pulls out of his embrace, then tucks the ditten into the crook of her arm and returns to the office. She blows him a kiss as she goes; he carries the promise of that gesture with him into the game room.

Marilyn is standing by a yellow machine, her pet carrier at her feet. "I thought I should leave you two alone," she says, her smile a quick curve of thin lips.

"Much appreciated." William tucks his hand into a pocket of his coveralls, feeling like a man who has just won the world's largest jackpot. In an overflow of goodwill, he throws an arm around Marilyn's soft shoulder. "Come to the back with me, good lady. I want to show you something."

Marilyn grins, then picks up her pet carrier and follows him through the break room and into the factory. The cavernous space is uncharacteristically quiet because he and Stan have been modifying the production line to manufacture copies of *Wondrous Raquel*.

William walks Marilyn toward his invention, then yanks off the concealing cover.

She blinks at the finely tuned instrument, then focuses on the video screen. The game is in attract mode, so the hologram is swaying and smiling to a faintly audible beat. "What—why, that's Raquel!"

"Isn't she lovely?" He fishes a gold coin from his pocket and presses it into Marilyn's palm. "I want you to be one of the first to play our newest game."

She barely glances at the coin; the three-dimensional image has captivated her. "How'd you get Raquel's picture into that thing?"

He laughs. "It's a hologram—a new type of technology. Pretty cool, isn't it?"

She steps back to take in the game's other elements. "My, my. It's so shiny."

"It's laminated wood."

"So many lightbulbs!"

"You haven't seen anything yet." With one hand on the machine, he leans down and shows her the slot. "Put the coin in here and watch."

After giving him a dubious look, Marilyn slides the coin into the narrow opening. The swaying hologram swings into action, a curved line of lightbulbs flashes, and music pours from the speakers—a lively samba beat in perfect sync with Raquel's dance. Three reels spin, their *clickety-clack* providing yet another feast for the senses, and finally settle on an apple, an orange, and a cherry. When the reels fall silent, the treasure chest lights up.

Marilyn's smile dissolves into a bewildered expression of disappointment. "That's all? I like the nightingale's music better."

William shakes his head. "It's not a musical reward, Marilyn. The machine didn't give you a prize this time. See this?" He touches the treasure chest. "Your coin went into the jackpot, along with other coins that Stan, Raquel, and I have put in. If you keep playing, you might win the entire load of coins. They're all in the treasure chest, waiting for someone to hit the jackpot."

She leans forward and frowns at the reels.

"You see, Marilyn," he tries to explain, "there are three reels with twenty symbols, so there are eight thousand possible combinations. Only twenty of those are three of a kind, but if you hit one of those, you win everything."

"Twenty out of eight thousand?" Her mouth dips into an even deeper frown. "Why—I can't beat those odds!"

"Yes, you can." He drops his hands onto her shoulders and bends to look in her eyes. "We programmed the machine, you see, so it will pay out at least 98 percent of what it takes in. So it *has* to pay out sooner or later. If you keep playing, you increase the odds of it paying out sooner."

She holds out her palm. "Another coin, please."

He sighs. "One more. But that's enough for today—this game isn't exactly official yet. Ramirez hasn't seen it."

As Marilyn slips the coin into the slot, Raquel eases through the doorway and pulls William out of Marilyn's hearing. "She loves the games, you know," Raquel whispers, her breath tickling his ear. "She's likely to become your best customer."

"I'm counting on it. I want to fill the entire game room with machines like this one." He tucks her arm under his and grins at the ditten nestled in the space between her shoulder and neck. "Have you named him yet?"

Her face brightens. "I'm going to call him Lucky, because that's what I am: the luckiest girl in Paradise, all because of you."

He tilts his head and studies the green-eyed beastie. Eager to snuggle next to the warm pulse in Raquel's neck, the ditten is practically turning himself inside out.

"I think I'm jealous," William tells her, meaning every word.

She laughs. "Trust me, as much as I want to cuddle this little guy, I want to cuddle you more."

He has to look away as his breath quickens and his face grows warm. Happiness has to be oozing from his pores; he must be glowing like a hundred-watt bulb.

"I don't get it." Raquel leans closer. "If you fill the game room with these machines and people start winning the jackpots, how are we going to make money? We need some way to pay salaries and bills—"

"The machine never pays out *all* the money in its drop box," he explains. "It will pay out according to its program, but it will never dispense everything it has taken in. Yet when players realize *they* could be the one to hit the jackpot—well, that enticement will keep them playing."

Marilyn has pulled a coin from her pocket and is about to slide it into the machine. "Now, Marilyn." William steps toward her. "I thought I told you this game isn't ready for public play."

"One more," she says, her gaze fastened to the dancing hologram. "What could it hurt?"

She slips the coin into the slot before he can stop her. He clamps his mouth shut, watching as the reels spin and stop: *cherry, cherry, cherry*.

The red siren atop the machine begins to whirl, and an ear-splitting wail lances through the factory. Marilyn's chin quivers as she rushes to his arms, and Raquel squeals, trying to cover both her ears and the ditten's.

Laughing, William pats Marilyn's shoulder, then pulls her toward the machine. "We'll need to lower the volume on the siren," he yells at Stan, who has stepped out of his cubbyhole to investigate the noise.

The siren stops as the *real* magic begins. William's best customer stands in open-mouthed silence as the Raquel hologram jumps for joy and fireworks light the screen.

Marilyn's squint tightens. "What happened?"

"You won, sweetheart. Put out your hand, 'cause here comes your prize."

Two gold coins slide into the coin tray—it's not the most overwhelming jackpot, but Marilyn gapes at the payout as if she's just won a handful of priceless diamonds.

Twenty-three

The room seems as restless as my thoughts.

I smooth the comforter over my chest, then lace my fingers and stare at the mottled ceiling. The curtains, drawn against a moonlit sky, stir in the breath of the ceiling fan, coyly allowing errant moonbeams to dance on the walls and mingle with the shifting shadows.

I can't sleep. Beside me, Carl breathes deeply and evenly, his cheek nestled into his pillow, his angular form cloaked by the comforter.

Irritating, the way he can doze off without even trying. He can be reading, then announce, "I'm fading," close his book, turn off the lamp, and be out in thirty seconds. I, on the other hand, have to lie in darkness for at least a quarter of an hour while my actual and fictive worlds settle into slumber. The real world tends to fade first; the realm of my imagination resists circadian rhythms. The clock on our dark bureau could chime the midnight hour while a noon sun glares at me from my story sky, forcing me to sweat and stir and struggle for the rest I desperately need.

Suddenly warm, I push the comforter away and roll up my pajama sleeves. I roll onto my side, pound my pillow, and study the stream of light outlining the shifting curtains. Beyond the window few creatures, if any, move on the lawn. A couple of owls are probably patrolling the dark skies, their sharp eyes searching for a careless rat or mouse.

On the rug beside the bed, Dubya snores like a pig in the sun. Some people might be bothered by the noise, but I find the sound comforting. We tried living without a dog after our first mastiff died a year ago. Carl said it would be easier to travel without a giant canine—we could pick up and go anytime we chose, and as we edged toward retirement, it would be nice not to have to worry about boarding a pet the size of a pony.

We endured two weeks of doglessness before Carl called the breeder and begged for a puppy.

Now, of course, we can't "pick up and go" because we aren't comfortable leaving our son. Zack might do perfectly well on his own, he *ought* to do well, but how can we be sure we won't come home to find him propped up against our front gate?

I snort softly. Dubya, our "replacement puppy," has eased the pain of my broken heart, but I don't think the pain surrounding Zack will be assuaged so easily.

Two weeks ago, after returning from Otto Glazier's office, I told Carl everything the counselor had said. We have never considered ourselves demanding parents, but since that time we've been letting Zack come and go as he pleases, careful not to push or pry.

A couple of times Zack has given me an odd look, but he seems to appreciate my new attitude—though he has no idea how often I bite my tongue rather than ask where he's going or when he expects to be home.

I only hope he doesn't take my hands-off approach for indifference.

My mind has no sooner formed the thought than I become aware of a change in my surroundings. Something in the room has shifted, or the sound of silence has altered—

Carl's drowsy voice cuts through the quiet. "Can't sleep, hon?"

Grateful for company, I roll to face him. "I was thinking about William."

"William?"

"I mean Zack." I laugh. "Sorry. Sometimes one world bleeds into the other."

Carl's hand falls on the top of my head. "He's doing okay, don't you think?"

I shrug and then remember he can't see me in the dark. "I think so. He seems to enjoy his talks with Glazier."

"He hasn't seemed depressed lately."

"No. He's been . . . chipper. I hear him in his room on the phone all the time."

"Who does he talk to?"

"People from Salt Lake, old friends from high school, I guess. He likes to talk."

Silence, thick as wool, wraps itself around us as Carl's fingers ruffle my hair. Then he pats my cheek. "It's going to be okay, hon. We'll make it through this."

As I close my eyes to stop a sudden swell of tears, the wail of the burglar alarm cuts through the quiet with the force of an air horn. I am upright and on the floor in an instant.

"What are you doing?" Carl asks.

"Either someone's broken into the house or Zack has tripped the system."

I pad out of the bedroom in bare feet, then cut through the living room. Through the moonlight streaming through the stained glass doors, I see our son in the foyer, his jacket on, his head tilted toward the security panel. The wailing siren stops as he finally enters the correct code.

He's about to open the front door when I call his name. He flinches, then brings his hand to his chest in exaggerated surprise. "Good grief, Mom. You nearly scared me to death."

I flip the light switch. "What are you *doing*?"

He gives me a look of disbelief mingled with hurt. "I'm going out with some of the guys."

I stand there, wavering between the desire to trust him and the urge to protect him. It's nearly one. The only places open at this hour are bars and clubs and all-night diners.

Please, Lord, let him be going to a diner.

"Mom," he says, his voice firmer, "I'm not a child."

No, he's not. But neither is he a responsible adult.

I hear the soft shuffle of bare feet, then I feel Carl's hand on my back.

"You're going out at this hour?" he asks, but his voice is mild and curious, a sharp contrast to my accusatory tone.

Zack jerks his head in a nod. "I'll be back soon. We're just going to grab a bite."

Carl steps forward, supporting me with his strength. "Be careful. It's easy to run into trouble at this hour."

Before I can think of anything to add, Zack has opened the door and gone. I hear the fading *chink* of his keys as he moves to the side of the house where he parks his Ford Explorer.

I collapse against my husband, who turns me to face him. "Lord," he prays, his arms firm on my waist, "protect our son. We can't be with him tonight, so you'll have to go before him. He knows what's right, so guide his path. Please, Father. We're begging you."

Without another word—what else could we say?—Carl leads me back to our bed. I settle onto my back, fold my hands across my chest, and lift my gaze to the shadowed ceiling, waiting for the rest that will come . . . eventually.

I lost Zack once. He was about eighteen months old and as independent as a hog on ice. We were shopping in a department store—or *I* was shopping, and Zack was fretting in his stroller. When he arched his back and pitched a screaming tantrum, I lifted him out of the stroller and tried to soothe him. When that didn't work, I set him on the carpet at my feet and tried to browse a rack of dresses, half-hoping curious passersby would wonder how such a rational, pleasant-looking woman could possibly attract a stranger's strong-willed brat.

Leaving Zack on the floor by the stroller, I moved around the circle, trying to think about dresses instead of my screaming child. I didn't worry about losing him; I could have heard him three departments away.

Finally, bereft of his audience, Zack grew quiet. I bent and saw him sitting on the floor, his thumb in his mouth, his cheeks and upper lip wet. He was alert and curious, looking around, but making no move to stand up and walk.

My nerves relaxed in the silence. I stepped to another carousel, flipped through a selection of sweaters and slacks. Every three or four minutes I'd glance over to check on Zack. The third time I looked, he was gone.

I ran to the stroller, fell to my hands and knees, and searched beneath the dresses. Nothing. I peered around carousels and wound through the aisles. The mall wasn't crowded, so he couldn't have gotten far, could he? I'd been checking every few minutes, unless . . . could I have been so relieved to be rid of his screams that more time elapsed than I realized?

"Zack!" In between each convulsive breath, I heard myself calling him, as if I had been stricken by an incurable case of Tourette's and would spend the rest of my life unable to stop shouting my son's name.

Panic was like a balloon in my chest, swelling and stealing my air. The sounds of the department store faded into a low buzzing; the view went dark and soft. *Oh God, help me find him . . .*

I was reaching for the cashier's desk to steady myself when I heard a hoarse chuckle. "See, now, isn't that better?"

I whirled to see Zack riding an older woman's hip. Along with my son, the salesclerk carried a crumpled tissue.

"Here you are, Mother," she said, slipping the tissue into her pocket. "We thought his nose needed a little swipey-wipey."

Something in me wanted to scream that "we" should ask permission before picking up a baby, but all I could do was scoop my son into my arms and hold him close to my heart.

I wake with the sun, then sit groggily on the edge of the mattress and try to figure out why my eyelids feel so heavy. Because . . . we were late getting to bed. Because Zack went out.

The memory washes over me like a tsunami, nearly sending me back beneath the covers. Then another thought strikes—Zack didn't come home. If he had, we would have heard the beep of the door alarm. I'm a solid sleeper, but a mother always knows when her children are coming and going.

I lean over and tap Carl's shoulder. "Did you hear Zack come in?"

The question startles him into wakefulness. "What?"

"Our son. Did you hear him come in last night?"

I'm hoping—*please, Lord*—that Carl heard what I could not. Maybe I was so tired I slept through the door alarm; maybe Carl got up for a drink of water and let Zack in.

Carl groans. "I didn't hear anything."

Without another word, I slide my feet into slippers and hurry to the front of the house. In the dining room, I push back the lace sheers and peer at the spot where Zack usually parks. It's empty.

Okay. So maybe he had car trouble and a friend brought him home. I climb the stairs at a quick clip and head toward his room, but the instant I see the open door, I know Zack's not inside. If he were, the door would be closed.

I lean against the back of the sofa in the family room and brace myself to accept the truth—Zack promised to be back early, but he hasn't kept his word. Which could mean he's been beaten and is lying in a ditch by the side of the road or he's drunk. Or both.

Sometimes a vivid imagination is a curse, not a blessing. My brain fills with horrific images, all of them in living color and numbing detail. A serial rapist has been terrorizing women on the north side of town; maybe Zack witnessed an attack and the rapist killed him. Or maybe Zack's been kidnapped by someone who heard him mention that he was related to Jordan Casey. Maybe he's been beaten up by gang members and suffocated with duct tape, a favorite torture employed by the murderous villain featured in *Unholy Tower*.

Maybe my son hasn't been the victim of a crime at all. Maybe he's been stringing us along for two weeks, putting in his time with Otto Glazier and taking advantage of his newfound liberty. Maybe he's tipping back another scotch-and-soda with his friends right now, high on Ecstasy and laughing as the world goes fuzzy before his eyes . . .

I don't know. I not only don't know where he is; I don't know who he's with.

I don't know anything about him anymore.

I roll up my drooping pajama sleeves and march into his bedroom, flipping the light switch as I enter. I walk to the window and lift the blind, then squint in the bright morning light. With the determination of a drill sergeant, I open Zack's drawers and begin to search for any clue that might tell me what my son has become.

Six drawers later, I have found nothing but shorts, socks, T-shirts, baseball cards, and assorted pairs of underwear. I press my hands to the small of my back and stretch, then attack the closet. Nothing but shirts, slacks, three pairs of jeans on the floor, and a collection of scuffed shoes. Zack's bathroom is similarly unhelpful—the medicine chest contains nothing but cold medicine, a bottle of vitamins, tubes of toothpaste, and hair gel.

That's when I think of the bed, the favorite hiding place of every boy in the movies. I pull back the sheets and run my hand between the mattress and box spring, half-expecting to find a pornographic magazine.

What I find is a blister pack of Xanax. I don't know much about the drug except that it's available by prescription only. No doctor I know has prescribed this for Zack.

I sink to the edge of the bed and hold the packet of pills on my palm. How did he get these? I suppose he could get them from a friend or even over the Internet. Lately I've been hearing a lot about the easy availability of prescription drugs from Canada.

Carl's voice makes me flinch. "What's that?"

I hold up the packet of pills. "Xanax."

He frowns. "What's it for?"

"I have no idea. But I can find out."

Ten minutes later, I've powered up my computer and found the answer we sought. Xanax is usually prescribed for panic attacks, so the drug must induce calm, maybe even euphoria if taken at a certain dosage.

When Carl places a steadying hand on my shoulder, I crumple the blister pack and scream through my teeth. "What was he *thinking*? What were *we* thinking? We've wasted all kinds of time and money on a counselor, and all the while our son has been using drugs!"

"We don't know that, Jordan."

"Don't try to placate me, Carl; here's the evidence. We've been fools."

My husband sinks to the edge of my desk. Watching him, I know he's come around to my way of thinking when I see something that looks almost like bitterness enter his face. "What do we do now?"

I shake my head. "What can we do? We wait, but I'll tell you this— I refuse to feel guilty one minute longer. We didn't intimidate our son. If he's making bad choices, it's not our fault. I refuse to feel ashamed because our daughters have made successes of their lives. I refuse to let Mr. Glazier fault you for not being a jock, and I will not let him make me feel like a failure because my books are best sellers."

Carl reaches to touch my shoulder again, but I'm not in the mood for embraces. I leap up and move away, only to hear him say, "What'd *I* do?"

"Nothing." Unable to look at him, I lean against the wall and cross my arms. "You didn't do anything; I'm just frustrated. I think I just have to feel this way until I don't feel this way anymore . . . or until Zack comes home."

Silence sifts down like a snowfall between us, then Carl slides off the desk and moves toward the door. "You'll let me know when we can talk again?"

I bark a bitter laugh. "You won't even need an appointment."

Twenty-four

At the machine company, William's work veers in a new direction. After a full week without a word from Ramirez, Raquel, Stan, and William take a vote: does *Wondrous Raquel* deserve to be in the game room?

The vote is unanimous (Raquel says that even Lucky the ditten agrees), so Stan and William wheel the prototype into the front hall and position the game next to the window. As they slide the machine off the dolly, Raquel cuddles Lucky and jokes about the sweat pouring from their faces.

"Did that thing suddenly get heavier?" she asks, leaning against a *Sahara Sunrise* game. "Or are you guys out of shape?"

They laugh, but William can't help wincing at the barb of truth. Marilyn doesn't notice that he and Stan are sweating like old cheese. She wants to be the first to play *Wondrous Raquel* in its officially approved status, so the men step aside and let her have the honor. An hour later, a line of customers stand behind Marilyn, all of them eager to try the new game.

William is sketching a new design in the break room when Stan goes into Ramirez's office, then immediately comes out. "We have a problem," he declares.

William feels Raquel's eyes rest on him briefly, but he doesn't meet her gaze for fear of betraying his unease.

She stops stroking her ditten to look up at the mechanic. "What problem, Stan?"

His voice is rough with disgust. "There are black things all over Ramirez's desk—I'm not sure, but I think they're rat droppings." He leans against the door frame. "Maybe we'd better call someone. Rats aren't supposed to live in buildings."

Raquel reaches for the phone, then hesitates. "Who do I call?"

"I don't know. The rats have always stayed outdoors." He looks at William with a flicker of awareness in the depths of his eyes. "I can't imagine what's brought them inside."

Raquel taps her nails on the top of the phone. "I could call Ruby Davenport—she lives next to the wilds and knows about animals."

"Good idea." Stan scratches his chin. "Maybe the silly animals are confused or something."

When Raquel has finished placing the call, William heads into her office. "Is Ruby coming?"

"Tomorrow. She's busy today with her own animals. She says they've been acting strange—skittish or something."

Not knowing what to say, William crosses his arms. "Heard anything from Ramirez?"

She shakes her head.

"That's really weird—him taking off like that. Has he done that before?"

"Not since I've been around." She pets the ditten in her lap. "He's always been odd, but walking out is odd even for him."

"And the wilds! Why would he go into the woods?"

"I've no idea. Unless he wanted to talk to Casey. Maybe it's easier for him to concentrate out there."

William forces a laugh. "I guess Casey isn't big on creature comforts."

Raquel looks at him, confident and approving, but a shadow of doubt flickers in her eyes. "You don't care much about Casey, do you?"

The unexpected question snaps like a whip. "Of course I care. He put me here, didn't he?"

She waits, silently urging him to continue.

"It's just . . . Well, so he put me here. I wake up and I'm in Paradise and everything's fine, but is this all there is?" William spreads his hands, gesturing toward the emptiness of the break room. "I think I can do and be more than a game designer."

She nods. "I feel the same way. I wanted to be sure, that's all."

"Sure of what?"

She hesitates, then turns the full wattage of her smile upon him. "Sure of you."

That night, after William turns the sign and closes the machine company, he pauses on the sidewalk. None of the businesses in Paradise lock their doors, but perhaps they ought to start thinking about security. After all, the celebrations of so many golden jackpots at Casey's Machine Company are bound to motivate someone to attempt an unlawful act.

He makes a mental note to ask Stan about a lock for the front door, then slips his hands into his pockets and crosses the street. When he steps onto the opposite sidewalk, someone whispers his name: "William?"

Raquel stands in the shadows of the elm outside his apartment. She is wearing a sleeveless dress that reveals the gracefulness of her arms, her small waist, and her slender white throat. Coils of curls have escaped from the knot at her neck and draped themselves around her flushed cheeks.

He hopes the yearning that shows in her face is not quite so apparent in his own.

"Here I am." That's when he notices the suitcase at her feet. From a woven bag by the suitcase, a furry face peers at him. She and Lucky have apparently come to stay.

He moves to her side and slips his arm around her waist. "It'll take time," he tells her, "to get the house and all the things you deserve—"

When she places a finger across his lips, her touch sends a shiver rippling through him. "For now," she says, passion radiating from the dark depths of her eyes, "let's just enjoy being together."

Unwilling to release what has taken so long to win, he tugs her toward his apartment door, then turns the knob with his free hand. The sound of her laughter is delicious, the taste of her lips even more so.

He won't be alone tonight. If he's lucky, he'll never be alone again.

 Twenty-five

My anger fades as the hours pass with no sign of our son. Carl goes out looking for the boy, searching neighborhood driveways and the parking lots of bars known to cater to the college-age crowd. I call Zack's cell phone repeatedly, then discover it on his dresser.

By noon I have called the police, only to learn that they will not file a missing persons report until Zack has been gone for twenty-four hours. "Look, lady," the woman on the phone tells me, "if he's twenty-one, he's an adult. He's probably sleeping off a late night at a friend's house."

That's part of the trouble—the days when we had to meet the parents of Zack's friends before allowing him to sleep over are long past.

Carl asks if I want to go out for dinner, but since we want to know immediately when Zack comes home, neither of us can bring ourselves to leave the house. We order pizza and eat in silence, pretending to watch the under-the-counter television while we listen for the beep of the door chime. After dinner, we watch a movie we've rented, a comedy neither of us finds funny. We dress for bed and watch television until eleven, then we turn out the lights and lie in the dark.

Someday, when Zack's a parent, he'll understand how torturous this is. My stomach has clenched into a fist. I roll from my right side to my left, trying to find a position that relieves my stomachache, but I can't get comfortable. I am about to ask Carl if he would recognize the symptoms of a gall bladder attack when we hear the beep of the door alarm.

Immediately, I sit up. Our son is home. Without saying a word, I fly to the foyer, where I catch Zack at the bottom of the stairs. I flip on the light to take in his appearance—his eyes are shadowed, his cheeks sunken, his skin pale, his hair disheveled. "Wait, Son." When he pauses, I lean forward to smell his breath—no scent of alcohol on him or his clothing, so either he has cleaned himself up or this burned-out look is the result of drugs, not booze.

"Mom, I'm tired." His words are heavy and slurred. "I wanna go to bed."

"Where have you been?" My voice is sharp, pointed, but it doesn't cut through his fugue.

"Your mother asked you a question." Carl stands behind me now, apparently sharing my mood.

"Dad." Zack waves his hand in a vague gesture, then leans on the stair railing. "Yell at me tomorrow. I need to go to bed." He starts climbing the stairs. Though Carl and I both demand an explanation, he ignores us.

When he has turned the corner, my husband and I look at each other. "At least he's home," Carl adds, ever the optimist.

Now that I'm no longer worried, I'm furious. I'm muttering that Zack's going to be sorry he came home when I see an object on the carpeted steps. It's an oblong box, dark blue, barely visible in the lights from the foyer.

I lean on the stairs and reach for the box. A gold-stamped name gleams in the darkness. "Carl, look. It's from Henry's."

I didn't think it was possible to surprise Carl at this point, but the mention of Reno's most prestigious jeweler widens his eyes.

I lift the lid of the hinged box. Inside, on a bed of blue velvet, is a diamond bracelet with stones large enough to choke a rat. In the corner, printed on a small, discreet sticker, is the price: twelve thousand dollars.

"Oh my." I hand the box to Carl as I lean on the stair rail. "What has he done?"

Carl has little appreciation for fine gems, but he fully appreciates price tags, no matter how discreet. When the number registers in his brain, he snaps the box closed and marches upstairs, his footsteps echoing through the house. "I'm getting to the bottom of this," he snaps, his voice as firm as I've ever heard it. "I don't care how tired he is."

Five minutes later, Carl comes back down with a bewildered expression on his face. He hands me the box without a word.

"What? Did he have an explanation?"

Carl stares upward and rubs the back of his neck. "He says he bought it for you."

For me? I hardly ever wear jewelry, and I'd never wear anything that cost twelve thousand dollars. Aside from my wedding band and an anniversary ring from Carl, I don't own anything but costume pieces.

"That's crazy."

"I thought so too. But he didn't get you anything for your birthday, did he?"

"That was two months ago."

"I know."

I hate to say what I'm thinking, but the question must be asked. "Did you see . . . Did he have a receipt?"

"I looked through his pants pockets, but I didn't see one."

"Did you ask if he had one?"

"He said it must have fallen out of his pocket."

I still have a dozen questions—where has Zack been, why didn't he call, where's the receipt, and why in the world did he think I needed a movie star bracelet?—but Carl takes my arm and turns off the foyer lights.

"We're tired." He leads me toward our room. "Zack's tired. We'll get nothing useful out of him tonight."

"And tomorrow?"

"We'll talk to him. And we'll hope he has a few answers."

Carl and I wake on Sunday morning with every intention of confronting our son, but since Zack is out cold and we're due at church, we let him sleep.

Carl and I attend the worship service, but it's hard to think about the holiness of God when our souls are stirring with anger, confusion, and fear. We don't know if the young man sleeping at our house is a victim, a criminal, a drug addict, or some combination of all three.

Even more difficult is greeting our church friends after the service, all of whom shake our hands or hug our necks after asking, "How are you?" and receiving, "Fine, and you?" in reply.

I'm wearing an artificial grin like the wax lips we bought at the dime store when I was a kid. I smile and hug, shake hands and smile, and all the while I want to spit off that fake expression and scream that I'm going crazy, hasn't anyone noticed?

I know it's my fault. My tendency toward introversion, combined with my celebrity, has caused me to hold even our church friends at arm's length. I'm not used to confiding in people; I'm not sure I want to. But that doesn't stop me from feeling like a wounded warrior beneath a veneer only one smile thick. If one person would take the time to look into my eyes and ask about the pain flickering there, I'd share everything.

But no one does.

We eat lunch at our favorite Sunday afternoon restaurant and then drive home. The house is quiet when we come through the door, but surprise whips my breath away when we walk into the kitchen and find Zack sitting at the counter.

"I know you're mad," he says, lifting his hands, "and I'm sorry. What can I say? I messed up again."

I stare at him, about to launch into a litany of accusation, but Carl stops me with an outstretched hand. "What we want to know, Son"— he slips into the seat next to Zack—"is where you were this weekend."

"And why"—I can't resist adding—"you came home with a diamond bracelet worth more than you've earned in the last two years."

When his eyes widen, I realize he is feeling the same astonishment we experienced last night.

Carl picks up on his reaction too. "You don't remember the bracelet?"

Zack shakes his head.

"But last night you told me you bought it for your mother."

Zack covers his ears with hands too big for the little boy posture he is exhibiting. "I don't remember, okay? I don't remember anything about the weekend. All I know is I woke up this morning and you were both gone."

"It's Sunday," Carl says softly. "You know where we were."

"Sunday?" Zack's hand rises to scratch the stubble on his chin. "That explains the beard, I guess."

"Don't you even remember leaving the house?" I slide into the third seat at the counter. "You went out late Friday night—actually, it was early Saturday morning. I caught you at the door, and you said you were going out to eat with friends."

Zack looks at me as if he's trying to decide whether the truth or a lie would be more merciful. Finally, he gives me what I *think* is the truth. "I don't remember, Mom."

I draw a deep breath. "I found pills under your mattress, Zack. Maybe they're the reason for your memory loss, because you weren't drunk when you left the house."

His forehead furrows and then clears. "Those aren't my pills—they belonged to my roommate. He stashed them in my stuff when his parents came to visit; then he forgot to take them back. When I realized I had them—" He shrugs. "I didn't think you'd be snooping under my mattress."

Two months ago, that comment would have embarrassed me, but I doubt anything could embarrass me now. "If you had no intention of taking those pills, why didn't you flush them?"

"Geez, I don't know. Seemed like a waste."

"That's the sort of thing an addict would say."

"I'm not an addict."

"But you *are* an alcoholic. And if you were drinking this weekend—"

"I wasn't drinking . . . I don't think." His defensive expression fades to confusion, but only for an instant. "Look, you guys have to trust me. I'm not your baby anymore. I'm twenty-one, and I have a life of my own."

"Mature twenty-one-year-olds," Carl answers, his voice rising, "do not disappear without telling someone where they are going. Mature people show consideration for others. Did you not think we would worry? Did you for one minute think that we might be concerned when you didn't come home for two days? We called the hospitals, Zack; your mother called the police. I spent half the day driving around town, looking for your car in bars and clubs and places where I wouldn't be caught dead—"

"I'm sorry I'm such a freakin' disappointment to you!" Zack's face contorts to a mask of rage as he stands and waits to face his father's response.

What happens next is not pretty; my face burns with shame as the action unfolds. I can't believe this scene is transpiring in the heart of a Christian home, but I couldn't have written anything more intense.

Helpless, I watch as the son curses and threatens to pummel his father; the father, red-faced, dares his son to "bring it on." I stand to intervene, but when I step between them, Zack moves closer and calls me a word I wouldn't put in the mouth of Tower's most nefarious villain. As automatically as I would smack a spider that has just inflicted a painful bite, I slap my son's cheek.

Zack's hand curls into a fist, ready to strike. I refuse to back down; I'll slap him again if that's what it takes to knock sense into his head.

"You will not threaten your mother!" Carl roars, and suddenly his arms are around our son. Zack is screaming, kicking; Carl locks his elbow around Zack's throat and is choking the breath out of him. Zack's face grows red, and I am about to scream for mercy when Zack goes limp—he hasn't passed out; he has given up, and not a moment too soon.

My son is weeping when Carl releases him. In the trembling aftermath of an adrenaline rush, my men sit on the floor, Zack with his head in his hands and his shoulders slumped in defeat. Carl hesitates, then drapes his arms around our son. Weak-kneed, I sink to the floor and join them, adding my tears to theirs as we acknowledge our brokenness.

We have become a family of lunatics, and I don't know why.

Father, you plot the course of our lives, but please, God, don't push us too far.

Monday, I shower and dress, knowing my writing will have to wait until after lunch. Leaving Zack in bed, I drive to Henry's with the diamond bracelet in a plain white bag, hoping the manager will take it back without pressing charges.

I've convinced myself that someone stole this bracelet and dropped it in Zack's pocket. It could have been snatched by someone he met at a bar; maybe he took it himself. All I know is I want the thing out of my house. I'm not even comfortable having it in the car.

Henry's is the sort of place where everyone talks in a whisper. The thick carpet muffles my footsteps as I sidle up to an illuminated display case and pretend to browse while I check out the staff. The people working here—two men and two women—are elegant and well coifed; any one of them could answer a casting call for "snooty salesperson" and get the job in a heartbeat. I approach the youngest woman, hoping that a ribbon of mercy still flows through her heart.

"May I help you?"

I pull the white plastic bag from my purse and decide to run with Zack's original story. "My son brought this bracelet home the other night—he said it was a gift for me, but I really don't wear this sort of thing."

The young woman—Lorna, according to her gold name tag—opens the box and fingers the piece. "Oh yes, the Victoria bracelet. I assisted him with the sale."

Surprise makes me forget my preplanned patter. "You did?"

"Young man, dark hair, brown eyes? He was really sweet."

"B-but," I stammer, "he can't find the receipt."

"I'm sure we have a duplicate on file. One moment, please."

She turns to access a computer while I regard the jewelry from a different perspective. My son actually bought this? For me?

"Here." She pulls a sheet from a printer and shows it to me. "He charged it to his Visa, and the amount was approved." For the first time, she looks directly into my eyes. "If you don't like this piece, perhaps I can interest you in something more . . . refined?"

I am scarcely aware of what she's saying because I'm still trying to picture Zack in this store. Since he can't remember coming here, he must have been drunk.

"My son," I say, hoping to sound nonchalant, "did he seem all right when you talked to him? I mean"—I force a laugh—"he wasn't with a group of guys who might have been playing a prank, was he?"

A dimple appears in her right cheek. "Oh no, he was alone. And he was quite charming."

I bite my lip as I absorb a new piece of information: my son is a charming drunk. That's something I never would have guessed.

"He said you were special," the clerk continues. "A writer, that's what he said—and you deserved something unique. That's when I showed him the Victoria bracelet."

"Did you show him the price tag?" I make this comment in a sharp tone that draws disapproving glances from two other clerks.

"Of course," Lorna says, unruffled. "He said it was no problem."

I snort. No problem for him, maybe, but Carl and I will be paying for this if the charge goes through.

"Thank you," I tell Lorna, "but I'd really like to return the bracelet and have you credit his Visa. My son is a college student, and while I do appreciate the gesture, he shouldn't be buying me expensive gifts."

"Of course." Lorna smiles as she accepts the box, but she can't resist another dig. "I asked if he had a girlfriend," she adds, "because I thought he might like to get her something."

Red flags sprout like dandelions in my brain. I'm not sure if Lorna is commission-happy or if she's volunteering to be Zack's girlfriend, but as soon as that refund goes through, I'm leaving this place.

As I make my way across the thick carpeting, credit slip in hand, my relief is tempered by puzzlement. If Glazier is right and Zack is intimidated by the women in his life, was this some outlandish attempt to buy my love?

Twenty-six

Ruby Davenport, the resident animal expert of Paradise, comes into the office with a bucket of kibble and a large plastic jar. She examines the trail of evidence around Ramirez's desk, then points to the edge of a box that something has nibbled into tiny wisps of cardboard. "It's a rat, all right," she says, a faint light twinkling in the depths of her eyes. "I'd say it's a whole family of rats. Poor things must have come in by mistake. They prefer the woods, you know."

William crosses his arms and leans against the door frame, grinning as Ruby the Wonderworker crouches on the floor—lips pursed, elbows bent, hind end jutting up like a well-padded footstool. She is blowing air in a barely audible whistle, and the sight is so odd he has to stifle the impulse to laugh.

Ruby settles back on her haunches and heaves a loud sigh. "They're not coming out."

"Maybe they're asleep," Raquel says.

Ruby shakes her head. "How could they sleep through all this noise? It's almost as though"—she shoots William a faintly accusing look—"they're afraid of something."

He lifts his hands in a *not me* gesture. "Hey, I haven't even seen the critters."

She frowns, then looks back at the trail of droppings. "Tell you what—I'll put some kibble in the jar and leave it on the floor. If they come out, they'll go into the jar, and you can screw on the lid. Call me when you've secured them, and I'll carry the little guys out to the wilds."

Raquel makes a face. "You want *me* to—"

"It's not like I'm asking you to hurt them." Ruby grunts as she rises to her knees. "Goodness, girl, where's your courage?"

Raquel steps aside as Ruby drops bits of kibble into the jar, then places the wide-mouthed container on the carpet. Before leaving, she cocks her index finger at Raquel—"Call me, okay?"

Raquel waits until Ruby has left the break room before she dissolves into giggles.

"Goodness, girl," William says, mimicing Ruby's high-pitched tone as he draws Raquel into his arms, "where's your courage?"

She laughs until her merriment dies away in an exhausted sigh, then she settles into his arms and rests her cheek against his chest. "It's here," she says, locking her arms behind his back. "You are all the courage I need."

Twenty-seven

"And that's enough for today," I say, lowering my manuscript. My students, who at midterm have dwindled to fewer than a dozen, wear the dazed expressions of time travelers jerked from one era to another.

I usually take a few minutes to discuss the story in progress, but William and Raquel are at a juncture I don't want to pollute by inviting other people's opinions.

"Since next week is spring break, we will not meet," I announce. "We will not meet the following week, either. I am going to hole up in my study until I complete the bulk of this book, and I suggest you take some time over the holiday to consider how your own story is developing."

A collective groan issues from my students, but I answer with a smile. "In the life of every writer, there comes a time when it is far more prudent for the writer, to apply his rear to his chair and concentrate on the task. That is what I plan to do, and I think it's time for some of you to do the same."

I nod as several faces register surprise. "We could spend hours analyzing novels past and present, but you will not possess the skill of a novelist until you spend time writing a novel. So I am releasing you from the next few sessions so you can creep into your caves and pour your hearts into the stories you've been dancing around for weeks. Paint your backdrops in colorful words; depict your characters with active nouns and verbs. Create unique, fascinating story worlds. And when we meet again, you can share what you have written and we will decide what is good—and what could be improved."

Sari Soutar looks at me with glassy eyes. "You want *us* to actually start writing a novel."

"I do. I don't expect you to *finish*, but I would like to see you begin."

"But—but—"

"Now, Sari." I wag a finger at her. "Don't you think I know how intimidating the blank page can be? I'm terrified every time I begin a new book. But over the last few weeks, you've written plot outlines, character profiles, and inciting incidents. You've created descriptive paragraphs and realistic villains. So go home tonight and type 'Chapter One' on a blank page. Trust me, the rest will follow."

Linda Frankel laughs aloud, while Kristal Palma looks at Dr. Bell with an expression that clearly says, *The woman has lost her mind.*

If they only knew how close to insanity I've felt lately.

For the most part, things have calmed down at home. Zack is still visiting his counselor and attending weekly AA meetings, and he's been getting to work on time. We haven't had any blowups, nor have we discovered any diamond bracelets around the house.

I want to believe Zack is getting better, but I'm not sure. Sometimes

I think we're living with Dr. Jekyll and Mr. Hyde—we adore Jekyll, but Hyde makes my skin crawl.

At least I have this class to take my mind off things at home. Grateful for each surviving student, I lean on the lectern and fold my hands. "Before we dismiss tonight, I want to thank Mr. Morley for providing the impetus that drove me to consider writing *The Ambassador*. By challenging me that first night, Ian prodded me to begin some of the most interesting work I've ever attempted. So thank you, Mr. Morley."

As the class applauds, the back of Ian's neck flushes as red as a rooster's comb. Grinning, he looks at me and shakes his head, then I glance around to see if I've missed any uplifted hands. "Anything else? Okay, then. Have a nice break, and I'll see you on the first Monday in April."

Twenty-eight

Ramirez stays away for over a month, but Raquel, William, and Stan cover his responsibilities with few problems. After a week, Stan and Raquel take a vote and declare William the interim manager. He protests, more out of a false humility than anything else, but Stan is adamant. "Ramirez always said you were the representative," he says, only half-joking, "so get busy representing. Ambassador William, I hereby award you with management of Casey's Machine Company."

With Ramirez out of the picture, Stan and William press ahead with their plans to fill the game room with new and improved machines. Stan takes to the project like a gull takes to waves, and within a few days he has tweaked the production process so they can produce the new models faster than they ever assembled the old machines.

Raquel makes signs for the front windows, urging people to come in and try the new games. Marilyn becomes a flesh-and-blood advertisement. For a full week they give her a fistful of coins to play

Wondrous Raquel. Play she does, often with spectacular results, and the people of Paradise are attracted to the high-risk games like plants to sunlight.

The machine company attracts more customers than ever—and more rodents too. The rats do not leave; in fact, they seem to multiply at a prodigious rate. Every morning William comes in to find Ruby's container empty of all edible material. "We might as well stop filling the jar," he tells Raquel. "We're only feeding them."

So the rat droppings continue to proliferate, and tiny teeth marks appear on the baseboards, the edges of desks, and the corners of cardboard boxes. Rat ravages also appear on delicate exposed wires. They don't lose any machines to rodent damage, but Stan is frustrated by their inability to catch the pests.

When the company employees are not resisting rats, they're improving their approach to mechanical games. William names one machine in honor of the diner—*Fallen Eden* features a holographic image of the waitress holding a cake, her pink hair flaming. If the spinning reels do not match, the cake falls to the accompaniment of a piano glissando. But if the reels stop at three of a kind, a circle of glowing candles appears atop the cake and an Eden holograph does a tap dance as coins roll into the well.

Eden was uncertain about the project until William let her play a couple of rounds on the *Wondrous Raquel* machine. After winning a jackpot, she gave her enthusiastic consent. "Who knows?" she quipped, looking out the window. "Maybe people will play so long they'll come over to eat at my place. I could become famous far beyond Paradise!"

After William sketches out the designs, he gives the schematics to Stan, who sets about creating the games on the production line. For each new model rolling off the belt, they manufacture at least four copies to sell outside Paradise. Why shouldn't they export their products?

After coming up with several new designs, William concentrates on improving methods of play. "Multipliers," he tells Stan one morning, "will bring in more profit because we'll encourage people to spend more with each play."

Stan chews on his thumbnail as he studies William's latest diagram. "Go on."

"It's simple, really." William taps a picture of the new backdrop. "We add another variable, which will be revealed when the coins are inserted. If a player drops two, three, or four coins, the payout is multiplied by a randomly selected number. So if a player puts in three coins and 3x comes up, he'll win *nine* coins in the payout."

Stan, who's been so busy he hasn't shaved in three days, rubs his hand over his rasping jaw. "That's cool."

Relaxing in Stan's approval, William rolls up the diagrams. "How many new games do we have on the floor now?"

"Twenty-two," Stan answers. "And about as many of the old models, which leaves us room to spare—"

He halts as Ramirez pushes his way through the swinging door. The manager glares at Stan, then focuses on William, his face going the color of a tomato.

William's thoughts dart immediately to the gold key in Ramirez's desk drawer. He returned it immediately after his encounter with the magician's machine, so Ramirez *can't* know he took it.

The man has to be ticked about the new machines and the unusually crowded game room.

"What," Ramirez asks, his voice clipped, "is going on here?"

"New games." William steals a quick look at Stan. "I've made some modifications to the old system, and people love the changes. Take a look at *Big Bertha* over there, and you'll see what I mean."

William points to one of the new models on a dolly against the wall. He and Stan were planning to move it to the entrance during the afternoon lull.

Ramirez closes his eyes, squeezing them so tight his face seems to collapse on itself. "*What* did you call it?"

"*Big Bertha*." William's words spill out like they're glued together. "She's a masterpiece, an absolute work of art. She's designed to be flashy and catch players' attention, but she's programmed to be tight with payouts because we don't want people to stand around and block the aisles. People are going to play her because she's big and beautiful, but after a couple of losses they're going to come farther into the game room and play one of the looser machines."

"It's the wave of the future." Despite the waver in his voice, Stan gives Ramirez a confident smile. "The new games are great; we're drawing a crowd even at lunch. People would rather play our machines than eat."

Ramirez's mouth curls and rolls like he wants to spit. He points to *Bertha*, his thick finger trembling. "That, and the others like it, are abominations. They are contrary to all of Casey's principles. Machines like that should never be found in Paradise. You must get rid of them and burn all the blueprints."

"Well," Stan drawls, affectionately propping one hand on *Big Bertha*, "that's easier said than done, Ross. We've already shipped a dozen of these beauties, and we haven't heard a peep of complaint."

Ramirez's face fades to the color of parchment. "You sent them . . . *out*?"

"Sure." Playing off Stan's confidence, William folds his arms. "And we're getting new orders every day. Raquel has hardly been able to leave the phone."

Ramirez inhales a deep breath, then lowers his gaze and shows his teeth in an expression that is not a smile. "William, I want you to remove those corrupt machines from the game room and destroy any in the assembly process."

Under the pressure of Stan's eyes, William stiffens his spine. Ramirez still sees him as an innocent newcomer who knows nothing about how things work in Paradise, but the naive William has disappeared. A wiser, more sophisticated man has taken his place.

The new William cannot retreat.

"With all due respect, sir," William says, unfolding his arms, "your instructions are no longer applicable to our work."

"They are *Casey's* instructions."

"Tell you what." William hooks his thumbs over the top edge of his belt and rests his hands on his hips. "When Casey shows up and demands control, I'll let him have it. Until then, you can handle the orders and oversee the bookkeeping, but you need to leave all design matters to me. Stan and I know what we're doing."

Ramirez's eyes blaze for an instant, then he shifts the focus of his gaze to some distant point William can't follow. The older man's body seems to deflate as he lowers his head.

"Hey, it's not so bad," Stan says, forcing a laugh. "Look at it this way, Ross. You said Casey called you to the wilds, right?"

Slowly, Ramirez nods.

"Well, maybe that was Casey's way of easing you into the changes we've made. You gotta admit, you can be pretty stubborn about things. But now the changes are made—all you gotta do is live with them."

Stan's words ripple over Ramirez like water over a rock. The man's stony expression does not change as he turns to leave.

Before passing through the doorway, he looks at William. "You don't know what you've done, do you?" His voice retains only an echo of its former power. "Nothing in Paradise will ever be the same."

William gives him a smile tight enough to restrain the guilty grimace threatening to appear on his lips. "I'm counting on it."

Later that afternoon, William looks up to see the big man in the doorway, his face a pale knot of apprehension. Without speaking, he sinks into the guest chair, then presses his palms to his face.

After a long moment he lowers his hands and sighs. "You went into the forbidden room. You played the machine."

William shrugs. "So what if I did?"

"That machine is off limits. Casey locked it up."

Ramirez's meddling is beginning to irritate, but William barks out a laugh. "If Casey didn't want me to enter the room, he should have chosen a manager who knows how to hide a key."

The older man grimaces as though William has slapped him. "You don't get it. I doubt you ever will."

"Look." William drops his pencil. "If Casey didn't want me to play that machine, he shouldn't have left it in Paradise. He shouldn't have made it in the first place."

"It is only a game. A game of choice."

"Okay, then, what's so bad about that? Why was it locked up?"

Ramirez narrows his gaze. "You were chosen to be the ambassador. You represented us when you broke Casey's rules. Now evil lives among us."

"Are you saying that machine is evil? Because I think it's great. It's brought me money, love, and success—and that's more than I got working for you."

Ramirez winces but doesn't look away. "Evil is the bad use of choice, William, and even now it is spreading through Paradise. You opened the door."

"And I locked the door behind me, so I'm not worried. But thanks for your concern."

"The door cannot be locked." Ramirez speaks in a hoarse whisper, as if his comment is too terrible to utter in a normal voice. "Our innocence has gone."

William picks up his pencil and pretends to study the order form on the desk. Ramirez sits without speaking, a towering hulk of disapproval, until the clock strikes the hour. Then he stands and lumbers out of the office.

When he has gone, William throws his pencil across the room and stares at the wall.

"Darling." Raquel twirls before the elegant oak entry door, then tumbles into William's arms. "It's absolutely the most beautiful house I've ever seen."

She is finally standing before her dream home. This afternoon William settled the details with his broker; a new set of keys now jingles in Raquel's hand. Dear William kept the negotiations secret as long as he could, then he coaxed her away from her desk and hailed a cab outside the machine company.

Joy bubbled in her laugh when the taxi deposited them at the threshold of a house even larger than the one of her dreams. "We'll have to buy a car," William said, helping her out of the cab. "But with the way things are going at the company, that shouldn't be a problem."

Now she plants a kiss on his cheek. "I know you said you'd do it," she whispers, "but I never dreamed—"

"Keep on dreaming, Rocky Raquel." She smiles, liking the pet name, and he squeezes her hand. "This is only the beginning for us."

Together they tour the luxurious estate, opening doors and windows and closets that belong to *them*. Raquel's delight grows with every step. When they discover the last and most intimate room, she lets Lucky the ditten run free while she slips into William's arms, warmed by the glow in his eyes.

"I'll make sure you're never sorry," she says, raking her fingertips through his hair as they sway by the fireplace. "I'll love you like you've always dreamed of being loved. I'll comfort you and listen to you and even cook for you—"

"Shh." He places his fingertips across her lips. "Just let me adore you now and forever."

Her mouth curves into a smile beneath his fingers. "That's a lot to ask."

"It's everything." Then he moves his mouth over hers, warming her with the promise of shelter and the hope of endless tomorrows.

Twenty-nine

I stretch my arm along the back of the swing, then squeeze Carl's shoulder. The melting sun has dripped golden radiance over our back lawn, giving even the privacy wall a gilded dignity that fades as the last minutes of daylight tick away.

I look at the lawn, the fountain, the stone-rimmed pool and waterfall. This estate is almost too much for three people, but it has been home for so many years. People seemed to expect a best-selling author to live in a mansion like this, but I would be content in a mountain cabin, as long as I had Carl and my computer. And my dog. And my phone and books and a newspaper and space for my kids and grandkids when they visit . . .

Maybe I'm not as committed to simplicity as I thought. Maybe I'm a bit like Raquel, yearning for all the things that make us feel secure in our surroundings.

Carl shifts on the swing, giving me a slanted brow and a pouting smile. "A penny for your thoughts?"

"Hmm?"

"You're wearing that face."

I squeeze his shoulder again. "What face would that be?"

"The one that says you're a million miles away. Where are you this time?"

I snort softly. "In Paradise—or a few miles away, actually. William and Raquel have moved into a house in Oceanside."

Carl reaches over to brush a stray leaf from my shoulder. "Why do they have to live outside Paradise? That complicates things, doesn't it?"

"A bit. But I wanted to broaden the scope of the novel as the consequences of William's actions spread beyond Paradise. When Adam fell, the entire world was affected. When we make bad decisions, our loved ones suffer as well."

"Were you thinking of Zachary?"

"Bingo."

Leaning lightly into me, Carl tilts his face toward mine. "Don't tell me—something bad is going to happen."

"Worse than bad, I'm afraid."

"Well . . . you could always change your outline. These things aren't set in stone, are they?"

"They're set in my outline—which I will change only with the greatest reluctance."

I bend and kiss the tip of my husband's nose, then look back at the horizon, where the sun has spread itself like a peacock's tail. "Do you remember when you decided to let Zack spend the night in jail?"

I feel Carl shudder through the swing's wooden frame. The memory is not exactly a shining moment, but one night in Zack's junior year we received a call from the Reno police. Our son had been picked up with his friends, one of whom had stolen a six-pack of beer from a convenience store. Because Zack hadn't actually stolen the beer, the police said we could pick him up. If we didn't, he'd spend the night in a jail cell.

Though the decision broke our hearts, Carl and I refused. We'd warned Zack about those kids; we knew they had bad reputations. So we stayed home and paced in the living room while Zack spent a sleepless night in the holding tank. The next morning, though, he embraced us for the first time in months.

"That experience was hard on all of us," I remind Carl. "We agonized every minute we left Zack in that jail, and he suffered plenty. But when someone disregards one authority, he's practically asking to confront a higher power."

"So this William character—"

"Isn't going to see the error of his ways if someone slaps him on the wrist. This story calls for higher stakes—and that scares me to death."

Carl chuckles softly. "You know, love, sometimes I don't have the faintest idea what you're talking about."

"I'm talking about William—and Zack. He's forgotten what he learned in that jail cell. It's a miracle he hasn't killed or maimed someone on the highway. It terrifies me to think that something truly awful might have to happen before he turns around."

We sit without speaking as the night creatures begin to buzz and chirp around us. From behind the fence comes the mournful cry of a coyote, lonely as the wail of a lost soul.

Carl shivers and nuzzles my neck. "God has a good plan for us, Jordy. For Zack too. You have to believe that."

I give my husband a reassuring pat on the arm, but a storm of apprehension rages in my heart. I know all things work for good in the long run, but how is that going to help us through the difficult here and now?

On Tuesday the weatherman calls for chilly weather, so I dress in jeans, an oversized sweater, and socks. I've just put a load of laundry in the washer and settled at my desk when the phone rings. It's Winston, and once again, he is buzzing about some big opportunity.

I could use some good news, but I try not to get my hopes up. Too many of Winston's deals have gone south at the last minute. "What is it this time?"

His disappointed sigh echoes over the phone line. "I'm crushed. Have a little faith in me, Jordan."

"I do. It's everyone else I wonder about."

"Well"—I can almost see him grinning—"I told Brian Cooper about your new project, and he was jazzed. *Really* jazzed. He wants to publish it."

For an instant the words don't register, then I'm aghast. "You told my publisher about my class project?"

"He thinks it's a great idea. The Tower line is strong enough to stand on its own, so he wants to pull you out and get you started on a line of gift books. And get this—he wants you to use your married name to keep your identity separate from the Tower novels."

"You mean keep my identity secret."

"Why not? But you'll finally be able to write about subjects that are close to your heart. You can indulge your sentimental side."

I can't speak. I stare at my computer, where the cursor blinks below William's name. Where did Winston get the idea I wanted to publish *The Ambassador*?

"Winston, thanks for thinking of me, but—"

"Uh-oh. I hear a no in that statement."

"It's not a no; it's a hesitation. I never meant to publish this project. It's a class demonstration, for heaven's sake."

"Are you saying it's not good enough to be published?"

"I'm not saying that, but—"

"Then why shouldn't we publish it? Look, I know that community college isn't paying you what you're worth. So consider this project a means of earning a few extra bucks for all your hard work."

"Money's not the issue, Winston. It's . . . Well, no one but my students and Zack will ever read this manuscript. I'm not sure I want anyone else to read it."

"Why would you write a story you don't want anyone to read?"

I roll my eyes and pray for patience. We're talking in circles, and Winston is *not* getting the picture.

"I'm writing this story for my son. It's *personal*."

Winston falls silent for a moment, then a smile enters his voice. "All the better! The perfect hook! 'A mother writes for her son, a story from the heart.'"

"Winston, no."

"We'll use a pseudonym. You can write as Lovey Lamore for all I care; just let Dalton & Sons have the book. They want it, they're excited about it, and that's why I'm calling. They want you to join them in a conference call tomorrow."

I'm not wild about the idea, but maybe I ought to hear them out. I owe a debt of gratitude to my publisher, and it'd be rude to blow them off without listening to their pitch.

I sigh. "When?"

"One o'clock eastern time. You'll be home?"

I glance at my calendar. All clear, except for work.

"I'll be here."

"Great. We'll call you. And hey—don't be so quick to respond, okay? Hear them out. Keep an open mind. I'm telling you, they want this project, and I'm sure there's a way to work around any objections you might have."

"You haven't even seen this thing, Winston. It may not be what you expect."

"The more surprising, the better, as far as I'm concerned."

I thank him for the call and hang up, then prop my head on my hands and stare at the computer keyboard.

What is Winston thinking? I never should have told him about the William story. I want to write it with singleness of purpose—though it is serving as a teaching tool for my class, more than anything I want it to be an arrow that flies straight into my son's heart.

Giving the manuscript to Winston wouldn't negate that goal, but writing with the purpose of publication is more constricting than writing from the heart. Besides, the story is an obvious allegory; no one with any religious background could miss the parallels between Paradise and the Garden of Eden. If the public knew that Jordan Casey authored *The Ambassador*, the veil between my public persona and my private life would be ripped open.

Would that matter?

Maybe. Because some men tend to resist books perceived as "female," those readers might never pick up another Tower novel. And readers who think of Christians as ignorant, narrow-minded, belligerent, and bellicose might not remain loyal if they learned that Tower's creator also invented William Case.

I draw a deep breath, then push the matter from my mind. I will think about Winston's offer later. Now I have scenes to write.

Thirty

Ramirez surprises Raquel by coming back to the machine company, but for the next two weeks all he does is test her patience. The manager returns to his office, but he does nothing but sulk. He refuses to take orders for the new machines, nor does he want to look at the ledger books Raquel offers.

Frustrated, she decides to confront him. "What are you going to do in here all day?" She drops the heaviest ledger on his desk and props one hand on her hip. "You can't sit here and pout forever."

His lower jaw juts forward. "I can sit here as long as it takes for wrongs to be made right. Look at you! Your leader is unfit for leadership, your mechanic is a treacherous snake, and you are no longer virtuous—"

Raquel swallows hard, feeling her cheeks burn as though they've been seared by a flame. "What do you mean by that?"

"I know." He looks at her, his eyes soft with pain. "I know you're living with . . . that man."

She stiffens, lowers her hands to the desk, and leans in to face him. "His name is William, and I love him. You have been like a father to me, Ross, and I appreciate all you've done, but I'm grown up now. I can make my own decisions."

His eyes flash a warning. "You can make decisions, but you can also make mistakes. Take care, Raquel."

"You don't have to worry about me." She straightens, then clenches her jaw to strangle the sob in her throat. "I'm doing fine."

She whirls away from him in a flurry of confidence she doesn't quite feel, then closes the door. Despite the closed door, Ramirez's voice continues to rumble through the walls, irritating her beyond endurance.

After several hours of Ross's muttering, she opens his door and delivers an ultimatum: "I am in love with William, and you are a muttering fool. If you don't like it here, you can take your stuff and get out."

To her surprise, Ramirez stands and walks toward her, his arms extended, his eyes bright and wet with tears.

She skitters out of his way and runs to the break room, where Stan is feeding coins into a machine. When the weeping Ramirez shuffles out of the office and approaches Stan, the mechanic gives the old man a disdainful look. "Buzz off, will ya?"

At that, Ramirez leaves. Raquel relaxes, hoping he's gone for good. But the next morning he's back, and this time he turns his attention to the customers, his only remaining friends. Raquel watches as he spends an entire morning haunting people in the game room, either drenching them with pitiful tears or scorching them with heated rebuke. He chastises Eden for allowing her picture to appear on a game; he weeps when Marilyn spends the last of her ditten money to play *Big Bertha*.

Eden immediately tells William about the old man's activities, and Marilyn complains to Raquel. "That manager used to be such a nice fellow," Marilyn says, idly scratching Carlo's head as she eyes a new model Stan is wheeling into the game hall. "But now he's a ding-dang pain in the neck. A nuisance, if you ask me."

Back in her office, Raquel props her chin on her hand and ponders their problem. William and Stan have their hands full with the growing company and scores of new customers. If something is to be done about Ramirez, she might have to do it.

William has proven himself to be a man of action. She would love to impress him with her problem-solving abilities, but how does she begin?

The machine company employees have apprehended their first cheaters.

William tells himself he should have known to expect crooks; after all, the evidence of their success is enough to provoke envy from every human heart on the island. But he has been surprised by the ingenuity of those who would rather steal than earn an honest gamer's income.

The first episode of cheating nearly slipped by him. A woman from Oceanside came up to him, her face flushed and her eyes wet with tears. "I won the jackpot," she said, twisting her hands, "and the machine short-changed me. Something must be broken."

Eager to assure her, he patted her shoulder and then walked with her to the game in question. Everything seemed to be in order, so he radioed for Stan, who could open the locked cabinet and check the counting mechanism.

While he waited, the woman slipped away.

"She was right here," he told Stan a moment later. William stood on his toes, struggling to see above the heads of the other players. "I don't know why she ran off . . ."

Stan's smirk filled in the missing pieces. "She was lying, kiddo. When you said you'd have to check the machine, she knew you'd realize that the payout mechanism hadn't been triggered."

The incident left William dumbstruck, but now nothing surprises him. In the last few weeks, he has also uncovered slugging (using worthless metal slugs in place of genuine coins), coin retrieval (gluing string to a coin and pulling it back up through the slot), and a band of silver miners (people who wander through the game room hoping to glean overlooked coins from other people's games—or pockets).

He is in the factory, struggling to design a comparator that can more effectively differentiate between a coin and a slug, when Stan bursts through the swinging doors. He watches, bemused, as Stan scans the noisy area with wide eyes, spots William, and hurries forward.

Stan mouths something William can't hear through his earphones and then yanks at his sleeve. William pulls the headset away from his ear long enough to hear Stan yell, "Come quick! Raquel needs you in the office."

A chill climbs William's spine as his brain imagines scenarios with the power to alarm stoic Stan. Terrified that something has happened to Raquel, William leaves his work on the table and runs.

Rocky stands in the doorway of Ramirez's office, protectively clutching the ditten to her chest. Stan hovers at her elbow, alternately crossing and uncrossing his arms.

"What is it?"

Wordlessly, Raquel points at something in the room. William slips past her and sees Ramirez writhing on the desk like a cut snake. His eyes bulge, his mouth gapes. Something foams at his lips, white flecks doing battle with red, while a keening wail lifts the hair at the back of William's neck.

He forces down the sudden lurch of his stomach. "What happened?" He turns to Raquel, who shields Lucky's eyes and looks away.

Stan wipes his hands on his coveralls. "I heard Raquel scream and ran in here. This is what I saw."

William looks again at the injured manager. Curled on the desk, Ramirez's hands flail at his neck as if beating back wasps of pain. The cry in his throat has faded to a hoarse whisper, less a scream for help than a plea for release from unimaginable agony.

William presses his hand to his mouth. The people of Paradise do not get sick and rarely have accidents. The only person he's ever known to need a doctor is Hank, who fell last week and sprained his ankle.

William turns to face the others. "You'd better call for a doctor."

Stan reaches for the phone while William hovers helplessly between Raquel and the man who was once his boss. He doesn't know how to help Ramirez, and he's not sure anyone can.

Raquel's quiet sobs break into his thoughts.

"Are you all right?" He takes her arm; again she avoids his eyes. "Please, Rocky, can you tell me what happened here?"

With a choking cry, she tears herself away. William runs after her, finally cornering her in the employees' break room.

He presses his hands to the wall, looming over her, and bends to catch her gaze. "You can tell me," he whispers. "You can tell me anything."

She runs a trembling hand over Lucky's head. "I did it for you."

Understanding dawns with frightening swiftness. "How did you—"

She sniffs, then jerks her head toward the office. "Bottom drawer. The recipe. I mixed it with his coffee crystals. He swallowed without suspecting a thing . . . until it was too late. I didn't know what it would do, William—but I thought it would shut him up."

Eager to understand, William walks into her office. Stan is on the phone with the Oceanside hospital; he doesn't even look up when William sits in Raquel's chair and opens the bottom desk drawer. There, with her purse and several empty file folders, he finds a canister of crystal drain cleaner.

His angel fed Ramirez *acid*? A sludge of nausea oozes through his gut, then he remembers—she acted to please *him*.

They are bound in this, so they must stand together, no matter what happens.

He closes the drawer and moves to the doorway. His beloved's face is locked in neutral; she's waiting for his reaction.

He crosses to her in three long strides. "When we get Ramirez out of here," he says, griping her arms, "you get rid of that can—throw it in the dumpster behind Eden's diner. We don't know how this happened; it has to be an accident. Ramirez ate lunch at Eden's, so maybe someone there put something in the food."

She nods, relief shining through her tears. "I love you, William."

He curls his arm around her neck and whispers fierce words: "This is going to be okay, you hear? Don't worry. You can cry if you want to; people would expect that. After all, the man was your boss."

She sniffs again, then swipes at her lower lashes with the back of her hand. "I didn't expect it to be so . . . messy. He started gagging, and then he tried to call out. With his mouth open, I could *hear* the acid eating at him—"

Now that he knows the truth, she wants to share details. "Shh, enough." William taps her lips with his fingertips. "You heard him in distress, you came in, you found him on the desk. Stan and I are going to carry him out; as soon as we've gone, you grab his coffee cup and wash it out in the bathroom. All right?"

Stan comes to the door, his face pale. "They're sending an ambulance. It'll take awhile to get here, though."

William releases Raquel and jerks his chin at Stan. "Let's get Ramirez to the sidewalk. Might as well save the drivers all the time we can."

The two of them reenter the office, their jaws set and their nerves steeled to their task.

Thirty-one

I'm admiring the gardener's winter-hardy flower beds from the front porch as Zack's car stops at the gate. When my shoulders tense at the sight of his Explorer, I'm surprised to realize I am physically bracing for an encounter with my son.

As the gate opens, I lower my gaze as if I've spied something interesting in the lawn. The house has been peaceful all day, a good place to work and relax. As soon as Zack steps inside, though, the tension level inside these walls will rise several percentage points.

How can a mother swing from enjoying her son to dreading him?

From the corner of my eye, I see Zack get out of the car and slam the door. He is carrying something, but not until he reaches the sidewalk do I look up and see what fills his arms—pink roses. Two dozen, from the look of the tissue-papered bundle.

"Hey, Mom." Smiling, he comes forward and places the roses in my lap. "I saw these and thought of you."

In astonished silence, I blink at the gift.

"I didn't do anything wrong," Zack adds hastily. "I'm not trying to suck up."

I look at my son, whose eyes gleam with uncertainty.

"They're beautiful," I say, my heart breaking. "Thank you so much."

I thought I'd die when Patty left home. As we packed her car with two trunks, a half dozen suitcases, and a laptop, somehow I knew my first-born would never live with us again.

Carl and I stood in the driveway, supporting each other and smiling bravely as we waved her off to college. Once Patty's car turned at the gate and sped away, I buried my face in my hands and sobbed.

I didn't cry long before I felt a tug on my pant leg. I looked down to see that nine-year-old Zack was crying too.

"It's okay, honey," I managed to mumble through my tears. "We'll see her again in a few months."

"I am never going to leave you," Zack declared, wrapping both arms around my legs. "I will never make you cry."

I'm still on the porch, the roses in my lap and tears on my cheeks, when Carl comes home. He parks in the garage and then comes around to join me on the front steps.

"Hey," he says, sinking onto the bricks. He lifts a brow at the sight of the bouquet. "You got a secret admirer?"

I lean into him. "They're from Zack. Can you believe it?"

He chuffs softly. "The boy's going to put his old man to shame." For a moment we sit in silence; then Carl asks if I had a good day.

"Fine. Got some writing done. Also got a call from Winston."

"What did Wonder Boy have to say?"

I roll my eyes. "Come on, now. He's not that young."

"Okay, what did Superman have to say?"

I give him a grudging smile. "He called to tell me that Brian Cooper wants me in on a conference call tomorrow. Apparently they want to talk about the book I'm writing for my class."

"How'd Winston know you were writing a book?"

"I guess I told him when he called about the Olympic project. I never meant for him to sell it, though."

"But Superman couldn't resist."

"Something like that."

"What's your hesitation?"

"I don't know, but I'm not comfortable with the idea. Winston, though, has an answer for all my objections."

Carl tilts his head and looks at me. "If you're not comfortable, maybe you shouldn't give it to him. Sometimes that's how the Lord speaks to us."

"Sometimes my stubborn nature speaks that way too. Part of me wants to keep the story private because it's so clearly a spiritual allegory; then I have to wonder if I'm ashamed of my interest in spiritual things. I'm not, but that's never been a part of Jordan Casey's public persona."

"You talk about Jordan Casey as if she is someone else. *You* are Jordan Casey. Maybe it's time you let the world see the real you."

I snort softly. "The world tends to be unforgiving when its expectations are crossed. They think Jordan Casey is some kind of recluse who only gives e-mail interviews and refuses to have a picture snapped for the back cover."

"The Jordan Casey I know"—Carl draws me closer—"is a beautiful, loving woman who can intelligently discuss any topic but sports and economics. She's a loving wife, a patient mother, and a devout believer."

"You might want to revise that 'patient mother' bit," I tell him. "When I'm dealing with Zachary, I'm not as patient as I should be."

Carl squeezes my shoulder. "He's had a couple of good weeks, though. Maybe everything we've said is sinking in."

I press my lips together, thinking about our son. Zack has been a pleasure lately, a genuine Dr. Jekyll. A couple of nights he stayed out until after midnight, but he always came home before I went to bed. I haven't smelled alcohol on his breath or seen him stagger into the house. Maybe he has turned a corner.

After all we've been through, it's about time.

"I love you." I lean my head on Carl's shoulder. "I don't think I could handle any of this without you."

Thirty-two

The ambulance draws a crowd, as William knew it would. The citizens of Paradise wear shocked and horrified expressions as they watch the emergency personnel load Ramirez into the back of the vehicle. As the ambulance pulls away, the whirling red light casts blood shadows over a once-sheltered Main Street.

Stan and William stand in silence, as stunned and disbelieving as the others. As the truck disappears in the distance, William turns the door sign to *Closed*, slides the new deadbolt into position, and switches off the lights in the game room.

He treads carefully through the darkness and then sinks into an empty chair in the break area. Stan collapses across from him—the last hour has drained him too. He sighs, rubbing the back of his neck with a grease-stained hand.

William props his feet on an empty chair and rests his wrists on his knees. His mind is thick with fatigue and clouded with worry.

Raquel steps out of the ladies' room, her hands empty and her eyes red-rimmed. She sits at the table, only occasionally glancing toward the office.

The hush is like the silence after a tempest, when leaves hang limp in the quiet and nature seems to catch her breath.

Finally, William stands and walks into the office, where nothing appears out of order. Raquel has cleaned like a dervish.

Her eyes follow him, alive with calculation. "What do you suppose will happen?"

"I have no idea."

They are interrupted by a pounding on the front door. Stan leans forward, hesitates, and then rises. "I'll see who it is."

He returns a moment later with a bleary-eyed Eden, who carries a crumpled tissue in her fist. She gives William a brief, distracted glance and tries to smile, but the best she can manage is a wobbly grimace. "William, do you know what happened?"

He shakes his head. "I was in the factory working on a coin

mechanism. Stan came to get me after he heard Raquel scream."

Raquel hiccups a sudden sob. "Ross had just come back from lunch," she says, her tears flowing again. "He'd only been in there a minute when I heard these awful sounds . . ."

Eden nods. "I saw the spilled coffee on his shirt, but he didn't spill it at the diner. I'd remember something like that."

"We can't imagine what happened." Carefully maintaining a neutral expression, William meets Eden's gaze. "Should we . . . I don't know, should we do something? Seems like someone ought to investigate."

A quick flicker of fear flashes in the waitress's eyes. "I don't know who would. I mean, nothing like this has ever happened."

Stan rubs the stubble on his chin. "If anyone investigates, seems like it should be you, Ambassador."

William blinks at him, too startled to offer an objection.

"Eden?" Raquel's voice snaps him out of his surprise. "Do you know what will happen to Ross?"

The waitress shakes her head. "I heard one of the emergency technicians say something had destroyed his tongue and most of the muscles in his throat. They think he'll pull through, but I don't know if he'll ever speak—or eat solid food—again."

Raquel lowers her head in an attitude of mourning. Apparently overcome by the thought of losing a big-spending customer, Eden brings her hand to her mouth and runs out of the break room.

Not until the bells above the front door signal Eden's exit does Raquel catch William's eye and send him a tremulous smile.

Thirty-three

I have no sooner typed the final period when the phone rings. I glance at the caller ID and recognize the New York area code.

My publisher's secretary greets me when I pick up the phone.

"Everyone's almost here," she says, speaking *sotto voce* as other voices echo in the background. "Winston's on the other line; can you hear him?"

"Hi, Jordan!" Winston's voice, more tinny than the others, rattles in my ear.

A moment later I hear the well-modulated tones of Brian Cooper, publisher and president of Dalton & Sons. "Jordan! So glad you could join us."

"Thanks for the invitation."

"Let me go around the table and introduce everyone. I assume you know Winston is also on the line."

"Yes, I spoke to him a minute ago."

"Yvonne Hackett, director of marketing, has joined us, along with Jess Medeiros, head of publicity. Francis is also here—we pulled him out of an editorial meeting."

I can't help being impressed that Cooper has rounded up nearly the entire team. "Hello, everybody."

A jumble of voices respond; then we settle in to attack the business at hand.

"Winston has told us a bit about your new project," Cooper says, "and we're interested in hearing more about it. We think it's time we took you into a new field, tapped into a new market."

I swivel toward the window, torn between sharing my enthusiasm for the William story and wanting to hold it close to my breast.

"Well . . . the story is the result of a dare, actually, from a student in my college class. It's a personal story, something I wanted to write for my son. Zack, who's twenty-one, has been struggling lately with some life decisions. I hope this novella will illustrate some basic principles without being preachy." I force a laugh. "For Zachary, lessons are caught rather than taught. He's what you might call a vicarious learner."

Cooper coughs out a laugh. "I think we're all a bit like that. Can you give us an idea of the genre?"

"It's sort of a speculative fantasy—surreal world, limited cast of characters, allegorical plot. I want to illustrate the sovereign plan of God and the significance of our choices."

Silence reigns for a full beat—I've referred to *God*, which brings an immediate halt to many a New York conversation. At least I didn't say *Jesus*, which would have brought out the PC police.

"Interesting," Cooper says, his voice fading as if he's turned away from the speakerphone to look for the others' reactions. "You said novella? How big a book is this?"

"Not big. Finished, probably not more than fifty thousand words."

I strain to hear as one of the others makes a comment: "Might make a nice gift book—we could put it in a rack for impulse purchases."

Brian agrees. "Well, Jordan, I think we're interested in seeing the finished manuscript. You will send it to us, won't you?"

I draw a breath. Why not send it? By the time it's done, the semester will be over and Zachary will have had a chance to read William's story . . . so the manuscript's ultimate success or failure will be decided long before it hits my editor's desk.

"I'll send it," I tell Cooper, "but you should know I'm not sure I want to publish it. If you read it and still want to proceed, we can talk again."

"Wonderful." Cooper's voice rings with approval. "By the way, we were sorry you had to pass on the Olympic project. Just so you'll know, we handed the idea off to Thurman Medina, who writes the Travis Dexter series. We're sending Dexter to the games in Tower's place."

A small dart of regret strikes at my heart. "I'm sure Thurman will do a great job."

"We would have preferred you—you know that."

"I know."

"Anything else going on in your life?"

My mouth twists in a sardonic smile. He's asking out of politeness. There's no way Cooper and the people around that table want to hear about my son, our struggles, and how many times I've had to remind Zack to meet with his counselor or attend his AA meetings.

"Everything's fine."

"Glad to hear it. Well, take care, Jordan. We'll look forward to getting a copy of that manuscript."

I hang up and stare at the phone. I don't know what they're expecting, but I doubt they're going to like what they get.

I'm up to my neck in bubbles when Carl comes into the bathroom. He grins when he spies me in the tub. "You must have had a rough day. You don't usually hit the bubbly before eight."

I give him a smile that's more like a grimace with teeth in it. "I had my conference call with the head honchos at Dalton & Sons."

"How'd that go?"

"Pretty much like I expected. They want to see the manuscript, so I said I'd send it when I'm finished. I told them, though, that I'm not convinced I want to publish it."

Carl sits on the edge of the tub, then scoops up a handful of bubbles and sniffs them. "They don't smell."

"The perfume's in the water, not the bubbles."

"Oh." He blows the bubbles in my direction and then wipes his damp hand on his trousers. "You know, Jordy . . ."

"Yeah?"

"Maybe this is part of the big picture."

"My bubble bath?"

He laughs. "This book. Maybe it's part of a grand scheme we can't see. Maybe there are other people who could read it and catch what you want Zack to realize—you know, that one bad decision can affect the rest of their lives."

I squint at him. "You've been reading my outline."

"You left it lying by the phone."

He waits for me to respond, but what can I say? I move my hand under the water, stirring the bubbles as my thoughts swirl in an eddy of confusing ideas. "Maybe. I know God can use anything, but I'm not sure he wants to use this."

"Why not? If he uses it to influence Zachary, why not someone else?"

I scratch my nose, which is rebelling against the perfume rising from the heated water. "What about the risks? Even if this is published under the name of Jordan Kerrigan, someone is going to figure out that Jordan Casey Kerrigan wrote it."

"So use another pseudonym."

"Won't work. The author's real name always leaks out eventually; it never fails. What will happen then? Everyone will realize that Jordan Casey is a woman. Then they'll realize she's a Christian."

"So what's wrong with that?"

I blink. "Are you kidding? I could take heat from *both* sides. The anti-religious people will hate me because they resent anything having to do with Christ; the Christians will attack me because Tower uses guns, tells the occasional lie in the name of national security, and kills people. Christians will doubt my salvation, and the intellectual elite will question my intelligence. It's a no-win situation."

One corner of Carl's mouth twists upward. "Isn't faith about trusting someone else to handle those things?"

If there's one thing I hate about being married to a seminary professor, it's that when he's right, he's right—and Carl is almost always right.

Especially now.

Thirty-four

Acting in his role as ambassador, William presents the findings of his official inquiry to a select gathering in his office. "It was an accident," he tells Hank, Eden, and Marilyn. "Apparently Ross spooned drain cleaner into his coffee instead of cream. You know how absent-minded the man can be."

They nod, wanting to believe, and so they do. Hank and Eden go back to the diner; Marilyn clutches her precious pets and returns to her pastel pink house.

As Ramirez recovers in the hospital, word of the amazing game room spreads throughout Oceanside, River's Edge, and towns beyond. What had once been a thriving little business quickly becomes a booming enterprise.

To celebrate their flourishing commerce, Raquel orders a new electric sign: *Casey's Machine Company* will soon glow above the door in red neon. They scrape the old lettering off the windows and install blinds to provide privacy for those who stay at the games a little longer than they should.

William also hires additional help. Though he hates to crowd the game room with non-playing, non-paying bodies, he has to admit they need additional pairs of eyes to stop cheaters and those who would pilfer a coin or two from the next player's pocket. So he hires two imposing newcomers to Paradise, Mac and Dodge.

Like most new arrivals, Mac and Dodge walk into the machine company with wide-eyed stares, but they soon make themselves at home. Both are brawny men, wide-shouldered and tall, but Dodge is black and bald while Mac is white and hirsute. Mac wears a scowl every minute he's not eating; Dodge's usual expression is a soft smile. Together they are exactly what William needs to keep things under control at the company.

Shortly after hiring Mac and Dodge, William learns that Ross Ramirez has left the Oceanside hospital and returned to Paradise. This news comes from Eden, who heard it from Ramirez's neighbor when she stopped by the diner.

Two days later, Ramirez walks into the machine company. William is astounded that the man apparently thinks he can assume his former position as if nothing has happened.

He intercepts Ramirez at the office doorway. For a moment they engage in a little side-stepping dance, then William braces his arms against the door frame and physically bars Ramirez's path.

The older man's gaze lifts to meet William's. For the first time William looks at the scarred face and sees the damage wrought by the corrosive chemicals. The manager's lips have been replaced by mottled red flesh. Ramirez opens his mouth, probably from habit, and in that instant William glimpses the raw and empty cavern of his mouth.

He turns away as a chilly dew pearls on his skin.

"Go home, Ross." He tries to keep stunned horror out of his voice but fails. "You are no longer needed here. Go home and rest."

Ramirez proves as stubborn in weakness as he had been in strength. He crosses his arms and plants his feet shoulder-width apart, physically daring William to resist him. His body is large enough to convey his intent, but still his jaws wobble as if he desperately wants to speak.

Stan appears in the factory doorway. Seeing the impasse, he stands at alert, ready to help if needed.

William gives the old man a wintry smile. "Ramirez, don't push me."

The old man sucks at the inside of his hollow cheek for a minute, his silver brows working, then he turns and points into the break room. William follows his finger, wondering why Ross is pointing at the sketches of the newest prototypes; then Ramirez rushes forward and pulls the diagrams down, tearing the paper and ripping tape from the wall.

"What the—" William tries to catch the man's marauding hands, but by the time he reaches Ross, the old man is gesturing once again—not to the crumpled sketches but toward the painted picture of the all-seeing eye.

Casey's eye.

For no reason William can name, the sight of that image raises the hairs at the back of his neck.

"Stan." He doesn't turn; he knows the mechanic is still watching. "Call Mac and Dodge, will you?"

Like a shadow, Stan streaks through the edge of William's vision on his way to fetch the guards.

"You shouldn't have come back," William tells Ramirez, politeness soaking his voice. "You no longer have a place here."

Ramirez thrusts his finger toward the emblem, his hand trembling.

"Casey no longer has a place here, either—as if he cares. So get moving, or I'll have Mac and Dodge escort you out."

Ramirez stares at him, a look of unutterable pain in his eyes, until Mac and Dodge barrel through the swinging door.

William acknowledges them with a jerk of his head. "Would you two gentlemen escort Mr. Ramirez out of the building? He should not be allowed in the employee areas."

As obedient as trained rottweilers, the two security guards grab Ramirez's elbows and drag him from the break room. When they have gone, William looks at Stan. "Do you think he'll be back?"

"Oh yeah." A reluctant grin tugs at the mechanic's mouth. "As sure as you live and breathe, he'll be back."

Stan's words prove prophetic. Ramirez continues to show up, but because the older people of Paradise are fond of him, William tries not to evict the man until the out-of-towners complain.

Now Ramirez haunts the brick sidewalk in front of the building. His suit grows dingier by the day, his hair longer, his body more emaciated.

Most visitors to the game room ignore him. A few Paradise people bend toward him out of pity or concern; he attempts to communicate by scratching quick messages on a notebook. Drawn by the lure of the games, few people wait to read his scribblings; even fewer heed them.

One afternoon William peeks through the blinds to read what Ramirez has written—"Don't play the evil games," he warns, and another time, "The road to ruin lies within."

William laughs whenever he thinks about that last sentiment. The machine company is enjoying record profits. If this is ruin—well, bring it on. Raquel works only one morning a week because she convinced William to sink a portion of the profit into new office equipment; now all orders and bookkeeping are computerized. A machine answers the phone and takes messages, allowing Raquel a life of leisure. Stan uses the latest technology to enhance the games and frustrate cheaters; William uses it to tweak the machines so they pay off more consistently in the company's favor.

William programs *Money Honey*, a gold-coin-only machine, with reels that can stop *between* two symbols, creating forty different stopping positions instead of the usual twenty. His little tweak results in 64,000 different combinations, of which only fifteen are three of a kind. People can play for hours, continually missing by a *fraction* of an inch—close enough to convince them to insert yet another gold coin.

He finds it incredible that people who won't play the gold-only machines will play six silver coins without hesitation—in a town where four silver pieces equals one gold. Likewise, people will whoop with joy when they win three coins, conveniently forgetting they've just parted with eight.

When players hit a big jackpot in the game room, the employees ring bells, blow whistles, and do their best to make sure the entire town knows about it. But though they pay out a lot, they never violate the basic principle of machine gaming: *the house always wins*. William keeps at least one coin of every ten played on the machines and earns a healthy income from models they rent to other businesses in town.

Eden's Repast, for instance, now has a *Taste of Money* machine by the front door.

Despite his growing expertise and increasing profits, William is troubled by a recent development in his work. He experienced a wonderful burst of creativity at the outset, but now he seems to be suffering from some sort of inventor's block. Compared to the originality of his early efforts, the games he sketches these days feel hackneyed and derivative—not a good thing when players continually clamor for new models and bigger thrills.

Has his well of ideas dried up?

When William tries to pick Stan's brain, the mechanic freely admits he's a beta animal. "You give me directions, I'll follow them," he says. "You give me a plan, and I'll put it to work. But dream up an idea? Come on, William, that's your department. It's your gift."

William is beginning to doubt it. "Come on, Stan, think—who came up with the ideas for the old games? It had to be you or Ramirez—"

Stan cuts him off with a lopsided grin. "They're Casey's, remember? We still have the original schematics. Casey dreamed up Paradise, the machine company, the games, everything."

Stan's offhand remark grates on William. Casey's name is like an echo of a long-forgotten acquaintance. William's memory of the creator grows dimmer by the day, obscured by activity and the blinding glow of prosperity. He's not sure Casey even remembers Paradise or its people.

If by some miracle the creator still cares, William doesn't know how to ask for help. Ramirez is the only person in Paradise who has talked to the creator, but after what William has done to Ramirez, he's more likely to sprout wings and fly than to get help from Casey.

Restless and irritable, William opens the door to the game room, leans against the door frame, and surveys his domain. Stan left an hour ago with a beauty he met at the machines; Raquel, who grows more aloof by the hour, didn't bother to come in today. Dodge and Mac, the peace-keepers, stand at opposite sides of the hall, their hands on their belts as they study the motions of players at long banks of machines.

It's late, 10:00 p.m. Most of the games are vainly burping out their attract-mode jingles. Only about a dozen people are still working the room, including several unfamiliar faces. New folks, probably out-of-towners who've driven into Paradise to try their luck.

William blinks when he recognizes the little lady playing *Spin and Win*. Surely that's not Marilyn! She wears a faded blue-and-white housedress with a torn hem and a definite stain on the front. Her hair, which has always been curled and tidy, stands like exclamation points over her forehead. Her eyes are intent upon the machine; her right hand clutches the useless skill button while perspiration sheens her forehead. William glances at the floor and frowns when he sees no sign of the pet carrier.

He pulls himself upright and strides into the ringing, tweeting cacophony. "Marilyn?" He calls her name twice before she answers, unable or unwilling to tear her gaze from the spinning reels. "Marilyn, where are your pets?"

She doesn't answer, but her bright eyes follow the revolving wheel at the top of the game. This was another of William's tweaks—those who play *Spin and Win* can win with the reels or the huge wheel mounted high on the cabinet.

Respecting the game, he steps back and watches with her. "Come on, twelve!" She clenches her fist and pulls on the skill button as the big wheel slows. The wheel clicks to the eleven, teeters for a second on the edge of twelve, then rocks back to the eleven.

"Rats!" She pounds the machine. "I *almost* had it."

William draws a deep breath, glad he doesn't have to tell her the machine has been programmed to stop at anything *but* the winning number 99 percent of the time.

"Marilyn." He catches her wrist as she is about to feed another coin into the slot. "Slow down, honey."

Recognition finally lights her face. "William! So nice to see you. Say, I really like this new game."

"Thanks. How are you getting on these days?"

"Oh, you know." She shrugs. "You win a few, you lose a few. But yesterday I won big." Her face brightens. "I won a jackpot on *Moons Over the Mountains*. Did you hear me screaming?"

"Sure I did." He hadn't, but winners want to be celebrated. He grins and tries to change the subject. "By the way, I've just noticed something about you."

Her smile vanishes behind a mask of uncertainty. "What?"

"Aren't you missing something?"

She checks her pockets, her watch, and her earrings, then blinks up at him. "If you found money on the floor, I'm sure it's mine."

"I'm talking about your pets. Where are Marlo and Carlo?"

Her face goes blank as her fingers twiddle a button on her house-dress. "Well, they were so much trouble, you know. Always having to be fed and tended to."

William leans closer, trying to comprehend what he's hearing. "Your pets . . . are gone?"

She sniffs. "Sold them. Got a pretty good price for the pair."

For an instant he's sure he's hearing things. It's loud in here; perhaps the noise has distorted her words.

Then he looks into her eyes and sees a hard intentness he's never seen before.

"Well." He coughs to cover his surprise. "I'm sure you found a good home for them."

"Have you had your spin today?" Interrupting them, the *Spin and Win* machine warbles a welcome. Because it hasn't been fed in the last thirty seconds, it has shifted into attract mode. When Marilyn's eyes wander back to the shiny wheel, William knows its magic is working.

"I sold the animals to a doctor who needed specimens for his taxi-dermy students." Her words come out double speed. "Gotta go, William. I need to play while this wheel is hot."

He lifts his hands and steps back as she drops another coin into the slot.

The game is a hit. It has trolled for hungry fish and hooked Marilyn Barron, but the realization leaves William with an inexplicable feeling of emptiness. When he first met her, Marilyn loved her animals more than anything. Now she loves . . . a machine.

She needs to change. *He* needs to change.

And William has discovered only one character in Paradise with the power to shake things up.

Thirty-five

At eleven, William chases the last of the players out the door, then thanks Dodge and Mac for a good day's work. After watching the twin mountains of machismo walk down the sidewalk, he closes and locks the front entrance.

The door to the forbidden room opens easily when he unlocks it, and beyond the concrete divider, red and yellow lights flash a welcome.

He turns the corner to find the magician waiting on the *You Bet Your Life* video screen, a knowing smile on his face.

"Well, look what the wind blew in," he drawls, his tone warm and familiar. "How ya been, Ambassador?"

"I've been good." William steps forward, one hand in his pocket, hoping to project a picture of casual confidence. "I'm wealthy, in love, and successful . . . thanks to you, I suppose."

The magician chuckles. "Of course. But things aren't yet perfect, are they? So you've come to try your luck again."

William smiles. What a relief to know the magician understands! "Lately I've been feeling drained and empty. I could use . . . I don't know, a spark of creativity or something. Things aren't going so well, and I could use some help."

He lifts a pointed brow. "Problems in Paradise? Imagine that."

William doesn't care for the imp's sarcasm, but he releases a hollow laugh. "No major problems, just . . . annoyances. Apparently our new games are *too* good. People can't stay away from them."

"Uncontrolled appetites, hmm? I know all about desire." His ebony gaze sharpens. "So, Ambassador, did you come to play or to chat?"

The abruptness of the question startles William. He came to find answers to his problems, but something in the magician's dark eyes assures him he'll get no help unless he follows the conjurer's lead.

"I guess I came to play."

"Then let's not waste time."

He flicks his gloved hand, and immediately three words appear: *health, wealth, love.* William touches his choice on the screen. "I guess I could use a guarantee of good health."

"So be it." The bank of lightbulbs slides to the side; the reels appear. William grips the lever, finding it hot against his palm, and pulls downward with all his might.

As the reels spin, he glances at the magician, who watches with a calculating expression. "Patience." The man catches William's eye. "Good things come to those who wait, right?"

The first reel slows and stops: *banana.*

The second reel stops: *banana.*

William catches his breath, imagining Raquel's reaction when she sees him with an unexpected glow of good health. Perhaps this prize will grant him bigger muscles or increased stamina.

The third reel teeters on the edge of *banana*, then slides back: *orange.*

The magician heaves a dramatic sigh. "Too bad. You came *sooo* close!"

William blinks at the reels, unable to believe he's been suckered like any other player. "So this means—"

"You wagered your health," the magician says. "So, sorry to say, you lose."

He speaks the word *lose* with a delicate ferocity that makes it abundantly clear he is thrilled with this unhappy result.

"Wait." William lifts his hand. "Last time you said 'satisfaction guaranteed.'"

"*My* satisfaction, not yours. Did you think you were playing a game you couldn't lose?"

William closes his eyes, expecting to be struck with a coughing fit,

a seizure, or some foaming and writhing event like the one he witnessed in Ramirez's office.

Nothing happens.

When he opens one eye in a cautious slit, the magician is peering
at him from beneath his top hat. "Would I hurt you, my friend?"

William opens both eyes. "I don't know."

"I wouldn't have much of a business if I chased away all my players, would I?"

"I guess not."

"When one of your customers loses a round, it's not because you
have something *personal* against them, is it?"

"Of course not."

"All right, then. Want to play again? Redeem what you've lost?"

The white face screws into a question mark. William can detect
no signs of villainy in the magician's expression or voice, so why not
play again?

He moves closer, eager to see his choices. "What's up for grabs?"

"Yours for the winning *or* losing," the magician says as words
appear on the screen, "are wealth, attractiveness, and fame."

William scratches his chin as he considers his options. Wealth he's
already debated; he can't risk losing his fortune. Attractiveness? As
long as Raquel isn't repulsed by his appearance, he's satisfied. To lose
what looks he has—no, not an option. He hasn't thought much about
being famous, but fame *does* seem a natural accompaniment of success.
And since his reputation extends only a little beyond the borders of
Paradise, what would it hurt to lose?

The magician looms toward him, his eyeball filling the screen in a
bizarre close-up. "Come on, William—what'll it be?"

"Fame." The instant the word leaves his lips, *fame* fills the screen
in living, throbbing color.

"The ambassador wants to be famous." The magician giggles, but his
laughter has a sharp edge. "All right, lad, put the pedal to the metal!"

William grabs the ball at the end of the lever and jerks it downward. The first reel: *apple*. The second: *apple*. The third: *apple*.

As his knees buckle in relief, the bubble siren above the machine
begins to spin while the word *Jackpot* fills the screen. His ears fill

with more ringing, dinging, and shrieking than he's ever heard in the game room.

"Lucky you!" William's heart jolts when the magician purrs in his ear. "You've hit the bonus round. Not only do you win fame, but you get to play for the *big* prize."

William squints at the video screen, but he can't see anything through the lights flashing from the game cabinet.

"And the big prize is . . . ?"

"The apogee, William. The eternal possession of your soul."

William turns, half-expecting to discover that the magician has materialized behind him, but he is alone in the room. Yet he can *smell* the odors of the magician's body: stale breath, grimy skin, a tang of sweat, and the coppery scent of blood.

He manages a weak laugh as the lights fade. "Why should I play for something so worthless?"

The magician reappears on the screen, his eyes wide. "How little you know, William. Your soul isn't worthless; it's everything you are. It's your heart and mind together, the part of you Casey called into being."

"Well . . . if you're right, why should I play for something I already own?"

"But you don't own it—I do." The magician's smile sends a shiver down William's spine. "*To play one day, your soul you pay*; don't you remember? How do you think you paid for the opportunity to win the wealth, the woman, and the wonderful success? You surrendered your life force, your very soul; but I'm giving you a chance to win it back."

The conjurer could be lying . . . but his words ring of truth.

What has he done? Like the fools who gamble away a mountain of silver coins and congratulate themselves for not parting with even a sliver of gold, has he surrendered the most valuable part of himself without realizing the cost?

Is this why his life has been fraught with problems? Before he entered the locked room, life was simpler . . . and much happier.

His mind vibrates with a thousand thoughts, but one resonates above all: *I don't want the magician to own my soul.* How can he be free to enjoy his winnings if the essence of who he is belongs to this trickster? He's not sure how these things work, but he is sure his recent problems have sprung from this subtle slavery.

He'll risk anything to make things right.

Though he has been perspiring all day, William feels suddenly damper, slick with the sour stink of fear. He grips the lever. "I'll play."

"Not so fast." The magician's voice scrapes like sandpaper against William's nerves. "I own your soul now. If you win, you get it back. But what do I get if you lose?"

William takes a quick mental inventory, but everything he values most has come from the magician's game. What can he offer that the game master doesn't already have?

Slowly, William lifts his gaze to the video screen. "What do you want?"

The magician's red lips curve in an expression that hardly deserves to be called a smile. "Another soul."

"Impossible."

"I want a soul, my stupid one." His voice is soft, filled with a quiet menace. "Oh, I could arrange not to take Raquel's, or even Stan's, but I want one. Call it a bonus."

The comment makes no sense, but William can't deny the silken thread of malice in the magician's words. What is he saying? Does he want someone in Paradise to become his slave? His puppet?

"I—I don't know what you mean. And I can't give that kind of permission."

"Yes, you can, because you are the ambassador. As you act, so they respond; when you eat sour grapes, their teeth are set on edge. You are the delegate; you represent the others. So if you lose, one of their souls becomes mine."

"How can I agree to that? I don't even know who you are!"

The magician's mouth twitches with amusement. "You didn't ask for my credentials before."

Silence sifts down with the dust motes as William considers his choices.

Why does the magician want a human soul? He's powerful enough to grant wealth, success, and love. He's a master showman, and he possesses technology far beyond mortal imagining. So why doesn't he generate a soul or two and leave William alone?

Maybe he's tired. Or maybe, like William, he's suffering from inventor's block.

When William opens his eyes, his thoughts have crystallized into a stunning realization: the magician can copy, tweak, and manipulate, but he can't create.

William would laugh if his situation weren't so dire.

He studies the machine with narrowed eyes. The magician will steal what he can't create, but he has promised to spare Raquel and Stan. William won the last round. Perhaps his luck will hold.

A bead of perspiration traces a cold path from his armpit to his waist; his throat tightens until he is forced to struggle for breath. But he desperately wants to be free of this trickster.

He lifts his chin to meet the specter's gaze. "I'll play."

The magician responds with a low, silvery answer: "Spin away."

William pulls on the lever, putting all his weight into the effort. The three reels rotate so fast they seem to be whirling in reverse motion. He waits, his bowels tumbling, for seconds woven of eternity, then the first reel slows.

Apple.

Apple.

Cherry.

William stares at the trio of reels, his heart pounding painfully in his chest.

"You lose." The magician's response isn't much above a whisper, but William winces as though the conjurer has shouted in his ear. "Your life force remains safe with me, and someone else's is forfeit . . . and yes, I will take it. Soon."

"Wait." William grips the lever. "Let's double the wager. Let me spin again, and we'll play for the best two out of three."

"Too late. Playing strictly by the rules, I have won your soul. At least it's in good company—I have the lovely Raquel's as well."

"No! You said you wouldn't touch her."

"I said I wouldn't take her life. Yet she surrendered her soul the day she poisoned Ramirez. She came here seeking an answer to the problem of the old man, and I gave her the solution—a recipe. A heaping helping of advice, you might say."

William brought his hand to his head as his brain swarmed with words. "But I locked the door!"

"Do you think you're the only one who knows how to steal a key?"

"That's not fair!"

"All's fair in love and war, Ambassador." The magician's voice is fainter now and lined with laughter. "Thanks to you, I will soon possess the souls of every citizen in Paradise. Watch, you'll see."

"Wait!" William yanks on the lever, which now refuses to budge. The flashing lights flicker and dim; the video screen zips to black.

Only one light remains, the emergency exit lamp above the door. By the red glow of its bulb, William feels along the underside of the machine's cabinet, searching for a power switch. "Not fair," he mutters between clenched teeth. "I need another chance."

His fingers find nothing but smooth glass. After five minutes of frantic searching, he steps away and rakes his hands through his hair. *Think!* The machine has power, so it has to connect to an outlet. If he can break the connection and plug in the machine again, he can manually reset the game cycle.

He crouches on the floor and slips his shoulder between the wall and the game. With an effort, he shoves the cabinet forward and fumbles for the cord. There! His fingers encounter something long and smooth, but as he follows the length toward the wall, a hiss shatters the silence. The rubber in his hand becomes slick, reptilian, and alive.

He drops the writhing cord and recoils as an odd coldness settles over him, a terrifying sensation like a gust of fusty wind from the dumpster behind Eden's diner. The hiss continues, accompanied by a rattle not unlike the sound coming from his tight throat.

What has he done? This game is far more despicable than anything he's wheeled into the front room, yet those games are the spawn of this monstrosity.

Ramirez's voice comes back to him on a wave of memory: *"Evil . . . is spreading through Paradise. You opened the door."*

William stands and kicks the machine, certain the screen will blink to life and he'll confront a hostile magician, but the game remains lifeless and dark.

And he has probably broken his foot.

He backs into the concrete wall and slides down it, collapsing in an injured heap. He tries to tell himself not to worry, the machine is harmless. After all, he supposedly lost his health tonight, and except for his throbbing foot, he feels fine. So perhaps the thing *is* only a game. Maybe the magician's predictions are nothing but toothless threats.

On the other hand . . . the conjurer delivered everything he promised in the first round. William received some things instantly, but he still is being rewarded with wealth, love, and success.

He grimaces as a painful twinge slices through his gut. In that instant, he knows: one day the trickster will take his life as a final payment.

Thirty-six

To the soft strains of Mozart and the comforting flicker of a gas fireplace, I curl on the sofa to read my students' papers. Across from me, in his easy chair, Carl holds the latest chapter of William's story. From the look of intent on his face, I suspect he is trying to envision William's world through our son's eyes. Will Zachary understand that substance abuse can steal his life as surely as William's magician?

Like a snail fitting into its shell, I wedge myself into the corner of the sofa and pluck a paper from the stack in my lap. My students returned from their extended break ready to work, so I asked them to polish and hand in their first chapters.

Some of their efforts surprise me. Linda Frankel writes with imagination and verve; Dr. Bell's paper isn't half-bad. Johanna Sicorsky likes the omniscient viewpoint, a technique more common to the nineteenth century than the twenty-first, and Sari Soutar has an ear for dialogue and an eye for fashion—every character wears fully detailed designer clothing and shoes.

I glance at the name on the next paper—Ian Morley—and feel the corner of my mouth twist. This might prove interesting.

A black MD530 "Little Bird" helicopter touched down at precisely 2210 hours. Michael Pierce joined Reed and Berger as they climbed into the open doors. The black rotors whirled overhead, chopping the air in a dull rhythm as Reed greeted four Navy SEALs and made quick introductions, then explained how the operation would go down.

Pierce leaned against a mesh barricade, impressed. Reed must have actually earned those four bars if he commanded instant respect from these guys. Like him, they were dressed in black and armed to the teeth, their eyes shining with the bold audacity that adrenaline produces in true warriors.

My mouth drops open. Good grief, where did the lad learn to write like this? Ian Morley is not as unpolished as I thought; this writing is *good*.

I look at Carl, who has just turned a page. "Listen to this, hon."

I read the next two paragraphs, then lower the paper. "Can you believe it? That's from Ian Morley, the kid who pesters me in class."

"Jordan." Carl gives me a look that puts an immediate damper on my rising spirits. "Think about it."

"About what?"

"Read it again, substituting the name *Rex Tower* for *Michael Pierce*."

I take a quick, sharp breath. "He didn't."

"He did. If I'm not mistaken, that's from *The Tower Falls*."

I stare at the page, reading *my* words and *my* plot ever-so-slightly concealed beneath false names. "Why, that little rascal—"

Carl rubs a finger over his lips, undoubtedly stifling the urge to laugh. "He got you, honey."

I take a deep, insulted breath, then exhale slowly. All right, then. Ian Morley has played the joke of all jokes. When, I wonder, does he plan to hand in an original chapter?

I look at Carl, who has gone back to his reading. "What do you think I should do about this?"

He doesn't answer but pulls the printed manuscript closer.

"Carl?"

"Hmm?"

"What should I do about Ian Morley?"

He gives me a blank look over the top of a page. "I thought you wanted me to read this."

"I do, but—"

"Then let me get through this chapter, will you?"

I sink back, both rebuffed and pleased that Carl finds the story engaging. That's when Zachary comes out of the kitchen, an apple in his hand and a curious look on his face.

I turn and, as is my habit, immediately study my son's face to gauge his mood. His eyes are calm, not overly bright or bleary, so apparently he's still clean and sober.

I give him a smile. "I didn't know you were home."

"Did I hear you say something about Ian Morley?"

"You know Ian?"

"Went to high school with him. Tall guy, reddish hair, kind of a jock?"

"That's him."

Zack sinks onto the armrest at the end of the sofa. "Morley's in your class? That's hilarious."

"Why is that hilarious?" I press my hand to my chest in an exaggerated display of hurt. "I happen to offer an incredibly interesting curriculum."

Zack bites his apple and manages to grin while he's chewing. "In high school Morley couldn't write his way out of a paper bag. I was in his English class, and he handed in maybe three assignments the entire year. He passed, but barely."

"That doesn't mean he *couldn't* write. Not handing in his work means he *wouldn't* write. Maybe he's learned to like writing since then."

"More likely that he's learned to like some babe in your class. Have you noticed him hitting on any of the women?"

The idea that Ian Morley has taken my class only to be near some girl is so amazing I'm at a loss for words. I stare at my son a minute, then nod slowly. "He does sit next to Kristal Palma. And Sari Soutar is adorable, so maybe—"

"Would you listen to yourself?" From the depths of his recliner, Carl frowns at me. "Are you at that school to teach or play matchmaker?"

I wink at my husband, who is probably more irritated by our distracting talk than by the subject matter, then I turn to Zack. "You should come to class sometime. I could introduce you or not, but there are some really cute girls . . ."

"No thanks." He stands and backs away as if I've just threatened him with a fate worse than death. Apparently mothers don't make good matchmakers.

"Want me to tell Ian hi for you?" I call as Zack heads for the stairs.

"Just because I knew the guy doesn't mean we were friends."

Once I hear the slam of Zack's bedroom door, I return my attention to Carl. I wait until his gaze slides over the last of the printed lines and he drops the last page to the pile in his lap. "Well?"

For a moment he stares at nothing, then his eyes blaze into mine. "It's different."

I can't stop a frown. "Good different or bad different?"

"Just . . . different." He looks at the last page again. "I can't see Dalton & Sons publishing this."

"That's the least of my concerns." I glance toward the upstairs balcony and lower my voice. "How do you think the story will affect Zachary?"

Carl blows out his cheeks as he gathers the pages. "I don't know, hon. He might see everything you want him to see; he might see nothing at all."

I lean forward, my elbows on my knees. "Do you think he'll understand that even our mistakes are part of a master plan? I haven't written this part yet, but I want to demonstrate how all things work together for good, that God uses our mistakes to mature us."

"Sure, but—" A melancholy frown flits across Carl's features. "Our son's not a believer, so I don't know if the spiritual content will resonate with him. I just don't know."

I slump against the sofa. Maybe I'm expecting too much of a simple story, pinning too many hopes on words and ideas.

"Jordan?" When I glance up, Carl's mouth has gone tight and grim. "You look tired, hon. Maybe you've been working too hard."

"I'm fine."

"Are you sure?"

"I'm *fine.*"

Silence stretches between us as the mantel clock chimes the hour, then Carl stacks the manuscript pages on the coffee table. "What happens next?"

I give him a rueful smile. "William takes a few knocks before he learns his lessons. He's thickheaded, you know."

"Like some people of my acquaintance." Carl stands and pauses to drop a kiss on my forehead. "If this story gets too complicated, you could put it aside and get to work on the next Tower adventure."

I catch his hand. "Rex is a good man; he'll wait."

Thirty-seven

Raquel sets a drink on the kitchen table, then crosses her arms and looks at William with what she hopes is a playful pout. "Come on, William. I hear there's a great new band at the Oceanside Tavern. Let's go out."

He winces and lifts his glass. "It's late, Rocky. And my stomach is killing me."

She tilts her head, unable to understand his reluctance. "It's probably all that fried food at Eden's. You should eat more fruits and vegetables. You could eat an apple in the car—"

"I don't want to eat, and I don't want to go out. Let me enjoy my drink, will you?"

She blinks, stunned by the irritated edge in his voice. What happened to the man she once knew? The old William would have climbed a mountain to be with her; this frazzled scarecrow looks as though his chief joy lies in counting out aspirin.

She drops into the chair across from him, her arms folded tight as a gate. "You're no fun anymore. I moved in with you because I thought we would have more time to be together, but I see less of you now than ever. The company could run itself these days, so why do you insist on staying away?"

"I'm not avoiding you. But the business needs me."

She waits as he gulps several swallows of his drink, then closes his eyes. A shudder crosses his face, and for an instant she's convinced that he shuddered because he is with *her*.

She clenches her fist until her nails dig into her palm. This isn't what she bargained for. She paid the magician's price to play because he said she could win an answer to the Ramirez problem. She won what she wanted, but her prize has not brought happiness.

She presses her lips into a straight line as her chin wobbles and her eyes fill with tears. She doesn't have to sit here and wait for William. Unless her mirror is lying, she still possesses beauty, and there are plenty of men who will appreciate it. She dressed tonight for William, splashed on the perfume he loves, but if he won't even look at her—

"The company can't run itself," he says, grimacing as he holds his stomach. "We're doing all we can to stay ahead of the game. Every day we get new orders, new customers, and calls for new models. No one wants to play *Wondrous Raquel* anymore."

Maybe he didn't intend that comment to sting, but it does. She narrows her eyes. "What do you mean?"

His head falls to the back of the chair. "Don't take everything I say so personally."

"How else am I supposed to take it?"

"As a general observation. In case you haven't noticed, lots of people make lots of comments that have nothing to do with you. I'm sure this will come as a revelation, but the entire world does not revolve around you or your blasted ditten."

Alarm and anger ripple along her spine as his words lacerate her heart. She trembles, startled by the sudden vehemence of her fury, but William seems oblivious to her feelings. His eyes are closed, his attention focused squarely on himself.

She swallows a hysterical surge of angry laughter. "I'm glad we had this talk. Now I know how you really feel about me."

He waves her away. "Not now, please."

"You think I'm an egotistical maniac."

"I didn't say that."

"It's what you're thinking! If this is what you call love, I'd hate to see how you treat someone you dislike. Wait—I *have* seen what you did to Ross Ramirez. Is that poor man still slumming on the sidewalk outside the company you stole from him?"

She strikes a nerve. William sits up, choking on his fury. With one hand protecting his stomach, he leans across the table and thrusts his finger into her face. "I did *nothing* to Ramirez. You're the one who put drain cleaner in his coffee."

"I only did what you wanted me to do!" She rises from her chair, rage burning her throat. Doesn't he realize what she has sacrificed for him? "You wanted Ramirez gone!"

"You did too! From the beginning, you made it clear you wanted this"—he waves his free arm, gesturing to the china on the buffet, the gleaming kitchen, the house—"and you would do anything for anyone who could get you out of the company. I was just the first dope to come along with a plan. You'd have offered yourself to someone else if the price was right. Just like you offered your soul to the magician."

A tremor touches her smooth lips as the truth crashes over her like a wave. *He knows.* Which means he has been back to see the magician, which means this time he has played and lost. If he'd won, he wouldn't be clutching his side and moaning in self-pity.

What did he risk and lose—his love for her?

She summons the courage to break the icy silence. "Who are you to accuse me?" Hurt beyond words, she scoops up a porcelain teacup and throws it across the room. It hits the wall and shatters into sharp shards.

Without another word, she spins and stalks out of the kitchen. If he is miserable, the fault is his alone.

Thirty-eight

Tax Day, the fifteenth of April, dawns bright and beautiful, so after breakfast Carl suggests we go for a drive. He has no classes scheduled, and I could use a break, so I tie a scarf over my hair and help him lower the top on the roadster.

After leaving our home in the southwest suburban section of Reno, we drive along the Mt. Rose Highway, heading for Lake Tahoe. While thin clouds suds the sky, mountains rise along the road like a series of folds in a rug. As Carl hums to the radio, I imagine floating above the earth and looking down on the topography. Reno must look like an oriental carpet—a bright and busy diamond surrounded by gentle patterns of gold, green, and brown, broken only by the emerald and turquoise spill of Lake Tahoe at the lower left edge.

My thoughts stray to my work in progress. I find myself examining Paradise from the air, swooping over the dark rocks of the northern cliffs and the wooded forest rimming the far eastern edge. Only the island's center has been developed, as if all of Paradise revolves around the machine company—and in my story world, it does.

Beside me, Carl props his arm on the car door and sings along with the Turtles on the radio. He loves traveling through Tahoe and admiring the luxurious homes along the lake. My thoughts are focused elsewhere, but I nod when he points to a lovely house and smile when he drums on the steering wheel just before breaking into the chorus of "So Happy Together."

When the Turtles have finished, he leans over and pats my knee. "It's okay, hon."

"What?"

"I know you're humoring me."

"I'm not—"

"You've got that look on your face, so I know you're not really here. But that's okay."

I shoot him an apologetic grin. He knows me too well. Truthfully, my thoughts center on only two things these days, my story and Zack. It's a lot less painful to think about my story.

I thought Zack had been making progress, but his behavior has deteriorated over the last few days. He's been testy and argumentative, and though I don't think he's been drinking, he's turned on us several times, cursing at us for no reason until we retreat to the safety of our room. These rages usually occur at night when we're all tired, and I have to wonder if they have anything to do with Zack's *not* drinking—maybe they're spurred by resentment. Instead of being out with his friends at a bar, he's home with the folks, sober and bored.

By morning Zack is usually calm, but I can't believe we've had to lock ourselves in our bedroom to escape our son's verbal abuse.

At midday we pull back into Reno, and Carl suggests we eat at our favorite restaurant, Archie's Famous Grill. The young hostess seats us at a small table on the outdoor patio. After placing two orders for Archie's famous Jamaican chicken, I fold my hands and look around. The usual mix of working people and college students cluster around the tables—Archie's is known for good food and reasonable prices.

I lift a brow when I spy a familiar face across the patio. "Hon." I reach for Carl's hand. "Remember the student I told you about?"

"Which one?"

"The jock, the kid who went to high school with Zachary."

His eyes twinkle. "The kid who handed in an excerpt of *The Tower Falls*?"

"He's sitting across the way—the guy reading."

In a movement that is anything but subtle, Carl turns and stares. "The thin—oh, now I see." He laughs as he turns back to face me. "Did you see *what* he's reading?"

I squint. "I can't make it out."

"It's *Tower to the People*. I'd recognize that cover anywhere."

How could I miss that familiar design? *Tower to the People* was written in the days when I was still cutting my teeth.

I can't help but laugh. "What do you know? Maybe he's getting something out of my class after all."

"How's his writing?"

I shrug. "Typical. Very macho. He writes about Navy SEALs and guns and detectives."

"I think he has a crush on you." Carl smiles his thanks to the waiter who brings his iced tea. "Who wouldn't?"

"Now you're being ridiculous." I accept my drink from the waiter, then slip the paper jacket from my straw. "Morley's a nice kid, though. I'm going to give his paper back and ask when I can expect to see something of his own."

Carl nods. "He'd probably be surprised to hear that you didn't recognize your own writing."

"I not only didn't recognize it, but the little editor in my brain was ready to clean it up. I don't think I've ever written a page I could call perfect."

The waiter slides a basket of tortilla chips onto our table. "Reminds me of a discussion we had in my class last week," Carl says. "Someone asked if it was possible to live a sinless life—say, for a week. Half the class believed it could be done; the other half said our fallen natures would consistently prevent us from achieving perfection." He picks up a chip and waves it as he thinks aloud. "If we start thinking we're perfect, we become full of pride."

I snort. "Send a couple of those sin-free people over to our house and ask them to live with Zachary for month. If he's in a mood, their perfect natures won't last two minutes."

Carl smiles as he dips his chip into a cup of salsa, but his eyes are as cold as glacier ice. "It's an awful thing to feel like you hate your kid."

The waver in his voice is slight; only the tightening of the muscles in his jaw betrays his emotion.

Now that we're confessing our secrets, I give him a grim smile. "There have been days when I told the Lord it'd be easier if Zack went back to school. I know he'd have a hard time, but at least he wouldn't be upsetting us." I hesitate. "Gee, that sounds selfish, doesn't it?"

"I don't think it's selfish to want peace in your home. And face it, we haven't known a month's peace since Zack came back from Salt Lake."

We nibble at the chips as our thoughts venture toward feelings we are only beginning to admit. Even now, I'm afraid to let Carl see everything in my heart—how much I have resented Zachary, how often I have wished he was as levelheaded as his sisters. Last night when he stood in the kitchen and raged at his father, I fled into our bedroom closet. With my face pressed into the softness of Carl's shirts, I confessed that if Zachary were to leave home and stay gone, my strongest emotion would be relief.

"I know that's wrong, God," I sobbed. "I know I'm supposed to love him. But when he acts like this, he exhausts every bit of patience and love I have."

A bright ha-ha-ha of laughter wrests me from the dark memory. I freeze, one hand reaching for the chips, as a rowdy group of college kids crowd the doorway.

Carl turns too. "Sounds like they're having a good time," he says, but he keeps staring because something has snagged his attention. With a jolt, I realize what it is—the laugh. The particular loud laugh that belongs to our son.

"It can't be Zachary," I tell him, but I can't look away, either. "Zack has to work until five. He left the house early this morning, so there's no way he's with that crowd—"

The group of college kids shuffle farther into the waiting area, and I see Zack come through the door, his hands in his pockets, his sweatshirt loose around his neck. His eyes are bright above reddened cheeks, and he laughs again, louder and brassier than before.

"He's high as a kite," Carl says, swiveling to leave the booth.

"Wait." I reach for his sleeve, catching it just before he stands. Something in me wants to march over there and box our son's ears, but perhaps there is a logical explanation.

"Wait," I repeat as Carl slumps back into his seat. "Wait until we leave, then we can walk by the table and get a better feel for the situation. Maybe he got off work early; maybe this is a party for someone."

Carl is only half-listening because he's pulled out his cell phone and is punching numbers on the keypad. I sink back, miserable, as he finishes dialing and glances again in Zack's direction.

"Jim!" Carl's voice booms across the table. "It's Carl Kerrigan, Zack's father. I wonder—could you put him on the line?"

I watch, scarcely daring to breathe, as the glitter in his eyes brightens, fed by the heat of anger. He gives me a warning look, then apologizes to Jim McNeil and thanks the man for his time.

I feel a shiver run up my arms as Carl drops his phone back into his pocket. "Zachary never showed up at work this morning," he says. "Jim says he's sorry, but he's going to have to let Zack go. Apparently he's missed several days in the last couple of weeks."

I swallow hard and wrap my arms about myself as old feelings bubble up and crack the thin coating of my composure.

Carl rises and strides toward our son. His shoulders are set, his back straight, and when he reaches Zack he speaks quietly, firmly, and briefly. Zack laughs and tries to slap his father on the back, but Carl catches Zack's hand and tosses it away as if it were diseased.

When the waiter approaches with our dinners, I give him a wavering smile and ask him to put them in to-go boxes. "You can bring the check right away," I finish. "We're not hungry anymore."

One Saturday afternoon I was busily at work when Rosalita, our housekeeper, bustled into my office. "It is too much," she said, her voice high and tight. "I don't mind picking up smelly sneakers and underwear and wet towels, but I will *not* wipe up chicken splatter."

Hunched over my keyboard, I blinked rapidly, trying to align *chicken splatter* with the world behind my desk. I could imagine *villain splatter* in the Tower novel I was writing, but what had my family to do with chickens?

I swiveled to face her. "Rosalita," I said, lifting a hand to calm her down, "what are you talking about?"

She thrust her arm toward the staircase. "Zack! His room. It is filled with chickens, and they splatter the walls."

I tilted my head and wondered if Rosalita had inhaled too many cleaning compounds.

"Do you not believe me?" she asked, her eyes widening. "In Zack's room, there are chickens."

I pushed back and stood. "Lead the way."

I followed as she stormed up the stairs. We passed Shannon's and Patty's empty rooms, then paused in the hallway before fourteen-year-old Zack's door.

Rosalita folded her arms and refused to cross the threshold. "I am not going in the room with chickens. I clean a house, not a farm."

I stepped past her. Zack's rumpled bed looked like it always did, two dresser drawers hung open as usual. But in the corner, in the empty space between the bureau and the dresser, came a series of high-pitched squeaks.

I crept closer and peered into the space. Zack's bedroom lamp burned there, deprived of its shade, and beneath its warmth stood an open cardboard box containing five or six yellow chicks. They were pecking at a sheet of grit-sprinkled newspaper, scurrying around the box in confusion, and yes, somehow they had managed to splatter the walls.

At least he'd figured out how to feed them.

I smiled at Rosalita and walked to the balcony railing, then bellowed out a summons: "Zack!"

Two minutes later he bounded up the stairs, but his steps slowed when he saw me and Rosalita at his door.

"Mom, I can explain," he said, his hands fluttering at his side. "We did an experiment in biology, see? We used an incubator and eggs, but when they hatched we didn't want to leave them at school over the weekend, so I told Mr. Forester that I could take some home, and he said they'd be okay if I kept a light on them and kept them warm, and it's only until Monday and then I have to take them back, but I want to keep them until then 'cause I think they think I'm their mother or something, okay?"

My son was so earnest about saving those chicks that I couldn't even be annoyed that he'd brought them home without asking.

"I think you should feed them again," I told him, then I patted Rosalita's shoulder and went back to work.

At home, Carl and I slide the to-go boxes in the fridge, then move to the living room and sit like parents waiting to interview a prospective daughter-in-law.

"What did you tell him?" I ask when the silence becomes unbearable. "*Exactly* what did you say?"

Carl shakes his head. "I asked why he wasn't at work; he said he didn't feel like going. I said that was a lousy reason, and he said, 'Deal with it.' I said we were going home and we wanted to talk to him. He didn't respond to that."

"Are you sure he wasn't impaired? I'd hate to think of him driving if he's—"

"He knew exactly what he was doing. And he knew I was upset."

I inhale a deep breath and try to maintain my fragile control. If Zack wasn't drunk, there's no reason why he shouldn't come home. He'll probably make us wait, if only to emphasize his unwillingness to jump at our commands, but he's smart enough to realize he's been busted. He should face the music.

Lord, please send him home.

I cross my legs and fold my hands in my lap while Carl opens a book and rests it on his knee. He appears to be reading, but time passes and he never turns a page.

Silence looms between us like a heavy mist as we wait. I flinch at the sound of every passing car. When Carl clears his throat, I look at him and find myself resenting my husband. Why did he have to speak to Zack at the restaurant? Why did he have to call Mr. McNeil? He could have ignored Zack and addressed the problem later. We could have let Zack breeze in at his usual time and confronted him after dinner. But now, knowing that we know, Zack may not come home. He may stay with that rowdy group, he may go with them to a bar, he may get into his car and drive drunk.

If he dies tonight, it will be Carl's fault.

I shake off the disloyal and illogical thought as soon as it strikes. Carl did what he felt he had to do; I'd have done the same thing. Over the last few months, I've done things I never dreamed I'd be capable of doing. I've screamed like a banshee and slapped my son and gone for long drives to nowhere, determined to stay away for days, if that's how long it takes to find peace.

But I always come home. Just as Zack will.

As the grandfather clock's minute hand drags us from one hour to the next, I stand and wipe my hands on my jeans. "Well." My voice sounds artificially bright in the high-ceilinged space. "I can't sit here all day. I need to get some work done."

Carl nods, but his gaze is fastened to his book. I'm not even sure he hears me.

"I'll come out when he comes in," I say, edging between the coffee table and the sofa. "You know where I'll be if you need me."

He doesn't answer, so I slip away and enter the sanctuary of my office. Dubya is sleeping at the edge of my desk, oblivious to the undercurrent of tension in the house.

I pause to nuzzle his ears. "What a life," I murmur. "Wanna trade?"

His answer is a long, rumbling snore.

I turn to my desk and power on the computer. As the aging machine groans and rattles, I close my eyes and thank God for a job that can take me away from this house, away from my life, if only for a little while.

William's world may be a mess, but at the moment it's a vast improvement over mine.

Thirty-nine

The sun fails to keep its dawn appointment the next morning. After breakfast, William drives carefully into Paradise, his car's headlights barely penetrating the black rain flooding the streets. The parking spaces in front of the machine company are already filled with eager customers, so he pulls into a place in front of Eden's, then waits for the rain to slow so he can make a dash for the building.

As he sits in the car, umbrella in hand, he notices what looks like a pile of rags on the sidewalk across the street. He makes a mental note to ask Dodge to keep the walkway swept. Then the rags *move*.

William peers more intently through the rain. Those aren't rags. As the unidentified object shifts into a cone of light from the street lamp, he recognizes Ross Ramirez. The fool has probably gotten himself evicted from his apartment and decided to live on the sidewalk. Several Paradise businesses have offered to employ him, but because the bum prefers to harass the machine company customers, he has no job and no income.

William shakes his head, then decides to run for it. By the time he locks the car, dodges the morning traffic, and splashes his way through the flooded street, he is nearly as wet as his umbrella. Safe under the shelter of the awning, he shakes himself off.

Ramirez sits on the bricks, legs crossed, arms resting on his knees, eyes following William's movements. He's grown a beard sometime in the last few months, probably in an attempt to hide his facial scars.

The beard isn't working.

William knows he should ignore the man, but the day is melancholy and his stomach pains compel him to crouch on the sidewalk. "Ramirez!" He shouts to be heard above the roaring rain. "Why did Casey leave it here?"

The man looks at William as if he's taken leave of his senses.

"The game, Ramirez. *You Bet Your Life*. Why did Casey leave it?"

There is a flash, like light caught in water, when the old man's gaze crosses William's, then he pulls a marker from a sodden satchel hanging from his shoulder. Moving slowly—why should he hurry?—he pulls out a legal pad. Rain spatters the paper, but he doesn't seem to notice. He uncaps a pen, then writes in block letters: WHAT DO YOU MEAN?

William wants to slap him for his impertinence. "You know what I mean!" he yells, cupping one hand around his mouth. "The game in the locked room. If Casey is such a genius, why'd he leave that machine where anyone could get to it?"

Ramirez's broad face and dark eyes, which once could intimidate men even from a distance, fill with shadows. A faint line appears between his brows as he tugs the legal pad closer and writes again. William tries to read over the man's shoulder, but the script is too small; this time he is writing more than a single line.

Finally, he rips off the top sheet and passes it to William. The paper goes limp in William's hand, raindrops smudge the ink, but he can still read the words: *Obedience without choice is servitude. Love without choice is not love.*

William fixes his gaze on Ramirez as the page tears in his grasp. "It's not fair. You can't dangle something in front of a man and not expect him to reach for it. That's human nature, it's part of who we are. We are designed to want more—look at Raquel, look at Stan. We all strive to improve our place in life."

Ramirez touches his chest, then shakes his head.

"Not you, huh? I don't expect you to understand; you were the company's big man. But the rest of us—it's not natural for people to be happy about living at the bottom of the social order. We were made for better things."

The scarred man lifts his chin to give William a bright-eyed glance, full of shrewdness, and in that instant William hates Ramirez as much as he hates his absentee creator. If the magician wants to take a life from Paradise, he's welcome to this one.

"Forget you." William rises from the sidewalk. "You're a crazy old man, and everyone knows it."

He turns and opens the door, grateful for the cheery atmosphere and happy sounds of the much-improved game room. Due to new lights and heavy window blinds, the machine company customers are virtually unaware of passing time. After dark or in the pouring rain, the game room is as bright and cheery as a June afternoon.

Dodge hurries forward to take the wet umbrella. "Thanks," William tells him, swiping wetness from his sleeves. "Get rid of the old man on the sidewalk, will you?"

Dodge's left brow rises a fraction. "We've tried to run him off. We can usually get him to move on, but he comes back as soon as we turn around."

"Then don't turn around." William tugs on his collar and adjusts his tie. "If you can't keep the bum away, I'll find someone who can."

Dodge touches two fingers to his forehead in a salute, then steps out into the rain.

William spends the next hour discussing production designs with Stan, then passes the rest of the morning checking on order fulfillment. By the time his watch beeps at noon, he realizes he needs to hire a receptionist and probably an accounts manager as well. He's proud of the way they've handled the business's explosive growth, but a man only has so many hours in a day. If he's going to spend any time with Raquel, he needs help.

He takes a few minutes to return calls from customers on the mainland, then leans back in his chair and closes his eyes. Correspondence and phone calls leave him feeling as used up as a piece of chewed gum.

He breathes deeply and feels a stab of memory, a remnant sliced from his past, as piercing as a sword. He is floating in a beam of light while someone whispers in his ear, giving him a name and a face, knowledge and language. Words wash through him; the voice and its memories envelop him, tingling his skin like the touch of a spirit.

"I have outlined a plan for you . . ."

Without warning, the light vanishes and he feels himself falling. Black emptiness rushes up like the bottom of a rocky ravine, and his heart congeals into a tight lump of terror. His muscles tense, anticipating the impact—

The warble of the fax machine snaps him back to wakefulness. William opens his eyes and clutches at the armrests of his chair, expecting to find himself in midfall. His adrenal glands hasten to counteract his panic and dump such a dose of adrenaline into his bloodstream that his heart pounds like a kettledrum.

The game room outside is packed with people, but he is alone with his memories, his guilt, and his uncertainty.

A sheet of paper, probably an order, is emerging from the purring fax machine. He sits up and places his hands on the edge of the desk, gripping it as if it were the only solid substance in a world of shifting shadows.

The fax shuts off; a page slides across the polished desktop. He glances at it, expecting to see the usual order form, but an unfamiliar hand has printed a simple message:

Help is on its way.

Pasting on a smile, William checks his hollow-eyed reflection in the restroom mirror, then crosses the break room and enters the gaming hall. Dodge stands by the door, his thumbs hooked on the edge of his belt, the eyes above his soft smile roving from player to player.

William stops by the guard, keenly aware that the top of his head barely reaches the bigger man's earlobe. "How are you, Dodge?"

The husky man doesn't break his pose. "Fine, Mr. Case."

William nods. "By the way, you mind if I ask a question? I've been curious about something."

The man's gaze flicks at William, then returns to the nearest bank of machines. "Fire away."

"All right—who's Casey?"

The guard's bald head rotates toward him. "I beg your pardon?"

William clears his throat. "Since you come from Paradise, too, I wondered what you could tell me about Casey."

Dodge's smile broadens. "Is this some kinda test? You gonna fire me if I mess up?"

William waves away the man's worries. "I thought I'd ask around and see if anyone actually knows who Casey is."

Lethal calm replaces the apprehension in Dodge's eyes. "Casey is the owner of this company."

"You say that because you saw his name on the building. But have you ever seen or heard from him? Ever met anyone who has?"

The guard's fists tighten. "Did he slip by me?"

"Lighten up. It's not like Casey's anywhere around."

Dodge's fists relax. "That nutcase out front says Casey is going to send someone to check up on us. That's what he wrote on his pad when I told him to move along."

Surprise siphons the blood from William's brain, leaving him light-headed. He steadies himself against the wall. "Ramirez said Casey is sending someone to Paradise?"

Dodge's jaw tightens. "Sorry, Mr. Case. I thought you knew about it."

"It's not possible." William shakes his head to clear Ramirez's delusion from his thoughts. He's got to get a grip on his emotions, because the old man is doing his best to drive William crazy. Ramirez has lied to William's guards and harassed his customers; now he's sending faxes to the office.

He lifts his chin. "The man outside doesn't know what he's talking about. I think the strain of his accident has left him softheaded."

The guard exhales a sigh of relief. "Good to know, boss."

William pats the man's granite shoulder, then strolls toward a bank of innovative new machines. He and Stan have dubbed the latest model *Cross My Heart* and printed the reel strips with pictures of colored hearts. These machines, for which they have high hopes, introduce the concept of *pay lines:* instead of winning only when three symbols match in a horizontal row, players at a *Cross My Heart* game will win if three symbols match horizontally, vertically, or diagonally. A beginner might think he can easily beat this game . . . and he *could* if William hadn't programmed the machine to hold 20 percent of all coins played.

"Less player risk equals less reward," he told Stan as they finalized the payout schedule. "A golden rule of gaming."

Now he's not surprised to see Marilyn with her palm firmly wrapped around the lever of a *Cross My Heart* machine.

William clasps his hands behind his back and waits until four gold coins spill into the well. She gathers them, her eyes sparkling, and holds them up. "Look, William!"

"You're doing well. How about taking a break with me?"

He grips her elbow and tries to lead her away, but she resists. "I'm not done! I can play these four coins—"

"Take a load off your feet, Marilyn, and I'll buy you a drink."

She tilts her head. "Will you throw in a sandwich?"

"For you, I'll toss in two."

She winks at him. "You're a good friend, William. A good friend indeed."

"Let's go to the break room."

He reaches out to guide her through the crowd, and when he touches her spine, he knows something's wrong. When he met her, Marilyn was as soft and cushy as a well-padded chair; today her spine feels knobby beneath his hand. To better look at her as they move through the crowd, he falls back a step. His gaze runs over her baggy blue sweat suit, taking in the unstitched hem, the sharp shoulder blades, the knotted elastic at the waistband.

Why is the woman not eating?

Once they reach the break room, William moves to the new vending machines and buys two sandwiches, a bag of chips, and a carton of apple juice. She thanks him profusely as she unwraps the first sandwich.

"It's nothing." He settles into the chair next to her.

She squinches her face into a question mark. "Are you eating?"

He lies. "I had a big breakfast, so you go ahead. I want to ask you something while you eat."

She tears into the sandwich with surprising gusto. William smiles and looks at the table, pretending not to notice that she is gobbling her meal as though she hasn't eaten in days.

"Marilyn." To keep his hands busy, he pulls a pen from his pocket. "You've lived in Paradise a long time, right?"

"Longer than you." A smile nudges itself into a corner of her mouth and pushes across her sandwich-stuffed cheeks. "Longer than most everybody."

"Then maybe you can help me. I'm looking for someone who knows Casey."

She stops chewing. "Knows Casey?"

"Yes. Did you ever meet him?"

She shakes her head and then holds up a finger with one hand while she reaches for her drink with the other. After gulping enough juice to wash down the sandwich, she gives him a stern look. "Why are you asking about Casey?"

"Maybe because his name's on the building. Everybody talks about him, or at least they used to. I thought it might be nice to find someone who actually knew him."

"You want Ramirez." She picks up the bag of chips. "He talks to Casey all the time."

William folds his arms on the table and leans closer. "Does Ramirez call Casey on the phone? Send a telegram? I've been through the old man's address book; there's no information for anyone named Casey."

She tosses a chip into her mouth and then wags a finger at him until she swallows. "You don't talk to Casey like you talk to normal people—he's the *creator*, for goodness' sake. He's bigger than us, and different. He doesn't need the ding-dang telephone."

William exhales and looks away, convinced that Marilyn is nearly as crazy as Ramirez. The woman has lived here a long time; she has probably absorbed all the local myths and tall tales. And, being Marilyn, she has accepted them without question.

"Excuse me, but I need to ask Stan about something." He rises and squeezes her shoulder. "Enjoy your lunch. Don't rush; take your time."

She bobs her head in a scared-rabbit sort of thank-you and then attacks the wrapper on her remaining sandwich.

Forty

William finds Stan investigating a new shipment in the factory. The mechanic is checking a huge crate for signs of damage while a uniformed delivery man waits, clipboard in hand.

William props his elbow on the crate and glances at the shipping label. "A painting machine?"

"Uh-huh."

"Oh. Well, I hope you don't find anything wrong. I'd hate to have to ship this thing back."

"Everything looks good." Stan takes the delivery man's clipboard and signs the slip with a scrawl. "Thanks, pal."

William waits until the back door closes, then turns to the mechanic. "What happened to the old painting machine?"

"Broke." Stan pulls a box cutter and a pair of pliers from his pocket. "I can't fix it."

William's mind reels. What is wrong with this place? None of the machines ever needed repair when Ramirez managed the company. Some of the equipment has given them trouble in the last few weeks, but nothing has ever been beyond help—until now.

Their mechanical problems are multiplying as fast as the rats.

Acutely aware of the expense, he presses Stan. "Are you sure you can't fix it? Can't you adjust the timing or clean the nozzles or—"

Stan looks at him, the glitter in his half-closed eyes both resentful and accusing. "It DIED."

William searches his memory, but the word doesn't register. "*Died?*"

"A handy little acronym I've been using a lot lately—Damaged Irreversibly, Ergo Done."

William sinks to a stool, disbelieving. "So . . . the old machine is DIED?"

"DEAD." Stan stabs the carton, then slices the heavy cardboard with a vicious stroke. "Damaged Extensively, All Done."

William presses his hand to his throbbing temple and looks around the factory. How much equipment will qualify for Stan's acronym this fiscal quarter?

"Sorry about the extra expense," Stan says, using the claw end of a hammer to rip cardboard from the crate's wooden supports. "But when you work machines hard, they wear out."

"None of the machines wore out when Ramirez ran things."

Stan takes his time meeting William's gaze. He's still smiling when they connect, but his eyes have hardened. "I don't think I need to remind you that Ramirez didn't run our kind of shop. The old machines were different."

"They were boring. I'm glad they're locked away."

"Whatever."

Remembering why he has come, William slips his hands into his pockets. "Mind if I ask you a question?"

Stan doesn't look up. "You're the big boss, aren't you?"

"If you say so." William glances at the ceiling, hoping to find words that won't tick Stan off. The man's mood seems darker than usual.

"I've been thinking. You've been around longer than me."

Stan pulls out the box cutter and slices the second side of the box. "So?"

"Since you've been in Paradise, have you ever met Casey?"

The mechanic looks up, derision and sympathy mingling in his glance. "You gotta be kidding."

"I'm serious. Did you ever talk to him? Know anyone who's met him?"

Stan chuckles as he pulls a heavy-duty staple from the carton. "I can't believe you haven't figured it out by now."

"Figured what out?"

Stan drops the pliers to the concrete floor. "There is no Casey, man. He's nothing but a figment of the imagination."

"But what about the town? And Ramirez talks to him."

"Ramirez talks to the walls, too, or haven't you noticed? The town grew up weird because we're isolated."

"You told me Casey designed the old games." William jerks his chin toward the drawer in Stan's small office. "You said he personally drew those schematics."

Stan laughs. "I was only parroting the company line—you know, being a good employee of Casey's Machine Company."

"What about the eye?" William points toward the all-seeing orb above the door. "If Casey doesn't exist, why is his eye pictured all over Paradise?"

Stan bends to pick up his pliers and uses them to loosen another hefty staple. "One of the town fathers probably thought the image would intimidate us into playing nice—and it did, before we knew better." He pries another staple loose and then knocks a cardboard wall away from its supports. "The picture's only a symbol. There is no all-seeing creator, and there is no Casey. Never was, never will be."

Something in the gleam of the mechanic's eye sends a quiver up the back of William's neck.

"Why—why didn't you tell me this sooner?"

His laugh is a cackle of ridicule. "I wanted to let you grow up. Some things you have to discover for yourself."

William smiles as if Stan's explanation makes perfect sense, then steps toward the exit. "I guess I'll go check on the invoice for this painting machine. Want to be sure we pay the right folks."

"You do that, Mr. Ambassador."

William turns and walks away, but as Stan whacks and another nail screeches in protest, he can't help but feel that Stan once believed in Casey . . . and is furious for having been duped.

Well, who wouldn't be? If Casey really is a noble creator, why'd he abandon them in a town where people can go crazy and machines can become Damaged Extensively and Totally Hopeless?

In all his creative musings, William never imagined anything like DEATH.

Forty-one

Mac catches William in the break room and says he and Dodge are having problems with Ramirez. They've been chasing the old man from the sidewalk all morning, but he's been going over to Eden's, who is apparently fortifying his spirits with bowls of broth and strong doses of sympathy. Until William hires someone to patrol the sidewalk, Mac wants to know, can't he at least ask Eden not to encourage the enemy?

William promises to take care of things, then sets out to keep his word. He steps onto the wet sidewalk and surveys the rain-washed street. Ramirez is nowhere in sight; perhaps he has walked over to the diner. Before crossing, William takes time for a look around as he braces himself for confrontation.

Because he spends most of his day in a windowless office, he has forgotten how the sight of a newly washed earth can refresh the senses. The strip of grass along the brick walkway seems a deeper shade of emerald; the cobblestone street looks polished and textured. Rain has washed the dust out of the carved sign above Eden's door, and a lingering breeze is thick with the scent of cinnamon rolls.

Smiling, William crosses the road and pauses on the opposite sidewalk to look back and see what improvements the rain has brought to his own place of business.

His smile fades as he beholds the effects of time and traffic. The building's windows, which once beckoned like bright eyes, have nearly vanished behind a layer of dust. The bare trees raise black, bony arms toward the sky. No flowers edge the sidewalk; dozens of careless foot-steps have trampled the marigolds into mud. The bricks of the build-ing, which had been the lovely color of beach sand, are edged in grime as dark as dried blood. The striped awnings hang in red and white tat-ters over the dusty windows, and several letters of Raquel's electric sign have burned out. The red neon loops which once spelled out *Casey's Machine Company* now glimmer as *Cas   in o.*

The building that used to welcome him each morning now regards him with accusation.

His lower lip trembles as he returns the glare.

Do the people of Paradise blame him for this sorry state of affairs?

He pushes his way into the diner and waves to Eden, who is pour-ing a cup of coffee for a man at a booth. She nods, then lowers her coffeepot and hurries to meet him at the end of the counter.

"Hey, William. You must be hungry."

He slides onto an empty stool and cranes his neck to look down the bar. No sign of Ramirez, unless he's hiding in one of the booths around the corner.

"A cup of coffee is all I need." He gives her a smile and folds his hands. "By the way, you seen Ramirez lately?"

She moves toward the coffee decanter, then glances over her shoul-der. "You mean Ross?"

She's playing dumb, but William forces himself to be patient. "We've had to ask him to move away from the building several times, and I'm worried about him—considering the wet weather and all."

She picks up a clean mug, then looks inside and makes a face. "Yuck."

"Let me guess," he says. "Rat droppings."

She shakes her head. "Are they bad over your way?"

"Awful. Stan is always complaining about them. The other day he found a nest inside one of the machines."

She dumps the droppings into a trash bin, then lowers the mug into the sink. "I tell Hank to set the clean cups upside down, but some-times he forgets."

She pulls another mug from the shelf. This one, William is relieved to see, has been stored properly.

"If you're worried about Ramirez," she says, setting the mug on the counter, "why don't you leave him be? He's not hurting a soul."

"But he spooks our customers."

"Nobody in Paradise is afraid of Ross."

"The people of Paradise don't concern me. It's the out-of-towners who don't understand."

"I feel sorry for him." She sighs as she pulls a clean saucer from the dish drainer, then she lowers her voice to a confidential whisper. "Did you know I asked him about his accident?"

Cold panic erupts between William's shoulder blades and prickles down his spine. "What'd he say?"

She leans against the counter, resentment flickering in her eyes like heat lightning. "He told me it wasn't an accident."

William can't speak. He can't imagine what will come next—will she call for help, ask for money to buy her silence, splash boiling coffee in his face—

She stands there, waiting, but William is too rattled to do anything but gape at her.

She steps closer, places her hands on the counter, and leans so close her breath tickles William's ear. "He said—"

"What?"

"He said Casey did it."

She straightens, crosses her arms, and gives William a *top that* look.

"C-Casey?" The name comes out as a strangled croak.

"Yessir. I asked him who did it, and he flat out wrote that Casey was responsible. Oh, he went on and on about how he was only an instrument in Casey's hand—you know how Ross is. That's when I knew the accident had touched him in the head. So we have to take care of the old guy; look out for him and all. He's not the same as he was."

William looks away, hoping she hasn't seen terror in his eyes. Sweat has beaded on his forehead and under his arms, but he'll be okay . . . as soon as his heart stops hammering his rib cage.

"I'm glad," he says, finally finding his voice, "you told me this. So now you have to understand why I want to find him. We need to put him someplace . . . safe."

She turns back to the coffeepot. "He was here, but I think he's moved on."

William frowns as she pours steaming liquid into the cup. "Any idea where he might be?"

She hesitates. "You aren't planning to take him away, are you? Paradise is his home."

William presses his palm to his chest, a picture of innocence. "I only want to talk to him."

"Well, he's busy."

"Doing what?"

"Talking, I expect."

William rolls his eyes. "Come on, Eden, you and I both know he *can't* talk. So where have you hidden him, and what's he up to?"

She sets the coffee decanter on a trivet and then faces him, one hand on her hip. "I never said he talks like you and I do. Somehow he manages to talk to Casey without words."

William scratches his jaw, amazed that an intelligent woman could swallow such an idea.

"He wrote all that out for you, did he? And you believe him?"

She parks both hands on her hips. "Now you listen to me, William. Ramirez has been around a lot longer than you, and everything was fine when he managed the company. Things were peaceful. And while I don't like to blame you for things maybe you can't help, you can't deny that we've seen an awful lot of trouble since you arrived in Paradise."

He shoves the coffee away, sloshing brown liquid on the counter. "Forget this. I'll not stay where I'm not wanted."

"I didn't say you weren't wanted. I'm only telling the truth."

"Well, this is truth, too—you tell Ramirez if he ever sets foot on our sidewalk again, I'm going to have Mac and Dodge stash him in the storage shed at the back of our building. If he wants to be near us so much, we might as well keep him under lock and key."

She stares at him, her eyes damp with pain, but William can't help marveling at her weakness and naïveté. He pushes at the coffee again, shoving the cup off the counter, and smiles in grim pleasure when a splash of brown liquid stains her white uniform.

Leaving the other diners in shocked silence, he strides back to the business where he is king. Though nothing remains of the neon sign but *Cas in* and *o*, he likes the changes time has brought.

So be it, then. Casey's Machine Company is no more; long live the Paradise Casino.

William's stomach begins to twist and burn as he hurries through the game room. By the time he reaches the office, pain has risen inside him like a wave, sending streamers of agony through his gut. Not knowing what else to do, he buys a package of crackers from a vending machine and stuffs them into his mouth. Might as well let his stomach torture a processed snack instead of his nerve endings.

He is swallowing the last cracker when Dodge runs into his office, his eyes wide and his forehead streaming with sweat. "Mr. Case, you gotta come quick."

"What's wrong?"

"I don't know, but you gotta see. Hurry!"

William wipes crumbs from his chin and follows the security guard into the game room. The machines are happily whistling, warbling, and ringing, and aisles three through six are packed with players. But Dodge leads him down aisle two, where the machines are cooing to themselves in full attract mode. Not a soul remains on these games, but a knot of anxious people stand at the far end of the aisle.

They part as William approaches. As the crowd shifts, he glimpses a familiar blue sweat suit. But something is wrong; the fabric shouldn't be on the floor . . .

When a heavyset man steps out of the way, William sees Marilyn, one arm over her head, the other curled at her side. Her eyes are half-open, but her skin has gone the color of a cloudy sky.

He kneels by her side and presses his fingers to her cheek. "Marilyn? Come on, honey, snap out of it."

Her skin is clammy beneath his fingertips, cold and thick and disagreeable. He lifts her hand and rubs it, then catches his breath when a silver coin falls from her grasp and rolls across the floor. A heavy silence falls over the onlookers as the coin rolls to the base of a *Wondrous Raquel* game and spins to a stop.

One of the women edges away. "If no one else is gonna grab that, I am."

In the next aisle, a player hits the jackpot and the siren sounds. William closes his eyes, snapped back to the past by the flashing red light: *If you lose, I get to take a life.*

Is *this* what the magician meant? *Marilyn?*

No. Please, not her. She never harmed anyone; all she wanted was to enjoy life and play a few games.

"She's not waking up," Dodge says.

William lowers Marilyn's hand and gently places it on her chest. "I think she's DEAD."

Dodge gapes at him like a man faced with a hard sum in arithmetic.

"Damaged Extensively, All Done," William whispers. "Marilyn is never going to wake up again."

Forty-two

Energized by one thought—*save our son, save our son*—I have written like a dervish, but the sound of a slamming car door breaks the fictive spell. I turn from the computer and glance at my watch—six o'clock. Zack has finally come home.

My anger gives way to relief. The confrontation in the restaurant could have sent Zack off the deep end, but he's home—and before dark, thank goodness.

I hurry to the living room and find Carl peering over the top of his reading glasses, waiting for the front door to open.

"He's back." I smile in an effort to calm my husband's simmering temper. "He's safe, and that's good."

The door opens. "Stupid people in traffic," Zack snarls, stepping into the foyer. "Guy cut me off at the corner, but I showed him—cut in front of him when the light turned green and nearly ran him into the median. You shoulda seen it, Dad. Serves the guy right for cutting me off."

I cut a look to Carl, who is listening with an uplifted brow.

"Son," Carl begins, speaking in a slow and steady tone, "we need to talk about what happened today."

"Guy at lunch said our government tried to kill Hitler," Zack says, moving toward the stairs. "Can you imagine that? I said no way, because if we'd meant to kill Hitler, we woulda killed him and spared everyone the trouble of the war, but he wouldn't listen. Guy is a geek who listens to the History Channel all the time—he has no life. Who does he think he is, anyway, dumping that load on me? I told him he didn't know who he was talking to. I live with a professor and a writer, so I know more about lots of things than he knows about anything—"

Carl stands, knocking the book in his lap to the floor. "Stop right there, Son. We need to talk about your job."

Zack blinks. "McNeil is an idiot. He said I haven't worked enough to earn full-time benefits, so I figured he wouldn't miss me if I didn't show up. I'd have gone to work anyway to tell him off, but this girl in the next car was waving at me, so I followed her for a while. Ended up at the mall, where we had a couple of Cokes. That's where I met Mike and Jason. We decided to grab a couple of burgers—"

Carl is striding toward Zack, every muscle tense and set, so I step between them. "Honey, listen to us. Mr. McNeil has every right to run his restaurant the way he wants to. But we need to know what you've been doing while you're supposed to be at work."

Zack brushes back hair that has fallen into his eyes, then gives me a look of disdainful tolerance. "What I've been doing is really none of your business."

Carl's face flushes. "As long as you're living under our roof, it's our business!"

"Fine." Zack turns to head up the stairs. "I'll move out. Just give me a minute to gather my stuff."

"Zack!" Carl slams his hand on the stair railing, but our son pays no attention. "Stop right there! You come down and talk to us, or . . ."

Or what? Carl looks at me, his jaw going slack as we both realize we can't threaten our son. We could take away his car, but he'd only go out with his friends. Short of locking him in his room and confiscating his credit cards, wallet, and keys, what can we do?

Carl turns to me, frustration evident in his face. "The kid is twenty-one years old. He ought to be responsible."

"Something's not right." I glance up to be sure Zack's not listening on the landing, then lower my voice. "He's not himself, Carl, can't you tell? He's on something. I don't know what it is; maybe Ecstasy. I read about that stuff in the papers all the time."

A tide of despair washes through Carl's eyes, and I'm sure he can see the same swift currents in mine. "So what are we supposed to do?"

I seize upon a sudden hope. "Maybe his AA counselor can talk some sense into him. Do you have that man's number?"

"He hasn't been drinking; I'd have smelled it on his breath. Besides, this isn't how he acts when he's drunk."

"What about his other counselor, Mr. Glazier?"

Carl snorts. "Try reaching him after hours. I called a couple of weekends ago, and his message said to either leave a message or call 911."

Not knowing what else to do, I pace in the foyer with my arms crossed. Maybe Zack is simply upset about the guy in traffic, and a good dinner will calm him down. I don't have time to make anything, but I could call Angellino's and have three orders delivered. Zack loves their lasagna.

"Hey, Zack!" I call up the stairs, injecting a cheerful note into my voice. "You hungry? What if I call Angellino's and have them deliver some lasagna?"

Carl's eyes brighten. "Do you have their number?"

"I'll get it." Grateful for even this simple distraction, I hurry into the kitchen, where the phone book is stashed in a drawer. Carl follows, moving to the refrigerator as I walk toward the telephone.

I'm propping my reading glasses on the end of my nose when I hear Zack's thumping step on the stairs. Thank heaven, the promise of a good dinner must have calmed him.

"Hey, Zack," I call, assuming he is on his way to the kitchen, "what kind of dressing do you want on your salad?"

ANGELA HUNT

Zack fills the kitchen doorway and responds with such a vile word that I halt, one hand on my glasses, the other on the phone book.

Carl drops the glass he's just filled with ice and turns to face our son. His hands curl into fists. "You will not speak to your mother that way! You will not use that language in this house."

"Oh yeah?" Zack drops the book bag in his hand and lifts his fists in a boxing stance. "I'll take you down in a second, old man."

For an instant I'm afraid Carl will accept the challenge, but he holds Zack in a steely gaze as he crosses his arms. "I'm not going to fight my own son. But I deserve respect, as does your mother."

Zack answers with an outburst of such violently abusive language that my knees go weak. Where has this come from?

I lift my hands to my ears as father and son yell at each other, Carl lifting his voice to be heard above Zack's cursing; Zack responding with even more vehemence.

Carl breaks off the attack with an uplifted arm. "Get out of our house if you're going to talk like that. If you can't live here and give us the respect we deserve, then you can leave."

"No problem." Sullen and narrow-eyed, Zack picks up his book bag and stalks toward the front door.

I reach the kitchen doorway as the front door slams. Our china rattles in the hutch; one fragile plate rocks from its upright position and clatters against the glass door.

I take a step toward the foyer, but Carl lifts a hand, stopping me.

"Let him go," he says, staring at the door as if he can see through the heavily beveled glass. "Let him do what he will and suffer the consequences. God knows we've done all we know to do with him."

I bend my hand into a fist and hold it to my heart as a flash of wild grief rips through me. The events of the day are colliding in my brain like the bits of glass in a kaleidoscope—Zack is William, William is Zack, both are stubborn and lost and hopeless . . . and who am I? With every passing day I feel less like Casey and more like Marilyn, a character steamrolled by the story.

Moving as slowly as an old woman, I step into the dining room. Where will Zack go? I open the door of the hutch and reach for the plate that has tipped forward. He will go to a bar or to a friend's house. My slow

207

and clumsy fingers knock another plate before I reach the one that has fallen. He may come home, but he'll be drunk and dangerous in a few hours. The plate escapes my grasp, spins on the shelf, and crashes to the floor.

Standing amid the shattered pieces, I realize I am crying only when I taste the salt of my tears.

Forty-three

Stan calls the hospital in Oceanside; they send an ambulance to take Marilyn away. William has no idea what will happen once the body leaves Paradise, and he doesn't want to know.

He is certain, though, that he doesn't want anything DEAD lingering in the game room.

As the ambulance pulls away, Eden, Hank, Stan, and Mac join him on the sidewalk. Hank wonders aloud if they should build a hospital in Paradise. Eden, who keeps her distance from William, says they don't need one; they've only suffered a run of bad luck. William sighs heavily and leaves them to their debate, preferring the quiet of his office to the overcast street.

He sinks into his chair and is filled with remembering: *"If you lose, I get to take a life."*

Later that evening William finds one of the EMTs in the game room. The man seems embarrassed to be caught playing the machines, but he laughs off his discomfiture and assures William he just needs to unwind after a hard day.

"I'd never heard of Paradise until this afternoon," he says, checking the game's well to be sure he hasn't missed a stray coin. "But this is a quaint little town. And I love this casino idea."

William smiles and extends his hand. "William Case."

"Jeb Carter."

William can't help feeling he owes this man something, so he invites him into the office. As they share a pot of coffee and a can of cashews from the vending machine, William asks about Marilyn.

The EMT shrugs. "As far as I can tell, her body simply wore out."

"But bodies don't wear out for no reason."

William's comment seems to amuse him. "Sure they do. People expire all the time."

"Not in Paradise, they don't. Marilyn's the first."

Carter's smile vanishes. "You're kidding."

"Afraid not."

The EMT frowns at the desktop and then lifts a brow. "I think someone's been pulling your leg. In any case, this afternoon's patient was severely malnourished. An inadequate diet can severely strain the heart."

William digests this answer in silence. He doesn't blame Carter for doubting what he's told him about Paradise; when he talks to out-of-towners in the game room, he often feels as though they are speaking different languages. Most off-islanders can't seem to grasp what the people of Paradise understand instinctively.

He gives his guest a grim smile. "If Marilyn's life could run out . . . does that mean something similar could happen to any of us?"

Astonishment touches the man's round face. "I'd say that's a safe bet."

"Wanna bet your life?"

Against William's will, his mind flashes back to the magician's insistence that he owns William's soul.

He reaches for another handful of cashews. "You know, Mr. Carter, I haven't been around long enough to know everything, but I'm beginning to think this entire town is based on fiction. Maybe someone put up the buildings, set things in motion, and went off to die—like all people apparently do."

Fresh misery darkens the visitor's face. "I didn't mean to contradict your local beliefs. If what you've been taught makes you happy, you should feel free to believe it."

William releases a hoarse bark of laughter. "It's okay. It's time we woke up to the truth. People die—maybe everything dies. Maybe our creator is already Damaged Extensively, All Done."

Carter stops chewing, a fistful of cashews in hand, and examines William's face with considerable concentration. "I certainly hope I haven't wrecked your belief system," he says. "Frankly, life itself is sheer misery. That's why I encourage everyone to pursue whatever makes them happy."

Happy?

William closes the office door and stands with his back to it in a childish effort to block the loneliness seeping into the room like a fog. Sadness pools in his heart, a dark depression unlike anything he's ever felt.

"Wanna bet your life?"

He wasn't honest with Carter—or with himself. The magician isn't a mere video image—he's a force William has *smelled* and *felt* in the forbidden room. Death came to Paradise because he gambled with this force—and lost.

Eden was right; he is responsible for everything bad in this once-lovely place. He shattered some sort of protective bubble when he broke the rules; now disgrace, discord, and death have entered Paradise. Worst of all, that gruesome threesome seems intent on sticking around.

His misery is like another body in the room, a laboring, pervasive presence.

Is there no hope? Is there no escape from the magician's malicious machine?

His face burns as he remembers Marilyn begging to borrow two silver coins last week. "Sweetheart," he'd said, slipping his arm around her narrow shoulders, "if I gave you two coins, what's to stop everyone from wanting the same favor? If I gave free coins to the entire town, we'd never make any profit. We'd have to shut down the game room. Dodge and Mac and Stan and I would lose our jobs. You'd have nowhere to play the games. You wouldn't like that, would you?"

Her wide blue eyes watered as she shook her head. She walked away, her palm as empty as her stomach.

Because she'd spent her last coins in William's machines.

Guilt strikes him like a blow in the gut. He pushes away from the desk and chokes back the heavy bile rising in his gorge. What can he do to make things right?

He could go into the forbidden room, humble himself, and beg the magician for another chance to win back what he's lost, but how can he forget the number one rule in gaming? *The house always wins.*

The magician has tainted everything he loves, and William cannot defeat him.

Swallowing a sob, he looks up at the painted eye above the door. "Casey? Do you see me?"

No one responds, but perhaps he doesn't deserve an answer.

He pushes back his chair and moves to the side of the desk. Ramirez believes Casey sees everything, so if the creator is watching, perhaps he will see.

As William's pride buckles, he sinks to the floor. "Casey," he cries, surrendering to the debilitating pull of despair, "I've messed up, and I can't see a way out. If you're really there, could you please . . . help me?"

Forty-four

I sit back in my chair, startled by the realization that I have just written my own heart's cry. I, the creator-author, the one who boldly holds the story in my hands, feel as lost as William, as abandoned as any of the souls in Paradise.

Like them, I know my creator loves me. I know far more than my story characters, for I've been a believer for ten years. God has proven himself faithful; he has blessed my marriage, my career, my faith walk. Both Patty and Shannon have fallen in love with my Lord, and my heart thrills to know that my grandchildren, Glynn and Kale, are being taught to love God.

So why hasn't God revealed himself to my son?

I lower my head to my hand, desperate to offer another prayer but wondering if it will reach any higher than the ceiling. I know the Spirit intercedes when we are too distressed to pray, but I'm not sure the Spirit has anything to do with the sordid mess my son has made. Since deciding to follow Christ, Carl and I have tried to be good examples, we have begged Zack to come to church, we have prayed over family meals, we have presented him with a new Bible every year at Christmas . . .

The boy has a stack of Bibles so new the gilt edging cracks when you turn a page.

Has he rejected *everything*? I see his stony face every time I close my eyes. I hear the anger in his voice and feel the heat of his glare. I didn't know my son's vocabulary included the words I heard him use tonight— obviously, I do not know my son at all.

I turn toward the doorway and lean forward to look down the hall. Though the hour is late, a light still burns on the foyer table. For Zack.

After his loud exit, I swept up broken china while Carl made sandwiches in the kitchen. I wanted nothing more than to go to the sanctuary of my office, but I had a class to teach.

I scarcely remember driving to the college. Wrapped in a numbing fog, I talked to my students about the mythic model of plot structure, and I dismissed them early. Johanna Sicorsky approached as I headed for the door, but I shook my head and told her I needed to get home.

The empty house offered no comfort. In my absence, Carl had gone to his office at the seminary, so after I slipped into my pajamas, Dubya and I went into my study and settled before the computer. I opened *The Ambassador* file but had to wait until the words stopped swimming before I could write.

Now I leave William on his knees and glance at the clock. Ten fifteen. Still early, if you're twenty-one. But Carl will be home anytime now.

I don't really expect Zack to come home tonight. We'll leave the porch lights on in case a miracle brings him back, but my hope has been superseded by weariness and my love is feeling threadbare.

I'm so tired my eyes burn. I press my fingertips to my eyelids and rub to ease the sting, then flinch when the phone rings.

Has to be Carl. He probably wants to know if I need anything at the grocery store. I could use a quart of milk and some eggs.

I pick up the receiver. "Hello?"

"Mom?"

The sound of Zack's voice startles me to alertness. He doesn't sound belligerent now, nor does he sound drunk. He sounds . . . frightened.

"Mom, I wrecked the car."

"Are you hurt?" I push aside panic and speak with that odd sense of detachment that arrives with the awareness of disaster.

"I'm okay. There's, um, a rescue unit here, and they looked me over." He's alive, check. Not hurt, check.

"What about the car? Can you drive home?"

"It's pretty messed up. The cop told me to call you."

The composed presence that has taken control of my body reaches for a pen and paper. "Tell me where you are, and I'll come get you."

He gives me an address that's not far away; I jot it down. "I'm leaving now."

I'm wearing pajamas and slippers, but who cares? I grab a raincoat from the hall closet and windmill into it, then slip my purse over my arm, making sure it contains my glasses and my keys.

I find Zack by the side of the road. A police car is parked on the shoulder; my son sits in the passenger seat, his head down, his shoulders bowed. At first I don't see the Explorer; then I notice the back door gleaming in the officer's searchlight. It looks like it's been driven into a mound of scrubby brush at the side of the road.

I get out of my car and cinch the belt of my raincoat; the police officer comes forward and catches me before I reach Zachary. When I realize she's female, I'm relieved. Perhaps, like me, she has a mother's heart.

"Mrs. Kerrigan?"

"Yes."

"Zachary Kerrigan is your son?"

I point to the police vehicle, where Zack's head is haloed by the dome light. "That's my son. Is he okay?"

"He's darn lucky, if you ask me."

Her remark puzzles me. Either he was drinking and she's decided not to give him a ticket despite his record, or he swerved to miss hitting a semi or something.

I meet her gaze and manage to smile. "Can you tell me what happened?"

With a practiced two-fingered gesture, she gestures me forward. "Follow me."

We walk past the police vehicle, my slippers crunching the gravel at the side of the road. There is little traffic at this time of night, and for that, I'm grateful.

"Your son was approaching at a high rate of speed," she says, pointing toward the north. "Looks like he picked out a tree and drove straight into it. Apparently, ma'am, he was trying to commit suicide."

Because I've learned a few things about accident investigation during my years as a novelist, I give her a tight smile. "That can't be right. First of all, you can't tell anything about his speed because you didn't witness the crash, and it's too dark to see skid marks on the asphalt. Second, what tree was he trying to hit? There are no trees in that brush. Third, I don't know how you came up with that theory, but it's more likely my son was leaning over to change the radio station and missed the curve. There's no way he could be suicidal, and frankly"—I give her an indignant look—"I think you're out of bounds to suggest such a thing."

The officer folds one arm across her chest and regards me with a no-nonsense look. "Mrs. Kerrigan—"

"Can I talk to my son?"

"Mrs. Kerrigan, you can't see the tree because the impact snapped it in two—that's probably what saved your boy's life. It fell to the right of the vehicle."

I squint into the darkness, but I can't see past the Explorer's back bumper. "All right, so he was fiddling with the radio station and hit a tree. That doesn't mean—"

"He told me what happened, ma'am. He was clear about his intentions."

When my frightened gaze flies into hers, her eyes soften. "The EMTs checked him out, but I should have asked them to take him to the hospital. That's what we're supposed to do for suicide attempts. He told me you'd come, though, so I thought I'd let you take him in." Her eyes are dark, soft with kindness. "If he were my son, that's what I'd want to do. It's better than having him brought in wearing restraints."

I glance back at the police car, where Zack's head remains bowed. "He . . . really said he wanted to kill himself?"

"You need to get him some help *tonight*." Her hand, calm and cool, rests on mine. "Don't disappoint me. You've got to do the right thing."

Numbly, I nod, then follow her to the side of the police car. When Zack stands and faces me, I can see the silvery tracks of tears on his face.

"Zack"—my voice breaks—"we're going to the hospital, okay?"

Raw pain glitters in his eyes. "They said I was fine."

"We're going anyway, honey." I tiptoe through the words, trying to avoid anything sharp or specific. "You need help, and I think we can get it at the hospital."

I put my hand on his shoulder, then reach up to touch his cheek. "Get in my car, hon. Let me thank this officer."

He nods without speaking, then walks toward my car. I turn to the officer, who has waited at the edge of the road. I am suddenly overcome with a sense of helplessness. "Where do we go?"

She props one hand on her gun belt, searching the horizon as if she's mentally mapping our course. "St. Mary's is the closest emergency room with a psychiatric screener on staff. I'd take him there and get him checked out."

The word *psychiatric* strums a shiver from me, but this is not the time to think about my own fears.

"Oh." I stop and knock my fist against my forehead. "His car. What do we do about that?"

"I'm going to put an emergency flasher by the side of the road," she says. "You belong to an auto service?"

"Yes. Triple A."

"Call them in the morning. This vehicle isn't going anywhere until then."

I thank the officer for her consideration and pull my phone from my purse. I'm going to get Zack to the hospital, have someone talk to him, then take him home and put him to bed. He is calm now, though a bit rattled, and for the first time in days he seems compliant.

I dial Carl's cell phone.

By some miracle, the emergency room is quiet on this Friday night. A nurse sends us straight to admissions, where a heavyset woman gives Zack a plastic hospital bracelet and asks for his social security number and insurance card.

He seems shell-shocked, and when he does speak, it's in a barely intelligible mumble. I provide as much information as I can, then stand aside as the nurse takes his blood pressure.

"What seems to be the problem?" she asks, her gaze shifting from Zack to me.

I wait for Zack to speak, but he only hangs his head. "We, um, had an accident with the car," I tell her, hoping she'll read between the lines and correctly interpret my oversimplified answer. "The investigating officer seemed to think Zack had the accident on purpose."

The nurse lifts a brow and looks at my son. "Did you wreck the car on purpose?"

I close my eyes, unable to watch.

"Yeah."

The nurse makes a note on the chart. "Have you been hearing voices in your head, seeing things, anything like that?"

"No."

Thank heaven.

"Were you drinking tonight?"

"A couple of beers."

"Did you take any pills? Any prescribed medication?"

"No."

"Height and weight?"

As Zack answers her questions, I lean against the wall and feel my composure begin to crumble. My young man looks like a child in that chair; the son I was ready to throttle a few hours ago has again become my precious baby.

"Have a seat in the lobby." The nurse closes the folder on her notes. "We'll call you in a few minutes."

Zack and I take seats in a row of hard plastic chairs. A television hangs from the ceiling in a corner; FOX News is replaying a story about a group of children missing in California. A man in scrubs comes through the sliding doors and barely glances in our direction. He presses a button and is buzzed into the treatment area.

I find myself thinking of Jeb Carter, the EMT from Oceanside.

A moment later, that same door opens. "Zack Kerrigan?"

He stands but looks back at me. "Will you come too?"

"You bet." I stand and slip my arm around his shoulder as we walk through the door.

A nurse in a brightly printed tunic top leads us past a group of employees who are gathered around a television set. I don't know if it's this part of Reno, the hour, or an off night, but this place looks nothing like the *ER* we watch on television.

"It's quiet tonight," I tell the nurse, trying to be pleasant.

"It's early yet," she says, glancing at the clock on the wall. "You should see this place after midnight."

She leads us into a curtained area and drops a gown in Zack's lap. "Shirt off, gown on, please." Her tone is bright and chipper. "You can keep your jeans on for now."

Zack pulls off his shirt like an old man whose joints hurt. I study his torso and the line of his jaw, looking for any bruises or cuts the EMTs might have missed.

He catches my eye. "I'm fine, Mom. The air bag, remember?"

"Oh, yeah." I give him a weak smile. "Thank goodness for that."

"Mom?"

"Hmm?"

"I'm so sorry." His voice breaks. "I know I was wrong—"

"Everything's going to be okay. We're going to find someone to help you." *Someone who knows more than Glazier and those people at AA . . .*

He takes a moment to compose himself, then he unfolds the hospital gown. "How in the world—"

"I think it opens in the back, though I don't suppose it really matters. Here, I'll fasten it for you."

I smile and keep my voice light as I tie the strings at the base of my son's neck. He is pale in the bright overhead lights, slender and shivering.

A nurse comes in, brandishing a syringe like a weapon. A smile that looks practiced flits over her face. "We need blood. Don't worry, this'll just take a sec."

Zack narrows his eyes. "I don't like needles."

"Then don't look."

Like a child, he turns away, his eyes clinging to mine as she ties a rubber strip around his left arm. She taps the vein at his elbow with a gloved finger, then slides the needle in.

Zack grimaces.

"You're lucky," I tell him, chattering away in an effort to keep things light. "I have thin veins. Remember Grandma? Her veins were so thin they had to take blood through her toes."

The nurse snaps the tourniquet free, waits another minute, then withdraws the needle. "Be back in a few minutes," she says, labeling the blood-filled tube. "We just want to run a few tests."

I know what she's doing, even if Zack doesn't realize. They'll test the blood for alcohol and drugs. The doctor will want to know to what extent my son's behavior has been chemically affected.

I'd like to ask about what comes next, but no one is around and I don't want to say the wrong thing in front of Zack. I'm still struggling to accept the fact that he told the policewoman he was trying to kill himself—how can that be? He must have underestimated how much he drank. Zachary would never try to kill himself if he were sober.

I sink into a plastic chair by the side of the bed. Zack leans against a stack of pillows and pushes hair out of his eyes in a gesture that floats up through the years. I tilt my head and see him at ten, climbing out of the pool and pushing back his waterlogged bangs. His toothy grin had the power to warm my heart . . . How long has it been since I've seen that carefree smile?

Other memories come crowding back like unwelcome guests:

Carl in the kitchen, telling me that our son has written about suicide.

Me clinging desperately to Zack's arm as he struggles to climb out of the car on our way back home.

Zack closeting himself in his darkened bedroom, avoiding friends and family for days.

Were all these things cries for help? Has my son been pleading for my attention in a language I've been too dull-witted to understand?

A shiver spreads over me, then I realize that the room is freezing. Zack is cold too; his skin is pimpled with gooseflesh.

I stand and look for a nurse, but the only staff I see are gathered around a television at the end of the corridor. "Excuse me," I call, "can we get a blanket?"

One of the women pulls herself away and grabs a thin blanket from a stack. I take it from her and tuck it around Zack's shoulders, biting back tears as I think of the little boy I used to tuck into bed. How old was he when I stopped that nighttime ritual?

I hear commotion from up front, followed by the buzz of the security door. Carl comes around the corner, his face dead-white and sheened with a sweat that has soaked his shirt at the armpits.

He takes one look at Zack and then manages a weak smile. "Hey, Son. You okay?"

Zack manages a tentative smile. "It's cool, Dad."

I catch Carl's eye. "We're going to see a doctor." Again, I pray my listener will pick up on everything I'm *not* saying. "We're going to see what the doctor recommends, because Zack has realized he needs help."

Carl nods slowly and then steps back as a doctor steps into our cubicle. The man in the white coat is surprisingly young, with sandy hair growing up and out in masses of curls. I'm not sure if this is the psychiatric screener who's supposed to be on duty, but right now I'd be happy to talk to anyone who can help us.

The doctor glances at Zack and then looks at the chart in his hand. "Zachary Kerrigan?"

"That'd be me," Zack quips.

"I'm Dr. Miranda." The doctor looks pointedly at me.

"I'm Zack's mother," I explain, "and this"—I point to Carl—"is his father."

I'm hoping he'll realize that we're solidly in Zachary's corner. We've been with him through court dates and rehab visits, long nights and tedious days. Some kids might come into the hospital escorted by police, but Zachary has a support system. We'll do whatever it takes to save our son.

The doctor looks at the admitting nurse's notes. "Your blood tests came back fine—no drugs, blood alcohol .02 percent. Because you're twenty-one, you don't qualify as legally drunk."

Zack's lips curve in a smirk. "I coulda told you that."

"Yet you had a deliberate auto accident?"

Zack hesitates. "Uh-huh."

"Have you heard voices? Anyone tell you to do that?"

Zack shakes his head.

The doctor stares at him for a long moment and then scribbles something on the chart. "Okay," he says, meeting my eye. "We'll send someone down for him in a few minutes."

I stand, assuming we can go with our son, but the doctor lifts his hand. "Sorry, but parents aren't allowed in the psychiatric ward except during visiting hours."

Carl frowns. "Can we at least walk him up?

"Sorry. By law, anyone detained on a Legal 200R must be escorted by security."

"A legal what?" I ask, but the doctor disappears behind the curtain. My mouth goes dry as two nurses approach. One points to Zack's sneakers and says they'll have to come off; the other lifts his smock and points to his belt. "That has to go too."

Ice spreads through my stomach as they take belt and shoes from my son, then a uniformed security guard walks up with a wheelchair.

"Mom?" Zack looks at me, his eyes wide. "Can't I go home?"

"Wait a minute, Son."

I step behind the curtain and find the doctor making notes. "Excuse me, but what's going on? I thought someone was going to talk to him, screen him, and refer him to a psychologist or something."

The doctor folds his hands over the top of his clipboard. "We are going to help him. But according to state law, we can hold anyone who's considered a danger to himself or others for up to seventy-two hours."

"Seventy-two—" I swallow the despair in my voice. "He's fine now. He's not about to kill himself."

"You don't know that."

"I know my son, and he said he was sorry! Look, he's been shaken up; I think he understands how wrong it was to run into that tree. Let me take him home, let him sleep, and we'll get an appointment with someone first thing Monday morning—"

"I'm sorry, ma'am, but it's out of my hands. You'd have to get a court order before we could release him. Now, if you'll excuse me—"

Wave after wave of shock slaps at me. What have I done? I turn and touch the curtain separating me and my son, wondering how I'm going to tell him he has to stay in this place.

The writer in me makes a mental note: *this is what panic and desperation and love feel like.*

I'm writing a novel to illustrate that God has a good plan for his children, but nothing about this feels good.

I grasp the last shreds of my courage, arrange my face into pleasant lines, and pull the curtain aside.

Zack is in the wheelchair, his shoulders bent, one hand over his face because he doesn't want us to see his tears. Grief shadows my husband's features, darkening the lines beside his mouth and eyes.

I lower my trembling hand to my son's head and bend to kiss his cheek, but he pulls away.

So . . . he blames me for bringing him here. He may blame me for all of this, but what choice did I have?

I withdraw and watch as the security guard wheels my broken boy toward another pair of locked doors.

With Carl's hand in mine, I stand in the silence and feel my heart break. God has supported us through trials before, but never has he asked us to do anything as difficult as this.

Neither Carl nor I sleep much that night. I lie in the darkness and feel my heart thump in my chest. A patch of moonlight spills from the partially opened curtains behind our headboard; when I look up, through the lace sheers I see that the stars are locked in place.

We have been trapped in an endless night.

On the chance that Carl has been able to doze off, I remain quiet and still, but my head is rioting with thought. Shannon and Patricia were not perfect children, but they grew to maturity in a predictable, frustrating, and exhilarating process. They tested the boundaries, they complained about life's hard lessons, but they *learned*. After absorbing those lessons, they left home and struck out on their own.

I have worried about them on occasion, but I worry about Zack constantly. Like a linebacker, he is always charging out of bounds, battering me and Carl as he passes. He gets knocked down, but he never learns. Sometimes I want to turn him out of the house, give him some money, and wish him well; at other times I want to hold him in my arms and shelter him.

My son is as predictable as a horse running back to the barn—if there's a bar within miles, he'll find it. He'll drink. He is one of the great loves of my heart, but sometimes I want to hurt him.

Yet I don't want anyone else to hurt him. I don't want him to be committed to a mental ward; I never intended for him to spend the night in the hospital. Somehow the situation spiraled out of my control, so when the sun rises, I'm going to make a few calls. I'm going to bring Zack home.

When the phone rings at seven thirty Saturday morning, I'm already awake. Caller ID reveals the name of the hospital, so I snatch up the receiver before it can ring again. "Hello?"

"Mom?" Zack's voice cracks. "They're moving me."

I glance at Carl, signaling an SOS even as that oddly detached aspect of my personality takes control. "Where are they taking you?"

I hear him murmur to someone else; then he's back. "West Lomas. They're taking me now."

"All right." I reach for a pencil and scribble the name on the *TV Guide*. I've heard of the place; it's a mental health facility for patients with chemical dependency disorders. "We'll call over there."

A sharp keening sound rises from Zack's throat. "You gotta get me out, Mom. I can't sleep. I'm going crazy in here."

Stay calm. Don't let your panic feed his.

"Don't worry, Son. Your dad and I will get on it. You get some rest, and we'll see you soon."

I hang up and look at Carl, who's pushed himself up. His eyes are puffy; the lines in his face have been deepened by grief. "They've moved him."

"I heard."

"He sounds scared to death."

"Wouldn't you be?"

I close my eyes. I've seen movies set in asylums, and I wouldn't want my dog to spend time in such a place. Yet my baby is in one of those mental wards because I put him there.

I shuffle into my slippers. "I need to call West Lomas."

After finding the number, I call the hospital, where a pleasant-voiced young man tells me that friends and relatives can visit from 6:30 p.m. to 7:30 p.m. only. Yes, my son will be able to use the phone, and yes, I can bring him some clean clothes, but no belts, nothing with drawstrings, hoods, or shoelaces. Toiletries? Sure, bring a toothbrush, but no razors or cologne. No medications.

I grab a pen and make a list. We will take him clothes, maybe some sports magazines, and the latest *Newsweek*. With nothing to do, Zack could go crazy in a place like that.

I also call Mr. Glazier's office. I bite my lip as the answering machine message plays in my ear: If it's an emergency, call 911. If it's not an emergency, leave a message, and someone will return my call when the office opens on Monday.

Some help *he* is.

Zack calls again after his arrival at West Lomas. He's crying again, but now his words are slurred and the edge of desperation in his voice makes me want to crawl through the telephone line to comfort him.

Instead, I speak in soothing tones and act as though everything is fine. "Get some sleep," I urge him. "Before you know it, we'll be there to see you."

While Carl busies himself taking care of Zack's wrecked car, I spend the morning doing research online. According to Nevada law, anyone who commits himself to a hospital voluntarily can leave whenever he wants to. Because he's an adult, Zack signed the consent for treatment form when we arrived at the emergency room, so doesn't that mean he committed himself voluntarily?

I call the admissions office at West Lomas. Speaking in the smoothest and most professional tone I can muster, I explain that a mistake has been made. Zachary Kerrigan signed himself in for treatment, and now he wishes to return home. "So I'll be picking him up in about an hour."

The man on the other end of the line clears his throat. "Ma'am, it doesn't matter what Mr. Kerrigan did. Once the doctor signs a Legal 200R, the matter is transferred to the authority of the courts. After seventy-two hours, the supervising physician will either petition for continued treatment or release the patient. But nothing's going to happen until then."

I've hit another brick wall.

The odd stillness in our house is broken by Zack's frequent phone calls. Carl answers the phone half the time; like me, he murmurs encouragement and promises that we'll see him later. Zack vacillates between begging us to get him out and moaning that he knows he is going to spend the rest of his life in the hospital.

Finally, about one o'clock, the phone stops ringing. Carl and I look at each other, realizing that our son must have finally fallen asleep.

At six thirty we stand in a line outside the locked doors of the adult wing. Two years ago we visited Zack in rehab, but that facility was more like a dormitory than a hospital. This place is undeniably a mental institution.

Two male orderlies look the line of visitors over, then confiscates all purses, car keys, book bags, and food items. I've brought a bag of peanuts, knowing how Zack loves to snack, but I'm asked to surrender them at the security desk.

"He can't have *peanuts*? What in the world could be wrong with a sealed bag of nuts?"

The no-nonsense woman at the desk looks at me with weary eyes. "You'd be surprised at the ways people will try to get drugs into this place. No outside foods are allowed, period."

After signing in at the security desk, we step into the wide hallway. Zack stands about halfway down, leaning against the wall, and at the sight of us, he breaks into tears. I want to sob as well, but for my son's sake, I smooth my expression and pull his stiff frame into my arms.

"Hey, bud." I rub his tousled hair. "How ya doin'?"

It's a stupid question; anyone can see he's not doing well. While Carl goes to find a visitors' room with three available chairs, I slip my arm around Zack's narrow shoulders and try to think of something encouraging to say.

My gaze, however, can't help roaming the hall. A middle-aged woman shuffles past us in slippers and a robe, her eyes wide and vacant as she trudges over the tiled floor and stares at nothing. An old man sits in a chair, his head in his hand, his eyes closed. He looks as though he hasn't moved in ten years.

Slippers, I notice, are the preferred footwear, since anything with shoelaces is forbidden. Zack, who hasn't owned a pair of slippers since his toddler days, is wearing his socks.

"I brought you some clean clothes." I hand him a pair of shorts and a T-shirt. I don't mention that an orderly pulled the drawstring from the shorts and confiscated the plastic bag I'd brought them in.

Carl waves to us from the end of the hallway. "Down here."

The room is large and open, with a TV rumbling in the corner and a divider separating us from another visitors' area. A man and a woman sit in front of the TV. Because they're both wearing flip-flops, I can't tell which of them is the patient. Zack, Carl, and I sit in three chairs in another corner, and then Zack covers his eyes and begins to weep.

I've often thought it would be good if he could cry instead of resorting to anger, but these tears claw at my heart.

He tries to say something, but between his tears and the clamor from the television, Carl and I have to lean close to hear him. "You—you, Mom," he says, hiccupping a sob. "You set me up!"

I bite my lip and look away so Zack won't see the shimmer of pain in my eyes.

"That's not true, Son." In a careful voice, Carl points out that Zack's situation is the result of his own actions. He then assures our son that we're working to get him released, that we're doing all we can because

225

we want to help him. When Zack calms down, he tells us that a doctor has been to see him, but the man only talked to him about five minutes. He's been taking medicines, too, though he doesn't know what they've been giving him.

Carl hands him a handkerchief. Zack holds it in front of his face until he gets hold of his emotions, then he wipes his cheeks and blows his nose.

Now that he seems rational, I cross my legs, prepared to spend the rest of the hour in this chair, but Zack stuffs the handkerchief into his pocket and stands.

"I want to go to bed." He moves toward the hallway.

Carl turns. "Really?"

"Yeah. I'm exhausted."

Carl and I look at each other. If he wants to sleep, what choice do we have?

We've already been told we're not allowed to enter any patient rooms, so we walk Zack to his room, then wait in the hallway as he enters.

Still determined to find a silver lining, I lean forward to peek inside. "It's nice. You have a window."

Zack curls on his bed and pulls the thin blanket to his chin. "I'm so tired." His voice is fainter than air.

"Then rest," Carl answers. "Go ahead and sleep."

I manage a halfhearted wave. "Bye, then. We'll talk to you tomorrow."

Zack's eyes fly open. "You're leaving?"

"Aren't you going to sleep?"

"Yeah."

I force a smile. "Okay. Good night."

"You don't have to go."

Carl laughs softly. "Son, if you're going to bed, we might as well go home."

Suddenly I understand—our son is dead tired, but he wants us to linger and watch over him as he drifts off.

I place my hand on Carl's back. "Go to sleep, Son. We'll wait here awhile."

So we stand in the hallway, silent and sober, as the wandering woman trudges over the tiles and our son surrenders to his weariness. When he doesn't stir for several minutes, Carl and I tiptoe toward the security desk.

When Zack was fourteen months old, he fell and hit his chin on the edge of a chair. I picked him up and wiped him off, but the sight of gaping flesh made me wince.

I knew he'd need stitches.

I drove carefully to the emergency room and then held my baby on my lap as a doctor confirmed my suspicions. "Not a big deal," the physician told me. "Two stitches will do the trick."

"Will it, you know, leave a scar?"

The doctor smiled. "Think of it as a badge of boyhood. I'll bet 70 percent of the men in this building have a similar scar on their chins. It's just one of those things."

Zack, who had calmed by that time, seemed more intent on studying the stethoscope around the doctor's neck than on listening to this positive prognosis.

The nurse lifted Zack from my lap. Alarmed, he began to cry, stiffening his little body and reaching for me as the nurse wrestled him onto a papoose board. I stood and folded my arms, every nerve tensing as they restrained my son's arms and legs with large Velcro bands.

I bit my lip as my chin quivered. I've never been tied down like that, but I could imagine how helpless my little guy was feeling. The boy only had about ten words in his vocabulary, so he couldn't even verbalize his fears.

I knew they would anesthetize the area before stitching the skin, but I couldn't watch anymore. I turned my head, studying a table loaded with medical supplies, as Zack shifted from screams to frenzied shrieks of the one word he had always used to summon help: "Ma-ma! Ma-ma! Ma-ma!"

By the time we arrive home, I think I have begun to understand what God is doing. From Zack's perspective, rehab was a drag, but it will seem like summer camp compared to being confined in a psychiatric ward. This experience may be what he needs to realize that he *cannot* drink—not a beer, not a wine cooler, not even a sip of alcohol. He will have to avoid all addictive substances for the rest of his life.

Before leaving, we stopped at the desk to ask about Zack's treatment. The staff psychiatrist wasn't around, but the charge nurse told us he had prescribed heavy doses of antidepressants for our son.

As we walked out, Carl slipped his arm around my shoulder. "No wonder Zack was so emotional and tired. The poor kid is drugged."

I resisted a wave of bitterness. How are we supposed to convince a psychiatrist that Zack's ready for release if the kid can barely hold up his head?

The situation is difficult—no, *surreal*—for me and Carl, but if Zack can endure this, so can we. We have crutches to lean on—Zack can sleep these seventy-two hours away; Carl and I can pray. Right now all I can do is beg the Lord to get my son out of that place, but I know God is sovereign. He knows what he's doing, even if I don't.

After returning home, I step into my office for the first time since Zack's frantic call. When I touch the computer mouse, the monitor wakes and displays my work in progress, William's waiting world.

But before I can get back to *The Ambassador*, I have to make a call. I open my personal contacts program, then scroll down to a name I never dreamed I'd call for personal reasons: Dr. Diana Sheldon.

I met Dr. Sheldon when I was writing *Tower of Terror*, the novel in which Rex Tower falls for his female psychologist. Diana is a local radio shrink, so she was able to give me lots of pointers about how mental health professionals operate and what Rex might experience in his sessions.

Now I need Diana to refer me to a local doctor who can help my son. From what the charge nurse told me, I know the hospital will not release Zack unless he has made definite plans to see a psychologist and follow through with outpatient treatment. Mr. Glazier, Zack's counselor, won't qualify. We need to schedule an appointment with a practicing psychologist or psychiatrist.

I dial Diana's number and wait until the machine picks up, then leave a message. I didn't expect her to be in her office on a Saturday night, but she'll get my voice mail—soon, I hope.

Now I lean toward the keyboard and pick up the thread of William's distressing cry. I'm beginning to see *The Ambassador* as more than a lesson for my students, a submission to my publisher, and an allegory for my son. The writing I do tonight and this weekend will be the lifeline that tethers me to sanity.

Like Zack, William needs help. Fortunately, my plot outline provides assistance. When Adam fell, God promised to send a redeemer. William is going to meet another kind of rescuer, a man I'm calling John.

As my heart twists in compassion for my poor protagonist, I insert a page break, draw a deep breath, and type:

Forty-five

Three days later, William looks up as a stranger enters the casino.

The game room has been busy this morning, so he isn't sure why he stops talking to Mac and glances toward the entrance. People from Paradise and Oceanside and even farther away have been streaming through the door all day, but for some reason the man at the entrance arrests William's attention. He's either an off-islander or a newcomer, but he lacks the bewildered look most newcomers wear for the first few days. The man is about William's height, not particularly striking, and he walks with an air of studied casualness, one hand in the pocket of his jeans. His eyes, however, are anything but relaxed. His gaze darts from face to face while the corners of his mouth twitch as if he's trying hard not to smile.

He stops next to Eden, who's playing the *Spin and Win* model, and whispers something in her ear. His words break her concentration; her green eyes widen as she stares at him. He doesn't give her time to respond but pats her shoulder and moves down the bank of machines, nodding when he catches a player's eye, smiling when he doesn't.

When he stops to ask Mac if business is good, William hears the stranger's voice for the first time. He speaks in a masculine baritone that is both powerful and gentle, and something about it sends a shiver down William's spine. Who is this man? And why does he act as if he owns this place?

William leans against the wall and studies the stranger's face, hoping some feature or gesture will spark a memory. Have they met in the diner? The man spoke to Eden, so perhaps he was sitting at the counter one afternoon when William dropped in for lunch. Or perhaps they've passed on the street.

By the time the stranger leaves Mac and ventures down another aisle, William would bet his last coin that he's never seen the man in the casino. New players usually drift as they scout out the area; returning players almost always head straight to their favorite machine. This man is coasting through the room like a newcomer, but instead of checking out the games, he seems to be checking out the *customers*.

William's brain clouds with uneasiness. The man must be a thief. He is watching the players, trying to gauge their levels of concentration, carefully choosing his mark and the moment he will pick a pocket or snatch a purse.

William pulls himself off the wall and steps to the spot where Mac stands sentry. "Mac—"

"Everything all right, Mr. Case?"

Without turning, William surreptitiously points over his shoulder. "You see the man who spoke to you a moment ago? About my size, brown hair, blue jeans?"

Mac's eyes narrow. "Yep."

"Escort him out, will you? Don't make a scene, and don't make any accusations. I don't think he's done anything, but the man is up to no good. I feel it in my bones."

Mac pulls himself up to his full six feet six inches. "Whadda I tell him if he asks why we're kickin' him out?"

William sighs, exasperated by Mac's lack of imagination. "Tell him we're at full capacity. He can come back when there are fewer people on the machines . . . when we're better able to keep an eye on him."

"Yessir."

William crosses one arm over his chest and chews on his thumbnail as the guard lumbers across the game room. With a smooth smile Mac takes the newcomer by the elbow and points toward the door. William expects the man to protest—most people do—but the stranger only gives Mac a rueful grin and follows the guard, meek as a lamb. Before leaving, though, his gaze rises and locks on William's, focusing with unnerving intensity.

He knows me.

A tremor of fear and anticipation shoots up William's spine as the stranger steps through the doorway. Mac waits until the door closes, then he catches William's gaze and brushes his hands together.

William nods his thanks, motions Mac back to his post, and strides toward the entrance. With both palms against the dark door, he presses his eye to the peephole to observe the stranger's reaction to his abrupt dismissal.

He doesn't see the man on the street. His pulse quickens; then he hears the baritone rumble of the stranger's voice. By twisting his head, William can see the man standing in front of the closed-off window, talking to someone. Now he's bending down. Who could he—

William groans as the realization hits home. Ramirez. The old man is sitting on the sidewalk with pen and notepad in hand, ready to flash stern words at anyone who glances his way.

William holds his breath and flexes his fingers until the urge to strangle the old man passes. He jerks the door open, intending to blast Ramirez *and* the stranger with the full force of his irritation, but what he sees on the sidewalk whips his breath away.

The stranger has knelt next to Ramirez. The scarred man's eyes close as the stranger presses his fingertips to Ramirez's face; then the newcomer lifts his head as if he is searching the sky for something—what, William can't imagine. He murmurs words William can't hear, then his fingers slide to the tortured skin and ragged beard around the old man's mouth. The stranger removes his hands as Ramirez's eyes open, and a shout breaks from his lips.

231

Through the half-opened door William stares wordlessly. Ramirez clasps the stranger's hands and proceeds to thank him in a voice rolling with thunder and assurance. Tears flow down his cheeks, and William gasps when he realizes that Ramirez's face has been restored—the red trails of marred flesh have been erased; baby pink skin gleams through the darkness of his beard.

Ramirez has no tongue; how can he speak?

"Thank you," Ramirez says again, his voice breaking. "How can I thank you? Everyone in Paradise will want to hear about this."

William opens the door wider, wanting to hear more. He's not worried about Ramirez seeing him; the old man is so focused upon the stranger he wouldn't notice if William started dancing in the doorway. But the stranger flinches as William's gaze strafes his back; he turns, and their eyes connect just before William dives back into the building and slams the door.

William stands in silence, his hand trembling on the doorknob, half-afraid it will begin to turn against his palm. A cold coil of regret tightens in his chest. Some sort of dark magic is afoot, some new kind of mischief. If this newcomer has the power to heal Ramirez, surely he has the power to punish those who caused the old man's injury.

He has come for William. And Raquel. And probably Stan. If Ramirez rates miracles and healing, then those who opposed him deserve agony and death.

"You okay, Mr. Case?" Dodge stands at William's side, a worried look on his round face.

"Yes—no, actually." Forcing a smile, William pulls a handkerchief from his pocket and swipes beads of perspiration from his neck. "Do me a favor, will you? Stand here and don't let anyone in for the next hour. Since we're operating at full capacity, I don't want to incite trouble by having too few machines for the players."

"No problem, Mr. Case." Dodge waits until William steps aside, then he crosses his arms and plants himself in the doorway, a human barricade.

William shoves the handkerchief into his pocket, tugs on his tie, and hurries to his office.

Forty-six

By mutual agreement, I stay home on Sunday morning while Carl fills our spot in the pew. My female intuition is confirmed ten minutes after Carl leaves—the phone rings and Zack is on the line. "Mom," he says, a plaintive note in his voice, "you guys are coming tonight, aren't you?"

At this moment, my twenty-one-year-old son is more boy than man. "Yes, honey," I assure him, "we'll be there."

"Can you bring somebody with you? It's boring here."

I know there are televisions and magazines and games in the visitors' rooms. Zack isn't bored; he's lonely . . . and frightened.

I force a laugh. "Who do you want me to bring?"

"Anybody. There's no one to talk to here."

I think back to the other patients we saw in the ward. Though several did not look capable of carrying on a conversation, I noticed several young people about Zack's age. He has people to talk to, but he wants the comfort of a friend.

"I'll see what I can do. Your dad and I will be there at six thirty sharp, okay?"

"Okay."

I shake my head as I lower the phone. Though I'd love to invite one of his friends to go with us, I also want to protect Zack. If I called one of his buddies, within a few hours everyone in his social circle would know where he was. I don't mind if Zack's peers know he's an alcoholic—in fact, I *want* them to know. But I don't want them thinking he's crazy.

Mental health care has come a long way in the last few years, but it's still a touchy topic. Before Carl left, I asked him not to mention our situation at church. As much as we need prayer, I don't want church members whispering about our son.

We are going to get through this. Zack is going to talk to a doctor who knows what to do, and this horrible experience is going to profoundly change him. By this time next year, we should be able to look back and realize this catastrophe was the event that forced Zack to realize the truth about himself.

Today could be the first day of his life as a sober, positive person.

I shower and dress, though three times I'm interrupted by Zack's calls. Each time he asks an insignificant question that I answer patiently, realizing that he's really calling to hear a familiar, supportive voice.

By the time Carl comes home with take-out chicken dinners, the phone has stopped ringing. "He has to be asleep," I tell Carl. "Let's hope he takes a long afternoon nap."

While my son sleeps in the hospital and my husband prays in the backyard, I return to my office. I want to finish this story so Zack can have it as he begins his treatment. Perhaps as he reads and listens to his doctor, the pieces will fall into place and he'll finally acknowledge the truths he's denied for so long.

At least that's my prayer.

Forty-seven

By keeping creative hours, using the back door, and asking Dodge and Mac to stay alert, William manages to avoid the stranger for two weeks. He can't avoid hearing about the man, though, and something in him is grateful to learn about the stranger without having to endure another frisson of familiarity.

Nearly everyone who enters the casino these days has either met the newcomer or knows someone who has. His name, Eden tells William, is John.

He forces a chuckle. "Ramirez acts like this guy is Casey himself."

Her eyes widen, then she snorts a laugh. "You *do* have an imagination. John does too. He's fascinating."

"The guy is living in my old apartment? He must be as poor as a church mouse."

"Don't forget, he *is* new," Eden says. "We all come into Paradise empty-handed. The other day I was telling someone that what matters most is what you make of yourself once you arrive, but John says the most important thing is discovering what role the author intends for you to fill. That's when—"

"Enough for one day." William holds up both hands, laughing. "Eden, you've lost me. You make it sound as though our lives are one big audition. For what?"

Her lips pucker in a tiny rosette, then unpucker enough to say, "Well, I don't know. I didn't think to ask."

"Here." William fishes a gold coin from his pocket and presses it into her palm. "Play a game on the house, okay? Don't take anything this newcomer tells you too seriously. Seems to me that life is for having fun while you can, because . . . you know." He arches his brow, reminding her of something he hasn't been able to forget: like Marilyn, any of them could find themselves Damaged Extensively, All Done.

Eden takes the coin and walks away, her thoughtful look replaced by a contented smile. Savoring this small victory over the newcomer's nonsense, William turns toward the office.

Raquel halts as William nearly runs into her. "Whoa!" she says, stepping back.

He looks up, surprise in his eyes. "What brings you here?" His gaze roves over her, taking in everything from her shoes to her hair. A jealous gleam enters his eye, a look she doesn't like or understand.

She feels her cheeks heat in a blush. "I was hoping to find you."

"Were you? I thought you might have gotten all dolled up for someone else."

She cuts a quick look at his eyes because she can't tell if he's joking. She has dressed up to please him, yet he seems to think otherwise.

"Of—of course I came to see you," she stammers, settling her purse more firmly under her arm. "When I didn't find you in the office, I thought I'd walk over to Eden's and—"

"We'd talk?"

"Sure."

William inclines his head toward the office. "After you, then."

She walks into the room, wondering what lies beneath his counterfeit expression. They have spent so little time together over the last few weeks that she has no idea what he's thinking. At home, he's either too tired or too preoccupied to share his heart with her, and here he doesn't seem to trust her.

She sinks into the guest chair before his desk and then settles her purse on her lap. "So," she says, trying to sound casual, "how are things at the machine company these days?"

"We call it the casino now." He perches on the edge of the desk. "The machine company is history."

"I saw the new sign. It's nice."

The brick building is now crowned by a twenty-foot tower featuring the word *casino* spelled vertically in dozens of flashing red and white bulbs. Against the night sky, the tower should be visible for miles.

Still searching for an agreeable topic of conversation, she gestures toward the game room. "I hear there's another newcomer in Paradise— an unusual fellow."

"I told you about him."

She catches her breath. "You don't mean the man who made it rain on Ruby's garden?"

"If you believe the rumors, the guy is working miracles all over the place."

She lifts an eyebrow. "This sarcasm isn't like you, William. You're usually the first in line to welcome newcomers."

He gives her a sharp look and then shrugs. "I don't like the look of this guy. Something about him isn't right."

She smiles. "Jealous?"

"Definitely not."

"Then why don't you like him?"

William looks down at his hands. "He's not like the rest of us. I think he's evil."

An inner alarm sounds as his words echo in the room. William has not mentioned her trip to the forbidden room since the night she confided in him, but his eyes flood with accusation every time he looks her way. Who is he to point a finger at her? He has gambled with the magician *twice*.

"Would you know evil if you saw it?" She tosses the words at him like darts. "Your judgment wasn't so hot when you were toying with the magician."

His temper, which must have begun to simmer when she appeared without warning, now boils over. "At least I never burned anyone's face off!"

"Shut up!" She glances over her shoulder, suddenly afraid Ramirez will appear to indict her. "That's over. We don't need to talk about it anymore."

A smile spooks over William's lips. "But the guilt carries on, doesn't it, my love?"

She closes her eyes. William knows her too well; he has heard her cry out in her dreaming hours. He understands her guilt, because he is guilty too.

But guilt is a burden that does not grow lighter when shared.

When she opens her eyes, the anger has vanished from his eyes. "Cheer up," he says, twirling a pencil between his fingers. "Your crime has been erased. John cured Ramirez."

She stiffens. "Don't joke with me. You've never had a knack for humor."

His eyes are flat, remote. "I'm not joking. Ramirez is as good as new."

Raquel looks away. A newcomer who has the power to heal the mess she made of Ramirez?

"What kind of man *is* this newcomer?" she asks. "Have you met him?"

"I've only seen him."

She hesitates. William can be stubborn, but he's not foolish. He'll need to know if John is a friend or foe. "Want me to check him out for you?"

He gazes at her as if weighing her intentions, then props his elbow on his bent knee and rubs the back of his neck. "Go ahead. Tell me if you agree there's something screwy about him. I've given Mac and Dodge a standing order not to allow him into the game room."

"Shame on you, William, locking out a customer." She tilts her head and gives him a teasing smile. "The man has to have a job. Where's he working?"

"Haven't heard. But I'm sure you'll find out."

"You bet I will."

William sinks into his chair. Raquel's offer to check out the newcomer was so sincere, so guileless and spontaneous, he almost laughed.

Didn't she realize he could see through her? She was bored with him, bored and lonely. Now she would turn her attention to the newcomer, the man who had razzle-dazzled the others with his tricks.

He clutches his gut as another pain shoots through his middle. Despite all he's done to safeguard all he's won, one of his most precious treasures is slipping through his fingers.

Groaning, he pulls a walkie-talkie from the desk drawer. "Mac?"

A hiss of static, then "Yeah, boss?"

"About that John guy—if he approaches the casino again, let him in. But before you allow him to play the games, escort him to this office."

"No problem, boss."

He clicks the receiver off. One of the things he appreciates most about Mac and Dodge is their reluctance to ask intrusive questions.

Forty-eight

Carl and I are standing in a line of visitors outside Zack's ward when I turn and glimpse a familiar face. "Is that Ian Morley?"

The young man stiffens. "Ms. Casey?"

I smile, not sure how to handle this unexpected encounter. If Ian is here, he is also connected to someone in this ward.

"Ian," I say, tugging on Carl's sleeve, "I'd like you to meet my husband, Carl Kerrigan."

Carl shakes Ian's hand. "I've heard a lot about you."

"Um . . . that's nice. I think." Ian slips his hands into his pockets as a flush shadows his cheeks.

For a long moment we stand in an awkward silence. I am wondering if I should ask what brings Ian to this hallway when I remember that he knows Zack. They aren't close, but Ian could still spread the story.

"Ian"—I force a pleasant note into my voice—"are you visiting a relative?"

His eyes flick away for a moment, then he nods. "My dad."

"Is he . . . doing okay?"

Ian lifts one shoulder in a shrug. "Who knows? He's been in and out of here so many times we've lost count."

Please, Lord, don't let that happen to Zack.

I give Ian what I hope is a sympathetic smile. "It's hard, coming here. We understand. Not something you want a lot of people to know about."

"You got that right." He turns and leans against the wall. "You got somebody in there?"

I look at Carl. "Our son."

"You might know him," Carl adds, picking up my thought. "Zack Kerrigan? I think you went to school together."

Surprise blossoms on Ian's face. "Zack Kerrigan is your son?"

We turn as the jangle of keys draws our attention. Through the glass inserts we see an orderly behind the locked doors.

"Yes." I toss the answer over my shoulder. "Zack is our son, and I think he could use some company. Feel free to say hello once we're inside."

Carl gives me a questioning look as we pass through the doorway; I squeeze his arm in response. "Ian's a good guy," I whisper as we stop at the desk to sign in and surrender any contraband. "I trust him."

Twenty minutes later, Ian and Zack are talking like old friends. I relax in my chair and rest my hand on Carl's arm—Zack was morose and despondent when we entered, but at the sight of Ian, he straightened and pulled himself together. It's one thing to break in front of one's parents, I realize, and quite another to be vulnerable before one's peers.

While the guys talk, I look over at the patient Ian came to visit. He spent only a few minutes with the man who sits staring out the window, and it's not hard to understand why. Ian's father wears an unbelted bathrobe, stained pajamas, and plastic flip-flops. His hollow cheeks are unshaven, his eyes wide and vacant. When an orderly stops to ask him a question, there is no response.

I'm not even sure Ian's dad realizes his son came to see him.

I prop my chin on my hand and watch as Zack and Ian laugh. Ian is telling a story about some kid they knew from high school, and Zack is smiling as he listens. One hand taps the table in a nervous rhythm; one leg is jiggling under the table. But this is good. God has extended grace in the form of Ian Morley, and for this unexpected shower of mercy, I am grateful.

Forty-nine

At lunchtime the next day, Mac raps on William's door. "Mr. Case?" His square head swivels toward the desk. "John's here."

Caught off guard, William stands and shoves away a stack of orders, nearly knocking over his coffee cup. "Okay—show him in, please."

As Mac holds the door for the newcomer, William tightens his tie and wishes he'd taken more time to plan an approach. He doesn't want to arouse the man's suspicions, but he needs to ferret out the newcomer's intentions.

After meeting John yesterday, Raquel came home, kicked off her shoes, and pronounced the man boring. She'd been introduced to him at Eden's, she told William, but he hadn't done or said anything unusual. No tricks, no miracles.

Now William steps around his desk and thrusts out his arm as John enters the office. At this distance, he can see that the man's brown eyes are cloaked in a secretive expression, while the set of his chin suggests a determined streak.

"John." William grips the man's hand. "I've been eager to officially welcome you to town."

The newcomer returns his handshake with an uplifted brow. "Really? I would say you've been doing your best to avoid me."

William blinks, as startled by the man's words as by the warmth of his grip. The newcomer's voice is low and confidential, the tone one friend uses with another.

William steps back and gestures to the guest chair. "Have a seat, please. I try to welcome all the newcomers to Paradise—"

"You don't have to explain, William. I know everything about you. You're the main reason I've been sent."

As John sinks into the seat, William moves to the security of his executive chair and hopes the newcomer can't sense the anxiety that must be radiating from him like heat from a fire.

"John," he begins, "I'm not sure what you're planning, but we're not going to let you interfere with our operation. You may be able to distract the others with your stories and well-timed tricks, but—"

John cuts him off with a wave of his hand. "My presence bothers you, does it?"

William meets his gaze. "Should it?"

The man's mouth curls as if on the edge of laughter. "That all depends on you. Why don't you tell me why you're afraid?"

"I'm not afraid."

"Aren't you?" John smiles and smoothes the fabric of his jeans. "I didn't come to rip you off, William, but I did come to interfere. Oh yes, I'm going to *completely* interfere with your operation."

William frowns, wondering if this stranger has mastered the trick of reading his mind . . . or if he possesses the magician's power. That trickster seems to have no trouble discerning human thoughts and desires.

"I think," William begins, "your power comes from the magician."

Amusement flickers in the dark eyes that meet his. "I'm not surprised you think so."

"So you admit it?"

"Of course not. Power never originates with the creation. It always springs from the creator."

"So these tricks you do—"

"I do what Casey allows me to do, nothing more. These abilities have been granted so you will know I speak for our creator."

William stares at his guest in a paralysis of astonishment.

John leans forward, his elbows on his knees, his eyes intent upon William's. "You want to know who I am? First, let me explain who *you* are. You are the representative through which evil entered this story world. Because you broke the law, the citizens of Paradise now live in a polluted city."

William forces a laugh. "You're talking gibberish. You sound like Ramirez."

"Maybe this will convince you: the other night you looked up and asked if Casey could see you. Do you think the creator is blind? Casey has watched your life unfold; the creator has heard every word you've ever uttered. Casey knows every thought that crosses your mind, unlike the magician, who is merely good at reading your expressions. Casey knows you, William, better than you know yourself. That's why I've been sent to Paradise."

A glint of humor fills John's eyes as he leans back in his chair. "You have questions. Ask away."

William gapes at him, his mind whirling. "Are you saying . . . that you are Casey?"

John laughs. "I'm a character, as are you."

They have been talking only five minutes, but already a trickle of crazy juice has begun to drip into William's brain. He closes his eyes. "You are insane."

Ignoring the comment, John continues to expound upon his delusion. "This world feels real to you, as well it should—Casey is pleased with the design. In the beginning, Paradise had everything—beauty, grandeur, structure, music, wonder. Then the creator added people." John's mouth quirks with humor when William looks up. "Characters always complicate things."

"Wait." William swivels in his chair and narrows his gaze. "You're saying a *writer* made us up."

"Exactly. You, Paradise, the world beyond this island—all were fashioned from Casey's words."

"So everything I see here"—William gestures toward the walls of his office—"doesn't actually exist. Paradise is only a figment of Casey's imagination."

A smile ruffles John's mouth. "Paradise exists completely, totally, and substantially within this story. Our actions have authentic consequences—in fact, *your* actions have brought about drastic repercussions. You broke the rules, William, as Casey knew you would, and now we have to do something about it."

William grasps at the strings of reality and holds them tightly. When people lose their minds, do they hear fantastic tales coming from the mouths of strangers?

Perhaps this man is a figment of his guilty conscience.

"You don't have to tell me what I've done." William looks away, unable to think under John's steady scrutiny. "You say Casey invented everyone in Paradise." Slowly, he meets the newcomer's gaze. "Why?"

At first John doesn't reply; then an almost rueful smile crosses his face. "Because the story will matter . . . to someone Casey loves."

John's answer hangs in the silence between them. William watches his guest for a long moment and then lets his head fall to the back of his chair. "How do you know so much?"

"I was created with knowledge, just as you were."

"I wasn't given the keys to the universe. No one explained the mysteries of the cosmos to me."

"You were given more knowledge than you remember. You have forgotten"—John's gaze shifts to the floor—"or you have chosen to forget."

His words fall with the weight of pebbles in still water, spreading ripples of pain and guilt.

Unable to meet John's gaze, William studies his hands. "I'm not sure I can accept any of this."

"What you think really doesn't matter. Casey has outlined this story; Casey will bring it to a close."

William has heard all he can stand. He works in a place where madness sprouts like mushrooms, and he has already endured his quota of crazy for the week.

"Mac," he bellows, standing so abruptly that his chair shoots back and slams against the wall, "escort this fellow out, will you?"

John stands as politely as if they are two gentlemen ending their conversation on a civil note. "We will talk again," he says, slipping his hands into his pockets, "before I go."

"Oh?" Not even this lunatic could miss the sarcasm in William's tone. "And how long will you be staying?"

"Until the story's finished," John answers. "Until the last chapter."

Fifty

My phone rings at precisely seven thirty on Monday morning. Zack is ready to come home, but only a doctor can release him, and the doctor doesn't make his rounds until late afternoon.

"Mom," he says, "I don't know if I can take another day in this place. You've seen it—you know what it's like."

I stiffen at something I hear in his voice, a ragged and desperate quality I'd expect from a man tied to a stake and left to die in the desert. My son is not the most stable person in the world, but I'm suddenly convinced he will suffer real harm if he spends another day in that ward.

"Honey, I've left a message with a doctor friend," I tell him. "We're going to get you out of there, but you have to be patient. When the doctor makes his rounds, speak coherently, try to be pleasant, and try to be positive. If he thinks you're unstable, he might want to hold you—"

"I can't stay here!"

His cry shreds my heart, but there's nothing I can do. His attempted suicide-by-car is not some minor infraction of family rules; it is serious business that could have major repercussions. Why can't he see that?

My heart is heavy when I hang up, but I am determined not to waste this day. In the shower, I consider my to-do list: place a follow-up call to Dr. Sheldon, prepare for my class tonight, write several chapters, and check with the insurance adjustor about the wrecked Explorer. If I haven't heard from Zack by three, I'll call the hospital and ask to speak to the charge nurse.

If the hospital won't release him today, I may have to engage a lawyer to fight the court order. I'll do whatever it takes to free my son.

An hour later, with hair still dripping from the shower, I sink into my chair and let myself slide back into William's world. Paradise is growing dark, but it's not as dark as my reality, where frustration follows every phone call and I am helpless to change our circumstances.

In William's world, at least, I am in charge. And maybe, if I am creative, I can darken William's world to the point that my troubles seem insignificant in comparison.

Fifty-one

Two days later, Stan raps on the office door and then thrusts his head through the opening. "Hey, we need a receptionist, right?"

William glances up, blinking to clear columns of figures from his field of vision. "Um . . . yeah. Why?"

Stan raises his chin and grins. "Found somebody I think you'll like. She's a newcomer, and she needs a job."

William glances at the clock. Nearly twelve. He doesn't expect Raquel today, but if she's going to show up, she'll arrive in the next few minutes.

"Tell you what, Stan," William says, pushing away from the desk. "Have the girl meet me outside the front entrance. I feel like driving up to the cliffs. Maybe she'd like to go along."

Stan wags his brows as his grin widens. "Whatever you say, Ambassador."

William pulls his coat from the back of the chair and shrugs into it, his heart stirring with an interest he hasn't felt in weeks. Dozens of women come to the casino every day, but he has disciplined himself to think of them as purses filled with the coins that keep his place in business. The thought of working with a new and pretty woman . . . is tempting.

He nods at Dodge as he approaches the front door, then steps outside. He yanks at his collar as a slow-moving car chugs by, stultifying black smoke pouring from its tailpipe. He turns, not wanting to inhale a lungful of soot, and that's when he sees her.

If Raquel is nighttime, this girl is daylight, as soft and glowing as a summer morning. Golden hair tumbles down her back like strands of sunshine, while her blue eyes peer at him over lips that gleam like honey. She wears a skirt she'll need a shoehorn to get out of and a perfume so inviting he takes an involuntary step forward.

Her unexpected beauty produces a momentary crisis in his vocabulary. "Um . . . hello."

Smiling, she extends her hand. "I'm Amber."

"Of course you are." He can't help noticing the warmth in her strong, slim fingers. "You're a newcomer to Paradise?"

She nods, and he sees uncertainty in her eyes, a common characteristic of new arrivals.

He smiles to put her at ease. "Interested in the receptionist's job? The work's not hard; a machine takes most of the messages. But someone has to return all those calls."

"Y-yes. I think I could do that."

"You're hired." Reluctantly, he releases her hand and then jerks his head toward the street. "On one condition, that is. I need some fresh air, and this isn't the best place to get it. Take a drive with me, will you? We can talk on the way."

She follows without hesitation, and the sight of her wide eyes reminds him of his own beginning. How innocent he was in those early days, how unsure of himself!

He seats Amber in his car, closes her door, and hurries to the driver's side. Soon they are leaving the town center behind, heading toward the steep cliffs at the northern boundary of Paradise.

As he drives, he glances at Amber from the corner of his eye. She rides with one elbow propped on the door, her face uplifted, her hair blowing in the breeze. One bare knee sways slightly to the rhythm of the road, moving toward him, away from him, toward him, and away . . .

He forces himself to focus on his driving. "So," he grips the steering wheel, "how long have you been in Paradise?"

She props her head on her hand. "Two days."

"Things have changed a lot since the day I arrived," he says, keeping his eyes on the road. "I woke up and found a note with my name, my job, everything I needed to know."

"Really?" He feels the weight of her astonished gaze, dark blue and deep as the sea. "I could have used that kind of help."

"Things weren't that great." He grins. "We had no freedom in the old days—everybody was told what they were supposed to do and how they were supposed to do it." He blows out his cheeks. "Like I said, things have changed. Nowadays people like to find their own place, make their own way. We'll set you up with a job at the casino; you can find yourself a man and make yourself a home. Anything can happen in Paradise."

She manages a tremulous smile, then reaches out to squeeze his arm. "It's really nice of you to take the time to talk to me like this. I was just feeling my way through things, you know?"

His forearm instinctively tightens beneath her grip, and his gaze falls to the creamy expanse of her neck. What would it hurt if he enjoyed a day with Amber—

Good grief, what is he *doing*?

He looks away as something tugs at his gut. He doesn't understand this feeling, but these days he doesn't understand a lot of things.

When they reach the end of the road, he pulls the car onto a graveled lookout point. "Here's a good place." His voice is huskier than he would have liked. "I come up here when I want to clear my head. It's quiet."

He gets out of the car and pauses by the back bumper as Amber steps onto the gravel. When she reaches him, he points to a narrow footpath winding through the dark boulders.

She clutches his arm again. "Are you sure that's safe? We're up so high."

"There's a ledge, a spot you can't see from here. It's worth the walk, I promise. Hang on to me if you feel woozy."

She clings like a barnacle as he leads the way down the trail. More than once she loses her footing and slips on the pebbled path, crashing into his back as she giggles and offers apologies.

William eases down the trail, using the jagged boulders for support and leverage as he follows the path to Lookout Ledge. Amber is telling him about her apartment when he stops and lifts his hand. Voices are flowing toward them on the wind, voices that do not belong on the cliffs.

"What's wrong?" Amber hisses in his ear.

"Shh."

With difficulty, he pries her fingers from his arm, motions for her to stay put, then creeps farther down the trail. Sliding with his back to the stony wall, he peers over the escarpment and glimpses the ledge below. Two people are sitting in his private place: John and . . . Raquel.

A hornet of jealousy buzzes in his ears. How could Raquel bring *him* to their special place? And why would the man who professes to know so much about everything in Paradise allow himself to be brought here? If he knows as much as he says he does, surely he knows Rocky's secret.

"What's going on?" Amber stands behind him, pawing at his back like an anxious puppy. "Can't we go on? Is someone out there?"

"Shh!" He pivots and glares at her. "Would you shut up so I can *listen*?"

Her countenance falls as she retreats, leaving him to eavesdrop in peace. He edges closer, pressing his chest against the cold rock, trying to catch words tossed pell-mell by the wind.

Useless. He can see John and Raquel sitting across from one another, more like friends than lovers. He sees Raquel's lips moving and John's head nodding; he thinks he sees the glint of a tear on Rocky's cheek. But to hear anything he'd have to leave the shelter of the rocks and expose himself as a spy.

Somewhere behind him, Amber begins to cry. As the wind carries the sound of her sobbing toward the sea, Raquel lifts her head and leans forward, searching for the source of the sound.

Mumbling beneath his breath, William races back along the trail to return his lost puppy to her pen.

With her bad news safely dammed within her, Raquel barely looks up when William comes through the door that evening. But when he drops into the easy chair and quietly asks about her day, she bursts into tears.

From the look on his face, she knows tears are not the reply he expected.

He braces his arms on the chair. "What's wrong now?"

She gulps hard and swipes at a trail of tears. "Lucky. He's dead."

"What?"

Her chin trembles as she meets his gaze. "I went for a run on the beach this morning. When I came back . . . The rats. They got to him."

His expression is more surprised than sad.

"I'm so sorry, William," she continues, forcing her words through her sobs. "I can't bear the thought of losing him . . . mostly because *you* gave him to me."

When he doesn't answer, she wipes her eyes. What is wrong with him? Didn't he hear her?

Finally, he answers. "I'm sorry, Rocky."

She dabs her eyes with a tissue, then hiccups another sob. "I didn't know what to do. I put him in a box and drove into town; the next thing I knew, I was at the cliffs. So I went down the trail to Lookout Ledge and threw Lucky's box over the cliff."

She hugs herself as the tears begin to flow again. At any minute she expects William to come over and pull her into his arms, but he remains in his chair as if something has glued him in place.

Her tears slow and stop. Sniffling, she wipes her face and looks at the stranger across the room.

"And after that?" he asks, his voice cold.

Bewildered, she wipes her damp hands on her slacks. "After that? I started to walk back . . . and saw John standing by the rocks. I don't know where he came from, but I guess he saw everything. He told me not to worry because Casey wanted to help us. I was wrong about him, William."

He crosses his legs at the ankles. "How so?"

"I thought he was boring. He's not. He's . . . amazing."

"He's only a man, Rocky."

"But he's different. He knows things. Even the things we don't talk about."

She lowers her head as a blush burns her cheeks. "I didn't think anyone but Casey could see everything we do. But John said Casey has told him things. He's come here to help us."

William flashes her a look of disdain. "Seems to me that he's come to lure you away. Lookout Ledge was our private place."

"Good grief, William, it's only a rock." She frowns, annoyed by his pettiness. "It's not like I invited him out there."

"You sure about that?"

"Yes." Her voice simmers with barely restrained anger. "Quite."

He looks away and laces his fingers, then meets her eyes. "You need to ignore that man. I don't know what he's up to, but he's not going to change anything. No one pays him any attention; most people think he's nuts."

"Doesn't matter." She stares into the fireplace and pulls her legs up to sit cross-legged on the sofa. "He's not crazy. I don't know what he is, but I think Ramirez may be right. Casey has finally sent someone to help."

"You'd better hope the old man is wrong. If John is from Casey, you and I are both in a world of trouble."

Her mouth twists. "You're not listening. John told me everything I've done; then he said he hasn't come to punish me. He said he's come to *rescue* me." Smiling, she meets William's gaze. "Wouldn't that be wonderful?"

William doesn't answer, but, watching him, Raquel can almost read his thoughts. Her dear William, ambitious and driven, has always wanted to be her rescuer, but he needs help as badly as she does.

"If your life here is so terrible," he finally answers, "why don't you leave?"

Her mouth clamps tight for a moment as his words ring in the silence. What has happened to the man she loved? Either he has gone completely insane, or guilt has hardened his heart so no trace of love remains.

"William, I didn't mean—"

"I'll be at the casino," he interrupts, standing. "At the company, where I am appreciated."

"William!" Raquel reaches for him as he leaves the room, but he does not turn again. Apparently he has no patience for her pain, sympathy for her sorrow, or love for her at all.

It's as if the magician took everything when he took William's soul.

Limp with weariness, Raquel lowers her head to the sofa and waters the pillow with bitter tears.

Fifty-two

Stan is showing Todd, his new assistant, how to splice a rat-damaged wire when William enters the break room. Stan looks up, a question in his eyes, but William urges him to stay put.

"Don't let me disturb you," he says, moving toward the vending machines. "I'm going to grab a quick bite before my meeting with the exterminator."

He has given up on Ruby and her nonviolent methods of coping with Paradise's rodent population. The exterminator from Oceanside assured William he could take care of the rat problem in only one visit.

"Will they . . . die?" William asked on the phone, half-afraid to hear the answer.

The exterminator snorted with the half-choked mirth of a man who finds little humor in his life. "You want the rodents gone?"

"Yes, I do. They're eating into our profits."

"Then let me do my job, mister."

William agreed to the man's terms and hung up. He's not thrilled with the idea of killing, but Stan says he should think of it as making the rats Disappear in Entirety. He can live with that.

Now Stan smiles without amusement. "That guy can't come soon enough, if you ask me. The rats have run rampant in the factory; last night they chewed through one of our main power cords. One of the little buggers fried himself in the process, but he blew power to at least ten motherboards that were running diagnostics checks. Todd and I had to start the process all over this morning."

William drops two silver coins into the juice machine. "Don't worry—this man seems to know what he's doing. Like you, I'm sick of rats."

He laughs, remembering Raquel's claim that John will help them get rid of the pests. Sure he will. The man can't even find a job.

William catches the can that rolls from the machine, then pops the top and turns to Stan and Todd. "So—what's new in town? Any interesting gossip?"

Todd, being a newcomer, only shrugs, but Stan's mouth curls in a one-sided smile. "They're all still talking about *him*."

William winks at their newest employee. "Todd's the latest buzz, huh?"

"Not Todd. John."

William pulls the plug on his smile. "Tell me about it."

Stan doesn't need further encouragement. "John's working his way through Paradise, talking to people about crazy things. He keeps saying Casey sent him to tell us the truth about who we are. He says everything we see is make-believe, that Casey lives in the only reality."

"This is a story world," William whispers, remembering what John told him.

Stan snaps his fingers. "That's it, exactly. He says the author sent him to Paradise. Eden actually asked John if he *was* Casey."

"What'd he say to that?"

Stan's mouth twists with irritable humor. "He laughed."

William runs his fingertip around the rim of his drink can. "What do you think, Stan?"

The mechanic's features harden in disapproval. "I think the man's ridiculous. You know why he doesn't have a job? Because he thinks he's *supposed* to wander around like the village lunatic. He's one of those people who actually thinks Casey put us here for some specific reason."

William takes a swig of juice and then lowers the can. "What about his miracles?"

Stan snorts. "Cheap tricks. You know how video works, William. You've seen what we can do with machines. He may have access to some technology we don't know about."

"How'd he get it?"

"Who knows? Who knows why I have a knack for production and you have a gift for seeing the big picture? Things just happen, that's all."

Todd lifts his head from the wire he's been studying. "Um . . . I heard something yesterday."

Stan grins at his protégé. "What'd you hear?"

"Eden asked John if he'd pull a few gold coins out of thin air—she said she wanted to come over and play a few games."

William leans forward. "What'd he say?"

Todd shrugs. "He said Casey cares more about how we invest in each other than how much we spend in the machines."

William's thoughts shift to Raquel. She'll never get serious about John if he expects her to give up all that money can buy. She's been too spoiled since moving in with William.

He hasn't heard from her since he walked out last night. She hasn't called or come by the company. For all he knows, she's left the beach house.

The thought feels like a blow to the stomach.

He's about to ask Stan if he's seen her when the door swings open. Mac appears, his face red. "Boss, you'd better come."

William's internal systems snap to full alert. "What's wrong?"

"The diner—it's burning!"

Billowing smoke has alerted people up and down Main Street, but no one has yet found the courage to enter the burning building. Mac and William are the first to cross the road and throw open the door to Eden's Repast.

For a minute William feels as though he is walking into a black cloud, then the hot odor of burning hair invades his nostrils. He waves his arms, fanning smoke, and as the billows roll onto the street, he realizes the fire is confined to one corner of the diner.

Sky high with adrenaline, he pulls off his jacket and moves toward the flames. His eyes slam shut when they encounter the heat, and through painfully forced glimpses he sees that the fire has consumed one of the tall wooden chairs Eden kept by the bar . . . and the burning chair is *occupied*.

He and Mac bat at the blaze with their jackets, fighting through smoke as thick as taffy. Heat sears William's shirt as he slaps at the burning seat, the edge of the counter, and bits of flying paper whirling like butterflies through the superheated air.

Finally, they smother the flames. William drops his smoldering jacket, braces his hands against his knees, and bends to catch his breath.

Beneath the crackle and pop of dying embers, he hears a low moan that chills his spine. He looks up to discover that the shape in the chair is Eden. Her wrists have been bound to the armrests with chain pulled from the stanchions she uses to control the overflow lunch crowd.

He glances at Mac. As color drains from the guard's face, he makes a noise sounding like every curse spoken at once, a strangled epithet that ends only when he shoves the back of his hand to his mouth.

Despite the heat, William feels a coldness in his gut. A horrible chill races up his spine and freezes his scalp to his skull. "What happened here?" He pushes his damp hair from his forehead and looks at the crowd beyond the doorway. "Who can tell me what happened?"

Mac groans and points to the burned body in the seat, and William sees one of Eden's green eyes peering at him from a canvas of charred flesh.

The line that once was her lips parts slightly. "Robbed." The word emerges as a croak. "They took the money—"

"Don't talk." He thrusts his hands into his pockets so he won't involuntarily reach to touch her. "We'll call the ambulance for you; they'll know what to do—"

He hears the rustle of the crowd as someone pushes forward. William turns, hoping by some miracle to find EMT Jeb Carter behind him, but John stands inside the soot-covered doorway. He doesn't glance at William or Mac but walks straight to Eden as if he hasn't noticed she is Damaged Extensively, All Done and can no longer be counted among the living.

"Eden." Gently, John's hand lowers to the frizzled patch that was once shining pink hair. "Eden, do you know who I am?"

A tear slips from her single remaining eye. Slowly, she inclines her head. "You are"—her voice breaks in a horrible, rattling gurgle—"the one Casey sent."

The grim line of John's mouth relaxes. "Cease your struggling, dear one. When you open your eyes again, you'll find yourself in a new story. Casey will take care of you."

The black mask that is Eden's face turns toward John's palm; he caresses her charred cheek as a slow exhalation rises from her lips. William watches, blood pounding in his ears, as the light in her eye dims and goes out.

After an interval of silence, John removes his hand. "Two men," he says, all traces of softness wiped from his voice, "came here for silver and gold. They waited until the diner emptied and Hank went out for his break, then they tied Eden up and took everything she had. Before they left, they splashed her with oil and set her afire."

He speaks as one who knows, but how could he?

William grabs his arm. "Where were you when this happened?"

"It doesn't matter. I know."

"Because you were a witness?"

"Because Casey has given me knowledge of the future." John speaks in a cool voice, but his eyes blaze into William's as if *he* is personally responsible for this crime.

William draws a long, quivering breath, barely mastering the rage rattling within him. He is about to walk away, but John catches his arm and holds it in a vise grip.

"How can you look at this and not see the result of your wrong choices? Evil always results in misery. Those who do not turn from wrong cannot escape dire consequences."

William lifts his chin and meets John's hot gaze straight on. "Let me go."

He is surprised when John obeys. The man steps back, his chest rises and falls, then he speaks loudly enough for the crowd to hear: "Someone needs to find Hank and tell him what happened. And check out the casino—the two who did this are there."

Without another word, John walks away through the gathering, leaving William and Mac alone with a burnt horror.

Fifty-three

I snatch the ringing phone from its hook and bark into the receiver. "What?"

"Are you all right?" Concern underlines Carl's voice. "I've called three times."

I blow my hair from my forehead and look through the lace curtains, where the sun is warming the window ledge. "Sorry I ignored you. I was writing."

"Have you heard from Zack?"

"Only about every twenty minutes, until they called him in for some kind of group meeting. I was trying to take advantage of the quiet."

"Oh." My husband is silent for a minute, then he sighs. "I don't know how you can get anything done. I tried to teach this morning, but I don't think I made a lick of sense."

His comment stabs at me—should I feel guilty for being able to work when our family is in crisis?—then I remind myself of why I'm doing this. For Zack. Everything lately has been for Zack.

"I'm not sure I'm making much sense, either." I manage a laugh. "I'm just connecting the dots, following my outline."

"You want to take a break for lunch?"

I look outside again, where the sun exudes a warm invitation. "Can't. I have chapters to write and a class tonight."

He hesitates. "Are you *sure* you're okay?"

I want to laugh. How can I be okay when my son is locked in a mental ward, I am unable to help him, and my always-dependable husband has just admitted that he can barely function? And those are the *major* problems. I could also mention the chapters I'm struggling to write before class, my headaches with the insurance adjustor who can't understand how Zack managed to hit a tree several feet off the road, and my stomach, which hasn't stopped churning in forty-eight hours . . .

I force a smile into my voice. "I'm fine. But I need to get back to work."

"See you later, then."

I exhale a deep breath as I return the phone to its cradle. Who am I kidding? I might be connecting the dots, but this story, like my life, is overpowering my intentions. My outline might be intact, but the nice little pony of a story I wanted to parade before my son, my husband, and my students has become a raging, belligerent bull.

The ultimate Outline Person is clinging to her grand plan by her fingernails.

When I began, I wanted Zack to learn from William—I hoped my son would see himself in my protagonist's desire to go his own way and ignore the creator's wishes. But lately, as I struggle to balance the real world with the one I have created, I find *myself* identifying with my stubborn main character.

How many times in the last few days have I looked toward heaven and demanded to know why I've been dealt such a difficult hand? Why did *my* son inherit a weak will, alcoholic genes, or whatever else might be causing his problems? We successfully raised two children, so why does this third child make me feel like a parental fraud?

I don't know. I don't understand. And I don't *like* not knowing and not understanding. I want details to be spelled out; I want the boundaries of my life path painted in fluorescent orange with easy-to-read road signs along the way.

I can't help thinking that God must be looking down on me and shaking his head. "Maybe I need one of those electric shock collars," I whisper, reaching for the next note card in my stack. "You could zap me before I take a misstep."

The heavens don't rumble in response, though the back of my neck tingles in psychosomatic sympathy.

I read my penciled scribbles on the card. In the next scene, according to my outline, William confronts John and the truth that he brings—truths I will soon place in his mouth.

But I can't help feeling there are bigger truths to be discovered, realizations beyond my present comprehension. There *must* be. Because when I consider the story of my troubled family, I can't begin to imagine a happy ending.

Fifty-four

William asks Mac and Dodge to search the casino players when he returns from the diner. They bring him two men from Oceanside—both have pockets full of silver coins; both smell of oil and smoke. But neither will admit to the crime. Without an eyewitness, what can William do? People always bring coins to the casino, and Eden's patrons always smell of grease and smoke.

He tells the pair to leave Paradise and never return; they laugh as Mac takes them by the arm and drags them to the street.

If those two *are* guilty, how can William be sure John didn't put the idea in their heads? He knew far too much, and though many people in Paradise have special gifts, no one has yet been able to foretell the future.

William punches the transmit button of his walkie-talkie. "Dodge— find John, will you, and bring him to my office. I'd like to have a word with him."

"Right away, Mr. Case."

While Dodge searches for the town imbecile, William leans back and lets his gaze drift to the painted eye above the door. He can't deny that life in Paradise is not what it was, but a sepia haze coats his memory of those early weeks. His biggest problem in those days was learning how to dress himself and cull the proper words from the stream of language in his head.

He startles as someone knocks. "Yes?"

Amber opens the door. "Dodge found the man you want, Mr. Case. He says he's been waiting to speak to you."

"Send him in, then."

John is smiling when he enters.

William frowns. "I can't imagine why you're feeling so pleased with yourself."

John's smile deepens. "I wasn't thinking of myself, William—I was thinking of you."

"You find me *funny*?"

"I find humor in this situation—you, commanding me to your presence, when Casey's is the only voice I obey. Still, I welcome this opportunity to talk."

Without asking William's permission, he lowers himself into the guest chair.

William decides to ignore the man's breach of manners. "I want to know," he begins, "what role you played in the fire. We found the two men you mentioned."

John's brow rises. "And?"

"They denied everything. With no proof, we kicked them out of the casino and told them they weren't welcome in Paradise."

The corner of John's mouth twists. "A half measure at best. Paradise will be fully restored only when evil is banished from human hearts."

William clenches his fist, feeling as though he's been hit in the stomach. An accusatory barb underlines John's words, stinging something deep in William's heart.

"We've never had any need to police our citizens," William says, his voice taut. "Perhaps we should reconsider."

"Anyone can find fault in others. But who among you has remained pure? Certainly not you, Ambassador."

William ignores the insult. "Ross Ramirez is never shy about pointing out our failures. Maybe we should ask him."

John's expression softens into one of fond reminiscence. "Ross Ramirez no longer lives in Paradise."

William bears no love for the old man, but his unease swells into alarm. "Is he dead?"

A secretive smile curves John's mouth. "For want of a better expression, you could say Casey wrote him out of the story."

"You are a lunatic! You killed him *and* Eden—"

"I didn't kill either of them." John studies William, his eyes dark and unfathomable. "Casey has other plans for them. But you wouldn't understand."

He's crazy, insane, nuttier than a pecan tree, but he's also rational, calm, and far too knowledgeable to be the village idiot.

Who is this man?

In an attempt to mask his inner turmoil, William picks up a pencil and idly taps it on the desk. "I don't know why you insist on blaming me for all the town's trouble."

"You entered the locked room when you knew it was forbidden."

"If I hadn't entered the room, someone else would have."

"Only if Casey had written the story that way. As it is, *you* broke the rules."

William responds to his ludicrous statement with a short bark of laughter. "You think I'm responsible for all this mess? Forget it. I'm not going to take the fall for that one. I don't know how someone so great and invincible could do such a horrible thing, but if Casey created that video villain, then *Casey* created evil."

Shadows fill John's eyes. He rubs the back of his neck and then spreads his hand in a broad gesture. "I don't know if you can under-stand—"

"Try me."

"—but I'll attempt to explain. First, evil is not an entity; it is a result. The author has a good plan in mind for you, but the creator can use anything—even the results ensuing from your bad choices—to accomplish a purpose. You don't play with knives because you could injure yourself if you're careless. In the same way, it is not good for you to toy with evil or encourage others to do so. But because the author sees the big picture, evil can be an effective tool in the cre-ator's hands."

"If Casey has my life planned out," William answers, keeping his voice light, "I hope my latter days are as pleasant as my first. I'd like to retire with Raquel in a mansion on the beach—unless, of course, the author wants to set me up with some other beautiful woman."

"The character does not dictate to the author. The author may lis-ten to his characters, but he already knows the ending to the story."

William leans toward his guest. "Do you know the ending of *this* story?"

"I can't say."

"You *can't* say, or you *won't* say?"

John smiles. "Casey always works with a detailed outline. You can rest in that."

"Why should I believe anything you say? I've never heard such nonsense."

"Because I'm giving you the truth . . . and because Casey has told me all about you. The author witnessed your struggle and watched as you surrendered your soul to the magician. Casey knew you, taught you, and loved you before you took your first breath."

William's mouth goes dry as John's voice stirs a memory within him. He is swimming in a sea of light while someone whispers his name . . . No, this is only déjà vu, the memory of a long-buried dream. This man knows things he shouldn't know, but he has been talking to Raquel and Ramirez. Bottom line, he is no more and no better than William.

John speaks again before William can protest. "When you broke Casey's law, you surrendered your innocence along with your soul. But your soul is precious to Casey because you were created to be an example."

"Of what? Failure?"

"A changed life. But before you can change, you must confront the thing you fear. That's why I'm here. I'm willing to go with you."

For an instant William is puzzled, then gooseflesh pebbles the skin of his arms. "You want to face the magician?"

"Why should I be afraid of another story character? Let's go."

He rises in one fluid motion, and for an instant William is too stunned to react. He has dreaded the locked room ever since the night circumstances peeled back the magician's friendly veneer and revealed the violent cruelty underneath.

John holds out his hand. "Come."

William stands, but he has to protest. "You don't know what's in there."

"Yes, I do."

"But you've no experience with him. He's ruthless, that one. He tricks you into risking more than you can afford."

John cocks his head toward the game room. "Isn't that what *you* do?"

Truth slams into William with the force of a fist. In the bright light of John's words, he sees himself as a grinning magician, complete with flashing lights, cheerful music, and a beguiling smile.

John nods slowly. "The magician holds no surprises for me."
He stands there, waiting, until William opens the door.

Fifty-five

My fingers are trembling when I drop the next scene card. This section
is so important; every word must carry my exact intention.

If ever I needed to capture *le mot juste*, today's the day.

I want my son to understand that I don't think of him as evil. He's
made bad choices, he has brought pain and suffering to our family, but
Carl and I would endure anything to save Zack's life. This is what love
demands and parenting requires.

Our son, like William, is not beyond redemption. God is not out to
punish him, nor are we.

We only want to love our prickly, hardheaded Zack. But rebellion
has consequences, and forgiveness comes at a price. A story without
those elements would be incomplete.

God, help me get it right.

I snatch a deep breath and begin to type.

Fifty-six

The employee break room is empty; their pale reflections gleam like
ghosts in the vending machines as John and William pass. William pulls
the waste bin away from the door of the forbidden room, padlocked
once again.

He snorts at the sight of the lock. A lot of good it has done—it didn't stop Raquel, and nothing has stopped the spread of evil throughout the town.

Without a word, John touches the lock's chrome hasp. It clicks and falls open.

William catches his breath. Another miracle? Or another trick?

He presses on the door. It swings open, revealing the familiar block wall and the flashing lights of the silent machine. He enters and peers around the corner, half-afraid he'll discover the magician standing before him in ghastly greasepainted flesh. But no, the trickster is still confined to the screen, still smiling and winking as William and John approach.

The imp's painted grin fades when his electronic gaze swivels toward John. "Who's this?" he asks, his tone low and seductive. "Another guest coming to bet his life?"

"He's called John." William waits to see if the name will register. "He's new—and he says he's not afraid of you."

The magician's mouth curves in the contemptuous smile of a pampered house cat. "How unwise."

"Wisdom," John says, "comes from Casey. Those who turn to you are the real fools in this story."

The magician purses his lips in a mocking expression of alarm. "Oh, I'm so frightened!" His face swivels closer until his slitted eyes dominate the screen. "I know who you represent, John, and I know why you've come. Ah, how vulnerable are those who exist only in thin story flesh! You think you have authority, but your creator has left you defenseless." His voice drops to a gravelly croak. "I reign over this room; you have no power here."

John smiles like a teacher amused by the antics of a student. "You think not?"

"I know." A twinkle sparkles in the animated eye. "I know your plan will not succeed. The people in Paradise have tasted my forbidden fruit, and they love it. They *crave* it. They would rather stand in that game room and feed silver coins into a machine than live out the stifling, tiresome plots Casey designed for them."

John's eyes flash. "How do you know they are not following Casey's plot even now?"

The animated eyes narrow. "If that's true, they are nothing but puppets."

"They are not! Consider William—since the beginning he has acted of his own volition."

"He is a slave to Casey's plot! The author decreed he would enter this room!"

"Yes, but he freely chose to play your game. I have been sent to release him from the terms of your agreement."

"His soul is mine; so is his life! I gave him what he wanted, I fulfilled his fantasies—"

"You enticed him from his first love; you blinded him to his true purpose. You have poisoned his mind, body, and soul."

William rakes his hands through his hair as their words clash and cut and compete. Through the din he can't help feeling he is missing something elemental—

"Stop! I am not a slave!"

His words echo in a sudden silence. The magician's mouth curves into a smirk, and John turns to look at him. "What are you, then?"

William summons every ounce of dignity he can muster. "I am the owner and operator of the Paradise Casino. I am Ambassador William Case."

"As the ambassador, who do you represent?"

"The people of Paradise."

"And *to whom* do you represent those people?"

The question startles, but after a moment's hesitation, he comes up with an answer: "The rest of the world, of course."

The ghost of a smile touches John's lips with ruefulness. "You have it backward, William. You are the ambassador, but you are to represent the people of Paradise before Casey. And yes, you are a man, but you are not independent."

"I certainly am. I can do anything I want."

"Can you?" John's eyes, alight with speculation, bore into him. "Can you count the morning stars or add another moon to the Paradise sky? Can you cross the sea on the breath of the morning or bring Eden back by the power of your word? You *are* a man, William, but you are a character in the author's story. As a character, your independence ends at the margin of the page."

William listens through a vague sense of unreality while the magician rocks with laughter, uttering spasmodic squeaks as tears run down his painted face. When his mirth finally dies away, he wipes dark smears from his cheeks and looks at John with something like appreciation in his eyes.

"They are revolting creatures, focusing on their dreary little lives with no appreciation for Casey's fascinating scheme. Go ahead with the plan, but know this—you cannot destroy me."

Ignoring the taunting fiend, John steps past William and kneels at the side of the machine. He has moved beyond the magician's range of vision, but that doesn't prevent the video maniac from continuing his tirade: "I have spread like a virus; I have infected everyone in this place. As long as choice remains, you cannot—"

The red and yellow lights flicker and fade; the magician vanishes as the screen goes black. John stands with the power cord in his hand.

William can't believe what he's seeing. "How did you—?"

"Unplugged." John yanks at the opposite end, straining to separate the cord from the machine. The heavy black length resists, appearing to stretch in his grip; then he gives the cord a quick jerk and the cord snaps free.

He turns and brings the frayed end to within two inches of William's eyes. William expects him to gloat—he feels like shouting himself—but John's eyes have become somber and shadowed.

In that instant William realizes the world beyond this room has changed. A thick silence has replaced the background noise; the game room's warbles and bells and sirens have been swallowed by a dread stillness. The cacophony of the casino, the pulse of his life, has vanished, while an awful vacuum has taken its place.

"What the—" He glances toward the door, half-expecting to find that they've been transported beyond Paradise. "What did you do? Did you destroy him?"

John's dark eyes gleam with a sheen of purpose. "I suppose you could say we've increased the pace of the plot."

Again he's speaking nonsense, but William doesn't have time to solve his riddle. They are definitely still in the casino, and when machines fail in the midst of play, people get upset about the coins they've lost.

The odd silence has evaporated by the time William strides into the game room. The machines remain quiet and dark, but the irritable and restless players are buzzing like a swarm. Many are jerking on the levers; others are beating on the cabinets and slamming the video screens. One woman is shrieking at *Hilarious Hank*, punctuating her words with well-aimed kicks, while across the aisle a man ends a blizzard of curses by spitting at *Wondrous Raquel*.

Where are the security guards?

William ducks into the office, where the new receptionist is trembling behind her desk. "Amber—have you seen Mac and Dodge?"

She shakes her head in a barely discernable gesture. "What's going on out there? It sounds . . . scary."

He grimaces as something slams against the office wall—a machine, judging from the heft and the sound of breaking glass.

"It'll be all right," he tells her. "But grab my radio and see if you can raise Dodge and Mac."

He slips back through the swinging door and rises on tiptoe to look above the melee. Neither security guard is in his usual position, but as he peers down the center aisle, he sees a flash of green and remembers that Dodge was wearing a green ball cap when he came to work.

Ignoring the commotion, William squirms through the rampaging crowd. He doesn't know what the guards are doing, but they need to coordinate their efforts if they're to control this situation.

A shock runs through him when he finally reaches Dodge. To the right of *Big Bertha*, Mac lies on the carpet. Dodge kneels beside him, his thick fingers probing for a pulse. Mac's eyes are closed, his face pale beneath the brim of his cap.

William winces at the sound of shattering glass. "What happened?"

Blood from a wound in Dodge's forehead has painted his visage into a glistening mask. "Someone cut me," he says, stating the obvious. "But I think some guy used somethin' heavy on Mac."

With the roar of the mob at his back, William strains to help Dodge turn Mac onto his side. He sees no sign of injury until Dodge tugs on his partner's cap. With a detachment that will horrify him later, William notices that only the hat has held Mac's brains in place.

Another friend of his is DEAD.

William wipes his mouth with the back of his hand as Dodge bellows in despair. His throat aches, but what could he have done to stop this?

He doesn't understand why power isn't flowing to the game room. Disconnecting the magician's machine shouldn't have anything to do with these games unless . . . Could they somehow be connected? This anger, the malevolence in these contorted faces, certainly *feels* like the magician's doing.

So John didn't destroy him. He only ticked the painted devil off.

"Pull Mac out of the way," William tells Dodge, "while I try to reason with these people."

A cold lump in his stomach sprouts chilly tendrils of apprehension as he stands.

His customers are not happy.

From across the room, Amber spots him. "Mr. Case," she calls, her high voice slicing cleanly through the din. "What do you want me to *do*?"

A red-haired woman stops beating a machine to focus on William. "*You* run this place?"

Like blood out of a wound, silence wells and flows into the game room. His face burns from the pressure of dozens of flaming eyes.

A man slaps a short club against his palm and stalks toward William. "What kind of racket are you running?"

William crosses his arms. "It's no racket. I'm sorry it took me awhile to get out here, but—"

"I want my money!" The feral redhead advances, looking as though she could claw out his eyes with pleasure.

"You'll get your money, but it'll take us awhile to restore power and check the status of the machines."

"I want my money *now*!"

William opens his mouth to reply, but they are hurling complaints like stones, their narrow eyes drilling into him.

"What's the meaning of this?"

"You cheat! I had five pieces of silver in that machine, and now it's dead!"

He shouts to make himself heard. "I'll fix everything if you will calm down!" He throws up his arm and glances around, hoping to find an escape route. To his right, Dodge has blocked the way with Mac's body; if he moves left, he'll be caught in a corner.

One glance at Dodge tells William he can't count on the security guard. The big man is squatting on the floor with his fingers laced together, his face shiny with blood and tears. Something inside him has snapped.

With terrible suddenness, William realizes he can't escape. These people don't want their money refunded; they want every coin in the cash box and every sliver of silver and gold in the machines. They have tasted blood and mayhem. They won't be satisfied until they have taken everything.

He looks toward the door at the back. Amber has disappeared, and John is nowhere in sight. The breaker box, which might allow him to restore power to the game room, is located in the factory, but the odds of his reaching it are as slim as a blade.

He takes a half step to the right as the crowd surges forward. Maybe he can distract them, let them have the money in the machines.

"People—" He holds up his hands, but the man in front of him isn't in the mood for explanations.

"Fifty gold ones," he yells, stepping toward William with his club raised. "I was *this far* from winning the jackpot, so that's what you owe me, you bum."

"Sir, if you'll wait a moment, I'll try to—"

Not waiting to hear his offer, the man slams the blackjack against William's skull. The blow sends a shower of lights sparking through his head like a cloud of fireflies. Color runs out of the room as the roar of the crowd fades, but his eyes focus in time to see the club rise again.

He lifts his hand and tries to protest, but his tongue refuses to cooperate. A fist comes out of nowhere and smacks his chin, cracking his head against the wall. He tastes blood as a cloud obscures his vision and other blows land at his gut, his chest, his ear. His nerve endings snap at each other, the room flickers like a faulty lightbulb, and William knows he is going to die. This is what the magician wanted, his soul and his life. He has exacted a heavy price for his temporary satisfaction.

The house always wins.

William folds gently at the knees and slides down the wall, resigned to paying for his folly. His body sings with pain as some still-functioning part of his brain registers three sharp kicks, the slamming of another fist against the side of his head, and the dazzling agony of a woman's stiletto heel grinding into the back of his hand.

His last breaths will be heavy with the smells of sweat and fury; his last sight will be this cursed game room. He is about to curl up and close his eyes, but through a tangle of knees and feet, he glimpses purposeful movement in a sea of confusion.

Somehow he struggles to his knees. Fending off blows, he widens his eyes and sees John moving amid the crowd with the hard grace of a man in total control. Without saying a word, the newcomer strides into the thick of the maelstrom and thrusts the broken power cord into the air like a hard-won trophy.

William's not sure who notices John first—perhaps the red-haired wildcat. But a woman calls, "Look—*that* guy ripped out the power!" And like a rippling wave, all heads swivel in John's direction. These people cannot possibly understand what happened in the forbidden room, but with fearful clarity William realizes John has stepped forward to save his miserable life.

With white-hot defiance the crowd meets the silent challenge.

"Look! *He* did it!"

"Who does he think he is, coming here to ruin our fun?"

"What'd he do, cut the cord?"

"I heard he had something to do with the fire at the diner."

"He doesn't belong in Paradise!"

William rises in protest, but the fickle crowd has forgotten about him. They rush at John, fists and feet and arms pummeling his slender frame. William squints around the room, hoping to spot a sympathetic face, but Dodge is still bent over Mac, and Amber has fled.

William can do nothing to help.

Grief wells in him, black and cold, as the atmosphere roils with rage.

The memory of the magician's voice edges his teeth: *Ah, how vulnerable are those who exist only in thin story flesh!*

Can John actually believe Casey sent him to Paradise for *this*? He may be a misguided newcomer, but he's brave, and now he is realizing how foolish it is to cling to Casey's principles in the face of full-throated evil.

Like a useless sack of skin, William listens to the rhythmic *thump* of kicks and blows and shouts. With every nerve tense and quivering, he eyes the door beyond Mac's body. He could try to run out and fetch Hank from the diner, but what could the two of them do to stop this?

In front of him, the mob seethes and shifts like a single-minded organism. Someone pushes William, and he topples forward, landing on his hands and knees before *Big Bertha*. By the time he pulls up on the machine, the mob has migrated toward the entrance, dragging John with it.

Dazed and shaken, William staggers to the doorway and watches as they prop the bruised and bloody newcomer against one of the bed-raggled trees. From where William stands, John seems barely conscious. His shirt is torn, his face a bloody canvas turned toward the dark clouds swirling overhead. His arms hang limply from his torso, while sweat and blood soak the hair of his chest and stain his ravaged clothing.

Oblivious to the coming storm, members of the mob throw rocks, dirt clods, and bricks, tearing up the sidewalk in their eagerness to do him damage. Their violence has escalated beyond reason; this is something William has never seen and doesn't understand.

Limping to the edge of the surging chaos, he draws near enough to see John's clamped jaw. The man is breathing hard through his nose with a faint whistling sound; then he looks up and finds . . . William.

Unspoken pain lives and glows in John's eyes, but something else flickers there too. A sense of déjà vu sweeps in, surrounding and warming and comforting William in the midst of carnage.

The long-repressed memory of his beginning passes through William like an unwelcome chill. He didn't enter Paradise through his own power; the one he thought of as *the creator* provided even the gift of language. Casey filled his brain with musical words, placed him in an apartment, and provided the clothing he would need. Casey prepared a job for him, a place, and a reason for his existence . . . as an author would. Because only the author would have the necessary authority.

Cold, clear reality sweeps over William in a terrible wave, one so powerful he nearly crumples to his knees. He can't fall, though, because he can't tear his eyes from John's. The newcomer has saved his life, and William wants to tell him he's grateful and so desperately sorry for the corrupted state of the world he entered.

Either his expression sends a private message or John reads William's thoughts; because as William gazes on him with gratitude and despair, John acknowledges those feelings with the smallest softening of his eyes . . . before his head falls forward.

William spins around, seeking any help he can find, and discovers that little remains of his casino. Through broken windows and ragged blinds, he sees machines tipped and turned like shells tumbled by the tide. Smashed video screens stare at him like lifeless eyes; shards of glass spangle the carpet.

But Amber may still be inside. And Stan. They can call for help; maybe they can summon the Oceanside police—

The thought has no sooner formed than a voice rises above the clamor. "To the cliffs!" someone shouts. "Let's throw him off!"

The crowd roars in approval.

In the hollow of William's back, a single drop of sweat traces the track of his spine. He was created to be the ambassador, they assured him. The envoy. The representative.

So he has to do something before Paradise is completely consumed by violence.

William limps to the back parking lot, slides into his car, and crosses the southern end of the road. Ignoring the headache blazing a trail behind his ear, he crunches the gears as the car tears its way through knee-high grass and weeds. He has to reach the cliffs before the mob; he has to stand in a spot where they can see and hear him before they go too far.

He sets out on a parallel track and glances in the rearview mirror. He can see the crowd advancing, John's body riding on their uplifted hands like a straw man. William waits until he is several yards ahead, then cuts toward the road and pushes northward, finally pulling off at the graveled spot where he recently parked with Amber.

Carried by the wind, the sound of the uproar fills his ears. He clambers onto the hood and ignores the pain cresting inside him like a wave. As he balances on the thin metal, his stomach drops and the empty place fills with a frightening hollowness.

What if they don't listen? They didn't listen to him at the casino. More than half of these people are from outside Paradise; they don't know Casey. They don't know he's the ambassador, and they definitely won't care.

How can he convince them he is to blame for the corruption of Paradise?

"Hey!" When the mob is within shouting distance, he waves his arms to snag their attention. "Listen to me!"

His hoarse voice cannot penetrate the fog of violence. The throng continues on its restless way, a sea of voices ragged with fury.

"Listen to me!" When no one answers, he climbs back into the car and honks the horn. When two long blasts fail to penetrate the swarm's collective consciousness, he lays on the horn for a full minute.

He might as well be a buzzing mosquito.

He is sitting in silence, his head against the steering wheel, when another car pulls up. Raquel spills out the passenger door, her eyes wide. "William! You've got to do something!"

With an effort, he raises his head. "What would you have me do?"

"Stop them!"

"I've tried."

"Good grief!" Her hand rises to her lips. "What happened to you?"

With his stiletto-bloodied hand, he points to the horde. "*They* happened to me."

He wants her to caress his swollen face, but she runs after the mob, her skirt flying in the wind.

Stan steps out of the driver's side of the vehicle and strolls toward him, his hands in his pockets and his eyes narrowed into slits. "So—they finally decided to do him in."

How can he be so nonchalant? William pushes hair out of his

swollen eyes and tries to wrap words around his regrets. "He saved my life. I tried to stop them."

"Why?" Stan's voice is laced with unmistakable venom. "It had to come to this, you know. The battle is always between the master and the slaves. Casey wants to control us; we want to be free. John allied himself with the wrong side."

William squints as one cold and lucid thought strikes: Stan resents Casey. Which means that despite his cynicism and claims to the contrary, *Stan knows the creator exists.*

William's right-hand man leans against the car, his mouth curving in a mirthless smile. "You chose freedom when you went into the forbidden room. As the ambassador, you brought freedom to all of us. This"—he gestures to the mob in the distance—"is only people expressing their right to do as they please."

William can't speak. He is a motionless lump of guilt watching the pack. Occasionally he catches a glimpse of Raquel's frantic waving. She is begging them to stop, pleading with them to calm down, but she'll be even less effective than he's been.

He focuses on the churning mob at the edge of the cliff. If chaos is the result of man's freedom, he would rather serve Casey.

Without a word to Stan, William pulls his aching body out of the car and hobbles after the others.

The effort is almost more than he can bear. With each step a shaft of blinding agony crackles behind his eyes; his lungs complain with every breath. He gasps as a sharp pain shoots from the inside of his right foot all the way up his leg. The muscles of his calves and thighs burn with exertion, his teeth are clenched hard enough to make his jaw muscles quiver.

Time slows and seconds stretch themselves thin as he hobbles forward, his nerves tightened to the breaking point. John's body flaps like a broken thing as they jostle him up and down, down and up. They are toying with him, taunting him, and at one point William sees John lift his head as if he wants to speak, but no one is listening. *William* would listen, and he would *make* them listen; but before he can command their attention, they launch John into the air. The man floats against the backdrop of gray sky for a moment, then his body spins and drops out of sight, tossed away like garbage, cast out of Paradise.

Silence, thick as wool, wraps itself around the black granite ridge. William screams and hears nothing, for even the pounding of his pulse has been muffled by the certainty that they have killed the one person on earth who could convince others to restore Paradise.

But the mob did not act alone.

He stumbles to a stop and shudders as his customers creep to vantage points where they can safely peer over the edge and stare at the broken man on the rocks below. The empty air above the sea vibrates; the silence fills with dread. The bravado that fueled the crowd dribbles from furious faces and clenched fists.

William finds Raquel weeping by the path that leads to Lookout Ledge. With his hand on her trembling shoulder, he peers into the chasm and sees John splayed over the rocks protruding from the dark, hungry water.

"By morning," he hears someone whisper, "the tide'll carry him away."

Tears brim behind William's eyes and swim in his head. He tried to save John, but as in everything else he's attempted, he failed.

What a sorry representative he is.

The rough wind scrapes his cheek as he considers the vast sea beyond Paradise. He lifts his gaze to the leaden sky. *Why darkness and death? If you could write any kind of story you wanted, why did you choose this?*

"William?" Raquel looks at him through tear-clogged lashes.

He nods because he can't trust himself to speak.

"Do you think . . . Does this mean Casey is finished with us?"

The question catches him off guard. "I . . . I don't know."

If he were Casey, he'd walk away. Patience has its limits, and people who murder an emissary from the creator don't deserve a second chance.

But John said the creator had a detailed outline . . . and the story would have a good ending. William, he said, had been created to be an example of a changed life.

Not certain what that means, he reaches for Raquel's hand. "John," he begins, his voice clotting, "believed Casey has a good plan for us."

The corner of her mouth twists. "After *this*?"

William tilts his head. "I don't know."

As much as he wants to believe all John said, the magician still prevails in Paradise—because he took John's life as easily as he took Marilyn's and Eden's and Mac's.

One day, he'll take William's and Raquel's. And they will be powerless against him.

William squeezes Raquel's hand. "For now, I think we'd better concentrate on living in the world we've made. Paradise is ruined . . . like us."

She stands and slips into the space under his arm. Together they turn and look at their fellow citizens. The assembly is scattering, their faces pale and drawn as they scurry for shelter from the approaching storm. The murderous mob has dwindled to a handful of pitiful people who run from the angry sky with fear-filled faces.

William leans on Rocky as they make their way across the stony ground. "We could go down," she says. "I don't know how we'd get farther than the ledge, but we could try to retrieve his body. Maybe we could use ropes."

"It'd be impossible. There are no footholds below the lookout."

"But we can't leave him there!"

"We have no choice."

Her eyes well with hurt, but she does not protest again as she helps him to the car.

Fifty-seven

I lift my fingers from the keyboard, hang my head, and let my arms fall into my lap. Tears roll down my cheeks, trails of pain that have as much to do with my life as with my story.

As I wrote of William's guilt about his fallen world, I couldn't help but think of my own failures. I didn't raise Zack in a Christian home. My grandchildren are learning how to sing "Jesus Loves Me" and "Deep and Wide," but I didn't teach those songs to Zack because no one taught them to me.

I'd heard about God and Jesus, of course—it's hard to be an American without hearing the gospel message at some point. But until my sister-in-law accepted Christ and demonstrated that breast cancer and death could not diminish a believer's joy, I had no idea faith could transform every aspect of a human life.

Last summer I listened in absolute awe as three-year-old Glynn asked Shannon where clouds come from. If Zack had asked me that question at Glynn's age, I've have scurried to the encyclopedia to research condensation and rain. Shannon simply said that God had designed a wonderful system that sent rain from the clouds to the sea and up again.

What more does a three-year-old need to know?

I didn't teach Zack anything about God when his heart was receptive and innocent. Now, like William, I am living in a world of my own making, suffering the consequences of what I've done . . . and what I didn't do.

The Author of Life is leading me through a painful plot, and like William, I'm ready to despair.

The phone rings; Zack is calling again. He wants to know if he can come home; again I tell him the decision rests with the doctor. I don't dare make promises I can't keep, but neither do I want to discourage him.

After hanging up, I tackle the other items on my to-do list. From repeated phone calls to the charge nurse, I know the staff psychiatrist has given only perfunctory attention to my son. Zack was admitted on a weekend, after all, and though on Saturday a therapist called to ask for Zack's medical history, no one else has volunteered even a scrap of information without my asking for it.

I call Diana Sheldon's office again, but her secretary tells me she's been in Nashville and is not expected back until early evening.

My frustration grows with each passing minute. I pull out the yellow pages and am looking for lawyers when the phone rings again. Zack's voice is heavy with relief when he asks if I can pick him up.

"Did the doctor say you can come home?"

"Yeah."

"I'll be right there."

An hour later, Zack and I are walking from the garage into the kitchen. I have attempted to make conversation as though nothing has happened, but Zack remains quiet. He walks through the kitchen and into the foyer, looking around as if he's never seen the place before. "It's good to be home." He caresses the stair rail as he climbs the steps. "So good to be back."

I ask Zack if he's hungry; he says no. "All I want to do is sleep," he calls over the balcony railing. "I think I could sleep for a week."

And so I let him rest, though I go upstairs at six and gently push on his door. My overactive imagination has already supplied me with a scenario where I step into his room and find him dead on the bed, but Zack is definitely sleeping when I check on him. I can hear his deep, regular breaths from the doorway.

When Carl comes home, flushed and worried, I tell him Zack is sleeping, but still he goes upstairs. Like me, he stands in the doorway and examines our sleeping son; then he joins me in the kitchen.

"I couldn't stand the thought of him in there," he confesses, meeting my gaze. "I know we tried to act like it was no big deal, but when I thought of him crying himself to sleep in that place—"

I squeeze his hand. "I know." I slide the sheet of discharge instructions across the counter. "They have given us prescriptions and made two appointments for us—one with a psychologist, one with a psychiatrist."

"Good grief." Carl looks at the list of drugs. "He needs all these?"

"I don't know—I suppose we can ask the doctors. I'm still waiting to hear from Diana Sheldon. If these doctors aren't good, I'm going to cancel and get Zack in to see whoever she recommends."

I glance at the clock, hating that it's Monday and I have a class. "Do you think I should cancel? I haven't missed a class yet."

"He's asleep, Jordy. You'll do more good at the college than you will haunting the upstairs hallway. Go on. Have a good time with your students."

So I go to my office and gather a stack of just-printed pages from my desk. As I stuff the new chapters into my briefcase, I remember Ian

Morley and his father. I wonder if Ian's father has been released—and if it'd be polite for me to ask about him.

After reading the latest chapters to my class, we take some time to talk about dramatic structure and character arcs. "Your character must change and grow over the course of the novel," I tell my students as they scribble on notebooks and legal pads. "William, for instance, has gone from being an innocent to . . . what, Mike?"

Michael Zappariello chews on the end of his pencil. "He seems awfully defeated, if you ask me."

"All right—what has made him feel defeated?"

I cringe when my cell phone begins to dance in my purse. "Sorry," I tell my class, "but I'm expecting an important call. Do you mind if I catch this?"

Apparently they don't, because almost all of them interpret the interruption as permission to socialize with their neighbors. Grateful for their willingness to ignore my breach of manners, I pull my phone from my purse. "Hello?"

"Jordan? It's Diana Sheldon."

"Thank goodness." I ask if she'll be available to talk in half an hour; after a moment's hesitation, she says yes. "But I won't be in my office. Let me give you another number."

I grab a pen and jot down the information she gives me. "I'll call you soon," I promise. "Thanks so much."

As I drop my phone back into my purse, my gaze passes over Ian Morley. As usual, he sits against the wall, but tonight he seems strangely subdued. He hasn't made a single crack or comment. Neither did he hand in an assignment.

If he's thinking about his father, I can't blame him for feeling melancholy.

I clap to regain my class's attention. "I'm giving you an unexpected treat," I tell them, smiling. "I'm letting you go early tonight so you can get started on your next assignment. I want each of you to draw an arc, a sweeping half circle, and show me how your protagonist will change throughout the course of the story. Remember—by the time the story ends, he or she will either be in a different place or be a different person. Any questions?"

There are none. Kristal Palma is about to fall out of her chair, she's so eager to leave, and Mike Zappariello has already edged toward the door. "Until Wednesday, then. Good night."

I'm eager to talk to Dr. Sheldon, but that's not the only reason I call from my car. I could have called from home, but Zack is there, and Carl . . . though I'm not sure why I wouldn't want my husband to overhear this conversation.

"Diana?"

"Jordan! How are you? You sounded worried when you called."

"I am." I have to stop when an unexpected bolus of emotion rises in my throat. "It's—it's my—"

"Take your time," Diana says, her voice low and soothing. "I'm not in a hurry."

"It's my son, Zack. He spent the weekend in a mental hospital. He told a police officer that he'd tried to kill himself in a car accident."

The words fall like bricks, and I feel ten pounds lighter for having said them.

Diana makes a comforting clucking noise. "No wonder you're upset. How's he doing now?"

"He's at home, asleep. He said he was tired, but I think he's still hung over from all the drugs they gave him."

"Hmm. Hospitals do tend to overmedicate patients, especially after their arrival. Keeps things quiet on the ward."

"He looked awful in that place. We visited him Saturday and Sunday, and it was all I could do not to break him out of there. Of course, we tried to act calm, but it broke my heart to see him. He was *crying*, Diana, and this is a twenty-one-year-old who practically never cries. Not until recently, anyway."

"What's happened recently?"

"Well . . . he's an alcoholic and he's been drinking. Once I found him by our front gate; apparently some of his so-called friends dropped him off because he was too drunk to drive home. It's a wonder a car didn't hit him."

"Has he been treated for alcoholism?"

"He goes to AA meetings when he remembers—and yes, once the court ordered him into rehab. Thirty days."

"DUIs?"

"Three—two here, one in Utah."

I breathe a silent sigh when she doesn't respond with outraged horror.

"Is he on any other kinds of drugs?"

"We found Xanax pills under his mattress, and sometimes I would swear he's high on something. He talks really fast, like his words are strung together. He's chipper at those times, sort of goofy. He buzzes around the house and then takes off. Later he'll come home drunk; then he crashes and sleeps for days."

"He sleeps for *days*?"

I nod before I remember she can't see me. "Yes. I've never seen anyone with that deep a hangover, but maybe it's the combination of drugs and alcohol."

"Xanax is not a stimulant." Her voice is low, as if she's talking to herself. "Neither is alcohol."

I rake my hands through my hair and look at the moon, high above the parking lot. "I know he needs help, but we've tried everything we can think of and nothing has worked. We sent him to a counselor, but that guy didn't help at all. The hospital wasn't going to release him until we made follow-up appointments with a psychologist, so that's why I called you. I was hoping you could give us the name of a really good shrink."

Please, Lord, let her know someone who can help us . . .

For a moment I hear nothing, then she clears her throat. "Your son is home now?"

"Yes."

"So the hospital hooked you up with someone?"

"Two people, actually." I close my eyes, trying to remember the names on the discharge form. "Doctors Hodde and Kraus—one's a psychologist, one's a psychiatrist."

"They're good. They're in the same practice, so they'll work together. I don't think you could go wrong with those two."

I exhale in relief. "Thank you."

I'm thinking Diana needs to rush off, but she continues.

"Do you mind if I ask you a few questions about Zack?"

"No, not at all. I'm grateful for any help you can give."

"All right. Listen to the question and reply as best you can. Don't stop to analyze; don't question my motives. Just give me an off-the-cuff answer, okay?"

I smile because she's speaking in her radio voice. "You're the doctor."

"That's right; I am." I hear her draw a breath. "When Zack is, as you say, *chipper*—"

"You mean when he's on stimulants?"

"When he's in this *up* kind of mood, would you say he can go without sleep for long periods of time?"

The corner of my mouth twists. "Yes. It's like he's full of caffeine or something."

"Is he more irritable at these times? More prone to aggressive behavior?"

I think back to a night last week when we were all in the kitchen together. Zack was running his mouth off about something, and Carl asked him to be quiet for a moment so he could listen to the television newscast. Zack slammed a plate on the counter so hard that the dish broke into four pieces.

"I'd say he's more irritable than usual. But isn't everyone when they're wound up?"

"When he's in this state, is he more easily distracted?"

"Sure."

"More reckless?"

"Definitely."

"Has he ever mentioned delusions or hallucinations?"

"You sound like those people at the hospital. He's not psychotic. He doesn't hear voices or have hallucinations."

"Okay." Her voice is soothing again. "When Zack is tired . . . You've already said he can sleep for days."

"Right."

"Is this when he's prone to suicidal thoughts?"

I'm about to say no, then I remember Zack's journal. When he's racing around, I can't imagine him taking the time to sit and write in that loopy handwriting, so he must have written those dark passages during his hangovers. "I think so."

"Have you noticed odd changes in his appetite and sleep patterns?"

"Goodness, Diana, he's an adolescent boy. How would you define *normal* for a kid his age?"

She releases a polite, professional laugh. "Just a couple of other questions. Does he get angry and yell at you?"

I want to say no, but I have to be honest. "Yes."

"When he does, does his anger seem way out of proportion to the event that ticked him off? If he's angry, is it easy for him to calm down?"

I press my fingertips to my mouth as memories come flooding back: Zack screaming, Carl having to physically restrain him, my son coming at me with his hand in a fist. I try to answer, but my throat tightens until I can't speak.

"Jordan," Diana says, "you still there?"

Through tears, I manage an answer. "Uh-huh."

"Does he rage at you?"

I whisper. "Yes."

"Has he ever become violent?"

"Yes."

"Is there any mental illness in your family?"

"No, no, none at all."

"Aunts, uncles, cousins, extended family tree?"

My mind serves up Uncle Joe. My father never talked about his older brother; apparently Joe Casey was the black sheep of the family. From what I've heard, he ran away at sixteen, joined the Navy, ended up in the brig, then got out and lived on the streets of Washington, D.C. When I was thirteen, I remember my father getting a phone call—his brother had been found dead in West Potomac Park, an apparent robbery/murder victim.

I never saw my father shed a tear for Joe. How could he mourn a brother he never really knew?

"No mental illness," I tell Diana, "but my father did have a brother who was . . . eccentric. He left home while my father was still a toddler and died in Washington after years of living on the street."

Diana digests this news and then makes a clucking sound with her teeth. "This isn't an official diagnosis, Jordan, but it sounds like Zack may be bipolar. The mood swings, the hyperactivity alternating with periods of depression and sleep—that's classic bipolar behavior."

"That can't be right." I transfer the phone to my other hand. "He's an alcoholic, a kid who's made a string of bad choices. We know this. That's why we need a doctor who's experienced with substance abuse."

"What you need," Diana says, her voice gentle, "is a doctor who can examine Zack and make an accurate diagnosis. Based on what you've told me, I think it's highly likely he's dealing with a mental disorder."

"Is it because of what I said about my uncle? He was never diagnosed as mentally ill, not even by the Navy. He just wanted to live on the street. The family always said he marched to his own drummer, but he was never declared insane."

"I'm not talking about insanity, Jordan. I'm talking about a fairly common condition that runs in families. You need to get Zack to see a psychologist as soon as possible. Dr. Hodde is very good."

"I think Zack needs a few days to recuperate from the hospital." I force a laugh. "I think he's sleeping now because he's suffering from post-traumatic stress."

"Jordan." Diana firms her voice. "There's no need to feel ashamed."

"If you could have seen that place, Diana—I couldn't wait to get him out of there."

"I *have* seen mental hospitals, Jordan, and I remember one thing from my residency in a psychiatric ward—when patients can't think of anything but getting out, that's a sure sign they need to be *in*. On the other hand, when patients are ready to accept help, that's when we're able to begin an effective treatment."

I slip lower in the seat as tears flow down my cheeks.

"Jordan." Diana's voice is softer now. "I hate doing this over the phone. Can you get away? Let's meet for coffee somewhere and talk."

"I need to get home."

"Tomorrow, then. Let me treat you to lunch."

"I can't." I force myself to stop sniffling. "I'll be okay."

"Remember—there's no shame in this."

"I'm not ashamed of my son."

"You don't need to be. Tell me this—did the police take Zack to the hospital, or did you?"

I sniff. "I did. The policewoman said it'd be better that way."

"Did Zack go with you willingly?"

"Yes."

I hear a smile in her next words. "At this point, it sounds like he's more ready for treatment than you are."

The house is quiet and dark when I pull through the gate. No lights burn in the living room, the kitchen, or my office. The entire upstairs is dark, which means either Zack is asleep or he's gone out . . . but Carl wouldn't let him go out tonight. Not after what we've been through.

I pull into the garage, put the car in gear, and turn off the engine. The walls are lined with shelves, half of which are crowded with boxes of books. The other shelves are littered with mismatched auto parts, cans of oil, skateboards, and deflated basketballs—the remnant of a boy's childhood.

As the engine ticks down, I sit in the car and review my conversation with Diana. I shouldn't have told her about Uncle Joe. The man was an eccentric, but he has nothing to do with us. The idea that he had any kind of condition that could show up in my son is ludicrous—unthinkable.

It's crazy.

Yet Diana is right about Zack needing help, and we can't afford to delay. How can we let him out of the house with a set of car keys if we can't be sure he won't run the vehicle into a concrete pylon? I have told myself again and again that he wasn't serious the other night—if he had meant to end his life, he could have done it. No, Zack's action was a cry for help, and we're going to get him to a doctor. I'll call Dr. Hodde and

Dr. Kraus; we'll do whatever they suggest. I am confident they will administer tests, talk to Zack, look at his high school academic record, and tell us that Zack's only problem is alcoholism.

I'm imagining my conversation with Dr. Hodde when the door to the kitchen opens. Carl comes down the steps, a worried expression on his face. He sees me behind the wheel and leans against the wall. "You okay?"

I open the door and pull my purse from the passenger's seat. "Just thinking."

"About?"

I stand and walk toward my husband. "I talked to Dr. Sheldon tonight—she finally returned my call."

When I reach Carl, he glances over his shoulder. "Should we talk inside or out here?"

I look toward the empty kitchen. No sign of eavesdroppers, but you never know. "Is he still asleep?"

"As far as I know."

"Still . . . we'd better talk out here."

I retrace my steps, open the roadster's door, and slide back into the driver's seat. Carl sits on the other side of the car, leaving the door open.

He props his foot on the running board. "What did Dr. Sheldon say?"

"She said the names we got from the hospital are good. She knows Hodde and Kraus, and she likes them."

"That's great news."

I open my hands, trying to gesture as if the next matter is inconsequential, but I can't continue. My chin wobbles, and Carl knows I'm about to cry.

He touches my shoulder. "What is it, hon?"

"She thinks . . . She thinks Zack might be bipolar."

Carl sucks in a breath.

"I told her I didn't think he was," I hasten to add, "because he's not crazy. He's an alcoholic; we know that. He's had problems with alcohol and drugs since high school."

"I've heard of bipolar disorder," Carl says, "but I've never known anyone who had it."

I lift one shoulder in a shrug. "She said Zack's mood swings sounded like bipolar illness. But she admitted she couldn't make an official diagnosis."

Carl stares out the windshield for a long moment. Finally, he braces one arm on his knee and inclines his head in a decisive nod. "We'll get him to a psychologist, then. We'll let the experts handle it."

"Zack's not mentally ill; I know that."

"How do you know?"

"Because God wouldn't do that to me."

Carl snorts a laugh. "How do you know that?"

"God wouldn't allow it because he knows I can't handle it." I swallow the sob that rises in my throat and then take a deep breath to still my racing heart. "When we accepted Christ, Alicia kept saying that God had a good plan for our lives. Remember? She quoted that verse about the Lord having plans for good and not for disaster, to give us a future and a hope."

Carl's eyes have gone soft with memory. "Jeremiah 29:11," he says. "I remember."

"Well." I spread my hands as if the answer is obvious. "I can handle a lot of things, but I can't handle mental illness. When Shannon got sick with meningitis, I handled it. When Patty shattered her arm in that car wreck, I handled it. When Zack got his heart broken over that girl he met at camp, I handled it. My kids could need surgery, they could lose their jobs, *I* could even lose *my* job, and I could handle it. But not this. Not mental illness."

Carl's eyes are shadowed and dark in the dim garage light, unreadable. "How do you know you can't handle it?"

I press my lips together and turn my face toward the window, waiting until I can control my voice. "Simple," I finally answer. "I have no experience with it. And God has promised not to send me what I can't bear."

Carl reaches out to push a stray hank of hair from my cheek. "We're not baby Christians anymore. You may be able to handle more than you realize."

I shrug. "Doesn't matter. He promised never to send more than we could handle, and I swear, Carl, I can't handle mental illness. This weekend nearly killed me. The only way I survived was by telling myself it was only one weekend. Soon Zack would be home, and we'd never have to go through anything like that again."

Carl reaches out to hold me. I lean toward him and submit to his embrace, but I'm so sure of my conviction I don't need to be comforted.

I know what I can handle, and so does God. A bipolar child is definitely not on the list.

Fifty-eight

My nose itches. I lift my hand to scratch it, and the movement brings me fully awake. I look into the brightness of an afternoon—impossible, since it was dark when I went to sleep—and discover I'm lying in a bed I do not recognize. Yet there is something familiar about this bed and this room.

I look to the left, where I see a bureau. A comb and hand mirror lie on its surface, exactly where I imagined them.

I throw off the white cotton coverlet and swing my feet to the floor. One window in the wall across from the bed, a closet, a bathroom with one porcelain sink and a matching white toilet. The closet—I fling open the door and see a basic set of men's clothing—two pairs of pants, two shirts, a jacket, a belt hanging from a rusty nail on the back wall.

I am in the newcomer's apartment. In Paradise.

I bring my hand to my mouth and choke back a surge of hysterical laughter. This can't be real, so this must be one of those lucid dreams where the dreamer knows he's dreaming and can somewhat control the events that take place.

The word *somewhat* makes me shiver. What about the events I can't control?

I step into the bathroom and look in the mirror. My hair is combed, though a bit disheveled. I am wearing a white cotton blouse and a white skirt. White, the color of—what, purity?

Not godliness, surely, though there's no telling what my subconscious meant to symbolize. As the creator of Paradise, I suppose I do fill a godlike role in this place, but I never intended to interact with these people. I only wanted to tell a story.

I sit down on the edge of the bed, then I lie back and close my eyes. Might as well go to sleep and wait to wake in my own bed, where plenty of problems wait for me. But though I lie still for what feels like ten minutes, my thoughts do not wind down, nor does my breathing slow to a sleeper's rhythm. I can't sleep.

Nothing to do, then, but get up. Dreams have a way of tapering off or breaking up when reality intrudes, so perhaps I should just explore awhile and wait for the alarm clock.

My lips tremble with suppressed laughter as I move into the kitchen of the newcomer's apartment. I've been writing for twenty years, but I've never dreamed myself into a novel. I make a mental note: *this will make a good story for my class.*

My senses are assaulted when I step onto the sidewalk. Writing from the safety of my office, I have enjoyed a certain distance from Paradise; now my story world looms before me in all its putrefaction and decay. An odor fills the air, a scent that reminds me of the Dumpster by the lake where I used to take Zack to feed the spring ducklings. A hot wind blows over the cracked sidewalk; scraps of paper rustle in the wind.

I squint at the litter, the weeds growing between the cobblestones, the charred doorway of Eden's Repast. I've lived in this world for hours each day; how could I have missed so much?

I lift my gaze to the machine company building. It sits, sad and furtive, behind a layer of graffiti. The windows are cracked from the recent melee; broken glass gleams on what used to be the sidewalk. Above my head, the neon tower hums and buzzes in a useless effort to advertise the casino.

The building itself looks deserted, as is the street. I'm not sure when I have arrived—at the point where I stopped in the story, or in some parallel time?—so I have no idea where I might find my characters.

Since the casino is the central location, I walk toward it, lowering my head to carefully pick my way through pebbles of broken safety glass.

I halt when a pair of rugged leather boots enters my field of vision. I don't remember writing a character who wears boots. Prickles of panic nip at the backs of my knees as I slowly lift my head.

A man stands before me, a tall fellow with puffy white hair, a fleshy face, and a knowing smile.

I am suddenly torn between wanting to run and wanting to embrace this fellow. I settle for standing still, my jaw dropped and my eyes wide. "Ramirez!"

He nods, his smile broadening. "I've been waiting for you, Casey."

"But—" I tilt my head, uncertain how to proceed. "Didn't I take you out of this place?"

"You wrote me out." He shrugs. "Your prerogative."

"So . . . what brings you to Paradise?"

He laughs. "You do."

"Me?"

"You made me a prophet. I spoke for you while I lived in this story; now I speak for an even higher authority."

This is crazy; this is pure insanity. I close my eyes and give myself a stern mental shake. When I lift my eyelids again, Ramirez is still there.

He continues as if he hasn't noticed my unwillingness to accept his existence. "You wrote an outline for *The Ambassador*; you set events in motion to work your will and develop characters. Don't you know that your creator has done the same for you?"

"Excuse me?" I squint at him, then close my eyes and pinch the top of my nose. "This is a dream. I've been working too hard; the situation with Zack has messed up my thinking—"

"The Creator of all doesn't delight in seeing you handle trials." Even though my eyes are closed, I can tell Ramirez has leaned closer; I can feel his warm breath on my face. His voice is uncompromising, yet oddly gentle. "The Creator of all delights in your surrender so *he* can handle your trials. His strength will be made perfect in your weakness, Jordan Casey. Don't resist his will."

His voice fades to a hushed stillness. When I open my eyes, he is gone.

I step forward, hearing the crunch of glass beneath my slippers. I look to the right and left, but no one else moves on the deserted street.

Did I imagine this? Have I experienced a dream-within-a-dream, or is my subconscious trying to tell me something?

Is *God* trying to tell me something?

Shivering in the cold wind, I hurry to the shelter of the machine company building.

The front room is a shambles. Sunlight barely penetrates the dangling blinds. The hulking games, which were bright and resplendent in my imagination, now look like poorly painted cartons. They stand silent in the gloom, their electronic voices muted because the power has been shut off.

I avoid looking at the corner where Mac died. The sound of buzzing flies issues from that area, and my gorge rises at the thought of encountering a corpse, even one of my own invention.

I come to the swinging doors and put out a hand. The painted surface is dirty; no one has taken the time to wipe away layers of accumulated handprints. The corner of my mouth rises in a smirk—*I should have written in a cleaning woman*—and then I examine the dark smudges. Which of these was left by William's hand?

I push on the door, hear a slight squeak, and freeze as a sound reaches my ear. I hear a low *thump*—no, a murmur. After passing into the gloomy employees' area, I spy a light through the office window. A candle burns on the receptionist's desk, and in its light a man kneels.

I'm not sure which of us is more surprised when William lifts his head. I bite my lip, amazed, as the photo I plucked from a JCPenney catalogue looks at me, his three-dimensional face marked with dirt, blood, and tears.

After an instant, his expression of surprise hardens. "You shouldn't be trespassing here."

I can't stop a smile from creeping across my face. His voice is lower than I imagined, and he has an accent—Bostonian, I think—that I don't recall writing into his description.

"I'm sorry." I move closer to the light. "I was wondering where everyone went."

He looks at me, his eyes gleaming with something that looks like resentment.

"Are you a newcomer? You've missed all the excitement." He places his hand on the desk as if to push himself up, but I catch his shoulder.

"You are William," I whisper. "I know you."

His gaze softens to thoughtfulness as he sinks back on his haunches. "Did Casey send you?"

I'm not sure how to answer; finally, I nod.

William grabs my hand. "Have you a message for me? John is dead, you know, and I couldn't prevent it. I tried, but the mob was out of control. You can see what they did to this place; maybe you saw what they did to Mac. I'm so sorry. Casey has to know how sorry I am."

Tears well within his eyes, so I step forward to comfort him. "Casey knows how you tried. You were very brave."

He dashes the tears away. When his gaze meets mine again, his eyes have widened with hope. "Do you know Casey well?"

Slowly, I search for words. "I know the author has a plan for you. From the beginning, your creator designed a plot that would make you strong and help you grow into the character you were meant to be. Rest in this, William—the author who created you loves and forgives."

He turns his head, looking past me to the ruined rooms beyond the doorway. "I want to believe that."

Suddenly he is clinging to me, one arm circling my hips, his head pressing into the folds of my skirt. I'm not sure if he thinks of me as a messenger, a newcomer, or a figment of his imagination, but his emotion is sincere and his regret genuine.

"Hush, now." Like a mother I stroke his hair, trying to console him even as my throat tightens at the sound of his sobs. My heart, which has been filled to the breaking point so many times in the last few days, overflows until my cheeks are wet and my eyes flood in an outpouring of emotion.

As my creation sobs at my feet, I look around the ruined building and weep at the depth of its corruption—and when I look down again, the slender man holding me tight is not William Case, but Zachary; not my creation, but my son.

My throat works, but no words come. Instead, I hear my own voice, sharp and tense:

"Someday when Zack's a parent, he'll understand how torturous this is.

"Someday when he's a father, he'll experience the sleepless nights, the worry.

"Someday he'll understand what he's put us through."

I cover my eyes with my hand as truth slaps me in the face. Have I been so focused on *my* pain that I've been blind to my son's agony?

If Diana Sheldon is right—and in the stark grimness of this place, I know she is—my son has been suffering in ways I can't begin to imagine. I've resisted mental illness because the thought of it frightens me spitless.

So how terrified must Zack be? Not only has he inherited a normal dread of mental illness, but he's suffered from its agony, buffeted by emotions that lift him to the crest of a wave one day and abandon him in a gully the next. He has known darkness and despair at one extreme, and frantic, out-of-control thoughts at the other.

No wonder my poor son wanted to end his life.

He's been desperate for years, but I've clapped my hands over my ears, unwilling to hear his cries and blind to his despair. Even when I tried to help, I sought quick fixes, simple solutions for what will probably be a lifelong challenge.

I sink to my knees and gather my sobbing son into my arms.

As I rub his back, I lift my eyes and promise God that I've learned a lesson. I can't handle mental illness. But he knows that, and he still has a good plan for my life. And for Zack's.

After a few moments, the sobbing youth in my arms grows quiet. I stroke his head and then pull back, experiencing an instant's shock when I realize that I'm once again holding William.

I give him a teary smile. "You know what? I used to think the creator tested me to discover how strong I was. Lately, though, I've begun to realize he has an entirely different purpose in mind. The author of my life knows everything about me, so he already knows how strong I am. The tests come to me—and to you—so we will know how strong the creator is when he carries us through what we can't handle alone."

William's eyes brighten as he looks at me. "You must know the creator well."

I laugh softly. "Not well enough. I've a lot to learn."

William pushes himself up on the desk, then he helps me to my feet.

I take his hand before saying good-bye. "Your story is not quite finished. Trust in the author; trust Casey's outline. Your trials have not been easy, but they have been suitable. They will result in good, for you and for Paradise."

William squeezes my hand and then moves back as I step carefully over the littered floor and make my way to the lonely street. A river of fog blankets the cobblestones, a swirling stream that rises and carries me home.

Fifty-nine

A deadly silence permeates the house. Like strangers, William and Raquel wander through a quiet as heavy as a wool blanket. The horrific incident on the cliffs united them for a moment, but grief and guilt keep them at arm's length.

William sits at the kitchen table and thinks about yesterday's encounter with the woman at the casino. She spoke of the creator, the one who wrote a plan for him and Paradise, but wouldn't it be better if he'd never heard of such a plan? How sad it is to live in Casey's world with no hope of reclaiming what has been lost!

He stumbles into the bathroom and stands under a steaming shower, conscious of the spreading black, blue, and green bruises on his body. A cut oozes above his brow, sending blood into the streaming water, and something stabs at the wall of his chest each time he takes a deep breath.

He doesn't want to look in the mirror. Raquel's grimace affirmed the mangled condition of his face, but the flare of compassion he saw in her eyes vanished as soon as she realized he was watching her.

He can't blame her for guarding her heart. The last time they talked in this house, he was so consumed by jealousy that he could barely look at her without clenching his teeth. She had tried to open up and share her feelings, but he had erected barriers against her, just as he had built a wall between himself and Casey. He used pride and desire as building blocks; ambition and jealousy as his mortar.

Raquel has spent most of the morning by the window, a weight of sadness on her thin face. She doesn't say much, and William can't help but wonder if she blames him for John's death. She probably thinks he should have been able to control the crowd, but not even Ramirez could have managed that mob.

That thought tows another in its wake—John told William that Casey had taken Ramirez away from Paradise. William wants to believe that, but something in him needs to be sure John spoke the truth.

He walks into the living room, where Raquel is curled in a chair. "Rocky, have you seen Ramirez in the last couple of days?"

Her gaze, remote as the ocean depths, shifts to him. "Why do you ask?"

"He was always hanging around John, but I didn't see any sign of him yesterday."

A frown works its way between her brows. "Since when do you worry about Ross Ramirez?"

"I'm the ambassador. Maybe I'm supposed to worry about the people of Paradise." He slips his hands into his pockets and forces a smile. "Want to get out of the house?"

"And do what?"

"Look around, see if we can find the old man."

She hesitates only an instant. "Let me get my purse."

They don't speak on the ride to town. William sips a cup of coffee and navigates with one hand; Raquel stares straight ahead, her eyes on some interior field of vision he is not invited to share. Is she reliving the horror of yesterday? Or is she wondering what she ever saw in him?

After crossing the bridge, William scans the horizon to check the tower atop the casino. The lights aren't flashing, but he has a hunch it won't take Stan long to restore power.

Without warning, Raquel slaps at his knee. "Good grief, what is *that*?"

He pushes on the brakes, spilling coffee onto his lap. Instead of the modest sign that used to greet visitors, a colossal billboard now welcomes guests to *Pair o' Dice, home of the world's finest wagering establishment.*

Raquel brings her hand to her throat. "Stan," she whispers, her voice flat. "He did this."

William is too stunned to reply. He had assumed Stan would be busy cleaning up the casino, but perhaps he hired help. The mechanic has never been one to let grass grow under his feet.

They continue into town. Because the casino is closed, few vehicles are parked along Main Street. Ramirez is not in his usual place on the sidewalk, nor is he in the diner, which is still closed for repairs.

William pulls over to the curb and puts the car in park. "I guess I'll see what's happening at the casino. You want to come in?"

Raquel shakes her head. "I want to drive to the cliffs—to see if there's anything we can do for John." She releases a choked, desperate laugh. "I have no idea what we're supposed to do, but somebody ought to do something. Even if it's only saying a few words."

William understands more than she knows. "Take the car, then, so you can go home afterward. I'll ask Stan to drive me home."

She nods wordlessly, then slides over the wide bench seat, closes the door, and pulls away, heading north.

He slips a hand into his pocket and turns toward the twin windows of the machine company. They stare back, grim with dark knowledge. A skein of evil unfurled behind those windows—he held it in his hands and toyed with it, but it has tangled into something he can't unravel.

Perhaps he can atone for his mistakes.

The door stands ajar, swinging on a broken hinge. He enters the game room, where the machines stand like tombstones, tall, dark, and silent.

Is the power still off? William fumbles for the switch on the wall and flicks it. A bank of fluorescent lights comes on, diluting the shadows and casting an eerie green tint over the walls.

He moves down an aisle and studies a bank of machines. They've been set upright and rearranged in a row. Since his last visit, someone has swept the floor, removed the broken glass, and touched up the scars on several painted designs.

Stan has been busy and probably Todd too. But the power to the games hasn't been restored.

A metallic *chink* breaks the silence, the sound snapping straight to the center of William's skull. He whirls, expecting to see someone in the break room doorway, but the door remains closed. Nothing stirs but dust motes floating in the strangely thickened air.

He must be hearing things. His nerves are too tightly strung because he hasn't had enough sleep. Shrugging off his anxiety, he pushes through the swinging door and enters the darkened employees' area, then flips the switch. He scans the room in the faint overhead light, and something in him shrivels to see Mac's empty cubicle. Someone has removed the man's cologne, his wadded handkerchiefs, and his thermos.

A raw and primitive grief overwhelms William as he stares at the vacant box. Is this Casey's grand plan? People arrive in Paradise, live a handful of turbulent days, then die. Nothing remains of their existence but an aching void.

He is about to step into the office, but another *chink* stops him in midstride. This time there is no mistake; he heard the sound clearly.

He swallows to bring his heart down from his throat and turns in the direction of the sound. Nothing has moved in the break room, but the padlock no longer hangs on the forbidden door. The trash can has been hauled away; the NO ADMITTANCE sign has vanished.

Hot as it is in the stuffy building, William feels as though a sliver of ice is sliding down his spine. He creeps toward the forbidden door, one arm raised in case something comes winging out of it.

He tentatively touches the wood. It feels cool beneath his damp palm, but when he pushes on the door, red and yellow light flares from the crack and bathes his arm in its glow.

He retracts his hand and chokes back a cry. What happened? Yesterday John killed the power to the magician's machine, yet *something* lives in this room.

His palms are slick with sweat, yet his mind has gone cold and sharp. He has to enter the room again. Evil still roams Paradise, and as the ambassador, he is responsible for restraining it.

Summoning his courage, he shoves the door open and steps forward. In an aura of pulsing red and gold light, Stan kneels at the back of the *You Bet Your Life* game. His tools are spread on the floor; a length of electrical cord dangles from his grip. He drops a pair of pliers on the floor; they hit a screwdriver with another metallic *chink*.

"Hi." He offers the greeting without looking up. "Wondered when you'd make it in."

William leans against the wall. His apprehension drains away, and he feels empty without it. "What are you doing?"

"What do you think of the game room?" Stan grins over his shoulder, his teeth yellow in the odd light. "Almost good as new, isn't it? We'll be open tomorrow. I think we should start staying open twenty-four hours a day. I know we could fill this place 'round the clock."

Some deep thought struggles to surface, but William is too tired to pull it up. "Actually, Stan, I was thinking of reorganizing the company. Maybe we ought to dust off the old games, put things back the way they were. Business will probably be slower, but—"

"Are you crazy?" The mechanic stands, his brows knitting in a scowl. "You think these people will go back to playing those senseless old machines? You've given them a taste of risk and adventure; they're not going back to safe and boring."

William gapes as the thought that would not come erupts in abrupt clarity: *How can Stan repair a game he's never seen?*

"Stan . . . do you know what you're doing? This machine is evil."

The mechanic ignores the comment. He plants his feet on the tile floor and then presses his palm to the dark video screen. Instantly, a thin red beam flashes from the machine, enveloping Stan in a narrow column of light. His head jerks back as though slammed with high voltage, his body spasms, his legs tremble within his coveralls.

William watches in open-mouthed horror as a pulse within the light rolls over the mechanic's body, growing as it takes his measure. When the beam has traversed his form, it vanishes; the machine growls to life, and music throbs from the speakers. Stan steps back, visibly shaken, and the magician smiles from the screen.

William can't conceal his terror. He trembles with it, shaking until his teeth begin to chatter, a fact that doesn't escape the magician. "Hel-*looo* again, William, my man," he crows, and like an electric jolt to his stomach, William feels the truth all at once.

Just as John drew his power from Casey, the machine has just drawn power from Stan.

William stumbles toward the door, finally understanding why evil persisted after John unplugged the game. John was right—evil was not created by Casey; it arrived when Casey's creations began to break the rules. William began to flirt with evil not long after his arrival; pride had infiltrated his thoughts long before he entered the forbidden room. *His* evil powered the machine on that first day. Since playing the magician's game, he has profited from evil, encouraged evil, empowered evil.

Horror snakes down his spine and coils in his gut. "What have I done?"

"Don't take all the credit," Stan says, wiping sweat from his brow. "I've invested plenty in this game. So has Raquel. Soon others will come and supply it with even more energy."

William steps back and scrubs his face with his hand. Is that it, then? Is Paradise to remain Pair o' Dice, a shadow of what the author intended it to be?

The magician is taunting him, tremors of mirth fracturing his voice, when William hears a noise from the game room. The tinkling sound of Ramirez's bells registers instantly, then he realizes—the bells no longer hang above the front door.

The magician's eyes narrow. "What is *that*?"

"Ignore it," Stan says, rubbing his brow as though he has a headache.

William draws a deep breath and swipes the wetness from his face. "I'll check it out."

Eager to leave the stifling room, he steps into the break area. A stranger in striped coveralls and a matching cap is pushing a huge carton on a handcart outside the office window.

The man peers around the edge of the box to be sure he's cleared the game room door. "Can you give me some help?"

William stands his ground. "What do you have there?"

"New model." The man's chewing gum snaps as he taps the address label on the carton. "This is Casey's Machine Company, right?"

"Yes, but—" William hesitates. No one has used that name in ages.

While the stranger lowers the crate to the floor, William walks over and peers at the sticker. The label has been printed with the business name and address, nothing else.

He straightens. "Well, I didn't order this, and I'm the manager. There must be some mistake."

"No mistake." The man grabs the handcart and grunts as he tilts the weight of the box onto the wheels. "If you'll just open that other door for me—"

"What door?"

"That one." He jerks his head toward the forbidden room, catches William's eye . . . and grins.

At the sight of that smile, comprehension dispels William's confusion. *"John?"*

"You didn't think the story was finished, did you?"

"So . . . you're back?"

John tightens his grip on the handcart. "I'd tip my hat, but this thing's heavy."

"You—you were DEAD."

"Casey wouldn't let death keep a good man down." He nods toward the forbidden room. "Casey wanted me to bring you another machine. So open the door, Mr. Ambassador, and let me install it."

William doesn't know what Casey's planning, but he pushes the door open and slides out of the way as John maneuvers the carton through the opening and around the concrete wall.

William doesn't know how it's possible, but he believes Stan and the magician are more surprised to see John than he was.

"Get that thing out of here." Stan's fists tighten. "This is our territory."

John turns to face his opposition. "This is Casey's room, Casey's company, Casey's town. You are here because Casey believes characters should have choice. I've brought this machine because Casey also wants them to enjoy *liberty*."

William stands in the clearing, fascinated by the battle of wills.

The pupils of the magician's eyes narrow into slits. "You think the creator will win, but Casey can't compete. I offer flashier prizes."

"But Casey's rewards don't sour over time." With a confident air of ownership, John yanks the cardboard packaging away from the game, then slides the handcart from beneath the base.

"Hang on to this, will you?" He rolls the dolly to William and grins at the video trickster. "You two need to watch what you say—Casey could write you into oblivion at any time."

Stan goes pale, and an animated drop of sweat runs down the magician's jaw.

John bends to plug in the cord, then stands and wipes his handkerchief over the smooth surface of the new machine. He grins at William. "So—what do you think?"

"I—I don't know what it is."

"It's a game, like the others."

"But how does it work?"

John leans against the wall and crosses his arms. "Your company is going to remain open, William, and people will continue to come to Paradise. They'll arrive here, drawn either by their love of pleasure or by Casey's love for them. Those who love pleasure will play the other machines; those who love the creator will wander into this room."

William turns to glance at the magician's game. Lights still pulse from that machine, but the noise has gone silent. "And when they come here?"

"They'll face a choice—that machine or this one. Just as you have a choice now."

William hears the finality in John's voice, and somehow he knows every moment of his past has pointed to this one; every moment of his future will be decided here. That game . . . or this one?

The decision is a no-brainer; even a child could make it.

He looks up, hungry for what his creator offers. "I choose Casey."

John's eyes bathe him in understanding. "Then come."

William walks toward him, amazed and trembling, as John taps a glass plate in the surface. "Remember the guiding principle of the old games? You always received something greater than what you gave. This machine is based on the same principle, but it's not to be played casually."

William bends, looking for some sort of intake slot. "What, exactly, do you want from me?"

John smiles. "Nothing that most people aren't happy to be rid of. Just place your hand here."

"You're taking my *hand*?"

John laughs. "I want you to place your hand here because this is a solemn occasion. What the machine takes is your stony heart—the unfeeling, desperate part of you that wants nothing to do with Casey."

William knows it's audacious of him, but he can't resist another question. "And what do I get in return?"

"A heart like Casey's, a living heart that loves and forgives."

The words open a door within him, releasing a realization that has been locked away. A loving and forgiving heart . . . Why, he knows this heart!

"John." He looks toward the door, through which lies the break room and the office. "Has Casey . . . been here?"

One of John's brows lifts. "What do you think?"

"I think I met . . . her. I had no idea who she was, but—"

William is ready to tell John about his strange encounter when Stan snickers. "A heart that *loves and forgives*? Come on, William, you think you can walk away from all you've done? Surely you haven't forgotten how you tempted Raquel to torture Ramirez. And I saw the way you looked at Amber. I know what's filled your heart lately, and those feelings aren't love and forgiveness."

Stan is right. Casey might forgive him, but the guilt will not go away. William closes his eyes. His hand must weigh four hundred pounds; it's dead weight he cannot move.

He can't even meet John's gaze. "I—we—none of us deserves this."

He opens his eyes to find John giving him a benign smile. "You're right, William, you don't deserve this. None of us do. But Casey doesn't bestow gifts because we are deserving; the author grants gifts because we are loved."

John catches his wrist. "Do you want to change your life?"

Of course he does. He's never thought of his heart as stony, but he knows it is heavy and hard and cold. So if by some miracle he can exchange it—

"I do."

John lifts William's hand and presses his palm to the cool glass. "A living heart will make all the difference, William. You'll see."

With a smile on his face, John reaches down and presses the start button. A strobe flashes, scanning William's palm from wrist to fingertips, then the room fills with a hot light.

He gasps and inhales a breath of brightness. The brightness takes William in and fills him until he can't catch a breath.

He is *William*, a voice whispers. He is William Case, and he has been fashioned according to a plan, a pattern, and a purpose, so he is not to fear. The one who willed him into being will continue to guide him.

What he is and what he's done . . . none of those things matter anymore. "*I, the author, have outlined a good plan for you.*"

When he blinks his bedazzled eyes, he knows everything about him is different. He looks around, waiting for his vision to adjust to the comparative gloom of the room. John is gone. But the two machines remain, as does Stan.

And William carries brightness within him.

Walking forward in a state of wonder, he moves into the break room. He presses his palm to his chest and feels the vital, robust beat of his heart.

He is clean. Unworthy. Forgiven.

And Casey has entrusted him with a responsibility far more important than the operation of a casino.

Overcome by the graciousness of the gift, William walks through the silent game room and steps onto the broken sidewalk. A rat scurries by, anxious to be away from the revealing daylight, but William lifts his face to the warm sun and breathes in hope.

He was created to fall, to mourn, and to be transformed.

He hasn't the authority to restore this town, but the author who created a beautiful Paradise can bring back all that has been lost. A warm wind will once again scissor the strip of grass along the road and evoke applause from colorful, leafy trees along the street. Golden marigolds will nod along the bricked pathway while ornate lamps sway above the citizens walking below.

As the author's representative, William will order new red-and-white-

302

striped awnings and repaint *Casey's Machine Company* on the wide windows. He can pull the old machines from the storage shed and let people again experience the author's creativity.

"You are the ambassador, the one who carries a message from one realm to another."

A smile creeps over his face when he recognizes the once-familiar voice. "I am."

"So tell the townspeople what you know."

"And who do I tell first?"

"The one who is ready to hear."

He hesitates a moment, then, with pulse-pounding certainty, he realizes who Casey has in mind.

Exhaling in contentment, he strides away from the casino and hurries northward in search of Raquel.

"The life of every man," wrote J. M. Barrie, "is a diary in which he means to write one story, and writes another; and his humblest hour is when he compares the volume as it is with what he vowed to make it."

I have written the first draft of a novella that remains reasonably true to my outline, but it is not at all what I imagined it would be.

I type "The End" at the bottom of the page and then use the mouse to click the print button. As the laser printer hums and begins to regurgitate pages, I lean back in my chair and close my eyes.

It's done—at least this draft is finished. I don't know how good the story is; I don't know if my editor will like it or laugh at it. But I didn't write this novel to please an audience; I wrote it to teach a class and change my son.

Yet God has used it to change me.

I now know that while I am not strong enough to handle Zack's illness, God is. He has promised to carry us through, and I am determined to be a character who trusts the creator's plan.

And Ian Morley—the thought of that red-haired rascal brings a smile to my face. He challenged me to open a vein, and I responded by outlining a spiritual allegory designed to teach someone else—as if I didn't need to learn anything. How foolish I was.

Ian may never realize it, but every page of *The Ambassador* is sprinkled with my heart's blood.

I glance at the laser printer as the last page rolls through the opening and the machine powers down. I gather the pages of this last chapter and tamp the edges on my desk, neatening the stack.

I'll send the manuscript to my agent because he asked for it. I'll read the last chapters to my class because I promised them a finished novella. I'll give the first copy to Zack, but not to convict him.

God already has changed a life through this book—mine. If the story has any impact on Zack—and I pray that it will—that impact will come from the working of a creative Spirit far more powerful than me.

With the full manuscript under my arm, I go to the bottom of the stairs. "Zack? You up there?"

The house echoes with my voice, then I hear the creak of his bedroom door. "Mom?"

"Hey, were you asleep?"

His head, tousled and sleepy-eyed, appears over the balcony railing. "I was listening to a CD." He jerks his chin toward the bundle under my arm. "That your latest?"

"Yes." I catch my breath and then grin up at him. "Want to read it?"

"Sure. Nothing better to do."

I hold up a warning finger. "It's not a Tower novel. It's different from anything I've done before."

He looks doubtful.

"There's a pretty girl in it."

He grins. "Bring it on up."

My heart is full as I climb the stairs. In the three weeks since I talked to Dr. Sheldon, Zack has been to see Dr. Hodde and Dr. Kraus, who, after evaluating Zack, have confirmed Diana's diagnosis of bipolar disorder, also known as manic-depressive illness.

We have further learned that Zack is what they call a "rapid cycler." Though he can move quickly from an episode of mania to an episode of depression, Dr. Hodde says most rapid cyclers can achieve a normal or near-normal mood state with the right kind of drug therapy.

So there's a good chance Zack will be able to stabilize his mood swings and live a normal life. Without medication, though, he will always be prone to emotional highs and lows, many of which could be dangerous.

"We're fairly sure," Dr. Hodde told us in a private meeting, "that Virginia Wolfe suffered from manic-depressive illness. As I'm sure you know, she was a brilliant novelist, but one day she wrote her husband a note and said she was certain she was going mad again. She then went for a walk, filled her pockets with rocks, and drowned herself in the nearest river. Between 15 to 20 percent of people with bipolar disorder end up committing suicide," Dr. Hodde said, "so it's crucial that Zack take his medication. It's also crucial that you remain involved in his activities. Bipolar patients who feel cut off are usually the ones driven to take their lives."

I have struggled with so many emotions over the past month—guilt, first and foremost, for assuming that my son's mood swings were brought on by drugs and alcohol. When Dr. Hodde explained that manic behavior usually includes drug and alcohol abuse, provoking of confrontations with obnoxious behavior, rapid-fire speech, irritability, and the purchase of outrageous gifts, I realized I had blamed my son for bad choices when I should have blamed a disease.

After hearing some of the symptoms of the manic and depressed states, I stopped Dr. Hodde. "In other words, it's possible our son hasn't been loopy because he's been taking drugs . . . He's been taking drugs *because* he's been loopy?"

The doctor smiled. "*Loopy* isn't the word I'd use, but yes, that's accurate. The slurred speech and physical uncoordination that follow a manic episode often look like intoxication."

Carl and I are enormously thankful that Zack survived our bumbling and misguided attempts to help. Now we have joined a support group for parents with bipolar children; both Carl and I are reading all we can to acquaint ourselves with the disorder.

Though Zack's illness may never go away, Zack, Carl, and I feel as though a tremendous burden has been lifted from our shoulders. We have grappled with the beast, looked it in the eye, and given it a name. It is still strong, still fierce, but because we know how it operates, we know how to resist it.

By the time I reach the top of the stairs, Zack has wandered into the family room, where a sofa and love seat face the television. He is sitting on the couch, his long legs propped on the coffee table, his hand restlessly pressing the television remote.

"Zack." I sink onto the love seat. "Can we talk a minute?"

I'm stunned when he turns off the television. "Yeah?"

I place the manuscript on the coffee table. "I want to apologize to you. For so long I blamed everything on you. I thought you were making bad decisions and purposely doing things to spite us—"

"Mom." He stops me with a look. "You don't owe me an apology. You and Dad have been great; you've always been there for me."

"But we didn't understand—"

"Neither did I." A shaky grin crosses his face. "But you're right; I did make bad decisions."

"We were blind."

"So was I . . . but I've seen some things in the last few weeks. Things I never realized."

I tilt my head. "What things?"

"You and Dad . . . You stuck by me when other parents would have kicked me out. I've got friends who are living on the street because their parents wrote them off a long time ago. When one of my friends asked why you kept taking me back, that's when I knew."

"You knew . . . what?"

"That you love me . . . like you've always said God loves me." He gives me a sheepish smile. "I prayed, you know."

"*What?* When?"

"In the hospital. I was so scared, I figured maybe it was time to start a dialogue with the guy upstairs."

Maybe it wasn't exactly a prayer of faith, but I will trust God's Spirit to draw my son. When the fruit is ripe, it will fall into my hands.

With a heart too full for speech, I open my arms. My son slips into them, and for a long moment we rock in each other's embrace without saying a word.

The road ahead won't be easy, but we know we are not alone. And I trust the Author's plan.

Our Paradise is not perfect, but neither are we. And that is how it should be.

As the prison guard points to his watch, I stand and look at the old man across the table. His face is like a stretch of sunbaked canvas, scarred with jagged seams—a map of vicious passions and unhealthy habits.

"I gotta go," I tell him.

He grunts in reply, but on the table, his hand crawls forward an inch.

Suddenly the world consists only of his hand and mine. Am I allowed to grasp it in a place like this? Is the old man reaching out for me, or is he merely flexing his fingers?

From across the room, the guard clears his throat. The old man says nothing, doesn't even meet my eyes.

But I take his hand and hold it tight. "I love ya, Dad."

I turn and walk away, not sure if he heard or understood. But sometimes you say these things for your sake as much as for the other person's.

Because love's the thing that holds us together.

Love's the thing that keeps us sane.

It's our last class, and to mark the occasion, I've been reading work from several of my students. I lower the last page of a first chapter and smile over the edge of the paper.

"Well?" I lift a brow. "What'd you think of that?"

Johanna Sicorsky begins to clap; the others join in with enthusiastic applause. Dr. Bell puts his pinkies in his mouth and whistles, while Sari, Kristal, Edna, and Michael glance around the room.

"Come on, Ms. Casey, tell us who wrote it," Joseph Thronebury demands.

I glance to the wall, where Ian Morley is the only student not applauding. He sits with his head bowed, his neck a flaming shade of crimson.

The student who dared me to bleed a few months ago has finally opened a vein of his own. He has learned to tap into something real —as have I.

"Ladies and gentlemen," I say, sweeping my hand toward him in a dramatic gesture, "I give you the author, Ian Morley."

Ian grins and waves in a show of bravado, but after the applause dies down, he looks at me and smiles, his eyes sending a private message of gratitude.

I return his smile in full measure.

READING GROUP GUIDE

Angela Hunt says she enjoys writing illustrative stories that answer a question or point to a moral or lesson. Her novelist, Jordan Casey, decides to write an allegory, an extended metaphor in which objects, persons, and actions are equated with meanings that lie outside the narrative itself.

- How do you interpret the elements of the interior story, the allegory involving William Case?

- How do you interpret the elements of the outer story, the situation with Jordan and her family?

- Jordan thinks of herself as a creator when she populates her story world. Yet how is she like William, a created being in another, broader world? What does she learn over the scope of the story?

- Theologians have listed several consequences of William's fall in the Garden of Eden. What are the consequences of Adam's wrong choice in Paradise? How does Jordan suffer the consequences of her choices?

Consider the story of the blind man whom Jesus healed:

> As Jesus was walking along, he saw a man who had been blind from birth. "Teacher," his disciples asked him, "why was this man born blind? Was it a result of his own sins or those of his parents?"
>
> "It was not because of his sins or his parents' sins," Jesus answered. "He was born blind so the power of God could be seen in him." (John 9:1–3)

Ramirez told Eden that Casey caused him to be injured. Zack Kerrigan suffers from a mental condition. In view of the above Scripture, why do Ramirez and Zack suffer? How should this comfort us when we experience physical difficulties?

- Church prayer lists are usually crowded with requests concerning physical difficulties, but how often do you read of people requesting prayer for mental conditions? What can we do to comfort and encourage those whose loved ones suffer from mental disorders?

- With which character in this story do you most identify? Why?

- How do the words of Psalm 139:15–16 apply to this novel?

> You watched me as I was being formed in utter seclusion,
>   as I was woven together in the dark of the womb.
> You saw me before I was born.
>   Every day of my life was recorded in your book.
> Every moment was laid out
>   before a single day had passed.

To read an interview with Angela Hunt about *The Novelist*, visit www.angelahuntbooks.com.

Expect the Unexpected—July 2006

ANGELA

HUNT

EXPECT THE UNEXPECTED

UNCHARTED